THE HANGMAN'S
SECRET

ALSO AVAILABLE BY LAURA JOH ROWLAND

The Victorian Mysteries

A Mortal Likeness
The Ripper's Shadow

The Sano Ichirō Mysteries

The Iris Fan
The Shogun's Daughter
The Incense Game
The Ronin's Mistress
The Cloud Pavilion
The Fire Kimono
The Snow Empress
Red Chrysanthemum
The Assassin's Touch
The Perfumed Sleeve
The Dragon King's Palace
The Pillow Book of Lady Wisteria
Black Lotus
The Samurai's Wife
The Concubine's Tattoo
The Way of the Traitor
Bundori
Shinjū

The Secret Adventures of Charlotte Brontë

Bedlam
The Secret Adventures of Charlotte Brontë

THE HANGMAN'S SECRET

A VICTORIAN MYSTERY

Laura Joh Rowland

CROOKED
LANE

NEW YORK

This is a work of fiction. All of the names, characters, organizations, places and events portrayed in this novel are either products of the author's imagination or are used fictitiously. Any resemblance to real or actual events, locales, or persons, living or dead, is entirely coincidental.

Copyright © 2019 by Laura Joh Rowland

All rights reserved.

Published in the United States by Crooked Lane Books, an imprint of The Quick Brown Fox & Company LLC.

Crooked Lane Books and its logo are trademarks of The Quick Brown Fox & Company LLC.

Library of Congress Catalog-in-Publication data available upon request.

ISBN (hardcover): 978-1-68331-902-3
ISBN (ePub): 978-1-68331-903-0
ISBN (ePDF): 978-1-68331-904-7

Cover design by Melanie Sun
Book design by Jennifer Canzone

Printed in the United States.

www.crookedlanebooks.com

Crooked Lane Books
34 West 27th St., 10th Floor
New York, NY 10001

First Edition: February 2019

10 9 8 7 6 5 4 3 2 1

To Marty

Chapter 1

London, January 1890

A loud rapping on my window awakens me. Groggy and disori-
ented, I sit up in bed. A yellow glow from the street lamp penetrates the curtains. The clock says 6:35. I crawl from beneath the
quilts and totter, shivering in the icy cold, to the window as the
long cane raps insistently on the glass. I fling back the curtains and
open the window. The air is so thick with fog, smoke, and swirling
snowflakes that I can barely see the man who stands in the street
four stories below my attic room.

"Miss Sarah Bain?" he calls.

"Yes," I reply. "Where is it?"

"Fashion Street, number forty."

I shut the window; dress in corset, flannel chemise, drawers, and
petticoats, and woolen frock; and splash water from the washbasin
on my face. As I braid my hair into a crown around my head, my
reflection in the mirror is tense with anxiety. I hurry down the
stairs and meet Mick O'Reilly on the landing. He always hears the
rapping before I do. A boy who's spent most of his fourteen years
as a street urchin sleeps lightly by force of habit, ever alert for
danger.

"I woke Hugh," Mick says. His red hair stands up in cowlicks.
His coat and trousers are too short; he outgrows his clothes so fast.

His freckled face and blue eyes are bright with excitement. "He's coming."

Downstairs, in my photography studio, my equipment is already packed. I check the large camera in its wooden case; the trunk that contains the T-shaped metal flash lamp, folding tripod, and light stand; and my leather satchel filled with glass negative plates and tins of flash powder. I spare a moment to glance around the studio, and smile. Furnished like an elegant parlor, with carved furniture, a gas chandelier, a Turkish carpet, a cabinet full of props, rolled backdrops on a stand, and a gallery of my photographs framed on one wall, it's much better than my first studio, which I operated for ten years before I was evicted.

Hugh comes in, yawning as he buttons his coat. His blond hair is damp from hasty combing, and whisker stubble glints on his jaws, but even while bleary-eyed and dozy, Lord Hugh Staunton ranks among the handsomest men on earth.

"Third time this week, and it's only Tuesday," he mutters. "Business is booming."

Fitzmorris joins us, clad in pajamas and slippers, carrying a plate of buttered bread. The thin, solemn, gray-haired man is officially Hugh's valet, in reality also our cook, housekeeper, accountant, and manager. Mick grabs a slice of bread and wolfs it down; he's always ravenous. Hugh and I never eat before these expeditions.

"Hurry," Mick says, flinging our overcoats at Hugh and me, jamming his arms into his own.

"Hugh and I can manage," I say. "You have to go to school."

"I'm done with school. I knows enough already."

This is an ongoing argument: I want Mick to get an education; he hates sitting still in a classroom, being treated like a child. His life on the streets, as well as the experiences that he and Hugh and I have shared, have made him precociously mature. But there's no time to argue now. Bundled in coats, hats, and mufflers, we lug my equipment out the front door.

Carriages and wagons are already rolling down Whitechapel

High Street. Snowflakes dance in the yellow haloes around the gas lamps. Coal smoke rising from chimneys mixes with the fog, the chemical fumes from the factories, and the stench from nearby slaughterhouses. People emerge like gray ghosts from the murky atmosphere that obscures my view of the street beyond twenty feet in either direction. As I lock the door, machinery clangs. A train rumbles into Aldgate East Station down the block; even in early morning, the East End of London is never silent. Although we're in a hurry, I pause to admire the studio.

It's in a row of the oldest buildings on the street, which date from the past century. Their three-story whitewashed stucco fronts and attics set in gables rise above the ground floors. Ours, located between a watchmaker and a jeweler, has "S. Bain Photographer & Co." painted in gold letters over the door and display window. This part of Whitechapel is the sprucest, most prosperous and respectable. To look at it, one would never know that it's surrounded by some of London's worst slums. I still can't believe my good fortune. I only wish I had time to use the studio and build up a clientele. The kind of work I'm doing today keeps me too busy.

"Come on, Sarah!" Mick calls.

Laden with my equipment, we hurry up the street, then down Brick Lane, entering the neighborhood of Spitalfields. The brick tenements look dispirited in the snow, smoky fog, and gas light. A layer of cold grime coats my face; I can feel my tongue turning black.

"At least this one's close," Hugh says.

They're always close. Whitechapel has an overabundance of violent deaths. Our house is conveniently situated. Trudging between Hugh and Mick, I can hardly believe I didn't know them until about two years ago, and now they're my dearest friends with whom I live and work. I glance at Hugh. Despite his looks and the fact that we're both single, our relationship is happily platonic. He's not interested in women, and my affections are engaged elsewhere.

Four blocks later, we turn left on Fashion Street, whose narrow, cobblestoned length divides terraces of three-story brick buildings. A small crowd is gathered outside the second from the corner. The people appear to be local tradesmen and housewives; dressed in dark winter garb, they resemble vultures huddled around carrion. The building is a public house, tall and narrow, with a door on the left, a large, mullioned window on the right, and a pair of smaller windows on each upper floor. The woodwork is painted dark red. Gold letters mounted across the front read, "The Ropemaker's Daughter." From a pole at the roofline hangs a flag illustrated with a picture of a red-haired girl in a white dress, holding a coiled rope. A young police constable with rosy cheeks is stationed outside the pub. Snow frosts his tall helmet and blue uniform. He rubs his gloved hands and stomps his booted feet to keep warm.

I swallow my fear of the law, which I've had since childhood and still plagues me even though my job puts me in daily contact with the police.

"We're not too late," Mick says happily. "There oughta be somethin' worth seein'."

Dread grips my stomach. Hugh says, "God, I hope it isn't too awful."

The constable sees us approaching the door. "Hey! What do you think you're doing?"

"Good morning, Constable," Hugh says with his most charming smile. "We're from the *Daily World* newspaper. We're here to take photographs."

The constable plants his feet wide and his hands on his hips. "This here's a crime scene. You can't go in."

"Then we'll just take photographs outside," Hugh says. "Would you like to be in one?"

"Well, all right." The constable seems pleased, flattered.

"What's your name?" Hugh asks.

"Mitchell, sir."

"If you'll just stand over there, Mr. Mitchell?" Hugh gestures away from the door.

Hugh's aristocratic bearing and accent command respect. The constable moves. "The wife would be tickled to see me in the papers." Then he sees Mick sneaking into the pub. "Hey! Stop!"

The crowd cheers. Hugh and I grab my equipment and scramble after Mick, but Constable Mitchell blocks our way. From within the pub, Mick exclaims, "Gorblimey!"

Another constable steps out of the pub. He has unruly dark hair, a slender but strong build, and an irate expression. Mitchell says, "Sorry, Barrett. They tricked me."

"It's all right," Barrett says. "Let them in."

Even though we're courting, when I see Barrett in uniform, I see the uniform first, and my fear of the law resurges. Then my heart flip-flops like it does every time we meet, despite the fact that we've been lovers for almost a year. I'm so smitten with him that I smile even though he doesn't.

"Fancy meeting you here." His carefully proper speech disguises his humble East End origins. Wry tenderness underlies the disapproval in his crystal-clear gray eyes.

This is the first time he's been at a death scene when Hugh, Mick, and I showed up. It's his duty to keep the public away from the scenes and protect evidence, but he's accommodating my friends and me because he loves me. I smile apologetically, knowing he doesn't like my job. He thinks it's unsuitable for a woman and only tolerates it because it's my livelihood. It's one reason our relationship is rocky.

"How did you hear about this so fast?" Barrett adds, "I only just got here myself."

"The *Daily World* has informants all over town." At every hour of the day, they hang around police stations and taverns in every neighborhood, ready to gather and pass on information about crimes and other newsworthy events. They include the man who

woke me up this morning. They alert the photographers and reporters who cover the stories for the paper.

"It's good to have friends in the right places." Hugh claps Barrett on the back and starts to enter the pub.

"Don't come in, Hugh," Mick calls. "You don't wanna see this."

"I'll take your word for it." Hugh retreats.

He has a weak stomach. I'm afraid mine will fail me; that's why
I didn't eat breakfast. I've endured viewing many terrible crime
scenes, both before and after I began photographing them last October, but someday there will be one I can't take. This could be it.

"It's bad, Sarah. Maybe you'd better skip it too," Barrett says,
trying to discourage me.

"I'll be all right." I avoid Barrett's gaze as he helps me carry my
equipment through the door. I don't want to see his ambivalence;
nor do I want him to see me struggle to muster my nerve.

When I step into the dim passage, the smell of blood and ordure
hits me like the foul wind from a slaughterhouse. A wave of nausea
churns sour bile up from my stomach. I drop my camera case at the
threshold and clap my hand over my nose and mouth—too late to
keep out the taste of iron and salt, meat and feces. The dark wooden
wainscoting and white walls swim dizzyingly around me. At the
end of the passage, beside a steep staircase, blood is spattered like a
thick red sunburst across the black-and-white tile floor. In the
middle lies the large, crumpled, bloodstained body of a man dressed
in a white shirt, black trousers, and black shoes. Instead of a head,
he has only a ragged, gory stump.

I've seen the corpses of four of Jack the Ripper's victims, who
were brutally stabbed and mutilated. This is just as terrible. I'm
glad it's so cold in here; otherwise, the smell would be even worse.

Mick, standing near me, says, "The bloke was hanged!" His
voice is shrill with horror and excitement.

I look up and see the thick rope that dangles from the railing
on the second-story landing. Caught inside the loop at its end is
the dead man's head, suspended about ten feet from the floor.

"His head came off!" Mick says.

The man's eyes are bulging, his mouth slack, and his cheeks bloated and purple. His short, smooth gray hair and beard look incongruously neat. Torn flesh under his chin oozes stringy red clots. I gag. It takes all my willpower not to vomit.

"I didn't know that could happen." Mick sounds awed.

Neither did I. Criminals are routinely hanged for offenses that include but aren't limited to murder. Stories about executions feature regularly in the newspapers, but I've never heard of anyone's head coming off.

Barrett peers up at the railing. He looks a little green. He's been on the police force for eleven years, patrolling beats in London's roughest neighborhoods, but the terrible things he's seen haven't prepared him for this. "He dropped at least ten feet before the rope pulled tight. The force on his neck must have been so great that it decapitated him."

I want to run away and forget I ever saw this—but I'll never forget, and I've a job to do. My hands shake as I set up my tripod and camera as close to the body as I can while avoiding the blood spatters. Working always calms me. My stomach settles enough for me to speak.

"Who is he?" I say.

"His name is Harry Warbrick," Barrett says.

"What happened?" Hugh calls from outside.

Mick runs to the door and tells him, sparing no details. I hear exclamations from the crowd as I load a negative plate into my camera and fill the flash lamp with powder.

"I've not had time to investigate yet, but this was probably a suicide," Barrett says. "So there's no need for you to take pictures."

I know from experience that things are sometimes far from what they seem on the surface. "Why do you think so?"

Barrett frowns; he doesn't like me challenging his professional judgment—or the sense of competition between us. Nor does he like the fact that Hugh and Mick and I, untrained amateurs who started a private inquiry service last year, have already solved two major cases. One was Jack the Ripper. Barrett is among a very few people in the world who know that we succeeded while the police failed, and he can't help taking the failure personally.

"It would have been difficult to hang a man as big as Mr. Warbrick," Barrett says.

"That's a good point." And it's hard for me to believe anyone would inflict such a violent death on himself. But he probably didn't know he would be decapitated. "Who found him?"

"The charwoman, when she came to clean this morning," Barrett explains. "The front door was locked. She has a key. There was no sign of forced entry."

"What about the back door?" I see it at the end of the passage, beyond Warbrick's body.

Barrett compresses his lips; his patience is wearing thin. "I was on my way to check when I was rudely interrupted."

I don't want to argue with him, but my experience with crimes has sharpened my instincts, and I sense something in the atmosphere—a lingering trace of malevolence? If I'm right, and this death proves to be murder, I'll live to regret leaving the scene empty-handed. I put my head under the black drape that covers the back of my camera, aim the lens, and focus. Holding up the flash lamp, I snap the shutter. Flash powder explodes, lighting up Mr. Warbrick's corpse. Sulfurous smoke overlays the reek of blood and death.

"It's not right for Sir Gerald to make you do this," Barrett says.

My friends and I work for Sir Gerald Mariner. One of the richest men in England, Sir Gerald made his first fortune in shipping, his second in banking, and ventured into the newspaper business when he bought the *Daily World*. I bristle at Barrett's insinuation that Sir Gerald has bought me.

"I chose to accept the job." But it's true that I'm at Sir Gerald's beck and call twenty-four hours of the day. That's the reason my studio sits unused while I photograph crime scenes.

"Working for him is dangerous."

I wince at the reminder as I emerge from the black drape, take the exposed negative plate out of my camera, and insert a fresh one. Last April, Sir Gerald hired Hugh, Mick, and me to find his kidnapped baby son. The investigation almost cost us our lives, although it earned us Sir Gerald's respect and further employment. "I just take photographs. Hugh or Mick or both of them are always with me. What could happen?"

"All sorts of bad things have happened to you three." Barrett's expression darkens; I know he's remembering the night in a slaughterhouse in 1888. "I'm only trying to protect you. And Sir Gerald is a monster."

I can't disagree; the kidnapping investigation had shown me the worst about my employer. I also know Barrett is protective of me because he loves me. "Sir Gerald pays well."

Barrett lowers his voice. "You wouldn't need his money if we got married."

Resistance flares in me even though I love him and want to be with him forever. I busy myself with adjusting the settings on my camera and taking more photographs. I can't explain to him why I'm reluctant to marry him. My reasons are so personal, so complicated.

"We're supposed to have dinner with my parents on Thursday," Barrett says. A crime scene isn't the best place for personal conversation, but we may not have another chance to talk later. "Do you think you can make it this time?"

I've canceled twice, on short notice, because of my work. I know Barrett is hurt, and it's another reason he dislikes Sir Gerald—my job has kept us apart, our future in limbo. But I was actually glad for an excuse to avoid the dinner. I'm shy, and I'm afraid his parents won't like me. I'm plain, thirty-three years old—two years his senior; he could get a younger, prettier, more charming woman. And meeting them is a step closer to marriage. "Yes. I promise."

Barrett smiles, but there's doubt in his eyes.

"I say, Barrett," Hugh calls from outside the pub, "do you know who Harry Warbrick was?"

"The pub's owner," Barrett says.

"He was also a hangman. That's what these good folks out here tell me." Hugh has a talent for striking up conversations and making friends wherever he goes. "Mr. Warbrick has hanged hundreds of criminals all over England. He's reputedly the best in the business."

"Well," Barrett says, disconcerted because Hugh has learned something that he himself hasn't had time to find out.

I'm interested to hear that a hangman has met the same end that he inflicted on others. It's as if his past has caught up with him, and fate has exacted justice.

"That's why his pub is called The Ropemaker's Daughter," Hugh says. "It's a polite name for the gallows."

It's said that when a man is hanged, he marries the ropemaker's daughter. I imagine hands that have tied nooses pouring me a drink, and I shiver. "Why was Mr. Warbrick running a pub?" I call.

"Hangings pay ten pounds apiece," says a woman outside. "Not enough to live on."

"So the poor fellow's head came off because he fell such a long distance," Hugh marvels. "After hanging so many people, wouldn't he have known to use a shorter rope?"

"I should think so." I focus my camera on Warbrick's suspended head.

"If he was in a disturbed state of mind, he might not have cared," Barrett says.

"He'd have cared," says a man in the crowd. "He always bragged that he'd never botched a hanging. He liked to tell the story of a hangman, named James Berry, who decapitated a bloke in 1885. Called Berry a disgrace to the profession. He wouldn't have botched his own hanging. It was a matter of honor."

I'd never thought of honor in connection with hangmen, but I suppose that every profession has its standards. I'm carefully composing these photographs, even though they may be too gruesome to publish in the newspaper.

"If Mr. Warbrick didn't hang himself, then this was murder." Hugh sounds excited.

"We better look for clues." Mick hurries toward the stairs.

Barrett blocks his path. "Oh no, you don't." He says to me, "This is why I don't want you and your friends here."

When we're confronted with a mystery, we feel compelled to solve it, even if it's none of our business. If we run roughshod over the crime scene, Barrett could get in serious trouble for letting us obstruct the police's efforts to catch the murderer.

Nimbly avoiding the blood on the floor, Mick runs through the doorway at the right of the passage, into the taproom. "Don't worry—I won't tinker with evidence."

Barrett stalks after him. I follow, eager to get away from the corpse and propelled by my curiosity. The taproom has a wood floor and wainscoting and contains a dozen wooden tables with benches. Framed pictures cover the whitewashed walls. At the back is the bar, with its row of taps; the bottles and glasses on shelves behind it; and the fireplace. A gaslight fixture dangles from the pressed tin ceiling.

"Look!" Mick says.

"Found something?" Hugh calls.

Mick points to the floor. "Bloody footprints."

I see smeared red marks on the floor. Barrett says, "Don't step on them."

"Somebody was here after Warbrick's head came off," Mick says. "They walked in his blood."

Something crunches under my foot. "Here's broken glass." I see more fragments under the tables and smell spilled liquor. "These may be signs of a struggle. Warbrick may have fought with his killer before he died."

"Maybe," Barrett says. "But fights and broken glass in pubs aren't unusual."

I point out damp, bloody streaks amid the glass. "I think that whoever tracked blood in here was trying to clean up. Why would he, unless he killed Warbrick and didn't want anyone to know the hanging wasn't suicide?"

"You're right." Barrett sounds grudgingly impressed by my deductions.

Mick is in the passage, tiptoeing between blood spatters and around the headless corpse. Barrett gingerly follows him to the back door. Mick opens it. "It weren't locked."

"Don't keep me in suspense," Hugh calls.

"Someone went out the back door after Warbrick died." I look outside.

Across the alley, trees with bare branches loom inside the brick wall that encloses the yard of Christ Church. Red footprints show on the thin snow on the cobblestones, getting fainter until they vanish amid other footprints. I hear the sound of hoofbeats and wheels rattling in the street.

Someone calls, "The police surgeon's here with the meat wagon."

"Time for you to go." Barrett points Mick and me toward the front door. "Out!"

Chapter 2

A crowded, noisy underground train takes Hugh, Mick, and me across town to Blackfriars Station. We carry my photography equipment to Fleet Street, where the major newspapers are based in tall buildings that rise like cliffs, and the loud, mechanical clatter of printing presses reverberates. Traffic adds to the din. Fleet Street is one of London's main thoroughfares, clogged with pedestrians. Carriages and cabs stall behind omnibuses pausing to let out passengers and wagons delivering huge rolls of paper to the presses. Snow, smoke, and fog veil the massive dome of St. Paul's to the east and the Gothic spire of St. Dunstan's Church to the west. The snow on the ground is already black with soot. So are the hems of my skirts by the time we reach the headquarters of the *Daily World*.

The five-story building boasts a stone facade, Greek columns, Moorish arched windows, and Baroque turrets. Above a giant clock on the curved corner is the Mariner insignia—a sailing ship sculpted in marble, a nod to Sir Gerald's past as a shipping magnate. On the ground floor, an army of men operates the presses and linotype machines. As we climb the stairs, I feel the vibration of the giant machines casting iron letters and rolling, printing, and cutting pages for the next edition. I breathe the distinctive odor of chemical ink, hot metal, and motor oil. On the second floor are the photography and engraving studios. The darkrooms contain sinks, running water, all the necessary tools, spacious worktables, modern enlargers, and cabinets full of supplies. I could leave my negatives for the staff to develop, as other photographers do, but I prefer to develop them myself and control their quality.

Hugh chats with the staff while Mick helps me pour chemical solutions into trays. When we started working for the paper, I worried that Hugh wouldn't fit in. A little more than a year ago, a different newspaper exposed him as a homosexual. His family disowned him; his high-society friends dropped him; and wherever he goes, he fears that people will shun him. Some here have indeed snubbed him and made unkind remarks, but most were willing to give him a chance, and his charm has won them over. He loves company, and he's happy to have new friends.

Mick and I develop, enlarge, and print the photographs. It takes awhile, because the newspaper keeps the negatives of the pictures it publishes, and I always shoot extras for my own portfolio. We're just finishing when Hugh knocks on the door.

"Sir Gerald wants to see you in the conference room. Bring the photographs."

I give the negatives to the engravers, who will convert the shades of gray into a halftone—a pattern of tiny black dots. They'll copy the halftone onto a metal plate coated with chemicals and etch it with acid. The finished plate, mounted on the press, produces amazingly detailed, realistic printed images. Wide-scale use of this method is a recent innovation in the newspaper business. I'm proud to see my work in the *Daily World*, but apprehension speeds my heartbeat as I carry the damp prints up the stairs, past the third floor where reporters, at long tables beneath hanging lamps, type on rackety typewriters amid tobacco smoke and clicking telegraph machines. These photographs of the murder scene, taken under less than ideal conditions, aren't my best, and Sir Gerald, who takes an active interest in the newspaper's operation, is capable of severe retribution when displeased.

On the fourth floor, where the top brass have their offices, I find Sir Gerald seated in the conference room with two men I know only by name and sight. One is James Palmer, editor-in-chief; the younger is Malcolm Cross, a reporter. My gaze fixes on Sir Gerald. Over six feet tall, his stout body clad in an expensive black suit, he dominates any gathering; he commands attention. He's more than sixty years old, his hair and beard iron gray, his broad features weathered by years at sea, but he's strong and robust. I hover outside the door as he gives orders to the two men. His rough Northern accent reveals his origins as a cabin boy from Liverpool. Now he notices me.

"Miss Bain. Come in."

He and the other men stand as I approach. The room is untidy, the table scattered with proof sheets; back issues of the newspaper are piled on the floor. Grimy windows look out on Fleet Street. Sir Gerald pulls out a chair for me and says, "Let's see what you've got."

We sit, and I spread the photos on the table. Even in black and white, the images of Harry Warbrick's decapitated corpse and his head suspended from the noose are stunningly explicit.

"Holy hell!" Sir Gerald says.

James Palmer and Malcolm Cross gape with horrified revulsion. Mr. Palmer is a gentleman in his fifties, thin of hair, face, and chest, wide of bottom. Spectacles frame his red-rimmed eyes. Despite the fire in the hearth, he wears thick layers of clothing, a wool muffler, and fingerless gloves. He's one of the few men in the upper echelon that Sir Gerald didn't fire when he bought the *Daily World*. I know this because Hugh tells me all the gossip. Shy with strangers, I've not cultivated new friends, and I prefer to keep a low profile, for reasons related to my past.

"And the poor bastard was a hangman?" Sir Gerald asks.

Malcolm Cross beats me to the reply. "That's right, Sir Gerald. My source is reliable." He has a round, rosy, boyish face, and a perpetual smile, but his blue eyes are as sharp as cut glass. He wears natty striped shirts with suits tailored to fit his trim figure and more expensive than he can afford. Hugh told me that Sir Gerald hired Cross away from the *Telegraph*, and although Cross is only twenty—the youngest of all the reporters—he's the rising star.

"Run the pictures in the morning paper," Sir Gerald says.

"Yes, sir." Mr. Palmer's face shows the same nervousness that I feel in the presence of Sir Gerald.

Sir Gerald's bold eyes gleam. "This could be a big story."

He has an instinct for big stories, even though he's only been in the newspaper business for the six months since he bought the *Daily World* and invited me to join the staff as a photographer.

"I'm ready for a new challenge," he'd said that summer day in his office at the Mariner Bank. "This is an excellent business opportunity. I've seen the power of the press."

I interpreted that as a reference to the kidnapping of his son Robin and all the public attention the press had generated. But he never talks about Robin, and it's a tacit rule that no one mentions the kidnapping in his presence.

"The *Daily World* was heading for bankruptcy," he said. "I got it cheap. If I can turn it around, I'll buy others and build a news-paper empire."

I think he had other motives besides a desire for novelty.

In the aftermath of Robin's kidnapping, Sir Gerald took ill—with pneumonia, according to an official statement. But rumors said he'd had a nervous breakdown. Hugh confirmed it with people who work for Sir Gerald. They said he had stopped sleeping and washing, drank too much, looked like a tramp, and frightened them with his erratic, sometimes violent behavior. He made rash investments. Customers and business partners lost confidence in him and withdrew their money from his bank. Friends and politi-cians distanced themselves from him.

Perhaps his new venture was an attempt to distract himself from the horror of the kidnapping and a way to regain his hold on his wealth and power.

His wife confined him to their mansion on Hampstead Heath and called in the best physicians to treat him secretly. When he recovered, he followed the same daring course of action as he had decades ago, when some ships in his fleet were wrecked at sea and he lost a fortune. He used his remaining funds to buy up banks and reinvented himself as one of England's richest men. When his banking empire faltered, he plunged into the newspaper business with the same ruthless determination to succeed. He poured money into the *Daily World*, buying new equipment, hiring new staff, and clearing out deadwood. The antiquated paper gained a modern, eye-catching design, with plentiful photographs, and he has increased circulation twenty percent. Hugh says the staff members are afraid they'll fail to live up to his expectations and lose their jobs.

I wonder if, in addition to a breakdown, Sir Gerald suffered an attack of conscience over black marks on his record. A cutthroat businessman who's destroyed his rivals, he's also a former slave trader and a murderer. Is he trying to make a fresh start, to outrun fate?

"Find out everything about Warbrick's death," Sir Gerald tells Malcolm Cross.

"I'll get on to my contacts at the police station right away." Cross's smile broadens with pleasure at this important assignment.

I clear my throat. "It was murder."

Cross and Mr. Palmer look at me as if the furniture had spoken. "How do you know?" Mr. Palmer says.

Uncomfortable in the sudden limelight, I describe the signs of a struggle hastily cleaned up, the open back door, and the bloody footprints in the alley. I mention that Mr. Warbrick, a proud expert hangman, would have avoided decapitating himself.

Mr. Palmer raises his eyebrows, impressed; Cross frowns because I've one-upped him.

"Murder," Sir Gerald says with relish. "The story's getting even better. Have the police any leads on who did it?"

"Not yet," I say.

"Incompetent fools." Sir Gerald has a dim view of the police because he thinks they mishandled the investigation of Robin's kidnapping.

Cross's smile hardens with his determination to regain the center of attention. "I'm sure I can dig up some new facts." He rises.

"Wait," Sir Gerald says. "I've an idea. Let's beat the police at their own game."

"What do you mean?" Mr. Palmer asks.

Dread gathers in the pit of my stomach. I think I know what's coming.

"We'll stage a contest. We'll investigate Warbrick's murder and solve it before the police do," Sir Gerald explains. "We'll run progress reports in the paper. It'll boost sales."

"We've never done such a thing . . ." Mr. Palmer subsides as Sir Gerald frowns.

I'm not the only one who walks on eggshells around Sir Gerald, for fear that the erratic, violent behavior that accompanied his breakdown will return.

"But what a wonderful publicity stunt," Cross says.

Sir Gerald ignores Cross's attempt to ingratiate himself. "You'll write the stories."

"I can do more than that," Cross says. "I'll find witnesses and suspects."

"Fine. However"—Sir Gerald points his thick, blunt finger at me—"Miss Bain, you're in charge of the investigation."

The dread solidifies into a cold, heavy weight as my memory echoes with gunshots. My last investigation for Sir Gerald ended in more than one death. But I thrill at the prospect of a new crime to solve, and all my life I've been attracted to danger. Fear makes me feel alive. It's a quirk of my nature. Still, I have strong reason not to want to be in charge of the investigation. Barrett is already upset about my photographing crime scenes. I don't want us on opposite sides, with me competing against the police to solve the murder.

"*Her?*" Cross regards me with scorn. "She's a woman."

Other women work at the paper, but they're low within the hierarchy. One writes an advice column for female readers; the others are secretaries or tea servers. There are some female reporters and editors at other papers, I've heard.

"She's not even a reporter," Mr. Palmer says.

"She's an experienced detective," Sir Gerald says. "She's worked for me before."

I can tell from their perturbed expressions that Cross and Mr. Palmer know Sir Gerald hired my friends and and me to find Robin. I'm sure they'd like to remind Sir Gerald that the outcome was hardly ideal, but they dare not break the rule about silence on the subject of the kidnapping.

"Perhaps it would be best if Mr. Cross leads the investigation," I say. My friends and I can assist while keeping a low profile. Barrett won't have to know we're involved.

Cross looks surprised that I would dodge what he considers a plum assignment. He and Mr. Palmer turn expectantly to Sir Gerald.

"It would be best if everyone followed orders." The warning note in Sir Gerald's voice quells further dissent.

I see another reason why Sir Gerald put me in charge: Hugh, Mick, and I are beholden to him, and he trusts us to look out for his interests; less so the ambitious, self-serving Cross.

"Now that that's settled, let's get something else straight," Sir Gerald says. "Whatever you find out, keep it quiet until it's published." He addresses Mr. Palmer: "Tell the whole staff that everything to do with the Warbrick murder is strictly confidential. No blabbing to the wife or chums or other papers. Especially not to the police. We don't want them using our information to get the jump on us. We need to be ten steps ahead of them by the time it's in print."

Now I'm really disturbed, for not only must I head this contest with the police, but I can't tell Barrett anything I learn; he'll have to read it in the newspaper along with the rest of London. Honesty has been a serious issue in our relationship since we first became acquainted, when Barrett was on the Ripper case and my friends and I conducted our own clandestine hunt for the killer. Later, Barrett worked on the Mariner kidnapping case, and Sir Gerald hired us as private detectives. Both situations required me to keep information to myself, and Barrett wasn't happy about it. And I have other secrets related to my family's past.

I speak up hesitantly. "Couldn't the police accuse us of obstructing justice?" That's a crime, but I fear losing Barrett as much as a jail sentence.

"They can accuse us. It won't stick," Sir Gerald says with calm confidence. He has connections with people in high places all over the world, but I can only hope that his wealth and power will shield his associates as well as himself from the law. "Time's a-wasting." He waves his hand in dismissal. "Go solve the murder."

★ ★ ★

I hurry after Malcolm Cross as he strides down the passage. He goes into the stairwell and slams the door in my face. Irritated, I yank it open and call, "Mr. Cross!"

He pauses halfway down the dim, cold flight of stairs. "What do you want?"

Our dislike is mutual, but we're yoked together nonetheless. "We should discuss how to proceed with the investigation."

"There's nothing to discuss. I'm not working for you."

"Sir Gerald expects us to solve the murder. We need to figure out what to do, divide up the tasks—"

"Cut the crap. You may be in bed with Sir Gerald, but you don't give me orders, no matter what he says."

I stare, offended. Behind my sedate facade, I have a temper, and it flares at Cross. "You don't talk to me that way." I wonder uneasily how many people think my relationship with Sir Gerald is improper.

Cross laughs, glad he's gotten a rise out of me. "I'll talk to you however I please."

The sound of footsteps echoes up through the stairwell. Hugh and Mick join us. "What's going on?" Hugh asks.

I tell them about the contest, and they react with exclamations of delight. "What're we waitin' for?" Mick says. "Let's get started."

"Glad to be working with you." Hugh extends his hand to Cross. "I don't believe we've been formally introduced. I'm Hugh Staunton."

"I know who you are." Cross eyes him with revulsion. "Get away from me, nancy boy."

Hugh's smile fades. I'm troubled to learn that Cross is among those who despise men like Hugh, and I think there's another reason behind his animosity. Cross's accent and manners peg him as working class, and Hugh unintentionally makes him feel inferior.

"Hey!" Mick says. "Take that back, or I'll belt you!" He once reviled Hugh himself; now he's Hugh's loyal defender. He grabs Cross by the arm and raises his own fist.

"Let me go, you brat!" Cross says.

They wrestle, stumbling down the stairs. Hugh and I pull Mick off Cross.

Cross smoothes his hair, straightens his clothes, and glares at us. "You don't belong here. I'm going to solve the murder by myself. And don't try to take credit for it. I'll make sure Sir Gerald knows it was all me, and he doesn't need the lot of you."

He stomps down the stairs. Mick yells after him, "Rotter!"

Then we look at each other in consternation. "We can't let him do that," Hugh says. Sir Gerald's money pays for our rent, our bread and butter.

"I'm supposed to take Catherine out to supper tonight," Mick says.

Catherine Price, a friend of ours, is a beautiful young actress, currently performing in London's West End. Mick is in love with her, no matter that she's nineteen and he's fourteen; he's determined to win her hand someday. He faces serious competition from her many other suitors, some wealthy and distinguished. I know he's desperate to grow up fast and become a man of means himself before she marries somebody else. For now, Catherine accepts Mick's company because he's the one who risked his life and killed for her. That's a hard act to beat, but wooing Catherine is expensive. Mick can't keep it up if he loses his employment with Sir Gerald.

Hugh gives Mick a look of sympathy. "You're not the only one who can't afford to get on Sir Gerald's bad side."

Hugh is engaged in a passionate love affair with Sir Gerald's son Tristan Mariner, a secret known only to themselves, Mick, Fitzmorris, and me. God only knows what Sir Gerald would do if he learned his son is a homosexual. He might blame Hugh for corrupting Tristan. Hugh has worked hard stockpiling good will with Sir Gerald in case the worst happens.

I state the obvious. "We'd better solve the murder."

"I've an idea where to start looking for the hangman's hangman," Hugh says.

Mick and I smile. Hugh always has ideas. That's one of the things we like about him.

"The murder didn't seem like a burglary gone wrong," Hugh says. "A common criminal wouldn't bother to cover it up by faking a suicide. Odds are, the killer is someone close to Warbrick. His family should be our first stop."

CHAPTER 3

We collect my photography equipment and return to The Ropemaker's Daughter to find out where Warbrick lived. Neighbors direct us to Church Street, one block north. Mick carries my camera, Hugh my trunk, and I my satchel, past Christ Church, the landmark that dominates the skyline of Spitalfields and Whitechapel. The snow has stopped, but the church's tall, pointed steeple looks as insubstantial as if made of the fog that still thickens the air. Beyond the church, the street contains rows of three-story Georgian brick townhouses. They're of a higher standard than the other houses in the area, once occupied by master weavers in the silk industry. Now the silk industry is defunct, and the houses belong to the neighborhood's wealthier citizens. We don't need to see the address to identify which belonged to Harry Warbrick. A crowd loiters outside a house with a front door painted black and decorative red masonry around the windows.

"The grapevine's been hard at work," Hugh says. "News of murder spreads fast."

Drawing near, we hear a man in the crowd say, "I'm a reporter with the *Daily World*. My readers will want to know what Mrs. Warbrick has to say about her husband's murder."

I recognize his young, belligerent voice. "That's Malcolm Cross."

"He beat us here," Mick says with chagrin.

"Well, you can't talk to Mrs. Warbrick. We have to interview her first."

This irate voice is familiar too. My heart sinks. My friends and I halt twenty paces away, grimace at one another, and say, "Inspector Reid."

We ran afoul of Reid during the Ripper investigation as well as the search for Sir Gerald's kidnapped son. Reid swore to get revenge on us. He thinks we know more than we're telling about both cases. He also thinks we're responsible for the fact that the Ripper has never been caught. He's right on both counts.

"How about letting me sit in on the interview?" Cross says.

"Get lost," Reid says.

"We'd better go," Hugh says. Reid swore to get the truth out of us, and if he does, it would be the gallows for us. But we're curious to see whether Cross gets the better of Reid.

"You haven't seen the last of me," Cross says. "The *Daily World* is challenging the police to a contest."

"What contest?" demands another man, hidden in the crowd.

It's Barrett. I murmur, "Oh no." I wanted to be the one to break the news to him.

"To see who can solve Warbrick's murder first—you or us?" Cross says.

Reid snorts with disgust. Barrett asks in an ominous tone, "When did this come up?"

"Today," Cross says.

"I see." Barrett obviously thinks I was already in on the contest when we met at the murder scene this morning, and deliberately neglected to tell him about it. He must be remembering other times I've kept secrets from him. I can almost feel his blood start to boil.

"I won't have you snooping around, getting in my way." Indignation raises Reid's voice.

"Seems like you need some new detectives on the job," Cross retorts. "You could have used the help while you were hunting the Ripper."

Laughter bursts from the crowd. I can't see Reid, but I sense the heat of his temper. The unsolved Ripper case is a sore point with the police, who have been widely criticized by the public and in the press. I can't see Barrett either, but I know he's thinking of the night at the slaughterhouse. That night bound us together forever, but it doesn't mean our love is indestructible.

"Mr. Cross, get off the premises at once or you'll be arrested," Reid says.

"Aye, aye, sir." Cross saunters away.

"The show's over," Reid says to the crowd. "Go home." The crowd scatters, leaving him and Barrett alone. "By the way, PC Barrett, I heard that you applied for a promotion to sergeant."

"Yes, sir," Barrett says. I know he wants to be a detective instead of patrolling a beat, to serve justice by solving murders instead of arresting pickpockets. He also wants a higher income, so he can support me in style when—if—we marry.

"Well, I blocked your promotion," Reid says. There's bad blood between him and Barrett as well as between Reid and myself. Barrett took my side in a dispute with Reid during the Ripper investigation, and Reid has never forgotten. Reid also suspects that Barrett was involved in some trouble he had with their superiors. He's right.

"That's not fair," Barrett protests. "I was due for a promotion two years ago."

"It's your own fault you're stuck in a rut," Reid says. "You'll be stuck for good if you help your girlfriend win the contest."

"Leave Sarah out of this." Anger tightens Barrett's voice. He's paying for his decision to cast his lot with me. His past catches up with him every day on the job with Reid.

Reid laughs. "You're going to have to pick a side—hers or your fellow police's. If you want a promotion, you'd better dump Sarah Bain."

I'm furious that Reid is making an issue of Barrett's divided loyalties, forcing Barrett to choose between his career and me, seeking revenge on us through destroying our relationship. Hugh tugs my arm. "Let's go before they spot us."

We duck around the corner and take refuge in the Queen's Head public house. "We'll cool our heels here until the police are gone," Hugh says.

"I'm hungry," Mick says. "What's to eat?"

★ ★ ★

After a lunch of bread, cheese, and pickles, Hugh and I return to the Warbrick house, leaving Mick to wait in the Queen's Head with my equipment. I suspect that if Mrs. Warbrick thinks we're going to take her picture, she won't let us in. The street outside the house is now deserted. When I knock at the door, a shrill female voice calls, "Go away. The missus isn't seeing visitors."

Hugh speaks in his most aristocratic, pleasant voice. "I'm sorry to bother Mrs. Warbrick at such a bad time, but we're from the Home Office."

I raise my eyebrows at Hugh. He shrugs and smiles at his ruse. The door opens to reveal a plain older woman in a housemaid's gray frock, white apron, and white cap. Hugh tips his hat and smiles. Her eyes widen, dazzled by his good looks.

"Please allow me to introduce myself. My name is Hugh Bain. This is my sister, Sarah." It's not the first time Hugh has posed as my brother. He avoids using his real name when someone might recognize it from his scandal. "To whom do I have the pleasure of speaking?"

"Mary Jenkins." She blushes bright red.

Hugh bows. "*Enchanté*, Miss Jenkins." He's an expert at charming women; he's done it all his life, to disguise his true nature. "If you could just tell Mrs. Warbrick we're here?"

"All right." The door closes.

Hugh holds up crossed fingers. A moment later, Miss Jenkins, who only has eyes for him, leads us through the foyer. It smells of the polish that gleams on the paneled walls and carved staircase.

It's so cold that when Miss Jenkins asks for our coats, I reluctantly let her hang mine on the stand. The parlor is barely warmer, despite the fire in the hearth, and so dim with the velvet curtains drawn over the windows and so full of furniture that at first I don't see Mrs. Warbrick. Dressed in black crepe, she hovers like a ghost. A black snood covers her hair and frames her delicate, pale face. As my eyes adjust to the dimness, I see that hers are red and swollen from crying. After the introductions, she says, "Please be seated."

Her voice is quiet, gentle. She's not what I expected. Not that I've ever thought about the kind of woman a hangman would marry, but I've seen many coarse, buxom, outspoken wives of publicans. She sits in a damask-covered armchair, Hugh and I on a velvet settee. The house, decorated with bouquets of dried flowers, seashells under glass domes, and figurines in curio cabinets, isn't what I expected either. Then again, what did I expect—a dungeon in a medieval castle? But this is the nineteenth century, not the fourteenth; a hangman is no longer the hooded brute at the village gibbet.

"Thank you for allowing us to speak with you," Hugh says. "The Home Office sent us to deliver condolences on behalf of Her Majesty's government. And please allow us to express our personal sympathy for the loss of your husband."

"Thank you. That's very kind." Mrs. Warbrick doesn't question our identity, and she must be one of few women oblivious to Hugh's looks. She seems overwhelmed and preoccupied by sorrow. I'm ashamed of intruding on her under false pretenses. She turns to Miss Jenkins, who hovers in the doorway. "Mary, would you please bring some tea for Mr. and Miss Bain?"

"Yes, ma'am." Miss Jenkins, with a backward glance at Hugh, reluctantly departs.

"I assure you that the police will do everything in their power to apprehend your husband's killer," Hugh says.

"Yes . . . They were just here."

"It would help if you could answer a few questions," I say.

Mrs. Warbrick sighs. "All right."

"Have you any idea who might have wanted your husband dead?" I ask.

"Inspector Reid asked me that. I said no."

Miss Jenkins bustles into the parlor, carrying a tray laden with cups, saucers, and teapot. She smiles at Hugh as she serves us. I ask Mrs. Warbrick, "How did your husband get along with the people he knew?"

"Fine. He was very well liked."

"Can you tell us the names of his friends and associates?" Hugh says.

"I'm afraid not. I don't really know them."

"May I ask how long you were married?"

"Almost seventeen years."

After seventeen years together, how could a wife not know her husband's friends and associates? "Was Mr. Warbrick worried or afraid recently?" I say.

"I couldn't tell you."

Although she seems genuinely grief-stricken by his death, she could be talking about a stranger. As I ponder Mrs. Warbrick, I sip my tea, which is weak because Miss Jenkins was in such a hurry to get back to Hugh that she didn't let it steep long enough.

"Weren't you concerned when he didn't come home last night?" Hugh says.

"No. He often didn't." Mrs. Warbrick rouses herself to make the explanation that she seems to think is required. "He slept in his rooms above the pub."

"May I ask why?" Hugh says.

"He worked late. He didn't want to disturb my sleep."

Hugh gives her a sympathetic but skeptical look. Perhaps many married couples lead such separate lives, but I think something was amiss between the Warbricks.

"He often traveled," Mrs. Warbrick says, and I presume she

means he went to perform executions. "It was more convenient for him to come and go from the pub."

I think that so many excuses add up to a lie. Hugh says gently, "Forgive me if I'm being intrusive, but were there problems in your marriage?"

Mrs. Warbrick presses her lips together; then her resistance dissolves in a flood of tears. "We grew apart after he became . . . after he began working for the government fifteen years ago." She obviously can't bring herself to use the word *hangman*. "But he was a good provider." Mrs. Warbrick gestures around the ornate room. "And I loved him. I can't believe he's dead. I just wish things could have been different." She covers her face and weeps.

Miss Jenkins pats her shoulder and says regretfully to Hugh, "Perhaps you'd better go."

"Mrs. Warbrick, have you someone to stay with you? A son or daughter or relative, perhaps?" I'm not just concerned about her; I'm also fishing for names of people who might have information relevant to the murder.

"No. Mr. Warbrick and I weren't blessed with children. Mary will look after me."

A sudden intuition tells me why the Warbricks have no children: Mrs. Warbrick couldn't bear to be touched by the hangman.

Miss Jenkins sees us to the door and hands us our coats. Hugh thanks her, smiles, and says, "I'm so glad to have met you."

"Yes, sir." She looks dazed.

After we're outside the closed door, I whisper, "I don't think Mrs. Warbrick killed her husband. She's not strong enough to have hoisted him over the stair railing."

"I don't either. And I think she's genuinely devastated by his death." Hugh tries the doorknob. The door opens. "Just as I hoped—Miss Jenkins forgot to lock it." He beckons.

"We shouldn't." I don't want to trespass, and we've already taken enough advantage of Mrs. Warbrick.

"Harry Warbrick may not have spent much time at home, but there may be clues here, and this is our chance to get them."

I follow Hugh back into the house. He eases the door shut. We hear Miss Jenkins in the kitchen, clattering dishes and humming a popular love tune. The parlor is vacant. Then Mrs. Warbrick speaks, too softly for us to discern the words. We glance up the stairs, frowning in surprise because she'd implied that she and Miss Jenkins were alone in the house. Hugh steals up the stairs even as I grab at his arm to stop him. Then I hear a male voice answer Mrs. Warbrick. Curiosity outweighs caution. I follow Hugh. The stairs creak under our footsteps; I wince.

"You shouldn't be here," Mrs. Warbrick says.

"I can't leave you alone." The man's deep voice is educated, but not upper-class.

Their next words are muffled. Hugh and I reach the second floor. The first door to the right of the passage is ajar. Hugh puts his finger to his lips as we peer inside the room.

Mrs. Warbrick and the man are sitting on the edge of the canopied, four-poster bed with their backs to us, kissing passionately. Hugh's eyes widen; I stifle a gasp. The bereaved widow isn't as bereaved as we thought. The man is big and strongly built, wearing a dark coat and trousers and white shirt. Mrs. Warbrick runs her fingers through his wavy brown hair. His silver-rimmed spectacles press against her face as he kisses her. When they break apart to catch their breath, I see that his nose is large, his profile rugged. He looks like a laborer, but his hands, unbuttoning the back of her frock, are clean, long-fingered, and gentle. I feel a sympathy for Harry Warbrick that I didn't when I saw his decapitated corpse and learned he'd been a hangman. His wife shunned him and cheated on him, and even if he was the best in his profession, his personal life was unhappy.

"We mustn't," Mrs. Warbrick says, but she's working her arms free of her tight black sleeves, shrugging the frock down to her waist, exposing her chemise and corset. She lies back on the bed, skirts and petticoats bunched around her hips; her legs, clad in black stockings, are parted. The man straddles her, pushing his trousers down.

A hot blush suffuses my face. I'm embarrassed to watch them, and they remind me of Barrett and myself. We make love at my house when nobody else is there and neither of us have to work. We—like Mrs. Warbrick and her paramour—are always in such a hurry to satisfy our desire before we're interrupted that we haven't time to undress completely. I feel the ache of arousal because it's been weeks since Barrett and I have had a chance to be together. It may be a lot longer until the next time, for he'll be angry about the contest.

Hugh raises his eyebrows and tilts his head to indicate that we've seen enough. We tiptoe down the stairs and out the door.

★　★　★

We find Mick waiting in the Queen's Head. When we tell him about Mrs. Warbrick and her lover, he says, "Maybe they bumped Warbrick off so they could get married."

"A divorce would have been easier," I say.

"Maybe Warbrick wouldn't let 'er go. Some men is like that."

I think of Mick's love for Catherine and his refusal to let go of his hope that someday she will love him in return.

"We don't believe Mrs. Warbrick is guilty, but let's be objective," Hugh says. "The adulterous wife and her paramour are good suspects."

"Perhaps he did it without her knowledge," I say.

"Who is he?" Mick asks. When Hugh and I say we don't know, he rises. "I'll wait outside her house, and when he comes out, I'll follow him. Oh, I almost forgot—while I was waitin' for you, I heard somebody say there's gonna be a wake for the hangman tonight. Seven o'clock at his pub."

CHAPTER 4

By the time Hugh and I emerge from Aldgate East station, it's one thirty. Whitechapel High Street is busy as usual, with people dodging wagons and omnibuses and crowding the shops. Peddlers hawk their wares, trains rumble underground, and the clang of machinery in factories has reached a deafening pitch. The snow has been trampled into a slush of manure, garbage, and cinders. The ragged men, women, and children who beg us for a bit of bread are more desperate than ever. Not for them the shiny red apples outside the grocer's or the sides of beef at the butcher shops. Some of them will be found frozen to death in the alleys tomorrow morning. Winter is Whitechapel's harshest season.

But Hugh, Mick, and I are glad to call Whitechapel home. I had my first studio here; Mick knows every inch of the streets where he once lived; and Hugh won't run into former friends who dropped him after his scandal.

At our studio, Fitzmorris greets us at the door. He must have been watching for us, as he usually does. His family has been in service to Hugh's for generations, and after his own parents died while he was a child, the Stauntons gave him and his siblings a home, an education, and affection. Fitzmorris has repaid the Stauntons with unstinting devotion to Hugh, whom he loves as a younger brother, and his devotion extends to Mick and me.

"You have visitors," he says.

My heart thumps. Have Barrett and Inspector Reid come to upbraid me about the contest? When Hugh and I go up to the parlor and see the man and woman who rise from their chairs, my relief is short-lived. The young woman is my half-sister Sally Albert. She's ten years younger than me, her blond hair more golden than mine, her face softer and prettier, but the resemblance between us still startles me, even after seeing her regularly for the eight months we've known each other. The man is Tristan Mariner—Sir Gerald's son and Hugh's beloved. He's the only man I've ever seen who equals Hugh in handsomeness, but where Hugh is fair and cheerful-natured, Tristan is dark of hair, complexion, and mood. He's dressed in black, from head to toe, except for his white collar.

Tristan Mariner is a Roman Catholic priest.

He and Sally both wear stiff, uncomfortable expressions. This is the first time they've met. I'm disconcerted to see them here at the same time, alarmed because something bad must have happened.

Sally hurries to me. "Sarah. Thank God you're back."

I take her hands in mine. "We weren't supposed to meet today, were we?" Sally is a servant in a mansion in Chelsea. She usually visits me every Wednesday, her regular day off.

"No, no. I'm sorry to show up like this without warning."

"Not a problem." Hugh gives Sally an affectionate smile. "It's always good to see you, Sally."

She looks at the floor as she curtseys and murmurs a polite greeting. She's shy with my housemates, despite their attempts to befriend her, and awed by my unconventional way of life.

Hugh turns to Tristan, his face lighting up as it always does in Tristan's presence. "This is a surprise. What brings you here?"

Tristan has never visited us before. He's afraid to be seen with Hugh, afraid their liaison will become public and he'll incur the wrath of the Church as well as Sir Gerald. Homosexual acts are crimes against nature and the law, punishable by a prison sentence on top of social ostracism. Hugh and Tristan usually meet in secret, at night, in places unknown to me.

"There's something I need to tell you." Tristan's manner is cold, formal.

The light drains from Hugh's eyes. I know he's afraid of losing Tristan, afraid that this is the day. Tristan nods to me. "Good afternoon, Miss Bain." He doesn't like that I know about him and Hugh; he doesn't trust me to keep their relationship secret.

"Good afternoon." My manner is as cool as his. I've told no one—not even Sally. She looks puzzled about who Tristan is, confused by the tension between him and me. For my part, I don't trust Tristan with Hugh. I'm afraid he'll drop Hugh—and break his heart—rather than continue to risk exposure as a homosexual.

"Sarah, I have to talk to you," Sally blurts.

Hugh says to Tristan, "Let's go upstairs."

"I'll start cooking dinner," Fitzmorris says.

Left alone in the parlor, Sally and I sit on the divan. I hope Barrett doesn't drop by. He and Sally have never met. She knows about him, but her existence is a secret I'm keeping from him. It's in my nature to keep personal matters private, and at first I needed time to get used to the idea of having a half-sister. Later, I found other reasons.

"What's wrong?" I ask. "Is it your mother?" Mrs. Albert—my father's second wife—is the housekeeper in the mansion where Sally works.

"No, Mother is fine." Sally twists her hands. "I saw Father today."

Shock jolts me. *"What?"*

Our father, Benjamin Bain, mysteriously disappeared—not once, but twice. The first time was in 1866, when I was ten. One evening he didn't come home. My mother and I looked for him for weeks. Then she told me he'd been killed in a riot. Recently, I'd learned that he was still alive, and last April I'd sighted him myself. When I went searching for him, I found Sally and her mother. They told me he'd disappeared on them in 1879. They don't know what became of him, and even if my mother knew, she can't tell;

she died sixteen years ago. I've since learned the troubling details about his past, but he hasn't reappeared.

Until, perhaps, now.

"It happened in the library," Sally says.

"Are you sure it was him?" I'm afraid that just because I've seen him, Sally imagined that she did.

"Yes! He looked so old, and his hair and his beard are white, but I would know him anywhere."

Although I'm not convinced, my skepticism gives way to excitement. "What did he say?"

"Nothing. But he recognized me. I could tell."

"Didn't you speak to him?"

"No, he ran away." Sally begins to cry. "Oh, Sarah, how could he?"

As I pat her hand, trying to comfort her, tears sting my own eyes. We love our father despite the fact that he abandoned us; we both long for a reunion with him. We also fear that he hasn't sought us out because he doesn't want us. But I know there's at least one other reason why he would stay away.

"He's a fugitive from the law," I remind Sally.

Benjamin Bain is the prime suspect in a case of rape and murder in 1866. The victim was Ellen Casey, a fourteen-year-old girl who lived near my family. My father was a photographer, and he took pictures of Ellen. I learned the story from his police file, which had come into my possession. At the time of his disappearance, I knew nothing of Ellen's murder or his connection with it. I did know he was in trouble with the police, who came to our house, interrogated him, and beat him. I thought it was because he organized protest marches for workers. My mother must have known the police were trying to make him confess that he'd killed Ellen, but she withheld the truth from me, and she let me think he was dead.

He'd outrun his past thus far. Why should he reappear now?

He's the reason I keep a low profile—to avoid calling attention to myself that could spill over onto him.

"But I would never report him to the police," Sally says. "Neither would you."

I didn't report my sighting—not even to Barrett. The fact that my father was the last person to see Ellen Casey alive is evidence against him, whereas there's none in his favor except Sally's and my gut feeling that he's innocent. Barrett might believe my father is guilty and feel obligated to report my sighting to his superiors, and they would mount a new manhunt for Benjamin Bain. Sally and I are loath to let him fall into the clutches of the law. Childhood loyalty dies hard. And here's my other reason for keeping Sally's existence a secret from Barrett: Sally is a potential witness in the case of Benjamin Bain. I mustn't put Barrett in the position of having to choose between shielding my sister and doing his duty by subjecting her to police interrogation. For Sally's sake, I can't gamble on what his choice would be.

"Father doesn't know he can trust us," I say. "Maybe he thinks we've turned against him."

"At least we know he's in London," Sally says.

We know something else that's more credible than her sighting of him. His two disappearances have one element in common—a man named Lucas Zehnpfennig. But at the moment, Lucas is as much a mystery as Benjamin Bain himself.

"Will you help me look for Father?" Sally's expression pleads with me.

I want to drop everything and track him down, but powerful misgivings override the urge. "If he doesn't want to be found, he won't go back to where you saw him. He could be hiding anywhere in the city." I've returned multiple times to the place where I sighted him, to no avail. It's as if by searching for him, I'm chasing a ghost from the past who runs farther away from me with every step I take. "And I have to work."

Sally doesn't seem to notice that my excuses are an attempt to weave a veil over the truth. "Oh. I'm sorry. I was so excited, I didn't think."

She's so honest and transparent that she never suspects other people of ulterior motives. I feel ashamed of deceiving her, even though it's in her interest as well as mine.

Sally rises. "I have to get back to the house. Mother thinks I went out to buy furniture polish. She won't like my being gone so long."

"I promise I'll help you look for Father as soon as possible," I say.

★ ★ ★

Soon after Sally leaves, Hugh and Tristan come downstairs. Hugh looks troubled. Tristan bows politely to me before he slips out the door. I stand by the window, look down at the busy street, and see him pull the brim of his hat low over his face and glance around to see if anyone has noticed him. Then he strides rapidly away. Hugh and I sit in armchairs by the fireplace.

"You first," he says.

When I tell him that Sally spotted my father, he smiles. "Why, that's wonderful! You should go look for him now, before his trail gets cold."

"But I can't leave the murder investigation to you and Mick."

Hugh gives me a fond, indulgent, but disapproving look. He, unlike Sally, doesn't buy my excuses.

"I'm afraid of what will happen if I find him," I confess.

"You're afraid he won't welcome a reunion with you?" Hugh says, ever perceptive.

"With me or with Sally." I'm more concerned about her feelings than mine. Facing death more than once has toughened me, but Sally seems so vulnerable.

"But if you did find him, he could clear up the Ellen Casey business."

"I'm not sure I want it cleared up. What if I discover he's guilty?"

"Sally would be devastated," Hugh agrees.

"So would I. And I couldn't let a murderer go free—not even if he's my father."

Hugh frowns. "Don't go assuming the worst, Sarah. You and Sally believe your father is innocent. So do I. Have a little faith in him and in our own judgment."

He looks on the bright side, no matter that the world has treated him so cruelly. Although his own father disowned him, he's ready to believe the best about mine. I smile, comforted. "Very well." But I'm still glad that investigating the hangman's murder will keep me too busy to look for my father. I'm also glad to change the subject. "What did Tristan have to say?"

Hugh expels his breath; his troubled expression returns. "Lady Alexandra had a miscarriage last week."

Lady Alexandra is Tristan's stepmother, Sir Gerald's wife. "Oh no." Sadness fills me.

"It's her third since Robin's kidnapping," Hugh says. "And the doctor told her she won't be able to have any more children."

Sir Gerald had let on nothing about this, but the losses must have been grievous blows. Maybe the *Daily World* is a refuge from personal problems that are beyond his ability to solve.

"The upshot of it is, Sir Gerald wants to mend fences with Tristan," Hugh says.

Father and son clashed many years ago over Tristan's decision to become a priest. Sir Gerald wanted Tristan to join his business empire and has constantly tried to coerce Tristan into quitting the Church. Tristan, just as stubborn, has resisted, and their relationship is stormy.

"Sir Gerald must have realized he'll never have another child unless he divorces Lady Alexandra and remarries, and even then there's no guarantee. Tristan is the only one left." I don't mention Sir Gerald's daughter. Olivia is another taboo subject. "He's not young, and he's decided to make the best of the present situation instead of gambling on the future."

"It does seem a little cold to me," Hugh says, "but I told Tristan I'm glad there's a chance for him and his father to reconcile. Which I truly am."

I hear in Hugh's voice his wish for a reconciliation with his own father. Sir Gerald is far from a perfect parent and so is Lord Staunton, but I envy Hugh and Tristan. They at least know exactly what, and where, their fathers are. "What does Tristan think?"

"He thinks it's his duty to meet Sir Gerald halfway."

"He would." I can't keep the tartness out of my voice. Tristan is big on duty, and I fear he'll eventually choose duty to the Church, God, and Sir Gerald over Hugh. Although society would deem that an honorable choice, I have Hugh's interests at heart.

Hugh's lips twist in a rueful smile: he wants Tristan and me to like each other. "I think Tristan has always craved Sir Gerald's affection and approval, and this is his chance to get it."

"Does this mean Sir Gerald will stop pressuring Tristan to quit the priesthood?" I know Hugh also wishes Tristan would quit. Carnal relations of any kind are prohibited for Roman Catholic priests, and homosexuality is doubly forbidden. To maintain his integrity, Tristan either must leave the clergy or leave Hugh.

"We don't know exactly what Sir Gerald intends."

"Does it mean Tristan isn't going back to his mission in India?" I recall that Tristan had, for love of Hugh, canceled his return last summer.

"He's postponed it indefinitely." Hugh says, "Sir Gerald wants him to move back home." Sir Gerald lives at Mariner House, his mansion on Hampstead Heath. Tristan lives at a residence for priests. "He wants them to spend time together. Rides on the heath, brandy in the study after dinner, etcetera. So they can figure out how to get along instead of getting at each other's throats. Tristan is moving in tomorrow."

I begin to understand the new problem. "Oh."

"Yes. It'll be even harder for Tristan and me to see each other,"

Hugh says glumly. "The guards at Mariner House watch every-body who lives there and report to Sir Gerald. If he were to find out about us . . ."

I modify the advice he gave me. "Don't go expecting the worst."

Hugh smiles. "You're right. I'm sure things will work out. In the meantime, we've a murder to solve. I'm ready." He goes to the lamp table by the chaise longue, opens the drawer, and removes a pistol. He bought the gun last spring, after our investigation of Robin Mariner's kidnapping put us in danger. "Shall I bring it to the wake tonight?"

"No! Put it away." After that night on Hampstead Heath, I know what guns can do, but Hugh and Mick treat this one as if it's a toy. I hope our new investigation won't require a weapon.

Hugh shakes his head, disappointed, but puts the gun back in the drawer. "If anyone assaults you, I'll just have to defend you with my bare hands."

CHAPTER 5

The Ropemaker's Daughter shines like a beacon in the dark, foggy night. People loiter on the pavement outside, and laughter bursts from the open door as Hugh and I approach. Mick didn't come home, so we're attending Harry Warbrick's wake by ourselves. The pub is packed. Warbrick was a local celebrity, and the manner of his death must have made him all the more famous, drawing friends, acquaintances, and curiosity seekers to his wake.

"Maybe the killer is here, cadging free liquor," Hugh says.

Inside, the foyer is so crowded that I can't see the floor from which Warbrick's body has been removed. The odors of ale and sweat mask any lingering smell of death. As we jostle our way to the bar, I look for Barrett and wonder if he knows about the wake. I feel guilty because I'm investigating behind his back and troubled because if I learn anything, I'll have to keep it secret from him or risk Sir Gerald's wrath. A bevy of women greets Hugh as if he were an old friend. They must have been among the crowd of spectators this morning. Perhaps he can get some useful information from them. I look around for someone I can talk to, but everyone seems clustered in groups, and I'm shy about intruding. I don't see Mrs. Warbrick. The room is warm from the fire blazing in the hearth and body heat. I remove my gloves, unbutton my coat, and find myself squeezed up against the wall. The framed pictures hanging there catch my attention. This morning I assumed they were cheap prints, the kind often used to decorate pubs. Now I see that some frames contain segments of rope perhaps twelve inches long, mounted on boards. The rope nearest me has a white label stuck below it, which reads, "10 s. per inch."

"Excuse me," I say to a red-faced older man standing beside me, "what are these?"

He shouts in my ear so I can hear him above the noise. "Ropes from Harry's hangings."

My jaw drops. Warbrick sold the ropes as souvenirs! Other frames contain newspaper clippings. One, from 1873, is about Mary Ann Cotton, a "black widow" who poisoned three of her husbands and eleven of her thirteen children to collect on their burial insurance policies. Others show Charles Peace, the crippled burglar who shot a policeman and was hanged in 1879, and Kate Webster, the Irish servant girl hanged that same year for murdering her mistress. Kate dismembered the body, boiled the flesh off the bones, and gave the "lard" to the neighbors. These are all criminals Warbrick executed.

"It's too bad about Amelia Carlisle's rope," the man shouts.

Amelia Carlisle, the most recent notorious murderer, was a baby farmer—a woman who took in unwanted babies for a fee and supposedly farmed them out to adoptive parents or raised them herself. In actuality, she killed them rather than take the trouble to find homes for them or spend money on their care. She was convicted of the murders of three babies and hanged in November. There wasn't enough evidence to convict her of the hundreds of other murders that she probably also committed over the years. Her past caught up with her, but she only had one life to lose on the gallows. Her infamy almost equals that of Jack the Ripper. The framed clipping shows the photograph taken after her arrest. Deep-set eyes glower from beneath slanted dark brows in her haggard face. She has black hair severely parted in the middle, and she wears a hat trimmed with satin ribbons and a coat with a fur collar. I don't recall any mention of who had executed the "Baby

Butcher," as the press had dubbed Amelia. I'm surprised to learn that Warbrick did the honors, but he obviously made no secret of it, and it's boosted the public's interest in his murder.

"What's too bad?" I ask.

"The rope was stolen." The man points to an empty frame on the wall.

All that remains on the board is the label, "Amelia Carlisle, £5 per inch."

"Must've been last night," the man says. "I was here yesterday until closing, and the rope was there then."

He sidles off while I wonder if the killer stole Amelia's rope. Was theft the motive for the murder? Looking around for someone else to talk to, I see a man standing alone. I weave through the crowd and step into the open space that surrounds him. He's about thirty years old, of average height but odd proportions—large head, broad shoulders and chest, and long arms; thin, truncated legs. His jacket is too tight, its sleeves too short; his baggy trousers puddle around his black boots. He has a pale, clean-shaven face with a heavy jaw, and he holds his bowler hat in his large hands.

"Hello," I say.

He stares at me without expression. His eyes are dark brown to match his cropped hair. They stay open for an uncomfortably long interval before he blinks hard and says, "Six feet nine inches."

"I beg your pardon?" I say, puzzled.

"That would be the ideal distance for you to drop if you were hanged."

"*What?*"

His unblinking gaze sizes me up. "You're about one hundred twenty-five pounds?"

I'm affronted because this complete stranger dares to remark on the personal subject of my weight. "Yes, but why—"

"Six feet nine inches, and your neck would break quickly and cleanly. If the drop were too much shorter, you would slowly strangle to death." He speaks in a flat, matter-of-fact voice. "If the drop were too much longer, you would be decapitated. Like Harry was."

If this is his idea of a conversational icebreaker, then I can see why the other folks are giving him a wide berth. "How do you know that?"

He takes a white calling card from his pocket and gives it to me. Plain black print reads *Ernie Leach, Assistant Hangman. 45 White Horse Lane, Stepney.* My fingers feel as if they've touched something unclean. I slip the card into my pocketbook.

"I'm, uh, glad to meet you, Mr. Leach."

Ernie Leach nods, stares, and blinks hard again—a tic, I realize. I wonder if he's picturing me swinging from the end of a rope. He's repellent, but maybe he has information germane to Warbrick's murder, so I'd better keep the conversation going. "I didn't know there were assistant hangmen," I say.

"Most people don't. Public executions were abolished in 1868, and nobody but a few of us ever gets to see a hanging."

"What do assistant hangmen do?"

"We help set up the equipment and strap the prisoner. Afterward, we help take the body down and clean up."

"Clean up?"

"When people are hanged, they usually empty their bladder and bowels. It's an involuntary physical reaction."

Remembering the stench of feces this morning, I feel nauseated again.

"We get paid three guineas plus traveling expenses," Leach says.

He must like his work so much that he's willing to do it for a pittance. "Have you another job too?"

Nod, hard blink. "I work for the gas company. They give me time off when I'm called to a hanging. It's a public service."

I attempt to turn the conversation to the murder. "Did you work with Mr. Warbrick?"

"Yes. We did twenty-seven hangings together."

The total number of executions performed by all the hangmen in recent years alone must be enormous. "Who do you think killed him?"

"I don't know. But I'm glad somebody did."

I'm surprised because I wouldn't expect anyone at a wake to say he's glad the deceased is deceased. "Why is that?"

"He tried to have me struck off the list of hangmen." Anger enlivens Leach's stoic face. "It took me seven years to get on the list. There are so many applicants, and the Home Office doesn't hire very many. I submitted my application fifteen times." His eyes glint with ardor. "I've always wanted to be a hangman. When I was a boy, I read everything about hanging I could find. I built a miniature gallows and hanged cats and dogs. It's a science."

I stare in horror. Was the science or the killing the main attraction for Ernie Leach?

Leach goes on, oblivious. "I've assisted at thirty-nine hangings. I'm reliable—I do everything by the book. I was up for promotion to hangman. But Warbrick gave me a bad reference."

"Why?"

"At a hanging last November, he miscalculated the drop distance. I corrected him. He had to go along with me. He knew I was right, but he didn't like it. He told the Home Office that I'm a pervert who enjoys killing. They don't want people of that sort."

I wonder if Warbrick was right. "What did you do?"

"I reported Warbrick for drinking the night before executions," Leach says. "It's against the law. But I saw him, twice. That's why he miscalculated—he was drunk."

I suppose there are rivalries in every profession.

"He wasn't sacked, but he was put on notice." Leach adds, "He was very angry. He came to my house and picked a fight. The neighbors broke it up. Which is a good thing, because I could've killed the bastard."

A normal person wouldn't admit so readily that he had a motive for murder, but Ernie Leach is clearly not a normal person. "Did you kill Mr. Warbrick?" I ask.

Leach recoils as if I've insulted him. "And make such a sloppy, amateurish mess of it? I should say not."

Before I can suggest that making a mess of Warbrick's hanging could have been a ploy to disguise the fact that it was done by a professional, Hugh joins us, carrying two pints of ale.

"Sorry, I got caught up in conversation." Hugh gives me one pint, and when I introduce Mr. Leach, offers him the other.

"I'm not drinking tonight. I've a hanging tomorrow. I'll be going now." Leach elbows his way through the crowd, toward the door.

I tell Hugh what Leach said. Hugh laughs. "It takes all kinds. Do you think he did it?"

"I certainly think he's capable. Have you learned anything?"

"Our host is the chap who tended bar for Warbrick when he was out of town for executions. He said the lease on the pub expires this month, and the widow isn't going to renew it. She told him to use up the stock." Hugh raises his glass to me.

The cold, tart ale washes away the bad taste that my conversation with Ernie Leach left in my mouth. "If Mrs. Warbrick gives up the pub, how will she live?"

"Her husband had a burial insurance policy. Quite a generous one."

I think of Mary Ann Cotton, who poisoned fourteen people for the insurance money. "So the widow had a financial motive for the murder."

"Plus the facts that she didn't like being married to a hangman and she has a lover."

I tell Hugh about Amelia Carlisle's rope and the possibility that its theft is connected with the murder. The sound of clinking glass interrupts our speculations. "Attention, please," shouts the bartender. The crowd quiets. "I propose a toast to our dear departed friend, Harry Warbrick."

Cries of "Here, here!" are drowned out by someone yelling, "Take your hands off me!"

The crowd moves back from the argument that rages by the door. I glimpse two men tussling. One is Ernie Leach. As the bigger man holds him by the lapels, he throws punches and shouts, "You're not getting anything out of me. Leave me alone!"

The bartender and another man wade into the fray, pull the combatants apart, and shove them out of the pub. Hugh sets our empty glasses on a table, pulls me toward the door, and says, "I'd like to know what that was about. Come on."

★   ★   ★

Outside the pub, the big man who accosted Ernie Leach hunches on his hands and knees. Leach is gone. The night is colder, the air a poisonous grayish-yellow from snowflakes, gas lamps, and smoke.

"I say, are you all right?" Hugh extends his hand to the man.

"Yeah," the man says in a surly, breathless voice. Grasping Hugh's hand, he pulls himself to his feet. "Thanks." His paunch bulges under his tweed overcoat. His puffy features and curly strawberry-blond hair give him the look of an aging, dissipated cherub.

Hugh picks up his fallen bowler hat and gives it to him. I see something else he must have dropped. I crouch, retrieve a notebook with a pencil stuck in the spine, and read the words printed on the cover: *The Telegraph.* "Are you a reporter?"

He nods as I hand him the notebook. "Charlie Sullivan. On the beat for twenty years and still getting my arse kicked for the sake of a story."

The *Telegraph* is the newspaper that Malcolm Cross once worked for, the *Daily World*'s chief rival. I flash a look at Hugh, warning him not to let on that we're with the competition.

"Hugh Richards and my sister, Sarah," Hugh introduces us. He's realized that not only would a veteran reporter like Charlie Sullivan know about his scandal, the man might recognize my real name from the newspaper stories about Robin Mariner's kidnapping.

Sullivan squints, as if he's trying to place us. Hugh distracts him by saying, "Are you covering Harry Warbrick's murder?"

"Damned right. It's a big story. I spotted three reporters from other papers at the wake."

"I'm sorry you were thrown out," Hugh says.

"Yeah, me too. I was following a big lead."

Hugh and I exchange covert glances as our interest perks up.

"Did you know Harry Warbrick?" Sullivan asks.

"Not personally," Hugh says. "We live in the neighborhood. We stopped by to pay our respects."

"Oh. Well, good night then." Sullivan obviously thinks we're not potential sources, and therefore not worth his time.

We need to find out what his big lead is. Hugh says, "How about if we buy you a drink someplace?"

Sullivan considers, then shrugs. "Won't say no."

We walk to the Queen's Head, where we lunched with Mick earlier. The pub isn't crowded, probably because the regulars are availing themselves of free drink at The Ropemaker's Daughter. We have a table to ourselves by the fire, under a portrait of Queen Elizabeth. Sullivan gulps his ale and licks his lips. His eyes are bloodshot, his nose red with broken veins.

"Why were you rough-housing with Ernie Leach?" Hugh asks.

"I wanted information from him. He wouldn't talk. Damned Official Secrets Act." Seeing our puzzled expressions, Sullivan says, "Executions are covered by the Official Secrets Act. Whatever happens during a hanging, nobody who was there is allowed to blat it about afterward. Anybody who does could go to prison."

"I assume you're interested in something that happened during a hanging?" Hugh says.

"You assume right." Sullivan drains his glass.

I signal the barmaid to bring him another. "Which hanging?"

Sullivan looks around the room, as if to check for eavesdroppers, and lowers his voice. "Amelia Carlisle."

I'm interested to hear her name crop up for the second time tonight. "But how do you know something happened when nobody is allowed to talk?"

"Nobody is allowed. But somebody did." Sullivan chuckles. "Old Harry had loose lips when he was hitting the bottle, which was pretty often lately."

I'm eager for a new episode in the Amelia Carlisle story. Everyone else in London must be too, and Sir Gerald would hate for the *Telegraph* to publish it first.

"Well, don't keep us on tenterhooks," Hugh says. "Do tell."

"Harry never said. He just hinted. That was his way—he'd string me along for a while because he liked the attention. Eventually he would give in. He's been my anonymous source for some juicy bits about other hangings." Sullivan's expression turns grim. "But not this time."

"Why not this time?" I say, disappointed.

"I'd been kissing up to Harry for weeks. We were supposed to meet at The Ropemaker's Daughter tonight, and I thought he was ready to spill. But then . . ." Sullivan pantomimes pulling a noose tight around his own neck.

Can it be mere coincidence that Harry Warbrick was murdered when on the verge of revealing a secret? Hugh and I avoid looking at each other, lest we betray our excitement. "What do you think happened at the hanging?" I ask.

"Haven't the foggiest," Sullivan says. "If the hangman had been anyone except Harry, I'd have figured he'd botched it. Ever heard of William Calcraft?" Hugh and I shake our heads. "He was the official hangman of London from 1829 to 1879. Many of the poor sods he hanged died slowly and agonizingly by strangulation because their necks didn't break. Sometimes he would pull on their legs or climb on their shoulders to hurry up the process."

I wince. Hugh says, "That's a picture I won't be able to get out of my mind."

"That was in the days of public executions," Sullivan says. "The mobs went wild. Nowadays, the whole process is carried out behind closed doors. More civilized. If hangings are botched, the government keeps it under wraps. But Harry was an expert, at least according to himself. If he'd botched Amelia's hanging, he'd have kept his mouth shut."

"Any other ideas?" Hugh asks.

"Whatever happened, it didn't take long. Harry bragged about how fast he could finish a hanging. His best time was forty-two seconds from when the prisoner walked into the execution shed to when he was swinging from the rope. While Harry was teasing me about his big story, he said, "'Two minutes and fifty seconds. You'd be amazed at how much can happen in two minutes and fifty seconds."

Two minutes and fifty seconds had seen the execution of a woman who'd murdered hundreds of babies. What else had it seen?

Charlie Sullivan voices my next speculation: "Could be, Harry's murder and the incident during Amelia's hanging are connected."

"An intriguing possibility," Hugh says.

"Now that Harry is gone, I'm looking for other sources," Sullivan says.

I perceive a reason for the fisticuffs at The Ropemaker's Daughter. "Ernie Leach is a source?"

"Maybe. The little creep wouldn't even tell me whether he assisted with Amelia's hanging. But I'm going to get to the bottom of this."

"How?" Hugh asks. We lean toward Sullivan, eager for tips to aid our own investigation.

Sullivan leans back. "Hey, wait. I know you." He points at Hugh. "Lord Hugh Staunton. You were caught in that vice raid about a year ago."

The vice squadron raided a party attended by homosexual men and caught Hugh in compromising circumstances. My heart sinks. This has happened before—someone recognizing Hugh and recalling the scandal. Hugh was once a popular, highly visible man-about-town in London's most fashionable set. Now he flushes and cringes as he waits for the insults that inevitably follow.

Instead, Sullivan points at me. "And you're Sarah Bain. Sir Gerald Mariner hired the two of you to find his kidnapped baby. And now you both work for him at the *Daily World*. You're trying to steal my story!"

"No," I protest.

"That wouldn't be sporting," Hugh says.

"Don't lie to me." Sullivan's puffy face reddens with anger. "I heard about your contest—it's all over Fleet Street."

He stands up, grabs the table, and overturns it. Glasses go flying and shatter on the floor. I jump out of the way, but the table hits Hugh, his chair topples, and he falls on his rear end. Sullivan stalks out the door, calling over his shoulder, "Find your own damn leads."

Hugh pushes himself to his feet and says ruefully, "I can take on murderers, but God save me from the press. At least we have something to report to Sir Gerald tomorrow."

CHAPTER 6

The next morning there's no new crime scene, thank heaven. While Hugh sleeps in, Mick, Fitzmorris, and I enjoy a proper breakfast at the dining room table. Fitzmorris, reading the *Daily World*, says, "Good Lord." He shows Mick and me the story written by Malcolm Cross, illustrated with my photographs of Harry Warbrick.

This is the first time that photographs I've taken of a murder victim have appeared in the paper. When I'd arrived at other crime scenes, the body had been removed or the police wouldn't let me near it, and I photographed only the site. These photographs are not only horrifying but obscene. I feel ashamed because they're disrespectful to the dead man, and they pander to the public's desire for lurid thrills.

"The police are asking anyone with information about the murder to come forward," Fitzmorris says. "Apparently, they've no clues yet."

"Me either," Mick says ruefully. "I watched Mrs. Warbrick's house all afternoon, but her man never came out. Either he left before I got there, or he stayed till after I left to meet Catherine at the theater."

Last night Mick came home after I was asleep. This is the first I've heard of his unsuccessful investigation. I'm disappointed because we still don't know who Mrs. Warbrick's lover is.

"How is Catherine?" I say.

Mick scowls at his plate and stops eating, as if he's lost his appetite. "She's seein' somebody."

"She's always seeing somebody. It never lasts long," Fitzmorris says in an attempt to cheer Mick up.

Catherine has been in love, and engaged, so many times I've lost count. "Who is he?"

"Don't know. She wouldn't say."

That's a bad sign. Catherine usually regales us all with talk of her suitors. I sense that she doesn't want to jinx her new relationship by publicizing it too soon. It could be serious.

"There was a big vase of roses in her dressing room," Mick says, "and she had a new bracelet."

This new suitor sounds wealthy, alas.

Mick pushes his plate away, stands, and says, "I'll go back to Mrs. Warbrick's house and watch for her man."

This isn't a good time to revive our old argument, but I've let things slide for weeks, and if I let them slide longer, I won't be doing Mick a favor. "Mick, you have to go to school."

Mick stares at me in wounded disbelief; I've hit him while he's down. "But I have to solve the murder."

Fitzmorris leaves, not wanting to be caught up in a quarrel. I say, "You can help Hugh and me after school."

"I don't wanna go back there," Mick says, angry and defiant. "The teachers are mean. The other kids are always pickin' fights and gettin' me in trouble."

I remember my own days at the charity boarding school. Quiet and shy, I meekly endured the discipline and bullying. But the Whitechapel public school is rougher, and scrappy Mick doesn't take abuse lying down.

"It's just for two more years," I say. Many people leave school when they're younger than Mick. If he stays until he's sixteen, the extra education will give him an advantage.

Mick bangs his hand on the table; dishes clatter. "I ain't got two years to lose!"

I know he hates the idea of languishing in class while Catherine waltzes away with her mystery suitor. I feel sorry for him.

Desperation shines in Mick's blue eyes. "If I solve the murder,
maybe Sir Gerald will keep me on. And maybe give me a raise."

He's counting on a position with Sir Gerald to give him an
advantage with Catherine, who knows how rich and powerful Sir
Gerald is and likes having a connection to him via Mick. "If you
want a permanent job and a raise from Sir Gerald, you need more
education." I know Mick is good at arithmetic and reads well, but
he's terrible at grammar and spelling. "He's not going to promote
you ahead of better-qualified men."

"I always done good work for him. He likes me. And he never
got no proper education either."

"I know." I think Sir Gerald sees his young self in Mick—the
poor, low-class boy making his way in the world by his own wits.
"But his top men are educated, and the higher you stand with him,
the better chance you'll have with Catherine."

Mick frowns as his contrariness battles with common sense.
"Oh, all right. I'll go to school."

★ ★ ★

"The Harry Warbrick murder could be an even bigger story than
I thought," Sir Gerald says. "A connection with Amelia Carlisle is
the icing on the bloody cake."

Hugh and I are seated at the table in the conference room at the
Daily World with Sir Gerald, Malcolm Cross, and Mr. Palmer, and
we've just described what we learned last night.

"We issued two thousand more copies than usual this morning," Mr. Palmer says. "Word from the streets says they'll probably
sell out. Should we double the print run for tomorrow?"

Cross snorts. "Not on account of a tip from Charlie Sullivan."

"Why not?" Sir Gerald asks.

"I know Charlie—he's a washed-up blowhard. Odds are, he
fabricated the story about Amelia Carlisle's hanging to make himself seem important."

I think Cross is upset because we were the ones who got the tip. "We missed you at the wake last night."

"I was there when you arrived," Cross retorts. "I saw you leave early to chase after Charlie."

"What have *you* been up to, Mal?" Sir Gerald's tone says he doesn't suffer fools who carp instead of contributing.

Cross's perpetual smile widens. "I'm working on a different theory about the murder."

"Care to share it with us?" Hugh says, irked by Cross's superior attitude.

Revulsion toward Hugh twists Cross's mouth. "Not until I've gathered evidence to support it. *I* know better than to jump on a bandwagon before I'm sure it's heading in the right direction."

I'm not liking Cross any better than yesterday, and I'm afraid we missed something important by leaving the wake early. I glance at Hugh, who shakes his head—he thinks Cross is bluffing. Cross and Sir Gerald face each other like two men about to duel. Something unspoken passes between them—an acknowledgment of kinship?

"All right," Sir Gerald says. "Run with your theory." I remember that he likes playing his cards close to his chest, and he must respect Cross for doing the same. My heart sinks and Hugh frowns as Cross rises in Sir Gerald's estimation. "Just don't come back empty-handed."

"Yes, sir." Cross grins, elated.

Sir Gerald stands and looks out the window. I picture him on his ship at sea, watching the horizon for land. "Sometimes, all the justice in the world isn't enough. Sometimes the hunger never goes away."

We all sit silent and tense, aware that he's not making a general observation, but alluding to Robin's kidnapping, the forbidden subject. The hunger he refers to must be his need to avenge Robin, and it must still rage within him even though the person responsible for Robin's fate is dead.

"Sometimes you have to take whatever you can get." His voice rings like hot iron struck on an anvil. "By God, we're going to solve this murder."

The Warbrick case is personal for him, not just a matter of winning a contest and selling newspapers. There's nobody else to punish on behalf of Robin, so Sir Gerald is gunning for the killer who hanged Harry Warbrick.

Sir Gerald flashes a glance at Hugh and me. "Competition is a good motivator." He hasn't missed the rivalry between us and Cross. "I don't care how the lot of you solve the case as long as you do."

I feel a sudden, unwelcome sense of camaraderie with Cross. Woe betide all of us if we fail Sir Gerald.

"In the meantime, we need to find out what happened during Amelia Carlisle's hanging," Sir Gerald says. "I'll call in some favors."

★   ★   ★

We never learned what favors Sir Gerald called in, but three hours later, after a flurry of communiques sent by telegraph and messenger, Hugh and I find ourselves lugging my photography equipment up to Newgate Prison. Located less than a mile east of Fleet Street, the prison is a massive vault constructed of granite blocks, akin to a medieval fortress. It houses both male and female prisoners, in separate wards, and Amelia Carlisle spent her last days there. All the executions performed in London take place at Newgate.

An icy wind whips the clouds and smoke around the great dome of nearby St. Paul's Cathedral. Horses and carriages skitter on frozen slush. I trod carefully so as not to slip as we head, according to Sir Gerald's instructions, to the central section of the prison, a four-story block with a row of arched, barred windows on each level. At an entrance on one side of the central section, police constables unload shackled criminals from enclosed wagons. At the other, a queue of people waits to visit prisoners.

"Mick will be sorry he missed this jaunt," Hugh says.

"I wouldn't be." I recall my own brief, terrifying incarceration in

1888. At that time, I had done nothing that I thought merited incarceration, but things have changed since then. The past I have in common with Hugh and Mick is a shadow that encroaches on our daily existence. If the police knew about the night in the slaughter-house, we would be thrown in Newgate and not come out alive. I can tell from his queasy expression that Hugh is thinking the same thing.

"On second thought, I wouldn't be sorry to miss it myself," he says.

Fear of prison isn't the only reason for my discomposure. Today's venture is yet another secret from Barrett. I almost hope we won't learn anything here and add more secrets to my guilty trove. Someday I may have to choose between Barrett and my job, and the choice isn't as simple as love versus money, or fear of losing Barrett versus fear of Sir Gerald.

Two brutish wardens dressed in gray uniforms and caps stand at the ironclad door of the central section. When we introduce ourselves, one says, "Governor Piercy is expecting you." They escort us inside, to a hall with a cracked tile floor, where empty chairs stand against the stained plaster wall and a police constable occupies a desk at the end. The cold air smells damp and stale like a cellar. The wardens tell us to put my equipment on the desk, then they search us for weapons or other contraband. They don't offer to fetch a female warden for me. Their hands squeezing and patting us seem deliberately rough and intrusive. As the warden touches my breasts, I flinch.

"Is this really necessary?" Hugh says. "We're here on business for the *Daily World*. We're not criminals."

"Everybody gets searched," the warden probing Hugh says. "It's the law." He and his partner open my pocketbook, satchel, camera case, and trunk. They manhandle the contents.

"Please be careful," I say.

They grin. This is our first inkling that everybody who works at Newgate knows the purpose of our visit and we're not welcome.

They lead us up a dingy, gaslit flight of stairs. The second floor resembles a not very prosperous business establishment. The wardens usher us into an office, then stand outside the door. A man rises from behind a massive desk. Tall and spare, with a slight hump on his back, a narrow face, and beaked nose, he has the look of a vulture. His thick gray hair crests from a widow's peak above his steel-gray eyes.

"Governor Piercy. Thank you for seeing us on such short notice," Hugh says.

"Lord Hugh. Miss Bain." His voice is unexpectedly suave. His courtesy doesn't mask his distaste; it's obvious he's seeing us only because Sir Gerald twisted his superiors' arms.

He glances at the equipment we're carrying. "No photography."

"Why not?" I say.

Piercy addresses his reply to Hugh, as if he thinks me unworthy of his notice because I'm female, plain, low on the social ladder, or all of those reasons. "Photography inside Newgate is a violation of security rules."

"Governor, there must be a mistake," Hugh says with his usual, good-natured confidence. "Sir Gerald Mariner sent us on an investigation for the *Daily World*, and the paper needs pictures to illustrate the story."

"Sir Gerald isn't in charge here."

I comprehend that Piercy means to obstruct us in every way possible. He says, "Follow the rules, or I'll have you escorted out right now."

Heaven knows what Sir Gerald would do if we got ourselves thrown out of Newgate before we've discovered anything to back up our theory that there's a connection between Harry Warbrick's murder and Amelia Carlisle's execution. I sense that Governor Piercy doesn't want her execution investigated. He must be hiding something related to it, something serious enough that he would rather risk Sir Gerald's wrath than have it exposed. We need to find out what it is.

"Very well." Hugh smiles, acting the graceful loser. "No photography."

Piercy motions us to the two chairs in front of his desk and takes his own seat behind it. His seat is constructed of thick dark wood, has a high back and curved arms, and resembles a medieval throne. "How can I be of assistance?"

I let Hugh do the talking because he's better at coaxing information out of people than I am. He says, "We'd be obliged if you would tell us what happened at Amelia Carlisle's execution."

"That's not possible. The Official Secrets Act forbids me." Piercy seems glad to disappoint us, perhaps gladder to have an ironclad excuse.

On the wall behind Piercy are framed certificates and photographs. I study the photographs on the wall, a habit born of professional interest. In one, a group of uniformed police constables stands outside a building. I recognize a younger Governor Piercy at the center. Another is a portrait of him in an inspector's uniform decorated with medals. So he's a former policeman who rose through the ranks to rule over this dungeon. The certificates look to be commendations for exemplary service, written in ornate calligraphy and embossed with metallic seals. I become aware of an unpleasant smell in the room. Through the gas fumes from the lamps and smoke from the coal stove drifts an odor of rot and decay.

"Why are hangings covered by the Act?" Hugh says. "I thought it was just for state secrets related to military maneuvers and foreign espionage."

The odor is coming from Governor Piercy. Now I notice that his gums are red and swollen, diseased. It looks as though his sharp, yellowish teeth have been chewing raw flesh. It's his breath I'm smelling.

"To protect the citizens," he says. "When hangings were public, the spectacles often provoked violent uproars. Releasing information could have a similar, dangerous result."

"Meaning the Act allows society to pretend that hangings are businesslike affairs," Hugh says, "and the condemned go placidly to their deaths—no muss, no fuss."

"Meaning this is a civilized age, and the government doesn't cater to those who crave morbid thrills." Governor Piercy's contemptuous expression puts us, and the *Daily World*'s readers, among that number.

Civilized society accepts death as the punishment for major crimes as long as it's meted out quietly and discreetly. Still, the death penalty sits badly with me, for a personal reason. How many people found guilty of crimes they didn't commit have married the ropemaker's daughter? Will my father someday join their number?

"Of course the government wouldn't want the public to know that hangings are sometimes botched," Hugh says, "like Harry Warbrick's."

Piercy remains composed, but I sense a change in the atmosphere, as if there's suddenly less air in the room. The stench from his diseased mouth grows stronger. As I turn away from it, another photograph catches my eye. It shows Piercy shaking hands with a man dressed in ceremonial robes. The other man looks to be about forty years old, and he's the same height as Piercy but somehow appears taller. Fair hair like a lion's mane crowns his handsome face. He exudes a vitality that seems to project him out of the photograph, into three dimensions.

"Harry Warbrick didn't let the Official Secrets Act keep him quiet," Hugh says.

"Harry Warbrick was reprimanded for leaking information about hangings. He didn't go to prison because he denied it was him and so did the reporters he leaked to, but I could tell he was lying." Revulsion twists Piercy's thin lips: he didn't like Warbrick. I wonder if it's only because Warbrick broke the law or because he had reason to fear what Warbrick might reveal.

"The thrill seekers would have a field day if they found out that Amelia Carlisle's head came off when she was hanged, whether it was true or not," Hugh suggests.

Governor Piercy smiles, further exposing his ugly red gums. "I can tell you that Amelia Carlisle's hanging was conducted according to procedure. As are all the hangings at Newgate."

"What is the procedure?" I ask, hoping to throw Piercy off guard.

Piercy stubbornly addresses Hugh. "After the prisoner is convicted, he's held in a condemned cell for about three weeks, under watch twenty-four hours a day. Then he's brought to the execution shed. The assistant hangman fastens straps around his body. The hangman puts a white cap over his head and a noose around his neck, and opens the trap door under him." Piercy spreads his hands as if to say, *"End of story."*

I remember Charlie Sullivan quoting Harry Warbrick: *'Two minutes and fifty seconds.'* I'm becoming more certain that something of consequence happened during Amelia Carlisle's last two minutes and fifty seconds alive.

"You've seen executions yourself?" Hugh asks.

"The prison governor always witnesses hangings. It's part of the job."

"So that puts you, Harry Warbrick, and Ernie Leach in the execution shed during Amelia's hanging," Hugh says.

"Yes, Ernie Leach was the assistant hangman."

At least we've confirmed that Leach was present. "Who else was there?" I say.

Governor Piercy flicks a glance in my direction, as though brushing off a fly. "The prison matron, surgeon, and chaplain. The sheriff of London—Sir Lionel Hargreaves."

"We'd like to speak with them," Hugh says.

Governor Piercy shifts on his throne; his hands, bony with long, curved nails, tighten on its armrests. "You would be wasting your time. They're bound by the Official Secrets Act too."

"We'll choose how we spend our time," I say.

"To see Sheriff Hargreaves, you'll have to go to Old Bailey." Piercy seems glad that at least one witness is out of convenient reach.

"We'll settle for the others," Hugh says, rising.

Piercy grimaces in irritation. "As you wish." He tells the wardens to take my photography equipment to the vestibule, then says, "It will be waiting for you when you're finished."

Dismayed, I stand between my equipment and the wardens. "It goes with us." Leaving my precious possessions at the mercy of hostile men is unthinkable.

"We promise not to take photographs," Hugh says.

"If you're not going to take photographs, then you won't need it," Piercy says.

An angry objection rises to my lips. Hugh cautions me with a glance and lies, "That equipment belongs to the *Daily World*. If anything happens to it, Sir Gerald will be furious."

"It will be perfectly safe," the governor says, "but if you're worried, you can leave now and take it with you."

Either I let them hold my equipment hostage to my good behavior or go back to Sir Gerald with nothing to report. I reluctantly nod. Watching the wardens carry away my camera, trunk, and satchel, I wonder if I'll ever see them again.

A man enters the office. He's big, clad in a physician's white coat over a white shirt and gray wool trousers. "Governor Piercy— oh, excuse me, I didn't know the reporters were still here."

"That's all right," Governor Piercy says. "Lord Hugh and Miss Bain want to speak with you." He turns to us. "This is Dr. Simon Davies, the prison surgeon."

Hugh and I gaze in astonished recognition at the man's rugged, youthful features, at the silver-rimmed spectacles pushed atop his wavy brown hair. Dr. Davies is Mrs. Warbrick's lover.

CHAPTER 7

Hugh and I hide our shock. Dr. Davies looks at us as if he's just stepped onto ground he thought was safe, but he's fallen off the edge of a cliff. His brown eyes are bloodshot, with puffy shadows underneath, and I see a patch of stubble on his jaw that he missed while shaving. He avoids our gazes and speaks to the governor.

"I came to tell you there's an outbreak of influenza on Ward Four. I can't talk now."

"You will." Governor Piercy's tone brooks no objection. Now that he's consented to our interviewing the witnesses to Amelia Carlisle's hanging, he seems to have decided to get it over with.

Dr. Davies puffs his cheeks and blows out his breath. "Yes, sir."

"Don't leave them alone for even a second," Piercy says. "They must be accompanied at all times while they're here." His gaze holds the doctor's for a moment, as if to convey a warning that he doesn't want to voice.

"Yes, sir."

Piercy turns his warning gaze on us. "Don't be tempted to wander by yourselves. Good day, Lord Hugh, Miss Bain."

Dr. Davies leads us down the stairs, into a labyrinth of passages lit by flames that flare from hissing gas jets mounted on the walls. Gas fumes mingle with the odors of earth, drains, and cesspools. Our footsteps ring loudly on a flagstone floor worn down in a rut in the middle. The granite-block walls seem saturated with fear, anger, misery, and insanity absorbed from inmates throughout the centuries. Voices echo from doors that lead to other passages, in which guards loiter, watching us go by. I shiver.

The corridor is wide enough for us to walk three abreast, but Dr. Davies edges ahead, as if to outrun us. "I'm sure Governor Piercy told you about the Official Secrets Act. I can't talk about Amelia Carlisle's hanging."

"How about showing us the execution shed?" Hugh says. We need to see where Amelia spent her last moments alive; perhaps it will furnish clues relevant to Harry Warbrick's murder.

"I can't take you there. It's against regulations. And I really haven't time to talk now."

"Then perhaps we could meet later at Mr. Warbrick's house," I say. "You must be eager to get back to Mrs. Warbrick."

Dr. Davies stops so suddenly that Hugh and I stumble to a halt behind him. He stands with his back to us, like a man afraid to face a firing squad. "What did you say?" His voice shrinks to a hushed mumble.

"We saw you with Mrs. Warbrick," Hugh says.

Dr. Davies turns slowly. In the yellow light from the gas jets, his face sags with shocked realization. "That was you who called on her yesterday. I didn't see you, but I heard you talking. Your voices are familiar." I can tell he wants to know what we saw or heard, but is afraid to ask. He looks as though he's crash-landed after his fall off the cliff, and he's wondering how badly hurt he is. "She said you were from the Home Office." Anger roughens his voice. "You lied."

I'm still ashamed of taking advantage of her, but we needed information from her, and we need it now from Dr. Davies. "Did Mr. Warbrick know about your affair with his wife?"

Two guards walk down the passage toward us. They slow as they approach, eyeing us with curiosity. Dr. Davies hisses, "Be quiet!"

They vanish around a corner. Hugh says, "How about that execution shed?"

Dr. Davies sighs, then beckons. We follow him to a courtyard surrounded by prison buildings. I hear the everyday sounds of carriage wheels, factory machinery, and cheerful voices from the world outside Newgate. The execution shed is a house made of brick, built into a corner of the courtyard. About twenty feet wide and ten deep, it has a slanted roof, a skylight, two large wooden doors divided horizontally in half like those of a barn, and a smaller door on the left. When Dr. Davies opens the smaller door, Hugh and I hesitate because we know that, except for the grace of fortune, we might have arrived at the execution shed under different circumstances. Morbid curiosity propels us through the door. I see a large shape dangling in midair from the end of a rope.

A hanged man!

My heart thumps. Hugh makes a startled sound. Then we discern that the shape is a burlap sack apparently stuffed with rocks. We sigh with relief. The rope is attached to one of three heavy metal pulleys that hang from a cross beam supported by two tall, sturdy wooden posts—the gallows. Beneath the gallows is a plank floor with two rectangular trap doors, one about ten feet long and divided crosswise in half, the other small.

"What is that?" Hugh says, pointing at the sack.

"Weights," Dr. Davies says. "There's a hanging tomorrow. The rope has to be stretched the night before, with a weight equal to the prisoner's. So that it doesn't stretch during the hanging."

I deduce that if the rope stretches, the prisoner's neck won't break, and death will be by slow strangulation. Everything looks clean, but I smell a faint sour, foul odor, like a latrine. I remember Ernie Leach saying that hanged prisoners involuntarily empty their bowels and bladders. Hugh puts his hand on a long lever that juts from the floor near the left-hand post.

"Don't touch that," Dr. Davies says—too late

The two halves of the large trap door fall downward with a

crash. Hugh and I start. The latrine odor wafts up on a cold gust from a pit that yawns below the open door. We stare down into the pit, sickened and fascinated. It's perhaps eight feet deep with a stone floor and walls. How many humans have met their deaths suspended there? The next condemned criminal is due to follow suit tomorrow. So might we, and so might my father, eventually. Dizziness whirls my head. I grasp a post for support, and when I regain my balance, I look up to see Dr. Davies slumped against the wall.

"Please don't put Isabella and me in the newspaper," he says. "It would ruin her reputation."

I think he's in love with Mrs. Warbrick; their affair isn't just a fling. They seem an unlikely couple—the refined lady who couldn't stomach bedding her husband the hangman, and the young prison surgeon who doctors criminals. "How did the two of you meet?"

"On a pleasure boat on the Thames last summer." A nostalgic smile leavens Dr. Davies's expression. "I was with some friends from my medical school days at Oxford. She was with her neighbors. We started talking. By the time we each found out who the other was, we'd already fallen in love."

I know from my own experience that love can happen like that despite all the reasons against it. "Did you kill her husband?"

Horror and revulsion show on Dr. Davies's face. "Good God, no!"

"With Harry gone, you can have Isabella all to yourself," Hugh says, "and you needn't worry about him catching on and giving you both what-for."

Dr. Davies flushes and hangs his head. "He'd already caught us. We thought he'd gone to Manchester for a hanging, but it was postponed. He was angry and threw me out, but nothing came of it. I think he preferred to let it go rather than divorce Isabella or make trouble for me. We had to work together."

Hugh and I look at each other, unconvinced. "Where were you the night he was murdered?" Hugh says.

"Here at Newgate. I had some seriously ill prisoners at the infirmary."

"And you couldn't let them die before they finish serving their sentences," Hugh jests with a straight face.

Dr. Davies frowns, offended. "They deserve the same treatment as any other patients—my best. I came in at eight that morning and didn't leave until nine the next. The nurses and the wardens can vouch for me."

By nine, Harry Warbrick's remains had already been removed from his pub. I wonder if Dr. Davies slipped out for several hours during the night when everyone thought he was on duty. "So you have an alibi. Does Mrs. Warbrick?"

"She's innocent. You leave her alone!" Fist balled, muscles bulging, Dr. Davies suddenly looks bigger, stronger. I'm uncomfortably aware that Hugh and I are alone in the execution shed with a man who may have hanged and decapitated Harry Warbrick. If he did, he may be ruthless or insane enough to kill us here inside Newgate and throw our bodies in the pit.

Hugh cranks the lever and closes the trap door. "Let's make a bargain. You tell us about Amelia Carlisle's execution, and we won't plaster your affair on the front page of the *Daily World*."

Dr. Davies's anger gives way to fearful obstinacy. "I can't." The shed is cold, but his face gleams with sweat. "You know I can't."

"If you do, what could happen to you that's so bad?" Hugh says.

"At best, I'll lose my post."

"What would be so bad about that?" Hugh's gesture encompasses the entire prison. "This ain't exactly Buckingham Palace."

"I wouldn't be able to get another one."

"Oh, come now—you're an Oxford man."

Dr. Davies colors. "Not quite. I was sent down. I finished my education here in London."

"Sent down?" Hugh says, alert for scandal. "What for?"

"I was caught with a girl in my room. She was drunk and unconscious. Later she said I took advantage of her, which wasn't true. She was willing." Chagrin tinges Dr. Davies's self-defense. "It didn't help that she was the dean's daughter."

"Well, that was a mistake," Hugh says, "but surely it won't affect your prospects now?"

"I got into a little more trouble on my first posting, at the Royal Hospital," Dr. Davies says sheepishly. "There were these female patients . . ." He sighs. "They made me resign."

He has a pattern of compromising affairs with women. Mrs. Warbrick is but the latest in the series.

"If I leave this post under a cloud, I could lose my medical license." Panic gleams in Dr. Davies's bloodshot eyes. "You're not going to print any of this in the newspaper, are you?"

"Not if you tell us what happened at Amelia's execution," Hugh says.

"Have a heart! I could go to prison!"

That's a serious penalty worth avoiding, but I say, "It could be worse. If something happened during Amelia's hanging, and one of the witnesses killed Harry Warbrick to keep it secret, then the other witnesses are in danger. That includes you." Unless he's the murderer.

Dr. Davies clenches his jaw and glares, adamant in his refusal to violate the Official Secrets Act.

I seek another route to the truth. "Did you meet Amelia Carlisle before the day she was hanged?" Perhaps the time she spent in Newgate can shed indirect light on the critical two minutes and fifty seconds.

"Yes." Dr. Davies looks relieved to change the subject, but still on his guard. "I examine all the prisoners upon their admission to Newgate."

"What were the results of your examination of Amelia?" Hugh says.

"She was in good health." Dr. Davies seems determined to reveal as little as possible.

"How did she behave?" I say.

Dr. Davies hesitates. I watch him decide that if he cooperates with this line of questioning, perhaps we won't resume the other. "She was very agitated. This was before her trial, but she knew she was going to be convicted. The evidence against her was overwhelming. She didn't want to be hanged. She pleaded the belly."

"The law prohibits executing criminals who are with child, I understand," Hugh says.

"Yes," Dr. Davies says. "Convicts can plead the belly to delay their executions until after the child is born. It buys them a few more months on earth, as well as sparing the life of the innocent child."

"There was nothing in the papers about Amelia pleading the belly," I say.

"The information was never released to the press," Dr. Davies says. "Amelia was kept under observation after her trial. During that time, I obtained proof that she was not with child. She was hanged ten days after she was sentenced to death."

"What other information wasn't released to the press?" Hugh asks.

Dr. Davies clams up, aware that Hugh's question refers to the taboo subject of Amelia's execution. I say, "Why is the prison surgeon required to be present at executions?"

"Good question," Hugh says. "It's not as if you're supposed to mend the broken necks."

"I verify that death has taken place," Dr. Davies says.

"Do you perform the autopsy?" The period that led up to Amelia's death seems devoid of clues about Harry Warbrick's murder, but I'm hoping the period afterward will provide enlightenment.

"There is no autopsy after a hanging unless the coroner specially requests it. In Amelia's case, he didn't."

"Does that mean her death was straightforward, no unusual circumstances?" Hugh says.

Dr. Davies frowns at Hugh's ploy to make him talk about the hanging. "There was no autopsy," he says in a flat voice.

If Amelia's corpse harbored any clues, it took them to the grave.

"We need something to publish in the paper," Hugh says. "If we can't get anything about the execution, it'll have to be a story about you and your checkered past and Mrs. Warbrick." He speaks reluctantly; I know he doesn't like threatening another man with the scandalous exposure that he himself suffered.

Resentful obstinacy joins fear in Dr. Davies' expression. "Publish what you will."

"You care more about your job and your professional status than about Mrs. Warbrick?" I think him a selfish lover as well as cowardly. "You ought to be ashamed of yourself."

Dr. Davies glowers, refusing to take the bait. Hugh says, "When the story comes out, both you and Mrs. Warbrick will become suspects in Harry's murder."

"You're out to ruin people's lives for the sake of selling newspapers. *You* ought to be ashamed of yourselves."

I flinch as Dr. Davies's accusation hits home. I can rationalize my motives however I please, but I work for Sir Gerald, whose motive is making money, and by investigating the hangman's murder, I'm protecting my own livelihood.

Hugh looks chastened but says, "This isn't all about the newspaper. It's about justice for Harry Warbrick."

"Harry Warbrick, a total stranger to you," Dr. Davies says. "Spare me your holier-than-thou attitude."

"Harry Warbrick, the husband of your mistress," I say, goaded by my discomfort with my own dubious position and a sense of responsibility to stand up for Harry Warbrick. He seems a victim of his own tendency to brag—a human flaw that didn't merit his brutal death. "The husband who had a very generous burial insurance policy."

I watch Dr. Davies comprehend my hint that he and Mrs. Warbrick conspired to murder her husband for the insurance money. Dismay and dread cross his features in rapid succession. Then his gaze hardens, his posture straightens, and he speaks in a cool, steady voice. "I've nothing more to say to you except 'Go to hell.'"

He seems suddenly older, more the master of himself—the real man behind the overworked doctor and the foolish lover, a man dangerous to cross.

"Before we go to hell, we'll stop and see the matron and chaplain," Hugh says.

"So that you can ruin their lives as well?" Dr. Davies regards us with contempt, then opens a door at the back of the shed.

As he leads us along a stone-walled passage, a breathless guard appears around a corner and says, "Dr. Davies, an inmate is having a fit in Ward Two. Come quick!"

"Stay with them." Dr. Davies points at Hugh and me, then tells us, "Wait here. I'll be back soon." He hurries away.

A moment later, the lights go out, plunging the corridor into darkness.

CHAPTER 8

Hugh and I exclaim in surprise. All I can see is the pale after-images of the flames from the gas jets on the walls. I don't hear the gas hissing; it must have gone off. With my vision disabled, my other senses sharpen. I hear quiet footsteps, detect the faint, tingling warmth of other human presences nearby. I feel hands groping me at the same time a scuffle erupts. I cry out, alarmed.

"Hugh!"

He shouts; he sounds far away. I hear grunts, pants, and scraping noises, as though he's being dragged. The hands propel me in the opposite direction. They belong to two men behind me—one gripping my left arm and my coat collar; the other, my right arm and my hair. I smell their loud, sour breaths as I struggle.

"Help!"

My voice echoes. No one responds. My eyes adjust to the darkness, which isn't total; faint daylight emanates from other passages. I try to turn to see my captors, but they prevent me. The assault is all the more terrifying because they're invisible, faceless. At the threshold of a doorway, they give me a mighty shove. I scream while tumbling, skirts over head, down a flight of stairs. I crash to a stop and lie stunned, gasping. When I flex my limbs and neck, my knees, elbows, and chin hurt where they struck the stone steps, but my heavy clothes and my bustle padded me; nothing seems broken. I sit up as my heart pounds with lingering terror. Gas fumes waft through the air; then the doorway above me brightens as someone relights the jets in the passage. Below, down a second flight of stairs, the black hole of a cellar gapes.

"Miss Bain? Miss Bain!" The anxious voice belongs to Dr. Davies.

I hesitate before answering. He could have been one of the men who pushed me. But I'm afraid I won't be able to get out of Newgate by myself. "I'm here."

Dr. Davies hurries down the stairs. "Are you all right?"

"I think so."

"Let me help you." He extends his hand.

"No, thank you." Despite his apparent concern, I don't trust him. I grasp the railing and pull myself to my feet.

"What happened?"

A male voice says, "She fell."

I look up at a warden standing in the stairwell doorway. He's the one Dr. Davies left in charge of Hugh and me before the lights went out. "No, I was pushed."

Dr. Davies frowns as if confused about whom to believe. "I told you to watch her," he says to the warden.

"She snuck away and got lost in the dark and had an accident," the warden says.

"The hell it was an accident!" Temper moves me to swear. "Someone pushed me. Was it you?"

"It was your own bloody fault, stupid cow."

I turn to Dr. Davies. His expression is apologetic but disapproving; he believes the warden. I'm furious, but there's no time to make a scene. "Where is Hugh?"

"I thought he was with you," Dr. Davies says.

I falter up the stairs with Dr. Davies at my heels, push past the warden, and look down the corridor. It's vacant.

"He must have left," Dr. Davies says.

"He wouldn't leave without me. Something's happened to him." I grab Dr. Davies by the arm. "We have to find him. Now!"

Either he's convinced by my panic or he thinks he's humoring a crazy woman, but he raises the alarm. Soon Newgate is like a fortress under siege as the wardens mount a search for the missing visitor. Dr. Davies and I rush through corridors noisy with the tramp of footsteps, the echoes of voices calling. There's no sign of Hugh. I hear the ear-splitting shrills of police whistles. We follow wardens stampeding outside, to a yard enclosed by buildings on three sides and a wall topped with iron spikes on the fourth. At the center of the yard, other wardens struggle to pull men dressed in gray prison uniforms away from what appears to be a riot. The prisoners roar like animals. Other inmates cheer from barred windows. I shrink against the wall as wardens drag dozens of hand-cuffed inmates to the cells. Four wardens remain, trying to separate two men who are fighting. One is blond-haired, disheveled, and naked to the waist; his clothes must have been torn off. He grips the other, a brawny prisoner with a shaved head, in a chokehold.

"Hugh!" I cry.

While the wardens tug at him, Hugh grits his teeth and hangs on. His face wears a ferocious expression I've never seen before. His opponent grunts and chokes, face purple, eyes bulging. Their feet trample bodies of fallen, unconscious inmates.

"Hugh, stop!" I say. "You're going to kill him!"

Hugh lets go of the prisoner, who drops to his knees, clutching his throat, wheezing. Hugh shakes the wardens off him and says to the prisoner, "That'll teach you to assault visitors." He addresses the prone men, whom he apparently knocked out earlier. "You too." Breathing hard, sweating, and his left cheek scraped, he grins with exhilaration.

I'm glad Hugh isn't hurt, proud that he got the better of his assailants. On past occasions, he's displayed combat skills learned, he claims, at Eton, but I've just seen something savage in him that's usually hidden. I already knew he's capable of killing, the same as he knows I am, but it's disturbing to see it in broad daylight while in my rational mind.

The uproar from the prisoners in the other cells dies down.

The wardens in the yard stand aside to let Governor Piercy through. "What's going on?" Piercy demands.

Hugh picks his hat, overcoat, jacket, and shirt up from the dirty pavement. The shirt is torn and bloodstained. "When the lights went out, some men dragged me out here." He dons the clothes and points at his defeated opponents. "Those fellows thought they'd have a little fun with me. They should have thought twice."

Piercy asks the wardens, "What really happened?" After they each swear that Hugh started the riot, he frowns at Hugh and me. "I told you not to wander around by yourselves."

"We didn't!" Sudden suspicion enrages me. "You turned off the lights. You sent people to attack us."

"That's a ridiculous accusation," Piercy says. "Gas interruptions are common."

"Gas interruption, my foot," Hugh says. "You didn't like us asking questions about Amelia Carlisle's execution. You wanted to stop us before we could get the answers."

Piercy shakes his head in disdain and says, "I think you went to the men's exercise yard and made obscene advances toward the prisoners. They were only defending themselves." He bares his diseased gums in an evil smile. "You wouldn't want that story in the *Daily World*."

As Hugh and I gape, stunned by the unjust accusation, Piercy says, "Oh yes, I know about you—Lord Hugh Staunton, the famous sodomite."

And he must have made sure that the prisoners knew, that when Hugh was thrown into their midst, they would treat him as they would any homosexual. Hugh's expression turns black with rage, and he lunges at Piercy. The governor recoils, frightened. I grab Hugh by the arm, restraining him as his outstretched hands graze Piercy's throat.

"Let go, damn it!" Hugh struggles to pull free, still hot-blooded from the fight. As wardens step between him and Piercy, he says, "Get out of my way!"

"Hugh, stop," I plead.

Piercy eyes us with contempt. "I ought to have both of you arrested for disturbing the peace."

Hugh subsides as he comprehends that his reckless behavior could get us locked in cells with more prisoners than we can vanquish. He pats my hand before I release his arm—to reassure me that he can control himself—but he's breathing hard, his expression still defiant.

"See that Lord Hugh and Miss Bain get out of Newgate without causing any more trouble," Piercy tells the wardens.

Much as I would like to leave before any more trouble befalls us, I say, "We're not finished here. Governor, where were you the night Harry Warbrick was murdered?"

"In my residence here at Newgate. With my wife. All night." Piercy speaks as if he'd anticipated the question and rehearsed the answer.

"An alibi. How convenient for you," Hugh says. "We still need to speak with the matron and the chaplain."

Because now we're virtually certain that the governor is hiding something related to Amelia Carlisle's execution, and we're determined to find out what it is.

"Suit yourself. But be careful." Piercy's mocking smile suggests that he was indeed responsible for the lights going out and the attacks on us. "Or you could get hurt next time."

★　★　★

Two wardens escort Hugh and me out of the men's quadrangle. Dr. Davies has taken advantage of the confusion and escaped. Hugh and I exchange wary glances; these wardens could be some of the very people who attacked us. In the women's quadrangle, rows of cells flank the wide corridor. Prisoners peer out through grilles in iron doors. Above, more tiers of cells rise on both sides to an iron-and-glass skylight. Odors of urine, mildew, and disinfectant sharpen the cold, drafty air. Women's shrill voices echo. A scream of agony chills my blood.

"Jesus!" Hugh says.

The chatter quiets for a moment, then resumes. I've heard that prisoners are no longer flogged, but that seemed a sound from a torture chamber. The wardens seem undisturbed, and so does the woman walking down the corridor toward us. She wears a blue-plaid wool coat over her bustle and full skirts, with a large ring of keys at her waist. A dark blue felt bonnet crowns taffy-colored hair curled in a fringe over her low forehead. She could be a respectable shopkeeper.

"I'm Dorothea Fry. The guv said you want to speak to me." Her Cockney voice is deep, resonant; if raised, it would drown out the noise in the quadrangle. She's in her forties, short, full of bosom and hips. Her face, with its double chin, pointed nose, and shrewd blue eyes, is intelligent rather than pretty. When Hugh and I introduce ourselves, her eyebrows lift as she notes Hugh's good looks, but repugnance briefly twists her mouth. Either she knows about him, or she distrusts attractive men.

"They're all yours, Mrs. Fry. Don't let 'em out of your sight," one of the wardens says, and I'm relieved to see him and his partner go.

The scream comes again. Hugh says, "What is that infernal howling?"

"One o' the prisoners is having a baby," Mrs. Fry says, her tone matter-of-fact.

"Here?" Hugh says in surprise.

"She was with child when she was convicted. Where else would she have it?"

Up until today, I'd never thought about the plight of pregnant criminals. The idea of giving birth in jail is disturbing. "What will happen to the baby?"

"Her sister's gonna take care of it till she gets out in two years. She's lucky."

"She won't see her child for two years? That's lucky?" Hugh says, incredulous.

"It's better than never."

It seems like a punishment for both mother and child, an even more painful form of torture than flogging.

"Heard you got into a scrape." Mrs. Fry's shrewd blue gaze studies our faces. "You're bleedin'."

Hugh touches the raw skin on his cheekbone, and I my sore chin, which struck the stairs when I fell.

"I'll fix you up," Mrs. Fry says. "Come with me."

The screams follow us up an iron staircase that rises from the middle of the corridor. We reach a narrow catwalk that connects the galleries of cells on either side, then climb two more staircases. I can see through the spaces between the stairs, all the way down to the bottom. Fear of heights makes my heart pound. I fix my gaze on the matron's feet, clad in sturdy black boots, stepping confidently above me. On the top tier, Mrs. Fry leads us along a walkway that fronts the cells. She uses a key from her ring to unlock a door and lets us into a chamber furnished like a bed sitting room.

"Is this where you live?" I ask.

"Comes with the job," Mrs. Fry says.

The walls are covered with framed pictures, the floor with rag rugs, the bed with a patchwork quilt and embroidered cushions. A sewing box and a basket of knitting needles and yarn sit on the table. An upholstered armchair and a cupboard filled with dishes stand near a coal stove that emits welcoming heat. The barred window gives a view of rooftops and spires.

"Don't you mind living in a prison?" Hugh says.

Mrs. Fry shrugs. "I could do worse."

I think of the tenements where people crowd a dozen to a room, without heat, light, or comfort.

"Isn't it noisy?" Hugh says in response to the screams, now distant but increasingly frequent, and the incessant chatter from the cells.

"Where isn't?"

Compared to the button factory where my mother and I

worked when I was a child, after my father disappeared, Newgate is blessedly quiet. With wardens on duty and the criminals locked up, it's probably also safer than many places in London.

Mrs. Fry seats us at the table, cleans my chin with cotton dipped in mineral spirits, and applies sticking plaster over the wound. Her touch is deft rather than gentle. While she attends to Hugh's face, I look around the room. The windowsill holds an assortment of photographs that I rise to study. One shows a wedding portrait of a younger Mrs. Fry and her husband. In a picture with a black frame, her husband lies in a coffin. Postmortem photography is a customary practice; I've done it myself. Even people who can afford to have family pictures taken at any time often want a last memento of the dear departed.

"Thank you, Mrs. Fry," Hugh says. "That was very kind of you."

She nods, indifferent. I don't know if she helped us out of kindness, but it was more aid than Governor Piercy or Dr. Davies offered. I'm reluctant to pressure her for information that the law forbids her to divulge, but my experiences at Newgate have made me suspicious of everyone here, and perhaps she meant to hinder us by putting us in her debt.

"I suppose you know that we came to find out what happened at Amelia Carlisle's hanging," Hugh says.

"I s'pose you know I'm not allowed to tell you." Mrs. Fry sits at the table and takes up her knitting.

I voice the idea that Charlie Sullivan's story planted in my mind and the attacks on Hugh and me substantiated. "I think someone killed Harry Warbrick to prevent him from talking."

"You think." Her tone dismisses my theory as a figment of my imagination.

"It had to be someone who was at the hanging," Hugh says. "Someone who's desperate to hide a secret and wants to scare Miss Bain and me away, if not kill us. Is it you, Mrs. Fry?"

"No." Her expression is calm; her hands steadily ply her knitting needles.

"Then you could be the next victim." I think that's a likelier possibility than that a woman hanged Harry Warbrick.

"If I am, then you can investigate my murder." The green scarf she's knitting grows stitch by even stitch. Perhaps a woman who's buried her husband isn't afraid of death.

"All the witnesses could be in danger," Hugh says in his most urgent, persuasive tone. "The best way to protect yourself is to put the story in the newspaper. Then there'll be no reason to kill anyone else."

Mrs. Fry shrugs once more. "So you say."

I again seek an indirect route to the facts. "Did Amelia ever talk to you?"

"They all do. They all have a sob story, usually about men." Mrs. Fry gives Hugh another look of repugnance.

"What was Amelia's sob story?" I say.

Mrs. Fry knits; her suspicious gaze studies me as if she thinks I'm trying to trick her. "Amelia was from a coal-mining town in the North. She married at sixteen and lost two babies to the typhus fever. Her husband got killed in a mining accident. She married again, but her second husband died of cholera." Mrs. Fry relates the tale in a flat, uninterested voice. "Her third was a railroad engineer. She moved from city to city with him. They had a daughter, and then he died of consumption. Amelia was on her own. She became a midwife's apprentice. The midwife took in unmarried women who were expectin' and delivered their babies. The mothers gave the babies to baby farmers. Amelia saw that baby farming was a way to make money."

"How can there be enough unwanted babies to keep all the baby farmers in business?" Hugh asks.

"They're illegitimate. Most orphanages won't take them," Mrs. Fry says. "The mothers want to get rid of their shame so they can marry decent men. Amelia put ads in the newspapers. She started takin' in babies. The mothers trusted her because she was a respectable widow with a child of her own. She was pretty too, before she lost her teeth."

"Why did she kill the babies?" I say. That was the question heard all around town after Amelia's arrest.

"There are plenty of women wantin' to give away babies, but not enough people wantin' to adopt 'em. And the five pounds she charged the mothers didn't go far enough. Babies need to be fed and clothed until they grow up. Amelia took in more and more babies to make ends meet. She couldn't take care of 'em all."

According to the newspaper stories, that was the explanation she gave at her trial, but I found it too simple. There must have been some deeper reason why a woman would kill babies.

"So Amelia strangled 'em, wrapped 'em in blankets full o' rocks, and dropped 'em in the river at night. That's how she was caught, you know. The police was already watching her. They saw her do it. When they went to arrest her, they found two other dead babies in her house. She said, 'I had no choice.'" Mrs. Fry's voice turns acid with contempt. "Everybody has an excuse. Things are tough all over. The other girls in here done all sorts o' things for money to live on." The woman giving birth screams again and again, and Mrs. Fry says, "She got two years for stealin' oysters. But most of these girls never killed nobody."

I know from personal experience that even people who think themselves incapable of killing actually are capable under certain circumstances. But I can't imagine killing helpless infants. People speculated that Amelia was possessed by the devil, and although I'm not superstitious, I can't help wondering if they were right.

"What else did Amelia talk about?" Hugh asks.

Mrs. Fry gives him a put-upon look. I feel a sudden, overwhelming fatigue as the clashes with Governor Piercy and Dr. Davies, the terror of the attack, and the tumble down the stairs take their belated toll. I struggle to gather my thoughts. Perhaps Dr. Davies isn't the only suspect with a personal motive for Harry Warbrick's murder.

"How well did you know Harry Warbrick?" I ask Mrs. Fry.

"I met him a few times, whenever he came to hang one of the girls."

"Did he ever talk to you?" I ask.

"He talked to everybody." Mrs. Fry adds with distaste, "He was that sort."

"What did he talk about?" Hugh asks.

"His trips around the country. The criminals he hanged. He was always hintin' that he knew things that other people didn't. I don't think he really did. I think he just wanted to make himself seem important."

I have to consider the possibility that her assessment of Harry Warbrick could be accurate. I'm beginning to wonder if Warbrick's murder really isn't connected with Amelia Carlisle's hanging. We've yet to find proof that it is.

"Harry invited me to his pub," Mrs. Fry says. "I didn't go."

"It sounds as if you disliked him," Hugh says.

"Not enough to kill him, if that's what you're gettin' at."

We should look for witnesses to confirm or disprove the lack of bad blood between Mrs. Fry and Harry Warbrick, but her placid manner makes her seem innocent. Maybe Hugh and I risked our lives to come here on a fool's errand.

"Did you see Harry after Amelia's hanging?" Hugh asks.

"No," Mrs. Fry says. "The hanging was the last time I ever saw him."

My doubts trigger a sudden, disturbing notion: the attacks on Hugh and me might not have been instigated by one of the witnesses to Amelia's hanging. Maybe they were personal, unrelated to those two minutes and fifty seconds.

"Who do you think killed him?" Hugh says.

"Likely some bloke he ticked off at his pub." Mrs. Fry puts her knitting in the basket and stands. "I have to get back on the ward. I'll take you to the chaplain now."

CHAPTER 9

The walk with Mrs. Fry to the central prison block clears my head, invigorates me. But I'm rattled by the new ideas that have taken root in my mind, still on high alert for danger. Two wardens fall into step behind Hugh and me in the passage, the same men who escorted us earlier.

"We'll take 'em from here, Mrs. Fry."

Did they attack us? If so, on whose orders? I walk as far away from them as possible. The next push down the stairs could be fatal.

The chapel is on the top floor of the prison, a large room where stone walls rise to a high ceiling and iron bars fortify the tall, arched windows, whose grimy panes darken the foggy daylight. It's stark, without decorations to uplift the spirits, and cold. The air smells of body odor and stale mops. Hugh and I have been in the prison all afternoon; it's now four thirty, and an evensong service is in progress. A huge wooden pulpit looms against the wall opposite the windows, elevated on a platform about ten feet high. Inside it stands the chaplain.

"O God, make speed to save us." Young, with curly light brown hair, dressed in dark clerical garb, dwarfed by the pulpit, he speaks in a cultured, nervous voice.

Male prisoners sitting in rows of benches along the walls, behind iron grilles, recite the response to the prayer: "O Lord, make haste to help us." Female voices issue from the two galleries, which are screened by tall boards that slant toward the pulpit so the women behind them have a view of the preacher, but nothing else. I suppose the seating arrangement prevents the inmates from flirting and disrupting the service.

"Glory be to the Father, the Son, and the Holy Ghost," the chaplain says.

"Amen," some of the prisoners respond dutifully. Others mutter, joke, and chuckle among themselves.

The organist, a wizened gray man, plays a hymn on a harmonium. Voices rise in song:

God that madest earth and heaven,
Darkness and light!
Who the day for toil hast given,
For rest the night.

The men clown, singing the next lines in exaggerated falsetto or bass. The women giggle. The chaplain winces with pained disapproval. "Please, remember that this is a house of God!"

The congregation only grows louder, unrulier. The organist shakes with suppressed mirth. One of the wardens escorting Hugh and me steps in. "That's enough. It's back to the cells for you rabble."

The men exit through a door behind their benches. A woman calls, "Buy me a drink when I get out, Father?" The other women titter.

"Better show 'em who's boss, Father, or you won't last long here," the warden says, then points at Hugh and me. "We'll be waiting outside. Behave yourselves."

Hugh and I stand alone in the empty space where, in an ordinary church, the pews would be. We're ill at ease, not only due to the possibility of another attack. Hugh hasn't attended church since he was exposed as a homosexual and his pastor repudiated him as a disgrace to God. I haven't attended since my father disappeared, when the folks at our parish church shunned my mother and me. I now know that they believed my father had raped and murdered Ellen Casey. The memory still hurts.

The chaplain descends from the pulpit. "You must be from the newspaper." Face-to-face with him, I'm surprised to discover that he's tall and husky. His posture, hunched with self-consciousness, makes him seem smaller, frailer. He has boyish features and a prominent Adam's apple. "I'm Timothy Starling."

Hugh and I introduce ourselves and shake hands with him. His hand is wet with cold perspiration, but its grip is strong.

"How did you get yourself consigned to this hellhole, Father?" Hugh's tone has a rude, unpleasant, and uncharacteristic edge. I think he sees every clergyman as a personification of the Church's disgust toward him, and he's lashing out at this one.

The Reverend Starling has the kind of fair, translucent skin that blushes easily. Red patches bloom in his cheeks. "I volunteered."

"It doesn't seem like your cup of tea." Hugh usually hides his hurt feelings about his social ostracism, but sometimes they breach the barrier of his admirable self-control. I suppose he needs to vent them or they'll eat away at him like acid. Still keyed up from his fight, spoiling for another, he says, "I thought perhaps that you couldn't get a better situation."

"After I was ordained six months ago, I inherited the living at my family's parish in Wiltshire." The Reverend Starling's blush turns even redder. "I came here because the most afflicted and desperate among us need Christian faith the most."

"How noble of you," Hugh says.

He might be jealous of the chaplain, who's in good standing with church and society, but I don't want him picking on a young, idealistic man who, if treated properly, might be more willing to cooperate with us than the rest of the prison staff. I touch Hugh's arm to quiet him and say to the chaplain, "We need to talk to you about Amelia Carlisle."

The chaplain's Adam's apple jerks. "I can't violate the Official Secrets Act."

"You're not the only one who's hiding behind it. Join the club," Hugh says in a callous tone. "But you're a man of God. Isn't lying one of the seven deadly sins? You ought to make a clean breast instead of lying by omission. Did something untoward happen at Amelia's hanging?"

"No! I mean, I'm not saying something didn't happen. I'm not saying it did." Flustered, the Reverend Starling waves his hands as his blush deepens. "I'm not saying anything at all."

He's a terrible liar. I feel more certain that Amelia's last moments alive are at the root of Harry Warbrick's murder.

"Come on, Father, just a hint," Hugh says. "You'll feel better. The secret is weighing on you like a ton of bricks, I can tell."

The Reverend Starling backs against the pulpit as if claiming the authority of his office. "There's no use badgering me. You might as well go home." He sounds like a schoolboy trying to fend off bullies.

"Let's talk about something else." Hoping that a gentler, indirect approach will lead us to clues, I ask the Reverend Starling, "Were you acquainted with Amelia Carlisle?"

He hesitates, as if afraid that any word he utters will let slip a bit of confidential information. "Yes. I see each prisoner upon admission and discharge. And I visit them all, as often as possible, to offer spiritual advice." He gains poise while talking about his work; his blush fades. "I pay special attention to condemned prisoners."

Hugh laughs. "What good can you do for people who are headed for the gallows?"

The Reverend Starling faces Hugh's hostility with dignified courage. "Ministering to the condemned is an ancient tradition. I help them repent of their sins and make peace with their fate."

"How can you manage that when you can't even control your congregation during services?" Hugh says.

I flash a warning glance at Hugh. "Did Amelia repent?" The

newspaper stories said she expressed no remorse at her trial, and I'd like to know whether she turned over a new leaf while in prison.

"I'm afraid not. The first step toward repentance is acknowledging responsibility for one's sins. Unfortunately, Amelia laid the blame for hers on other people. Such as her husbands, God rest their souls." The Reverend Starling is confident now that the conversation has strayed from Amelia's execution. His voice gains volume and resonance. I think he would be a good preacher if he had a tamer audience. "She said her first husband should have been more careful and not let himself be buried under falling rocks in the coal mine. She said that if her second husband had been more than a clerk at the mine office, they could have lived someplace where he wouldn't have caught the cholera. Her third saddled her with a daughter to support on her own. She seemed less grieved by their deaths than resentful because they'd left her in the lurch. If they hadn't died, she wouldn't have become a baby farmer."

It sounds as though Amelia considered herself a victim. She must have been an unpleasant person as well as a murderess.

"The person she blamed the most was Faith Ingham," the Reverend Starling says.

"Isn't that the woman who tipped over Amelia's deadly apple-cart?" Hugh says.

"Yes. She set the police on Amelia."

"She was the star witness at Amelia's trial." I recall newspaper stories I read about Faith Ingham. Her photograph showed an emaciated young woman with big, dazed eyes. A governess and unwed mother, she'd given her baby boy to Amelia. Three weeks later, she changed her mind and went back to reclaim him. Amelia gave her a baby, but Miss Ingham knew it wasn't hers; hers had a birthmark on his leg, and this one didn't. Then Amelia told her the baby had been adopted. She gave Miss Ingham the parents' address, which turned out to be false. When Miss Ingham confronted her, Amelia said she'd made a mistake and gave Miss Ingham a different address. It too was false. Miss Ingham went to the police. They investigated Amelia and questioned her neighbors, who said they'd seen many babies go into her house and none come out. The police spied on Amelia and caught her throwing a dead infant in the Thames. When they searched her house, they found the two other murdered infants and cupboards stuffed with baby clothes, including a nightshirt that had belonged to Miss Ingham's son. It's certain that Amelia killed him and threw him in the river, but no trace of him—or the other babies she must have killed—was ever found.

"Amelia said that Miss Ingham had no right to come back for her baby," the Reverend Starling continues. "They had an agreement, and Miss Ingham broke it. Amelia also said that if Miss Ingham had cared about her baby, she should have kept him. If not for Miss Ingham raising a fuss, Amelia wouldn't have been caught. Amelia even suggested that all the mothers who gave their babies to her were at fault. If not for their mistakes, there would be no baby farmers."

"What a sweetheart," Hugh says.

I'm despising Amelia more and more myself. That she would blame the mothers of the babies she'd killed!

"Amelia wanted to sue Miss Ingham for breach of contract." The Reverend Starling shakes his head in disapproval. "She asked me to help."

She was not only a blame passer; she was vindictive.

"Why sue?" Hugh says. "Even if she'd won, she couldn't have taken the money with her."

"She said it would support her daughter. To her credit, she did care about her daughter."

"Oh, well, that should have gotten her a pardon." Hugh's voice drips sarcasm.

According to the newspaper stories, Amelia's adult daughter, Jane Carlisle, didn't testify at the trial and vanished afterward. Curiosity makes me wonder if she might be worth looking for. Then again, she wouldn't know what had happened at her mother's execution.

"Amelia thought that if she had to be punished, so should Miss Ingham," the Reverend Starling says. "But I think she also believed the world owed her compensation for the way her life turned out."

"Do you think Harry Warbrick deserved the way things turned out for him?" Hugh deftly turns the conversation to the murder.

"No one deserved such a terrible death." The blush spreads across the Reverend Starling's cheeks again. Wringing his hands, he seems even more nervous than when asked about Amelia's execution. "I shouldn't talk any more."

"Why not?" Hugh says. "Harry's murder isn't covered by the Official Secrets Act."

The Reverend Starling glances at the door. "I've prisoners to visit."

"Why so jittery, Father? Did you kill him?"

"What?" Starling is as crimson as a beet, his eyes wide. "No!"

"Well, you look guiltier than the cat that ate the canary," Hugh says, pleased that our investigation may be getting somewhere for our pains. "How well did you know Harry?"

Starling raises his chin in an attempt at defiance. "I don't have to answer your questions. You're just reporters, not the police." He turns to walk away.

"Would you rather talk to the police?" I say.

"When they read in the paper tomorrow that you got all het up when you were asked about Harry, they'll be on you like a dog on fresh meat."

Starling freezes, then turns to face us, his cheeks flaming. "I'm innocent. If you accuse me, you'll look awfully foolish when it turns out that someone else killed Harry." His voice resounds with conviction that his color belies.

Hugh sneers. "Next you're going to tell us that you hadn't any reason to kill Harry because the two of you were best chums."

Starling is silent while his Adam's apple jerks.

"Hah, my instincts were right on the money," Hugh says. "You did have reason."

I'm excited by the possibility that we've identified the killer, but not ready to believe it's Starling. "What happened between you and Warbrick?"

Cornered, Starling responds as if in the hope that if he spills the beans, we'll leave him alone. Or maybe he's succumbed to an urge to unburden himself. "All right. I didn't like Harry. He was the reason I got off on the wrong foot at Newgate. The first time I witnessed a hanging, I got sick after I left the execution shed. Harry saw me. He laughed and said I needed to develop a stronger stomach. Then he told some of the wardens. Pretty soon it was all over Newgate. Nobody who works here respects me. Neither do the prisoners. And Harry ribbed me whenever he saw me. At every hanging he did, it was, 'Are you going to lose it again this time, Father?'" Misery, resentment, and humiliation shine in Starling's brown eyes.

Hugh grins with satisfaction. "Sarah, remember that crime scene we photographed at the Wapping Docks? One longshore-man had killed another for bullying him on the job and turning their colleagues against him. Sounds like we've a similar situation here."

"No. It isn't," Starling protests. "I would never kill anyone, no matter how he treated me."

"Oh, right—'Thou shalt not kill,'" Hugh says.

I remember that motive is only one element of a murder. I feel sorry for Starling because I was bullied at boarding school due to my shy, solitary nature. Furthermore, I can't credit that the murder had nothing to do with Amelia Carlisle's hanging.

"If you have an alibi for the night of the murder, you've noth-ing to worry about," I tell Starling.

I didn't think he could blush any redder, but he does, as if all the blood has risen to his head. Hugh walks closer to Starling and says, "Just as I thought—no alibi. My instincts are in tip-top form today. Sarah, I bet we can find a witness who'll place the good father at The Ropemaker's Daughter that night."

Backing away, the chaplain blurts, "He was alive when I left him."

My mouth drops. The chaplain has dug himself a deeper hole by admitting he was at the scene of the crime.

Hugh advances on Starling. "Do you expect us to believe that you went there for a nice, friendly drink?"

"I did!" Desperate and pleading, the chaplain is physically taller than Hugh but shrunken smaller now by fright. "I thought that if I had a chat with him, I could get him to like me and stop teasing me."

Now I'm amazed by his naivety. I learned as a child that efforts to ingratiate oneself with bullies only earns more scorn.

"Did it work?" Hugh asks, doubtful.

Pinned against the pulpit, Starling speaks with rancor. "No. He told everyone in the pub how I got sick after the hanging."

"He impugned your honor in public. I wouldn't blame you if you stuck around until after closing and put a noose around his neck." Hugh thrusts his face at Starling. "Why don't you just confess? Isn't it supposed to be good for the soul?"

"Leave me alone!" Without warning, Starling punches Hugh in the jaw.

Hugh yelps, reels backward against the harmonium, and slides to the floor.

"Hugh!" I rush to him and help him to his feet. Although he provoked this second attack of the day, I turn to Starling, ready to do battle.

Starling gazes at Hugh, appalled by his own actions. "I'm sorry."

"No need to apologize, Father." Hugh laughs, sheepish yet triumphant. "I deserved it for needling you. I'm sorry about that. And you told me exactly what I wanted to know—you've a motive for murder, an opportunity to commit it, and no alibi. Oh, and a violent streak. That's worth a little tap on the jaw."

CHAPTER 10

In the front hall of the prison, the wardens are waiting with my camera, trunk and satchel on the desk. They grin at Hugh and me. Uneasy, I open the camera case while Hugh inspects the contents of the trunk. Everything is accounted for, undamaged. Then I pick up my satchel and hear an ominous tinkle. When I open it and shake the flat cases of glass negative plates, they rattle. All the plates are broken.

I glare at the wardens. "You broke them on purpose."

They shrug, not denying it. Hugh says, "We're going to lodge a complaint against you."

"Lodge it where the sun don't shine."

Still hot-tempered, Hugh lunges at the men. I restrain him, hand him the trunk, grab my other things, and pull him toward the door. "Let's just go."

Outside Newgate, an icy wind stirs the quagmire of drizzle and soot that immerses the city. Church bells ring five o'clock, but it's as dark as midnight. As we trudge toward the station, we stay close to the prison walls in case the boys leading horses and carriages through the murk accidentally wander onto the sidewalk.

"I'm sorry I lost my temper with the Reverend Starling and those guards," Hugh says. "I could have gotten us both arrested."

"It's all right. I'm just glad we got away before anything else bad happened."

"I shouldn't have grilled the Reverend Starling so hard." Hugh seems genuinely contrite. "It was cruel of me."

I can't disagree. "You apologized. And it did get results."

"The chaplain and the doctor didn't exactly have a personal interest in keeping Harry Warbrick alive. We don't know about Governor Piercy or the sheriff. But I'm not ready to call it quits on the Amelia Carlisle angle. Somebody in Newgate wants to hurt us. It must be one of the witnesses to her execution."

"I've been thinking maybe not."

"Who else could it be?" Hugh sounds puzzled.

"Someone who has a grudge against us. Someone with connections inside Newgate."

"Who—?"

Two men emerge from the fog, walking toward us. One wears a police constable's uniform, the other an overcoat and derby. It's Barrett and Inspector Reid. We stop abruptly. Hugh says, "Oh. I see."

The attack could have been Reid's belated revenge on us.

"Sarah?" Barrett says, his voice a mixture of surprise and dismay. My heart plunges.

Reid favors us with an unpleasant smile. "Here are the bad pennies, cropping up again." Framed by his fluffy, graying mustache and beard, his mouth is pink, his teeth sharp. There's no surprise in his cold brown eyes.

"We could say the same about you," Hugh says.

"What are you doing here?" Barrett asks.

I wanted to see him alone, explain, and smooth things over between us. All I can do now is tell him the truth. "Investigating Harry Warbrick's murder."

Barrett's expression hardens. "I should have guessed." I can tell he wants to upbraid me for going behind his back, but he won't make a personal scene in front of Reid. Then he notices the bandages on Hugh's and my faces, and concern replaces his anger. "What happened to you?"

"I was pushed down the stairs inside Newgate," I say.

"I was thrown into a boxing match with some very unfriendly prisoners," Hugh says.

"Who did it?" Barrett demands. He's not so angry with me that he'll excuse anyone who hurt us. His fists clench as if he wants to thrash our attackers even though he thinks we were doing something we shouldn't have been.

"We couldn't see. The lights were out," I say.

Confused, Barrett looks up at the jail, then back at us. "Why were you in there?"

"They think the murder has something to do with Amelia Carlisle," Reid says. "Sir Gerald pulled strings to get them interviews with the people who were at her hanging."

"Who told you that we would be in Newgate?" I ask Reid.

"A little bird."

Barrett turns his anger on Reid. "You knew? And you didn't tell me?"

Reid smirks. "I just did." Because his superiors won't let him fire Barrett, he instead plays every possible dirty trick on him; he's not content just to block Barrett's promotion.

"So that's why we're here," Barrett says. "You wanted to catch them when they came out and wanted me to see."

Reid points his gloved finger at Barrett. "Smart lad." Then he asks Hugh and me, "So what did you learn about the Baby Butcher's hanging?"

Hugh ignores the question. "Maybe that's not the only reason you're here. Were you responsible for the attacks on us? Did you come to admire your handiwork?"

"Is it true?" Barrett demands.

Reid holds up his palms and widens his eyes in an exaggerated pose of innocence. "This is the first I've heard of it. But I'll buy a drink for whoever did the deed."

"It certainly seems like something you would do, setting prison guards on us," Hugh says in disgust. "You're too much of a coward to fight us yourself."

Reid bristles. "If I'd wanted you done in, you wouldn't be standing up talking now."

Barrett takes a step toward Reid. "If it was you, I swear I'll—"

Reid chuckles and pats the air. "Take it easy. Lay a hand on your commanding officer, and the top brass will have to pull your badge, even if you're their blue-eyed boy. Don't ruin your career for *her*." He sneers at me. "She'll do you dirty to win the contest."

He's trying to drive a wedge between Barrett and me. If he can't get Barrett off the force and me thrown in prison, he'll settle for splitting us up. Barrett looks from Reid to me, his eyes stormy. He walks a few paces away, as if he doesn't trust himself not to lose control, and stands with his back to me. My temper is ready to explode at Reid, who's not the only one with a grudge. In the past, he terrified me, tormented me, and delivered my friends and me into the hands of Jack the Ripper.

"Hate to interrupt this little chat, but Sarah and I should be going." Hand on my arm, Hugh propels me along the sidewalk before I say or do something regrettable. "Barrett, why don't you come to our house after you go off duty? We'll talk things over."

Reid steps in our path, forcing us to halt. "Not so fast. Tell me what you learned about Amelia Carlisle."

"Read about it in the newspaper tomorrow." I shan't save Reid the trouble of interviewing the prison staff.

"I could arrest you for obstructing justice," Reid says.

"You and who else?" Hugh says.

Reid glances at Barrett, who doesn't move. Although Barrett is furious, he'll let the bad blood between him and Reid get worse rather than lay the hand of the law on Hugh and me. Reid knows it too, and his vexed expression says he hasn't forgotten the occasions when we resisted arrest and he came out the loser. As Hugh and I resume walking, Reid moves backward, facing us and keeping in step with us while Barrett stays behind. I'm glad not to be arrested, but I feel bad because Barrett is risking his own welfare for my sake.

"Spill the beans," Reid says. "Then get out of my case."

"If we do, Sir Gerald will just put someone else on it," Hugh says. "He's going to win the contest with or without us."

"I'll settle for that." Reid seems as angry about being pitted against us as about the contest itself. He doesn't want us to complicate the Warbrick investigation as we did the Ripper and the Mariner cases. Now he raises his eyebrows as if at a sudden, pleasing thought. "Let's talk about Mr. Benjamin Bain."

My heart seizes. I stop in my tracks.

Reid grins, pleased by the dismay I can't hide. "He murdered a little girl in 1866. What was her name? Oh yes—Ellen Casey. Then he absconded."

"My father didn't murder her." My voice wobbles, for I've no evidence to banish my own doubts about his innocence, let alone the police's belief that he's guilty.

"The investigation is on hold because we haven't enough manpower to devote to a twenty-four-year-old unsolved murder," Reid says. "But I thought it worth pursuing in my spare time. I've dug up some new clues to your father's whereabouts."

Shock and alarm clutch my heart. I look over my shoulder at Barrett. He's standing half a block away, out of earshot, almost invisible in the fog.

Hugh comes to my defense. "Leave her father out of this."

Reid chuckles. "Here's the deal: you quit the contest, and I'll let the Ellen Casey murder stay on hold. If you don't, I'll follow up on those clues." He tips his hat in mock courtesy, says, "A pleasant evening to you, Miss Bain, Lord Hugh," and strolls away.

★ ★ ★

On the underground train, Hugh and I stand in the aisle, clinging to straps. The swaying motion jolts us against the other people crammed into the car, which is dimly lit when the train passes gas lamps in the tunnel, then pitch-dark between them. Hugh shouts in my ear so that I can hear him above the racket of the wheels on the tracks and the thunder of the engine.

"Reid is bluffing. He doesn't really have any new clues."

How I long to believe it! "But if he's been hunting my father, he might have found some."

"Reid couldn't find his own backside at night."

I'm still afraid that the shadow of the past is coming closer, getting darker. "Sally saw our father in London yesterday. Maybe he ran into someone who knew him from the past, someone who tipped Reid off."

"Maybe Sally was mistaken," Hugh says.

Yesterday I was torn between hope that she really did see Benjamin Bain and fear that when we finally reunited with him, we would learn that he'd murdered Ellen Casey. Now I only hope he was a figment of Sally's wishful imagination. "If he falls into Reid's hands, he'll be railroaded to the gallows even if he's innocent."

"Then you know what this means."

"Yes. I have to find my father before Reid does." And ask him, at long last, whether he killed Ellen and why he abandoned Sally and me.

"You will," Hugh says. "You found Jack the Ripper when Reid and all of his horses and all of his men couldn't."

The train arrives at Blackfriars Station with a screeching of brakes and a push toward the doors. Hugh says, "I'll report to the *Daily World* office. You go look for your father."

I'm still reluctant. My father's answers to my questions will determine whether I warn him that Reid is on his trail. I can't in good conscience let a murderer go free. If he says he wants nothing to do with Sally and me, would that make turning him over to the police easier? "I'll go with you. It shouldn't take long."

Hugh and I weave our way, carrying my equipment, through noisy crowds in Fleet Street. Light from the buildings, gas lamps along the street, and lanterns swinging from carriages lend the dark, foggy scene the aspect of a carnival at night. Whistles shrill as police constables direct traffic, and people flock to the warmth of the public houses. Inside the *Daily World* headquarters, we find

Sir Gerald, Mr. Palmer, and Malcolm Cross seated at the conference table as if they've been awaiting our return.

"Well?" Sir Gerald says.

Hugh and I describe what happened at Newgate. When we're finished, Malcolm Cross scoffs. "So you didn't prove that Amelia Carlisle's execution has a smidgen to do with Harry Warbrick's murder. You're barking up the wrong tree."

Mr. Palmer hesitates before he says, "They did identify Mrs. Warbrick's lover." He sounds reluctant to give us any credit at all. "But his motive for the murder seems personal rather than related to the hanging."

Sir Gerald narrows his eyes in thought. "I think Miss Bain and Lord Hugh are right about the attacks—someone at Newgate thinks they're getting too close to a dirty secret. 'Witnesses keep mum about shady business at the Baby Butcher's hanging. Reporters attacked for trying to investigate.' Run something like that in tomorrow's paper."

Mr. Palmer raises a feeble protest. "But we don't know whether it's true."

"When has that ever stopped us from printing a good story?" Sir Gerald says.

I experience a sudden qualm. I'm glad Sir Gerald is taking our side, but his opinion isn't evidence that we're right. Maybe he likes our theory about Amelia Carlisle because it will inflate the Warbrick murder and the contest into an even bigger story. Or maybe his recent nervous breakdown has impaired his judgment.

"We don't want a libel suit," Mr. Palmer says.

"Just don't openly accuse anybody of anything," Sir Gerald says in a tone of overtaxed patience.

Hugh and I don't mention my alternate theory—that Inspector Reid was behind the attacks. If the *Daily World* accused Reid, he would retaliate by airing the story of Ellen Casey's murder and name my father as the prime suspect. I don't want it published, and I wouldn't trust Sir Gerald to withhold it for my sake. An article in the *Daily World* could put everyone in London on the lookout for Benjamin Bain.

"You're on the right track," Sir Gerald tells Hugh and me. "Keep up the good work."

His praise only adds to my uneasiness about keeping secrets from him. I hate to imagine what he would do if he found out. I think of Barrett and wonder what to say to him the next time I see him—if there is a next time.

"Miss Bain was clumsy. Lord Hugh picked a fight," Cross protests. "They made up a story about an attack so you wouldn't think they were incompetent fools."

Hugh's eyes glint with the same heat as during the fight. "What did you learn today, Mr. Cross? Have you solved the murder?"

Cross's face takes on a sulky expression. "I'm still following my lead."

"Follow it faster," Sir Gerald says. "Dig up something soon, or I'll put you on investigating Amelia Carlisle's hanging."

"Yes, Sir Gerald." Cross glowers at Hugh and me, irate because our stock with Sir Gerald has risen while his has fallen.

"We're going to solve this case. We'll keep shaking trees until something falls out!" Sir Gerald bangs his fist on the table.

We recoil from the blaze of zeal in his eyes. The temperature in the room seems to rise ten degrees. He's like the sun—he has the power to change the atmosphere. I was right: this case means more to him than just a good story; the contest is more than a game to win. And it's not on account of Harry Warbrick, a man he wouldn't have given the time of day when he was alive. Sir Gerald has a sense of unfinished business due to Robin's kidnapping, no matter that justice was served in the bloodiest, most personal fashion. His need for revenge is so insatiable that he'll exact it from a stranger who killed a stranger.

"By God, we're going to get the bastard," he says.

And heaven help anyone who fails to do his part or stands in Sir Gerald's way.

CHAPTER 11

That evening I hurry along Cheyne Walk in Chelsea. Ornate gas lamps glow in front of tall, stately brick townhouses. Across the street, beyond the green, the river hides beneath the fog. I hear the water lapping at the rocks; smell its fishy, fetid breath; and shiver in the chill wind. The house where Sally works and lives belongs to her employer, who owns a shipyard. It has a white marble facade on the first story, and its large windows glitter with light. I bypass the gate in the black iron fence and walk around the corner to the narrow, cobblestoned alley behind the house. The smell of manure issues from stables across the alley. I knock on a plain wooden door flanked by dustbins. Sally isn't allowed to receive visitors at the front entrance. Long moments pass before a woman opens the door. In her forties, she has gray-streaked brown hair coiled atop her head; she wears a black frock and white apron. She's the last person I wanted to see.

The feeling is mutual. "What are you doing here?" Mrs. Albert, Sally's mother, demands. Hostility deepens the lines in her pretty oval face.

"I need to see Sally."

"You can't," Mrs. Albert snaps.

She's hated me since the day we met. We got off on the wrong foot, and I'm a reminder that Benjamin Bain—whom she knew as George Albert, his false name—already had a wife and child when she married him. No matter that my mother is long dead and my father's deception isn't my fault; she bears a grudge against me. I suppose that because she can't punish my father for abandoning her and Sally, I'm a convenient target for her anger.

"Sally is busy helping with dinner," Mrs. Albert says.

I hear pans clattering in the basement kitchen and smell the savory odors of cooking food. My stomach grumbles. I've not eaten since breakfast. "This is an emergency."

Mrs. Albert glares as if I'm trying to fool her. "Isn't it enough that Sally spends her days off with you? Can't you leave her alone?"

My temper heats up, but I clamp a tight lid on it. "Sally and I are sisters. We have a right to see each other."

"You don't have the right to fill her head with nonsense. You told her that her father is alive and in London. And now she thinks she's seen him!" Mrs. Albert is spitting with rage.

"He is alive."

"Even if he were, he wouldn't be hanging around you and Sally. Remember, he left you. He left all of us." Mrs. Albert's brown eyes brim with pain.

Sally has let on that her mother prefers to think Benjamin Bain is dead because it's more comfortable than dredging up the past, opening unhealed wounds. I think Mrs. Albert is afraid of what will happen to her and Sally if his past catches up with him. I wonder whether she knows something about him that she's not telling.

"Why can't you let sleeping dogs lie?" Mrs. Albert's question is a plea for me to do exactly that. Before I can try to explain, she says, "It was an evil day when you turned up out of the blue. Sally used to be a good girl, content with her place. Now she's full of silly notions. She wants to be a writer and have her own house and live her own life."

I gape in surprise, for Sally has told me none of this, and I've never said anything to encourage her to change her situation.

"Go away," Mrs. Albert says through clenched teeth, "before you do any more damage."

"Mother, who's there?" Sally appears in the passage behind Mrs. Albert, drying her hands on her apron. She sees me and smiles. "Sarah!"

"Miss Bain was just leaving," Mrs. Albert says. She never calls me by my first name. She knows my father named Sally after me, and it galls her.

"No!" Sally holds the door open while her mother tries to close it. "Sarah, is something wrong?"

"We can't wait to—we have to go—" I can't say that we have to look for our father, starting at the place where Sally saw him. Mrs. Albert would never let Sally out of the house.

Sally takes the hint. "I'll get my coat." She runs down the passage.

Mrs. Albert fumes at me. "Sally is going to get in trouble, and it's your fault."

Sally returns, carrying her coat and hat, and pushes past her mother. We run down the alley like children running away from school. "Sally! Come back!" Mrs. Albert shouts.

On the main road, amid people hurrying to the shops before they close, we slow down to catch our breath. Misgivings fill me. "I'm sorry I came. You could lose your post."

"I don't care," Sally says. "I've been working in that house for eleven years. I don't want to spend the rest of my life there."

I consider the prospect of adding another person to my household. Sally could share my bedroom, but even with the generous salary Sir Gerald pays us, I come up short. "Your mother said you want to be a writer."

"Well, yes." Sally ducks her head, abashed. "I was good at writing when I was at school, and I love to read novels from the library. Some are wonderful, but others aren't at all, and I said to myself, 'I could do this.' Mother caught me scribbling at night. She was furious. She said I was stupid to think I could write novels, let alone earn money from it."

My mother had reacted much the same when I said I wanted to

be a photographer. Now my heart contracts with remembered pain and humiliation. She also criticized my looks, my manner, and everything I did. She often said I would need to earn my own living because no man would ever want to marry me. If she loved me, it was difficult to tell. Her harsh treatment of me has left scars as permanent as those caused by my father's absence.

"She says she's telling me for my own good," Sally says. It's exactly how my mother justified her behavior toward me. "But I'm not going to let anybody stop me."

I'm the last person to tell someone else not to pursue her dream, but I warn Sally, "You may have to work for a long time before you succeed. I operated my photography studio at a loss for the first year. You had better keep your post and save up your wages. There could be some hardships ahead."

"I know, but I just can't resign myself to emptying other people's chamber pots." Sally adds bashfully, "I want to be independent, like you."

My example speaks louder than my words, but maybe her notions aren't entirely my fault; maybe we were both born with an independent streak. "I'm sorry I've caused trouble between you and your mother."

"It's all right. She needs to realize that I'm old enough to make my own decisions. I'm glad you want to look for Father tonight, but why are you so urgent all of a sudden?"

I explain about Inspector Reid's threat. I've already told Sally that Reid hates Hugh, Mick, and especially me for meddling in police business. She's safer not knowing the whole truth about Robin Mariner's kidnapping and the fate of Jack the Ripper.

"Oh, dear," Sally says. "But I'm sure we'll find him before Inspector Reid does. We won't let him get arrested."

I'm not so sure he doesn't deserve to be arrested, but I'll let Sally believe in his innocence until, heaven forbid, he's proven guilty.

We arrive at the library, an elegant building so new that its bricks are still red instead of black with soot. A domed portico mounted on white stone columns embellishes the entrance. We climb the steps. The library is dark except for a lamp glowing in the vestibule. As Sally opens the door, a man inside says, "We're closing."

"Please, Mr. Roscoe, can we come in just for a moment?" Sally says. "It's very important."

The man is short and thin, with a bald head, a waxed brown mustache, and silver-rimmed spectacles. "Oh, hello, Miss Albert." He has a surprisingly deep, rich voice. He smiles and says, "For a regular patron like you, I'll bend the rules."

He lets us into a large room that smells of leather, wood, fresh paint, tobacco smoke, and floor wax. The dark shapes of furniture inhabit the shadows. The clatter of our footsteps on the parquet floor echoes up to the high ceiling. Sally says, "Mr. Roscoe is the head librarian." She introduces me to him. "This is my sister—Miss Sarah Bain."

I'm touched by the pride in her voice. I've shied from meeting her acquaintances for fear that she would be ashamed of me because I'm part of her father's dark, secret past.

"A pleasure to meet you, Miss Bain," Mr. Roscoe says as we shake hands. "How can I help you ladies?"

Sally's brow knits as she gropes for words. "The last time I was here, I saw . . . a man." She's obviously reluctant to reveal his name or connection with us. She and her mother have kept their history as much a secret as my mother and I did ours. "May I show Sarah where?"

Mr. Roscoe looks mystified but intrigued. "Certainly."

He lights gas lamps, illuminating dark, heavy wooden tables and chairs, the librarian's desk, and shelves filled with books. I follow Sally up an iron staircase to a gallery that circles the room and contains more rows of ceiling-high bookshelves. "I was here." Sally stands in the narrow aisle between two rows. She paces some fifteen steps halfway down the aisle. "He was right here. We looked straight at each other." Her voice resonates with the shock she must have felt. "Then he turned and ran." She leads me back to the staircase, leans over the railing, and points down at the door. "He hurried outside. By the time I got there, he was gone."

"I've been meaning to ask you." Mr. Roscoe's rich voice echoes up to us. He's standing below the gallery, his small figure dwarfed by the height. "Why were you chasing that man?"

Sally gasps. "You saw him?"

"Yes. Heavyset fellow with a white beard. He ran past me, and a moment later you did."

"See? He really was here," Sally says to me, breathless with triumph. "I didn't just imagine it."

I want to believe her, but it's possible she mistook a stranger for our father. We hurry down the stairs to join Mr. Roscoe. He asks, "Who was he?"

"I—I don't know." Sally blushes and looks at the floor. She's not a competent liar.

Mr. Roscoe turns his quizzical gaze on me, but my countenance is impenetrable; I've had many more years' practice at concealing secrets. I ask, "Had you ever seen him before?"

"Once or twice. I noticed him because he didn't borrow any books. He's not a member." Mr. Roscoe turns to Sally. "Was he bothering you?"

She lifts her puzzled gaze. "Bothering me?"

"At the time, I thought that was why you chased him and he was in such a hurry to get away," Mr. Roscoe says. "Because you were angry and meant to report him."

"No," Sally says, still confused. "He didn't do anything. He didn't even speak to me."

"That's good. It happens sometimes—an unsavory character notices a young lady and follows her around the library. When I see it, I put a stop to it and tell him in no uncertain terms never to come back. If that fellow ever does bother you, just let me know."

Sally and I look at each other, stunned as we absorb the implication of his words. *"He was following me?"* Sally says.

"Yes," Mr. Roscoe says. "He came into the library right after you, and he hid behind the stacks while you were browsing. He pretended to be looking at books, but he barely took his eyes off you."

★ ★ ★

As soon as we're outside the library, Sally exclaims, "It had to be Father! And he knew who I was! Why else would he follow me?"

I think of my own sighting of him, which I'd thought to be a coincidence. "My God, maybe he was following me too!"

"He tracked us down," Sally says, jittery with excitement. "He hasn't forgotten us. He wants to reunite with us, but he's afraid."

Even as my heart leaps to embrace this interpretation, other possibilities disturb my mind. Maybe it was a coincidence; maybe our father didn't recognize Sally or me. He is the prime suspect in the rape as well as the murder of Ellen Casey. Maybe he happened onto us and viewed us, his own daughters, as prey to molest. The idea is so sickening that I can't voice it to Sally.

"Did he think I wanted to catch him and turn him in to the police? Is that why he ran?" A mournful sob breaks Sally's voice. "Did I scare him away?"

That seems a real possibility. I look around the foggy street, where a lone carriage rolls. We and the few other pedestrians walk bent against the cold wind that buffets us. Our father has left no visible trace.

"He'll never come back," Sally cries. "Sarah, we've lost him forever!"

"Let's not give up," I say, to raise my own morale as well as Sally's. "Inspector Reid claimed to have clues to his whereabouts." Dreadful news at the time, it's encouraging now. "And we definitely do," I remind Sally.

Her face brightens. "Lucas Zehnpfennig."

We walk in silence as we think of the link between our father's disappearances in 1866 and 1879. Shortly before he disappeared on

Sally and her mother, he received a letter from a man named Lucas Zehnpfennig. He was very upset, burned the letter, and made Sally promise she wouldn't tell anyone about it. But she told me, and the news unearthed a buried memory of a day when I was ten years old and came home from school to discover a strange man in the parlor with my mother. *Hello, Sarah. I'm Lucas Zehnpfennig.* His last name was so odd that I giggled. He was holding me on his lap, stroking my hair, when my father came in. My father ordered Lucas to get out of the house, and that night I heard my parents having one of their many whispered arguments. Soon afterward, my father disappeared. I'm sure Lucas was the same man who sent the letter Sally saw. Sally and I believe that finding Lucas is the key to finding my father and the truth about the past, but I've let time slip by for fear of taking the next step.

"How would we go about finding him?" Sally asks.

"I have an idea." An idea that entails returning to a place where I never wanted to go again.

CHAPTER 12

When I arrive at home, I find Hugh, Mick, and Fitzmorris at the dining room table, eating a supper of bangers and mash. Mick listens, rapt, as Hugh says, "Then I punched him in the mouth. He went down on his knees, spitting out blood and teeth."

"Aw, and I had to miss it!" Mick says.

"It was quite a victory." Hugh preens.

I frown. He's making the attack at Newgate sound like fun and games. Mick says, "Can I go with you and Sarah tomorrow?"

"No," I say from the doorway.

"Sarah. Welcome home," Hugh says with a smile.

"You have school tomorrow," I tell Mick.

"It wouldn't hurt to skip just this once," Mick says.

"You've already skipped weeks. Besides, we're not going anywhere interesting tomorrow." I signal Hugh with a glance. "You might as well go to school."

Hugh doesn't take the hint. "We've one more suspect to interview—the Sheriff of London."

"Criminy!" Mick says. "Don't make me miss that."

"We could go to Old Bailey in the morning," Hugh says. "If you promise to go to school in the afternoon, maybe Sarah will change her mind." He's a pushover for Mick, whose company he loves. He always undermines my efforts to act as a parent to Mick.

"If we don't solve the murder and Sir Gerald fires us, Mick needs an education to fall back on," I say.

"Have a little faith, Sarah. We'll solve it." Hugh is forever the optimist despite his own misfortunes. "Mick will be a big help." The two exchange grins.

"It's dangerous," I say. "Look what happened today."

"If I'd been with you, it wouldn't've been so bad," Mick says. "They'd have had a harder time takin' all three of us."

"Besides, Newgate is a perfect place for an attack in the dark," Hugh says. "Old Bailey is more civilized. What could happen there?"

I drop into a chair. It's been a long day, I'm hungry, and I haven't the strength to keep arguing. "Oh, all right."

Mick cheers, clapping his hands. "You won't be sorry. We'll solve the murder. And we'll give whoever attacked you their comeuppance."

"That's the spirit." Hugh switches the subject before I can change my mind. "Did you and Sally find any clues to your father's whereabouts?"

I'm just finishing my supper and my description of our trip to the library when the doorbell rings. "Who could be calling so late?" I hope it's not a summons to photograph a new crime scene.

"I'll get it." Fitzmorris goes downstairs and returns with Barrett.

Barrett is still in uniform, helmet in hand. His black hair is unruly, as though he's been raking his fingers through it, his habit when he's riled. A whiff of cold air, rain, and smoke accompanies him. I'm glad to see him, relieved that he's not so fed up with me that he would stay away forever, but the gaze he turns on me is so reproachful that my heart sinks.

Barrett says, "Hello," to Hugh and Mick but doesn't speak to me. I try to smile at him and fail.

Fitzmorris says, "I'll leave the washing-up for later."

Mick says, "I better do my homework."

"Bedtime for me," Hugh says. "Good night, Barrett." They all go upstairs.

Barrett drapes his overcoat on a chair and sits. I say, "Are you hungry? Would you like something to eat?" I gesture toward the leftovers, delaying the inevitable. "A cup of tea?"

"No, thanks." Barrett cuts to the chase. "Why didn't you tell me about the contest?"

"I'm sorry. I wish I had." My regret impassions my voice. "But I didn't know about it when I saw you yesterday morning. I couldn't have told you then. Sir Gerald thought of it later. Afterward, there wasn't time."

"The reporter from the *Daily World* had time."

I cringe inside. If he knew that Hugh and I had been lurking near Mrs. Warbrick's house, eavesdropping on him and Inspector Reid and Malcolm Cross, he would be angrier than ever.

"You could have found a minute to stop by the barracks and tell me last night," Barrett says.

But last night I was at Harry Warbrick's wake. "You're right, I should have. But I was afraid you would be upset."

"I'm not upset," Barrett says in the stiff tone that people use when they don't want to admit they're upset. "I'm frustrated because here we go again—you're keeping secrets from me."

Our old issue has reared its ugly head. "I apologize." Feeling wretched, aware that I'm in the wrong, I nonetheless have to say, "But I warned you that there will always be things I can't tell you."

"That doesn't mean I have to like it," Barrett says. My warning, conveyed more than six months ago under happier circumstances, has ill prepared him for the present reality. "You must have known I would find out about your trip to Newgate. You could have told me before Reid made a fool of me."

I hate that he was caught off guard, but I explain, "Sir Gerald made Hugh and me sign a confidentiality agreement when he hired us. And he ordered us to keep our findings under wraps until they're published in the paper."

"It was your decision to take the job." Rancor permeates Barrett's voice. "And now your whole life depends on staying on Sir Gerald's good side."

Here's our other issue—whether I should do this work and what it means for our relationship. I'm exhausted and don't want to have this argument now, but Barrett obviously isn't ready to quit, and I mustn't refuse to discuss something that's important to him and to us. "It's not just my life. There's Hugh and Mick to consider."

"They can work for Sir Gerald if they want. You don't have to."

Barrett is hinting that if I marry him, I won't need to earn my own living. He proposed to me last spring, but problems arose, and we haven't made any progress toward marriage since then. Although I'm glad it's still a possibility, my feet are just as cold as they were then. After my father disappeared, my mother and I worked in the button factory and shifted for ourselves in a series of cheap lodgings. Even now all my imaginings about marriage end with my husband leaving me, and our children, to a similar fate. Barrett has always shown himself to be loyal and dependable, but I can't help placing more faith in my own ability to eke out a living than in a man's love.

These thoughts are too private and painful to confess. Instead, I say, "I can't abandon Hugh and Mick." After my father disappeared and my mother and I lost all our friends, it took me decades to open myself up to new friends, and now that I have them, I won't forsake them. "They're my family." The weight of my guilt toward Barrett gets heavier because he doesn't know they aren't my only family. I avert my gaze from his as I think of Sally.

"Hugh and Mick would want you to be settled and secure. And happy," Barrett says.

"I know." They've hinted that they think I should marry Barrett. Hugh once said, *"He's a good chap. Don't let him get away."* Mick said, *"If you're gonna be a copper's wife, you could do a lot worse than him."* "But I'm worried about what will become of them if I leave."

Barrett nods, reluctantly conceding my point. I've told him about the spells of black depression that Hugh has suffered since his family disowned him, although lately they're infrequent, and Hugh hasn't repeated his attempt to commit suicide. I think that's because of his job at the *Daily World* as well as his relationship with Tristan Mariner. The job gives him purpose, a sense of accomplishment, and the money to support himself. Barrett also knows that Hugh and Mick are so impetuous that they make me seem sensible. If they run afoul of Sir Gerald, they could both end up on the streets.

"You should encourage them to find another line of work," Barrett says. "Look what happened to you at Newgate."

But our unconventional job suits my friends and me. No matter that I'm deeply in love with Barrett, I wouldn't be content to keep house; nor can I picture Hugh working in an office. I can picture Mick returning to his old life as a street urchin and petty criminal. And our inclinations go deeper than an urge to solve murders. I've always had an affinity for danger. When I come across someone or something that frightens me, I feel an urge to draw nearer, as if it's a sleeping wolf that I can't resist poking and waking up. That's one reason I keep searching for my father, no matter what I might discover. And I've learned that there's no exhilaration like facing death and surviving. I think that our investigations have taught Hugh and Mick the same lesson. Our deal with Sir Gerald isn't the only reason we'll continue pursuing Harry Warbrick's killer, and justice for the hangman isn't the only reason we won't stop. We tempt fate because it's become a habit that's hard to break. But that seems too perverse to admit to Barrett, and it's not going to convince him that my friends and I should continue working for Sir Gerald.

"The attack at Newgate suggests that we're getting closer to the truth about Harry Warbrick's murder," I say.

Barrett frowns, skeptical. "Reid questioned the governor, the matron, the surgeon, and the chaplain today. They kept mum about Amelia Carlisle's execution and said they didn't tell you and Hugh anything either. You got yourselves hurt for nothing."

I shake my head. "I'm sure there is a connection."

"As far as Reid and I could see, not one of the witnesses had any motive for murdering Harry Warbrick."

Although I hate keeping Barrett in the dark, I can't tell him about the affair between Dr. Davies and Mrs. Warbrick—or the Reverend Starling, his grievance against Harry Warbrick, and his visit to The Ropemaker's Daughter on the night of the murder—until the information is published in the *Daily World*. Guilt, regret, and conflicting loyalties aggravate my temper.

"You're ruling out my theory just because you're angry with me," I say.

"Yes, I am angry, but I'm not stupid enough to let my feelings dictate which theories to rule out or accept," Barrett retorts. "Give me some credit, why don't you?" Then the anger in his expression changes to sadness. "I don't want this case to come between us, Sarah. I don't want us to be on opposite sides of a contest." He looks into my eyes. "I love you. I want us to be together—in everything, all the time."

His sincerity disarms me. My heart brims with love for him, and I feel my gaze soften. Barrett cautiously reaches his hand toward my cheek. I lean into his touch. Then we're kissing passionately, our lust as hot as the first time. Deprived for so long, too aroused to care about privacy, we stumble to the parlor. Barrett sits on the sofa, and I straddle his lap. His hands caress my breasts, grasp my hips. We've never completed the carnal act—I'm too afraid of getting with child—but we've found other ways to satisfy our need. Our kisses stifle our moans as we move in quickening rhythm.

The sound of footsteps descending the stairs freezes us. Then I scramble off Barrett and push my skirts down. He tugs the jacket of his uniform over his lap. We sit side by side, breathing hard. My heart is still pounding when Fitzmorris walks into the room seconds later.

"Oh. I'm sorry. Mr. Barrett, I didn't know you were still here,"

Fitzmorris says. I can tell that he knows what we were doing. He and Hugh and Mick probably know that we do it whenever we're in the house and they're not. I look at the floor, embarrassed.

Barrett clears his throat, stands, and says, "I'd better go."

With our desire still unsatisfied, I don't want him to leave, but I say, "I'll see you out," and accompany him downstairs to the studio, where we steal one last, long, fervent kiss. Our lovemaking has defused our tempers and postponed our quarrel about Sir Gerald, his contest, and the murder investigation for the moment.

"I'll stop by for you at six o'clock tomorrow night," Barrett says.

"Tomorrow night?" I don't know what he's talking about.

"We're having dinner with my parents." Barrett pauses. "Aren't we?"

Trepidation is cold water dashed on my lust. I still don't want to go, but I've already upset Barrett enough, and I can't disappoint him and his parents again. "Yes," I say.

CHAPTER 13

The next morning is so dark with fog that when Hugh, Mick, and I emerge from the studio, the man loitering by the front door is a mere blurry shape crowned with a bowler hat. We don't realize that he's waiting for us until he says, "Hey, you!"

I'm surprised to recognize his tweed overcoat, puffy features, and curly strawberry-blond hair. "Charlie Sullivan?"

The reporter from the *Telegraph* draws back his fist and punches Hugh in the face. Hugh cries, "Ow!" and reels against the door. Mick and I exclaim in dismay.

"Good morning to you too, Mr. Sullivan." Indignant, Hugh rubs his cheek. "Why did you do that?"

"Don't play dumb. You stole my story about Harry Warbrick's murder and Amelia Carlisle's execution!" Fists clenched, panting like an angry bulldog, Sullivan lunges at Hugh.

Mick and I grab Sullivan. He turns on me and yells, "You thieving bitch!"

I let go and scramble away, lest he hit me too.

"If you don't want your stories stolen, you shouldn't blab them to strangers," Hugh says.

Sullivan curses as he strains toward Hugh, trying to break free of Mick's grasp.

"How did you know where we live?" I say.

"I have my sources. I'm not telling you another goddamn thing!" Sullivan slips on a patch of ice on the sidewalk.

Mick shoves him. He falls on his buttocks and slides into a puddle of dirty slush. Picking himself up, he says, "Bugger you and Sir Gerald's contest." He trudges off.

As my friends and I gape at one another, stunned by the turn of events, a newsboy's cry rises above the racket of wagon wheels and factory machinery. "Amelia Carlisle and her hangman! Read all about their shocking connection!" Proprietors and customers gather outside the shops, reading newspapers, talking in excited voices.

"I'll get one for us." Hugh disappears into the fog and returns with a copy of the *Daily World*.

The front-page headline reads, "WHO HANGED THE HANGMAN?" The illustration shows the inside of the execution shed at Newgate. Five men and a woman stand by the gallows, a hooded female figure dangles from a noose, and a sixth man poses with his hand on the lever of the trap door. The faces are indistinct, but one of the men wears a physician's white coat, another a priest's collar. They represent Harry Warbrick, Ernie Leach, Governor Piercy, Dr. Davies, Matron Fry, the Reverend Starling, and Sir Lionel Hargreaves, sheriff of London.

I read tidbits from the article under Malcolm Cross's byline: "What happened at the Baby Butcher's execution? Did it incite someone to murder her hangman? What dangerous secrets did Amelia take to her grave?"

"The story doesn't name the witnesses or accuse them of murder, but Sir Gerald is treading too close to libel for my comfort," Hugh says. "Although he must be happy that the story is a sensation. He'll want a new episode to keep the public on tenterhooks."

"We better hurry to Old Bailey," Mick says.

★ ★ ★

Old Bailey, the courthouse where criminals are tried and verdicts rendered, is conveniently situated adjacent to Newgate Prison. The ground floor of the massive building is surfaced with masonry blocks. A stone wall topped with a high, spiked iron fence surrounds the front courtyard. Fog shrouds the men and women queued up by the gate, where police constables ask them what their business is before letting them in or turning them away. Hugh, Mick, and I join the queue. Eavesdropping, we learn that some of the folks are solicitors or barristers coming to defend or prosecute clients; others are spectators.

"I've met Sir Lionel Hargreaves," Hugh says.

"Oh?" I'm not surprised. When Hugh was a popular man-about-high-society, he rubbed shoulders with London's most prominent citizens. "Where?"

"At the Metropolis Theater. He's the owner. He hosts parties after the performances. His guests get to mingle with the stars."

"The sheriff owns a theater?" Mick says. "How come?"

"He started out as a bit-part actor with a theater troupe that toured the provinces," Hugh says. "He became the star and married the producer's daughter. He had a flair for writing, directing, and producing plays too. When he brought the troupe to London, it was a smash hit. He made wealthy friends in high places, and they invested in his new project—the Metropolis. Now it's the biggest moneymaker in the West End. Melodramas, Shakespeare, musicals, and Christmas pantomimes—something for everybody. Sir Lionel retired from acting and hired big stars to perform. He was knighted for his achievements."

"How did he get to be sheriff?" I say. A journey from the stage to the government seems improbable.

"He took an interest in politics, and he won a seat on the London County Council. His influential friends got him elected sheriff. Now his people run the Metropolis while he assists the Lord Mayor and officiates at Old Bailey. Rumor says he'll be the next Lord Mayor."

"He won't be if we find out he killed the hangman," Mick says.

"That would wreck a political career," Hugh agrees.

When we reach the gate, we give the constables our names. Hugh says, "We're with the *Daily World*. Sir Gerald Mariner sent us to call on Sheriff Hargreaves."

Sir Gerald's name is like a magic password. Soon an official whisks us through the gate and the courtyard and beyond the semicircular brick wall that barricades the entrance to Old Bailey. Inside the cold, dank hall, we cross a stone floor worn down from centuries of footsteps. The smell of cesspools and unwashed human bodies seems soaked into the scarred, soot-stained walls. Voices resound from two big courtrooms already filled with people gathering for trials. A staircase leads us to the top floor, a different world that the public never sees. Gas sconces in the passages shine on gilt red wallpaper and polished parquet floors. White-wigged judges stride past us. Our escort shows us into a large office with paneled walls, a brown Turkish carpet, and glass-fronted bookcases. Heavy chairs upholstered with leather stand in front of the fire burning in a hearth beneath a marble mantelpiece. Windows overlook a courtyard where carriages and horses wait. Above the courtyard, rooftops spread to the great dome of St. Paul's. A closed door leads to an inner chamber. The air smells richly of expensive coffee and tobacco. Hugh takes it all in stride, accustomed to such elegance, while Mick glances around with bright-eyed curiosity. Old Bailey's inner sanctum may be safer than Newgate, but I feel uneasy, out of place.

Three gentlemen stand conversing by a large mahogany desk. Two are in their fifties, dressed in ordinary business attire, their voices a civilized murmur directed at the third man. He's a decade younger, tall and broad-shouldered. He wears a long scarlet robe trimmed with dark fur over a black velvet coat, waistcoat, and breeches, and black stockings and buckled black shoes. An ornate jeweled brooch hangs from gold chains across the ruffled white lace jabot at his throat. He breaks off the conversation, dismisses his two subordinates and our escort with a nod, and strides toward my friends and me.

"Miss Bain. Lord Hugh Staunton. Mr. Mick O'Reilly." His voice is a pleasant baritone, cultured but not haughty. "Sir Gerald let me know that you would be calling on me. It's good that you came before I'm due in court. I'm Lionel Hargreaves."

I've seen officials look puny and uncomfortable in their archaic garb, as if it's wearing them. Sheriff Hargreaves carries his with nonchalant dash. In figure he resembles portraits of the young Henry the Eighth, but his face is strikingly individual—less like the lion that his name and mane of fair hair suggest and more like a fox, with its narrow shape, pointed chin, and neatly trimmed reddish-brown mustache and beard. I recognize him as the man I saw posing in the photograph with Governor Piercy.

"Honored to meet you, Sir Lionel. Thank you for making time to see us." Hugh speaks with his usual, confident good manners, but I know he's wondering, as he's told me he always does when he meets someone from his old life, whether the sheriff knows about his scandal.

"It's my pleasure." If Sheriff Hargreaves knows, he's too polite to let on. When he shakes hands with me, he smiles. His lips are full and sensual, his eyes a pale, glinting blue circled by a ring of gray, like aquamarine gems set in steel.

I'm not immune to his charm, even though he could be a murderer.

Mick looks impressed in spite of himself, and when it's his turn to shake hands with the sheriff, he gulps before he says, "Sir."

"Let me take your coats." Sheriff Hargreaves hangs them on a brass coat tree, then says, "Would you like some coffee?" He gestures at a cart laden with an urn, cups, and a tray of assorted pastries.

"Sure," Mick says, never one to pass up free refreshments.

I move toward the cart, anticipating that I, the only woman present, will be asked to serve, but Sheriff Hargreaves says, "Please allow me."

Soon we're seated in the chairs by the fire, cups in hand, plates on our laps. The coffee is delicious, and so is my lemon-filled puff pastry. Mick smacks his lips, then looks embarrassed by his bad manners. Hugh says, "This is very kind of you, Sir Lionel." It's a far cry from the treatment we received at Newgate.

Sheriff Hargreaves takes his seat. "I'm always glad to cooperate with the press. However, you must understand that I can't talk about Amelia Carlisle's execution. My lips are sealed by the Official Secrets Act." He speaks with what seems like genuine regret.

I wonder if he deliberately buttered us up before letting us down. Still, I'm not surprised by his refusal to talk.

"We do understand." Hugh's tone implies that of course a high official who's a candidate for Lord Mayor can't break the law.

"I'm ready to be of service to you in any other way I can."

I think of the Thames when the sun shines on it, when I know that dark, unsavory things are submerged beneath the brilliance. I wonder what, if anything, the sheriff's charm hides. "Have you any idea who killed Harry Warbrick?" I ask.

Sheriff Hargreaves, unlike Governor Piercy, answers me instead of ignoring me. "I haven't, Miss Bain. But the crime seemed quite personal. That suggests a grudge on the part of someone close to Harry."

"Were you close to him?" I ask. Then I want to bite my tongue; the sheriff might perceive my question as an accusation, take umbrage, and throw us out.

"I hardly knew the man." Sheriff Hargreaves seems unoffended and sincere.

"Could it have been someone at Newgate?" Hugh asks. "What about Governor Piercy, Dr. Davies, Mrs. Fry, or the chaplain?"

Mick nods in approval at the question. I too hope that even if Sheriff Hargreaves won't incriminate himself, he'll dish dirt on the other suspects.

"I doubt that they knew Harry well enough to have a personal motive for murder. Executions are hardly occasions for getting acquainted."

If a conspiracy of silence unites the execution witnesses, they all have to keep mum to sustain it. I remember that there's another suspect besides those Hugh mentioned. "How about Ernie Leach?" I say.

"The assistant hangman? An odd little fellow. I've never heard any ill of him, but I know he and Harry worked together often."

Although Sheriff Hargreaves speaks in casual manner, I wonder if he's trying to direct suspicion onto Leach and away from himself. I also wonder if my experiences have made me so suspicious of everybody that I see guilt where there is none. Or perhaps Sheriff Hargreaves's good looks and charm have biased me in his favor and caused me to doubt myself.

"By the way, I heard about your trouble at Newgate. I apologize for Governor Piercy. He ought to take better measures to prevent accidents." Before we can say that the attacks were no accident, Sheriff Hargreaves says, "Maybe you need a police escort to keep you safe while you're investigating Harry's murder. I'll be happy to lend you a pair of constables."

Hugh and I glance at each other. We never expected this kind of assistance, but does Sheriff Hargreaves intend for the constables to protect us or to report our every move to him?

"We don't trust coppers," Mick says.

Amusement crinkles the sheriff's eyes. "Spoken like a man of experience. Has any particular one done you wrong?"

Mick shifts in his seat, nervous at being put on the spot, unsure whether Sheriff Hargreaves is making fun of him. "Inspector Reid gives 'em all a bad name."

"Edmund Reid can be difficult. He's heading up the Warbrick murder investigation, isn't he? Suppose I tell him to leave the three of you alone?"

"Can you really do that?" Mick sounds awed.

Sheriff Hargreaves smiles. "I really can."

Hugh frowns, and I can tell that he's thinking what I'm thinking: What does the man expect in return for the favor? Is it a bribe to get us to leave him out of our investigation and the *Daily World* to omit his name from stories about the Warbrick murder?

"That's very generous of you," Hugh begins, "but—"

The door to the inner chamber opens, and a young, drowsy female voice says, "Lionel? Who's there?" The voice is familiar and so unexpected that I start. I turn to see the young woman who stands at the threshold. Her pale blonde hair hangs in long, disheveled ringlets. She wears a blue wool dressing gown that's too big for her, the sleeves covering her hands and the sash loosely tied around her slim waist. The gap at the front shows the top of her bare bosom. Her lovely face is dazed with sleep; her cerulean-blue eyes blink at Hugh, Mick, and me. We jump to our feet, staring at her in shock.

"Catherine?" Mick blurts.

It's Catherine Price, the actress with whom Mick is desperately, unrequitedly in love.

"I thought I recognized your voices." She looks as disconcerted to see us as we are to see her. "What on earth are you doing here?"

It's obvious what she's doing here naked under a dressing gown that must belong to Sheriff Hargreaves. She's his mistress.

Hugh recovers his manners and speaks with forced gaiety. "Good morning, Catherine. How nice to see you. We're on an investigation."

"So you know one another?" Sheriff Hargreaves rises, studying the four of us with keen interest.

"Yes. We're old friends," I say.

I've known Catherine for four years, since the day she came to London from her country village to make her fortune on the stage. I was at Euston Station, taking photographs, when I saw her on the platform. I rescued her from a shady character who was about to carry her off to a house of ill repute. Hugh and Mick have known

Catherine for less than two years, but the events associated with the Ripper case have bound us all together with a strength that other relationships of longer duration can't match. Now my protective instinct toward Catherine revives.

She flushes with embarrassment and casts a guilty look at Mick. Although she doesn't share his feelings, she's not heartless, and he once saved her life. He glares at her, angry and betrayed. Hugh regards Mick with somber sympathy.

"What a coincidence." Sheriff Hargreaves smiles as though glad to discover a mutual acquaintance.

I sense that his actual thoughts are more complicated. Is he calculating how to exploit the situation for his benefit? Maybe I only think so because I've taken a sudden dislike to him on Catherine's account.

Sheriff Hargreaves gestures for Catherine to take the empty seat between his and mine. The gold wedding ring gleams on his finger. "Come and join us, my dear." He seems proud to flaunt his beautiful mistress who's more than twenty years younger than himself, unashamed of his adultery.

"I'll get dressed first." Catherine backs into the bedroom and shuts the door.

We all sit down. Sheriff Hargreaves is the only one of us who's at ease. His benign gaze studies us, lingering on Mick. Mick scowls. Hugh breaks the silence. "How did you and Catherine meet?"

"I saw her perform at the Oxford Music Hall," Sheriff Hargreaves says. "I'm always on the lookout for new talent for the Metropolis."

Maybe Catherine is sleeping with him in hopes of a star role. The possibility doesn't lessen my concern for her, and Sheriff Hargreaves's charm has worn thin for me. Suspicion makes me bold. "Are you taking advantage of Catherine?"

"Let's just say that my arrangement with her is mutually beneficial." His jovial manner has an edge that warns me that I don't want him for an enemy.

Hugh puts his hand on mine to calm me as I say, "What are your intentions toward her?" I must sound like a mother interrogating her daughter's suitor.

Sheriff Hargreaves chuckles. "I thought you were covering crime for the *Daily World*, not my personal affairs."

Catherine returns, having dressed so fast that her hair is pinned crooked atop her head, and when she sits beside me I see gaps on the back of her mint-green silk frock where she's missed the buttons. She smells of lavender-and-rose perfume. Pretending that nothing is amiss, she smiles at my friends and me. "So, what are you investigating?"

"The murder of Harry Warbrick, the hangman," Hugh says.

"Oh, I heard about that. Wasn't it gruesome?" Catherine giggles, her habit when she's nervous.

"Yeah," Mick says, suddenly belligerent. "And he's a suspect." He points at Sheriff Hargreaves.

Catherine's mouth drops. *"What?"* She says to Hugh and me, "You can't be serious." When we remain somberly silent, dismay clouds her expression. I myself am dismayed because Mick as good as accused Sheriff Hargreaves of murder.

The sheriff's manner is calm but a shade less jovial than a moment ago. "I thought you wanted to talk to me because I witnessed Amelia Carlisle's execution. It's a big leap from witness to murder suspect."

"Big leaps are our specialty," Hugh says with a cheeriness that doesn't relieve the tension in the atmosphere. "But don't take it personally. As far as we're concerned, everyone who knew Harry Warbrick is guilty until proven innocent."

Sheriff Hargreaves's smile doesn't reach his narrowed eyes.

"Lionel can't have done it!" Catherine says.

"What makes you so sure?" Mick demands.

"I know him."

"Oh?" Jealousy blazes in Mick's blue eyes. "For how long?"

"Since October."

Even though he knows she regularly sees other men, Mick looks stricken because this affair has been going on behind his back all that time. His thoughts are heart-wrenchingly transparent: Sheriff Hargreaves is rich, knighted, and powerful—everything that Mick himself is not. "Three months, eh?" Mick takes refuge in contempt. "An' you think you know everything about the bloke."

"Lionel isn't a killer." Flustered, Catherine glances at Hugh and me, uncomfortable about siding against us.

"Thank you for your faith in me, Catherine." Sheriff Hargreaves gives her a warm smile, then addresses the rest of us. "I don't have a motive for the murder."

"That we know of yet," Mick says.

I recall that of the other execution witnesses, only Dr. Davies, Ernie Leach, and the Reverend Starling have any apparent motive—which puts Sheriff Hargreaves in the same boat as Governor Piercy and Mrs. Fry.

"So where were you when Harry Warbrick was murdered?" Mick says.

"He was with me." Catherine stares at us with nervous defiance. Sheriff Hargreaves nods.

"All night?" Mick asks.

"Yes," Catherine says.

"Where?"

"Here." She glances toward the closed door.

"What were you doing?" Mick says.

Catherine sputters, angry and embarrassed.

"Couldn't he have left after he were finished, while you was sleepin'?"

Indignation sparks in Catherine's eyes. "How dare you!"

Sheriff Hargreaves says, "Catherine and I were here together the whole night. She's my alibi. That's all you need to know."

"You did it!" Mick lunges out of his chair, at the sheriff.

My heart seizes. "Mick, don't!"

"Whoa!" Hugh snatches at Mick and misses.

Catherine jumps up. She stands in front of Sheriff Hargreaves, her arms spread to shield him from Mick. "What's the matter with you? Have you lost your mind?"

Sheriff Hargreaves rises, puts his arm around Catherine, and draws her to him. "Why don't we all settle down?"

"Take your hands off her!" Mick grabs Sheriff Hargreaves by the fur-trimmed lapels of his cloak.

I rush to Mick and pry his hands loose. Hugh propels Mick out of the room, calling to Sheriff Hargreaves, "We'll be on our way. Thank you for the coffee."

As I follow Hugh and Mick, I snatch our coats from the stand and look over my shoulder. Catherine clings to Sheriff Hargreaves. The look she gives me is at once smug and defensive. He wears an enigmatic smile. If forced to hazard a guess as to what's on his mind, I would say he's not sorry about the drama that just occurred.

CHAPTER 14

Mick runs out of the building ahead of Hugh and me. We don our coats and spot him leaning against the wall that surrounds Old Bailey, almost invisible in the dense fog, a picture of utter dejection. I hand him his coat. He jams his arms into the sleeves and mumbles, "Sorry."

Hugh and I don't have the heart to scold him. "It's all right," I say.

"No it ain't." Mick says in a tone filled with self-reproach, "If not for me, you mighta got somethin' out of the sheriff."

"He wouldn't have told us anything that would incriminate him," Hugh says. "He's too smart."

"Yeah. Smarter than me." The doleful look on his face says that Mick is aware of all the other ways in which the sheriff is superior to himself. "I really cocked it up."

As we walk toward the train station, Hugh says, "Catherine has made a mistake by hitching her wagon to Sir Lionel. I know he picks up actresses, uses them, and then throws them away as if they're dirty handkerchiefs. She must have seen him do it. If she thinks she'll be any different than the others, she's a fool."

"She's not a fool! She's just innocent." Mick always leaps to Catherine's defense.

I could tell him that Catherine is far from innocent and doesn't deserve his loyalty, but he stubbornly clings to his belief that she's perfect and brooks no criticism of her. And he remembers, as we all do, that she risked her life to help us catch Jack the Ripper.

"I didn't mean to insult Catherine," Hugh says gently. "I just wish she weren't involved with Sir Lionel. Aside from the fact that he's a murder suspect, he's married. I once met his wife at a ball. Lady Anne is an attractive, sweet person, if a little too earnest. She devotes herself to noble causes, and she's chairwoman of the Society for the Prevention of Cruelty to Children. She bent my ear for half an hour, talking about her efforts to rescue neglected and mistreated children. She's a big political asset for Sir Lionel, knows the wives, sisters, and mothers of all the most important men. Word around town says he'll never leave her. Maybe I should have a word with Catherine."

"Yeah," Mick says. "Tell her he done it. He killed the hangman."

"But we don't know that," I say.

"*I* know."

"Then you must be a mind reader," Hugh says. "I didn't see any evidence."

"I don't need no evidence." Mick is adamant. "I just know he's guilty as sin."

I'm sad to see the past repeating itself. I don't want to make Mick feel worse, but I have to say, "You thought you knew who kidnapped Robin Mariner."

"So I was wrong then. I got a gut feeling I'm right this time."

"I'm all for gut feelings," Hugh says. "I place great reliance on them myself. But they're not enough to convict Sir Lionel."

"We need proof," I say.

"Then we'll get proof." Mick spots an empty beer bottle in a heap of trash and kicks it along as he walks.

I know what he's thinking: if Sheriff Hargreaves is convicted, he'll be marched off to the gallows and out of Catherine's life. "He has an alibi."

Mick scowls at my unspoken reminder that Catherine was the one to provide the alibi.

"I'd take it with a grain of salt," Hugh says. "Catherine is trying to protect him. She may be lying because she believes he's not a killer even if she knows she faked his alibi."

Now Mick looks torn between hoping the alibi is false and not wanting to believe Catherine is a liar. I say, "One of the other witnesses to Amelia Carlisle's execution could be the killer. And there may be other suspects we haven't run across yet. It's too soon to make up our minds."

"My mind's made up." Mick gives the beer bottle a final violent kick. It flies through the fog and shatters somewhere out of sight. "I'm gonna get the bastard." He runs off.

"Let's give him time to sort himself out," Hugh says. "He'll come around."

"We have to find out whether Sheriff Hargreaves is guilty." I feel more pressure than ever to solve the murder. The idea of Catherine at the mercy of a man who hanged and decapitated Harry Warbrick sends a stab of dread through me.

"If he is, we'd better prove it and get him behind bars fast," Hugh says. "Because if Catherine knows his alibi is fake, her life is in danger."

★　★　★

Hugh and I spend the rest of the morning and the afternoon in the neighborhood around The Ropemaker's Daughter, looking for witnesses who can place any of the suspects there at the time of the murder. We dodge police who are also investigating the crime. Once I glimpse Mick on the street, talking to passersby. He's broken his promise to go to school in his eagerness to pin the crime on Sheriff Hargreaves. At five o'clock, Hugh keeps at the search while I go to the *Daily World* to tell Sir Gerald the latest.

I'm hurrying up Fleet Street when a woman calls, "Miss Bain?"

Her voice barely audible above the racket of carriages, printing presses, and crowds, she hovers by the *Daily World* building. In the thick fog and the dim light of the streetlamps, it takes me a moment to recognize the matron of Newgate Prison. She wears a plain black coat instead of the blue plaid, and a veiled black bonnet hides her hair.

"Good evening, Mrs. Fry." I'm surprised that she's apparently been waiting for me.

She hunches her shoulders and puts a finger to her lips, bereft of the calm indifference she displayed at Newgate. She beckons, and when I move close, whispers, "I gotta talk to you."

"About what?"

Mrs. Fry glances around. "Not here."

Curious to know what she has to say, I lead her a few blocks down the street to Peele's Coffee House, a popular haunt of reporters, but not crowded at the moment. When we're seated at a back table, with steaming cups of coffee at hand, Mrs. Fry pulls the veil on her hat lower over her face and her coat collar up to her double chin. She speaks in a low, furtive tone.

"It's about Amelia Carlisle's hanging."

Excitement and suspicion mingle in me. "You refused to talk about it yesterday. Why are you willing now?"

"Because something wrong happened at it." Her deep Cockney voice trembles. "Last night I went to church and prayed to the Blessed Virgin, and she said I had to tell."

Thank heaven for divine intervention. "What happened?"

Mrs. Fry fidgets with her cup and sips the scalding liquid, as if for courage. I wait in suspense, unable to imagine what I'm about to hear.

"There weren't no hanging," Mrs. Fry says.

Startled and confused, I laugh. "How could there not have been a hanging? Amelia was sentenced to death."

"She got away with it." Rancor sours Mrs. Fry's voice.

"But the hanging was announced in the newspapers. Everybody thinks she's dead."

"Everybody but us who was there that day." Now Mrs. Fry looks wise and smug. "We knows better."

I'm astounded by the idea that there is indeed a conspiracy of silence, and this is what the witnesses to Amelia's execution are hiding. "So you're telling me that Amelia isn't dead?"

"Yeah. I am."

Even more suspicious now, I say, "Why should I believe you?"

Mrs. Fry looks me straight in the eye. "Because it's true. Because I could get in a heap o' trouble for sayin' it, and I'm sayin' it anyway."

Although unconvinced, I'm willing to give her the benefit of the doubt for the moment. "Then what happened the day of Amelia's supposed hanging?"

Mrs. Fry gathers her breath, drinks more coffee, then leans across the table. I lean toward her so that I can hear her whisper, "I fetched Amelia from her cell. She were acting mighty odd—smiling as if she hadn't a care in the world. I never seen a condemned prisoner act like that. I asked her why she seemed so happy. She just laughed. I thought she'd gone out of her mind. When we got to the execution shed, the others were waiting there—Harry Warbrick and Ernie Leach, Governor Piercy, Dr. Davies, Reverend Starling, and Sheriff Hargreaves. Harry was holding the noose. He looked at his watch. He always timed his hangings."

She pauses. I envision the solemn men, the incongruously cheerful Amelia.

"Then Governor Piercy said, 'There's not going to be an execution.'"

I picture the surprise on all the faces except Amelia's. Mrs. Fry says, "Well, that explained why she was so happy. She knew she wasn't gonna die."

If the story is true, did anyone besides Governor Piercy and Amelia know before he spoke? Were any of the others really not surprised?

"You coulda knocked me over with a feather," Mrs. Fry says. "She killed those babies, she was caught red-handed, and she was getting off. Reverend Starling said, 'Has she been reprieved?' Governor Piercy just repeated, 'There's not going to be an execution.'

Then Harry Warbrick said, 'But I'm supposed to hang her. I was chosen over all the other hangmen in England.' He seemed madder about losing the job than about her getting off."

I remember the rope that he'd supposedly used to hang Amelia, the prize souvenir that had been stolen from his pub the night of his murder.

"Governor Piercy didn't look no happier than Harry, but he said, 'The hanging is canceled.' Harry said, 'Will I not be paid?'" Mrs. Fry chuckles. "That was Harry—always lookin' out for himself. Governor Piercy said, 'You and Mr. Leach will be paid.' Ernie just stood there blinking, like usual."

"How did the others react?" I say.

"Someone said, 'This is an outrage!' I don't remember who. And I didn't see the looks on anybody else's faces. I was too busy watching Amelia. *She* looked like the cat that drank the cream." Mrs. Fry says, "Governor Piercy said we weren't to tell anybody, because it was an official secret. If we told, we would lose our jobs and go to prison."

Incredulity makes me skeptical. "But why would he do such a thing? Why spare Amelia's life?"

Mrs. Fry shakes her head, bewildered. "I don't think he wanted to. An order must've come from higher up."

Governor Piercy might have been coerced, but who would have wanted to rescue the infamous Baby Butcher, and why? I ask another crucial question: "If Amelia is alive, where is she?"

Mrs. Fry looks out the window, as if she expects to see Amelia walk by. "I don't know. Governor Piercy sent me back to work. The others stayed."

If her story is true, there's a conspiracy within a conspiracy. All of the witnesses knew that the hanging didn't happen, but only the men were privy to what became of Amelia. Mrs. Fry says, "They musta smuggled her out of Newgate. After I finished my shift, I looked all over the place for her, and she were nowhere to be found."

And Harry Warbrick had been murdered less than two months later.

"I think they killed Harry because they were afraid he would talk," Mrs. Fry says. "He had a big mouth, Harry did."

My friends and I had believed that one of the suspects was the killer; now they could all be partners in the crime. But I challenge Mrs. Fry. "Your story removes you from the list of suspects who supposedly know what became of Amelia. Did you make it up to protect yourself so that I won't think you killed Harry to keep it secret?"

"I didn't make it up!" Mrs. Fry answers so vehemently that I lean back from her hot, coffee-smelling breath. "And I didn't kill Harry. I told you because I'm scared that I'll be next."

We had considered the possibility that the other witnesses' lives were in danger, but I'm not ready to believe Mrs. Fry. "Why did you come to me about this?"

"Because you seem like a good lady. Because I don't know who else to trust."

My skepticism persists even though she seems sincere. "You only met me yesterday. Why not the police?"

"They might be in on it, and if I tell, then they'll know I'm a blabbermouth, and I'm dead for sure."

If there is indeed a conspiracy, it could reach far outside the circle of witnesses at the execution. "What do you expect me to do with your information?"

"You work for Sir Gerald Mariner. He's a big, important man. Couldn't he do something?"

"Perhaps. Come with me and tell him your story."

"You mean, now? To his face?" Mrs. Fry shrinks down in her seat.

"Yes." And let Sir Gerald, with his sharp instincts about people, be the judge of whether she's telling the truth.

"Will he put it in the newspaper?" Mrs. Fry doesn't seem to have considered the fact that Sir Gerald is in the newspaper business to make money, and hers is the kind of story that would sell many, many copies.

"Probably," I say.

"I can't have my name in the paper. I'll get in trouble."

"If your story about Amelia is true and you really are in danger, the best way to protect yourself is to get the secret out in the open. Then it won't do the killer any good to kill again."

Mrs. Fry kneads her hands. "I—I don't know." If her story is a lie, perhaps that's the real reason she doesn't want to tell it to Sir Gerald—she's afraid that she can't pull the wool over his eyes, afraid of what he'll do to her when he finds out he's been deceived.

"I thought you came to me because it was wrong that Amelia Carlisle got away with murdering babies and you wanted to set things right," I say. "Have you changed your mind?"

"This is too much." Mrs. Fry seems upset because things are moving too fast, beyond her control. "Just forget I said anything." She gets up to leave.

Indignant, I grab her arm. "You tell me Amelia Carlisle is alive, and you expect me to keep quiet?"

"Please! If you've a heart, you won't tell." Mrs. Fry wrenches free of my grip and runs out of the coffeehouse.

★   ★   ★

There's a moment when I debate with myself whether to tell Sir Gerald about the tip, tell Barrett instead, or tell neither. The tip seems like a hot potato that could burn the hands into which it drops. In the end, I decide I must tell Sir Gerald because he's paying me for this investigation.

At the *Daily World*, after I relate Mrs. Fry's story to Sir Gerald, Malcolm Cross, and Mr. Palmer, they behold me with dumbfounded stares. The rumble of the printing presses fills the silence in the conference room. Cross and Mr. Palmer look to Sir Gerald, to see how he reacts, before they say anything.

Sir Gerald chuckles. "Mrs. Fry's having a joke on you, Miss Bain."

Cross and Palmer burst out laughing—they're relieved because that's what they thought, and Sir Gerald agrees.

"The very idea that Amelia Cross walked away from her own hanging!" Palmer wipes his eyes.

"And that Sheriff Hargreaves, Governor Piercy, and the others were in on it." Cross shoots a disdainful gaze at me. "She must have thought you were an idiot to fall for such a load of crap."

"I didn't say I believed her." I should have known Cross would seize the opportunity to ridicule me. "But I don't think it was a joke."

Sir Gerald frowns, displeased because I've contradicted his judgment. "Why not? How could it be anything else?"

"Mrs. Fry was afraid," I say.

Cross sneers. "Afraid her trick wouldn't work, you mean."

"That wasn't it." I'm certain.

"She wouldn't have tried it on a man." Cross's tone implies that men are too sharp to be duped, himself in particular.

Perhaps Mrs. Fry did approach me because I'm a woman and she thought I would be more sympathetic than sharp. After all, she could have brought her story to Hugh. I hasten to defend the opinion that's taken root in my mind. "Even if she lied when she said Amelia Carlisle wasn't hanged, I think there's something to her story."

Sir Gerald listens silently, chin in hand, his eyes narrowed in speculation. Mr. Palmer says, "What could it be?"

"A conspiracy between the witnesses," I say.

Cross regards me with unabated scorn. "A conspiracy for what purpose?"

I'm forced to admit, "I don't know." I still think the witnesses are hiding a secret, and one of them killed Harry Warbrick to prevent him from blabbing it. But if the secret isn't Amelia's escape from justice, then I can't imagine what it is.

"*I* think the conspiracy is all in Miss Bain's head," Cross announces.

I compress my lips to prevent myself from saying that his head is so stuffed with pride, there's no room for new ideas. It would do me no good to lose my temper.

"Thanks for the levity, Miss Bain," Mr. Palmer says. "Now, have you any news we can publish?"

Stung by the dismissal, I say, "Lord Hugh, Mick, and I met with Sheriff Hargreaves. He refused to talk about the hanging, and he has an alibi for the night of Harry Warbrick's murder." I leave out the part about Catherine, keeping yet another secret from Sir Gerald.

Sir Gerald nods as if he's checking Hargreaves off his mental list of items to take into account. "Who says we're not publishing Mrs. Fry's story?"

Cross and Palmer gape at him in disbelief. I stifle a laugh. I'm used to surprises from Sir Gerald and not as unprepared for this one as they are.

"But it's just hearsay," Cross says.

"And entirely unsubstantiated," Mr. Palmer says.

Sir Gerald's eyes glint with amusement at their dismay. "So?"

Everybody knows that newspapers are full of rumors and speculations, which are often more interesting than facts, but I'm as dismayed as Cross and Mr. Palmer.

"This is big news whether it's true or not," Sir Gerald says.

"Wouldn't it be a crime to set a murderess free after the court sentenced her to death?" I say. "Mrs. Fry's story says Governor Piercy and the other witnesses did exactly that and covered it up. That's a serious accusation."

"The *Daily World* could become party to a libel suit," Cross says.

"Not only the *Daily World* but us as individuals," Mr. Palmer says.

I imagine Hugh, Mick, and myself on trial in court, and our

worldly goods seized. For once I'm in agreement with Cross and Mr. Palmer. Now the hot potato seems like a bomb with a burning fuse. "We mustn't run the story."

"Of course we won't run it verbatim." Impatient, Sir Gerald says to Cross and Palmer, "Word it so that it doesn't sound like an accusation. Say it came from an anonymous source."

They exchange a glance and shrug in defeat. We all realize that Sir Gerald has made up his mind, but my intuition warns me that running the story is a mistake whose consequences none of us can predict. "At least let me investigate Mrs. Fry's story," I say.

"Of course," Sir Gerald says, "but the story runs tomorrow morning."

The deadline for the morning edition is midnight. "But I have to ask Sheriff Hargreaves, Dr. Davies, Ernie Leach, and the Reverend Starling about Mrs. Fry's story and hear what they have to say." Cross and Mr. Palmer nod, backing me up for once.

"Then you'd better get to work." Sir Gerald's impatience is like a spear prodding me. "Light a fire under those people. Make one of them tell you what the hell really happened at that execution and who the hell killed Harry Warbrick."

Here's more evidence that the kidnapping of his son has permanently affected Sir Gerald. A man obsessed with vengeance in whatever form attainable, willing to risk the reputation of the *Daily World*, has replaced the shrewd businessman of yesteryear. Winning the contest with the police is beside the point.

I can read those thoughts on Cross's and Palmer's faces, but none of us dares to voice it.

Now I have less than six hours to corroborate or debunk Mrs. Fry's claims.

Then I remember: I'm having dinner with Barrett's parents tonight. And I'm already late.

CHAPTER 15

Irush home to find Barrett loitering in the cold fog outside the studio. He's wearing his good wool overcoat, trousers, and felt derby instead of his uniform, stamping his feet to keep warm. "You're late." His expression mixes annoyance and relief.

"I know. I'm sorry," I say, breathless because I ran all the way from the station.

"I thought you were going to cancel again."

"Why didn't you wait inside the house?"

"I rang the bell. Nobody answered."

Fitzmorris must have gone out, and Hugh and Mick must be still searching for witnesses near The Ropemaker's Daughter. I haven't time to find them, tell them what's happened, and ask them to investigate Mrs. Fry's story. "Just a minute."

I unlock the door, run inside, scribble a note to them, and prop it on the stairway. When I run back to Barrett, he says, "What's up?"

"I had to remind them where I'm going." I feel guilty because I just lied to him, but if I told him Mrs. Fry's story about Amelia Carlisle, he would want to know where I heard it. My reluctance to expose a frightened woman to the police dovetails with my duty to keep Sir Gerald's confidence and my habit of secrecy.

"We'd better hurry," I say.

★ ★ ★

Barrett's family lives in Bethnal Green, not far from Whitechapel. I haven't been to the area recently, but my mother lived there when I was twelve and at boarding school. She had a tiny flat in one of the new tenements built for the poor, near the Club Row Market, where live animals are still sold on Sundays. Walking through the crowd during holidays, looking at the dogs, cats, birds, snakes, and monkeys in cages stacked along the street, is among my few good memories from the bleak time after my father disappeared. On this cold winter evening, Barrett takes me to Cambridge Heath, a more affluent area near the shops along Columbia Road. His parents' home is in a clean, well-maintained terrace of narrow, two-story brick houses. It's similar to the house where I grew up in Clerkenwell, and I feel a pang of nostalgia. For the first time, I think that marriage with Barrett could be a sort of coming home to a situation where I'm loved and secure, after years of lonely, precarious wandering. I realize how lucky I am to have him, but I'm still deathly nervous, fearful of making a bad impression tonight.

Barrett's parents, gray-haired and in their sixties, greet us at the door. "Hello, Mum and Dad," Barrett says, all smiles. "Here's Sarah."

"It's a pleasure," his father says. He leans on a cane but seems in good health; he has Barrett's average height and tough handsomeness.

"Miss Bain, at last!" His mother is small, slender, and pretty, with Barrett's keen gray eyes. She and her husband seem dressed in their Sunday best—she in a mauve-and-indigo-striped frock, her hair curled in a fringe across her forehead; he in a brown jacket with matching trousers, tie, and starched white shirt. They obviously view this dinner as an important occasion, but although their welcome is sincere, they can't hide their unflattering surprise. I can tell that my looks haven't met with their approval.

"Thank you so much for having me." As we shake hands, I glance at Barrett. He doesn't seem to notice anything wrong.

"Let me take your coat. Come in and sit down," Mrs. Barrett says.

The parlor is modest but comfortable, with a braided rug, striped wallpaper, and framed prints of landscape paintings. A fire crackles in the hearth, and the savory smell of food issues from the kitchen. Barrett and I sit on the flowered divan, his parents opposite us in matching armchairs. A vase on the table holds fresh pink hothouse roses.

"Your home is lovely," I say, touched because his family went to some trouble for my visit.

His mother smiles, pleased. "Oh, it's not much, but we're happy here." Barrett smiles too, glad that we're getting along.

"Would you like some sherry?" his father asks.

"Yes, thank you." I need a drink to help me get through this.

Mr. Barrett pours full glasses. "A toast to our honored guest." We drink. The sherry is good quality, smooth and not too sweet. I like his parents, and I want them to like me.

"Thomas tells me you're a photographer," Mrs. Barrett says.

"Yes. I work for the *Daily World*."

"How interesting! What sort of pictures do you take?"

Barrett evidently hasn't told his parents that I photograph crime scenes. He shoots me a glance that warns me not to say so.

"I photograph places, mostly," I say.

"We read the *Daily World*," Mrs. Barrett says. "Which pictures were yours?"

My image of the Harry Warbrick murder scene flashes through my mind. "Well, uh, you probably wouldn't have seen mine. I'm new at the paper, and they don't get published very often." I used to be sorry that my name wasn't printed alongside my work, but now I'm glad.

"Oh. I see." Mrs. Barrett seems puzzled by my evasiveness. I begin to feel irate toward Barrett, who looks relieved that I've managed to sidestep troublesome issues.

"How did you two meet?" his father says. "The lad's been a bit close-mouthed on the subject."

Barrett grimaces; this subject is another danger zone. He once told me that his father is a retired police officer whose beat was the Nichol—the slum in east Bethnal Green, one of London's worst. Before he went lame, Mr. Barrett spent his career rousting hardened criminals. The story of how his son and I met—when we crossed paths during the Ripper investigation—wouldn't delight him.

"Sarah lives in Whitechapel," Barrett says. "That's on my beat, you know."

Why didn't he prepare for these questions? I suspect it's because he's not used to keeping secrets from his family and inventing cover-up stories.

"Whitechapel!" His mother speaks in the tone of horror and fascination that many people use when they mention Jack the Ripper's stalking ground. "Those horrible murders."

"Wish I were still on the force," Mr. Barrett says. "I'd help you boys catch the Ripper."

Barrett and I avoid looking at each other, knowing we can never tell his family that the Ripper is gone.

"Thomas said you're an orphan, Miss Bain," his mother says. At least he's told his parents that much, although I would wager he's kept them in the dark about my father. "Do you live on your own?"

Barrett's eyes pop in alarm. We can't tell his parents that my housemates are three men, including a famous homosexual and a former street urchin. "I live with friends," I say.

"Uh, why don't we go in to dinner," Barrett says.

In the dining room, at a table set with a lace-trimmed cloth, flowered china, and polished silverware, we eat split pea soup flavored with onion and bacon. The conversation turns to the big news of the week—the hangman's murder.

"I heard about the contest between the police and the *Daily World*. So now reporters are in the crime-solving business?" Indignation raises Mr. Barrett's voice.

"Yes," Barrett says with a pointed glance at me.

The tension between us constricts my throat. I put down my spoon.

"Well, you go beat them at their game." Mr. Barrett is oblivious to the fact that his son and I are on opposite sides of the contest. "Show them who the real detectives are. Make them eat crow on the front page of their own paper."

"We will," Barrett says.

"That's my boy. Now tell me what's going on with the case."

Father and son discuss the Amelia Carlisle angle. Mr. Barrett says, "I don't believe there's a connection between her hanging and Warbrick's murder. I think the reporters made it up, to send you on a wild goose chase so they can get the jump on you."

"Maybe so." Barrett avoids my gaze.

"It's always shop talk with those two," Mrs. Barrett says to me, exasperated but proud. "I stay out of it. Best leave crime solving to the men, don't you think?"

"Yes." I squirm with guilt.

"Any new developments today?" Mr. Barrett asks his son.

"Not that I'm allowed to talk about."

"Come on, you can tell your old dad," Mr. Barrett says. "Once a policeman, always a policeman, that's me."

If the police have discovered anything new, Barrett won't talk about it in front of me, the competition. "You know Inspector Reid will have my head," he says in a falsely jovial tone.

Mr. Barrett nods but can't hide his disappointment. Now I feel bad because I've driven a wedge between father and son.

"Any luck with the promotion?" Mr. Barrett says.

"It's still in the works."

"If only I'd stayed on the force long enough to get promoted myself, I might've had friends in high places who could give you a boost," Mr. Barrett says with regret. "You're our hope of making a name for ourselves in the police service. 'Chief Inspector Barrett.'" He smiles. "That would do us proud."

Barrett is silent and concentrates on eating. My spirits sink as I realize that his wish for promotion is about more than money or prestige; it's about family honor, and his relationship with me could ruin his parents' cherished dream.

Conversation lapses, and Mrs. Barrett tries to revive it as she serves a pie made of beef, gravy, onions, carrots, and turnips, topped with mashed potatoes. "Have you any family, Miss Bain?" she asks.

The evening is riddled with danger zones. "No," I say, unable to tell her about Sally when I've yet to tell Barrett. And if his parents knew about my family's shameful history, they would think me even less an appropriate bride for their son than they already do.

We chat about the weather and other trivia. After the baked custard dessert, I'm glad when nature calls and I can excuse myself. When I return, I hear Barrett and his parents talking in the parlor. I stop outside the door.

"Are you sure?" His father sounds doubtful.

"Yes, I am." Barrett's tone is defensive, adamant.

My spirits plunge. I gather he's just told his parents that he wants to marry me, and they aren't thrilled.

"She's not as pretty as the other girls you've gone with," his mother says.

"I think she's beautiful."

Barrett says it as if he means it, but I'm upset to hear his mother disparage my looks.

"She seems kind of stand-offish," his father says, "like she thinks she's better than us."

"She's just shy," Barrett says. My spark of anger at him flares. He must know that my behavior tonight is at least partly his fault. "When you get to know her, you'll like her."

"Did she say yes?" his father asks.

"Not yet."

"That's good. You can change your mind."

"I'm not going to change my mind!" Barrett sounds less certain than defiant. Our strained relations have taken their toll on him. "I'm going to marry Sarah—if she'll have me."

His mother sniffs. "She would be lucky to have you. If she doesn't know that, then she doesn't deserve to be your wife."

"Let's not talk about it anymore." Anger tightens Barrett's voice.

I feel hurt and rejected, my hopes for our future sinking. Barrett loves me, but he also loves his parents. Can he stand firm against their disapproval? I wish I could sneak out the back door and run away. Instead, I paste an artificial smile on my face and walk into the parlor.

★　★　★

An hour later, Barrett and I are riding toward Whitechapel on top of an omnibus. Icy wind swirls the fog around our open-air seats. My head aches from the strained atmosphere at his parents' house and my effort to pretend everything was fine. Barrett, slumped beside me, massages his temples. I take a deep breath, preparing to break the silence that's as thick as the fog. I should tell him about Mrs. Fry's tip. It will be in the morning paper, and surely Sir Gerald won't mind if Barrett hears of it a few hours early. But that's not what comes out of my mouth.

"If we were to break up, that would kill two birds with one stone."

Barrett turns to me, confused. "What are you talking about?"

"You could mend fences with Inspector Reid, get promoted, and please your parents." My voice cracks. "Or does that count as three birds?"

"Sarah. I'm not going to throw you over just to make Reid happy and get ahead." Barrett's voice is irate, emphatic. "And what have my parents got to do with it, anyhow?"

"They didn't like me."

"They did like you," Barrett says, as if trying to convince both of us. "It just takes them time to warm up to new people."

"They think I'm too plain and stand-offish and I don't deserve to be your wife." The humiliation stings.

"You heard what they said? Oh, God, I'm sorry." Then his eyebrows draw together into a suspicious frown. "Were you spying on us?"

"No!" I'm offended that he should accuse me, the injured party.

Barrett shakes his head in disbelief. "Of all the sneaky things!"

Everything that's happened today is suddenly too much. My temper snaps. "That's the pot calling the kettle black. Don't you think it was sneaky not to tell your family anything about me and then drop me on them without warning me to expect questions?"

Barrett has the grace to look ashamed. "I'm sorry. But I knew they wouldn't—"

A fireball of anger with hurt at the core grows in my chest as I complete his sentence. "You knew they wouldn't approve of my looks, the work I do, or how I live."

"No." His expression says yes.

"And you figured I could make up lies about myself that they would like better than the truth."

"That's not it. I thought you would—well, just bend the truth a little."

"What's the difference between that and lying? You want me to be honest with you but to keep secrets from your parents." I'm shamefully glad that the shoe is on the other foot. His behavior doesn't justify my past treatment of him, but I can't help feeling that it should. "You're just as dishonest as you think I am."

Barrett looks contrite. "Sarah, I said I'm sorry. Let's not quarrel."

"That's what people say when they're losing an argument. Well, I'm not finished." I'm in serious danger of saying something I'll regret, but my temper overpowers me, and my hurt fuels its flame. "You knew that if you introduced me to your parents, I would make a bad impression. You brought me anyway."

Now his eyes flare with a temper as hot as mine. "Well, if you insist on arguing, you could have tried to make a better impression. But you didn't try. You were stiff and cold, and you didn't even pretend to like them. So if they don't like you, it's your own fault."

His words sting like a slap across the face. They're true, never mind that the circumstances weren't conducive to my being my most likeable self. A lump rises in my throat. Fear, pain, and anger override my inhibitions. "I suppose you're happy that I made a bad impression. Isn't that what you wanted?"

"Of course not. What the devil are you talking about?"

"It's not only your parents who think I'm not good enough. So do you."

"That's nonsense!"

Is Barrett telling the truth or trying to spare my feelings? "If your parents don't like me, it gives you an excuse."

"Excuse for what?"

"To end it between us." As soon as the words are out of my mouth, I realize that they hint at the reason I've been so reluctant to meet his family and confront my deepest fear—that Barrett will leave me. And when he does, it won't be due to my lack of honesty; it will be because I'm not good enough in all the ways that a man wants a woman to be good.

My mother was right when she said that no one would ever want to marry me.

The omnibus stops on Whitechapel Road. I have to get away from Barrett before I start crying. As I falter down the staircase, he calls, "Sarah! Wait!"

I run to the studio, and he catches up with me before I can unlock the door. Lights shine in the upper windows; Hugh, Mick, and Fitzmorris must be home. Barrett seizes my shoulders. "I don't want to end it."

My ears are ringing with my desperation to escape. I can't tell whether he's being sincere or not. I twist to avoid his gaze.

"Sarah, look at me."

In some deep, buried part of me, I understand that I'm trying to make Barrett leave me now, to self-fulfill the prophecy—better than waiting in dread for the inevitable to happen. My traitorous body overcomes my will. I turn and see that his expression is drained of hostility, filled with urgent pleading. "Sarah. I love you."

He kisses me so hard that his lips crush mine. I resist; I don't want him to let me down easily by making love to me before he tells me it's over.

Barrett pulls back but holds my shoulders tight. He looks straight into my eyes and says in a quiet, intense voice, "You're good enough for me. You're more than good enough. You're better than I deserve."

I want to believe him. He kisses me, and this time I melt against him, soothed by the warmth of our desire. When we pause to catch our breath, Barrett whispers, "Don't worry about my mother and father. Things will work out."

I smile, but I doubt that I can counteract his parents' bad first impression of me. Even if I exert myself to be friendly, I can't change my looks, and my background, work, and manner of living are all black marks that they'll find out about sooner or later.

It's only when we've parted, when I'm telling Hugh and Mick about Mrs. Fry, that I realize I forgot to tell Barrett.

CHAPTER 16

The next morning, Hugh and Mick and I run outside and buy a copy of the *Daily World*. We eagerly read the front-page story while standing in the cold, foggy street. The headline reads, "Did the Baby Butcher Get Away with Murder?" Below Malcolm Cross's byline, the illustration shows a dark, sinister scene of Amelia sneaking out of Newgate Prison at night. "Only seven people know the truth!" declares the line above a row of portrait sketches. They're not captioned, and the faces are blank, but one is a woman. One of the men sports a doctor's white coat, another a minister's collar. The sheriff's jeweled brooch adorns the last. The line below the sketches reads, "One was Harry Warbrick, the hangman, murdered the seventh of January."

"Bloody hell," Mick says.

"This is already causing a flap," Hugh says.

Newsboys invisible in the fog shout, "Amelia didn't hang!" "She's still alive!" "Read all about it!" I hear our neighbors buying papers, chattering and exclaiming. The story is already being exaggerated, and Mrs. Fry's allegations bandied about as though they're facts.

"The article is risky stuff even for the *Daily World*," Hugh says. "It virtually accuses the witnesses of subverting justice and covering it up."

The watchmaker from the shop next door joins us. "Miss Bain, is this you?" He holds up a copy of the *Daily World* and points at the text.

We take a second look at our copy, and my own name leaps out at me. I read aloud, "'Last night our reporter, Miss Sarah Bain, received a shocking tip from an anonymous source who claims that Amelia Carlisle was never hanged and was instead smuggled out of Newgate Prison alive.'" Alarm stuns me. "Malcolm Cross used my name!"

"You're famous! I can say I knew you when." Chuckling, the watchmaker returns to his shop.

"That scum Cross is tryin' to get you in trouble," Mick says.

If the story isn't true, I'll take the brunt of the repercussions even though it wasn't my decision to print the story.

"A pox on Cross," Hugh says. "I should have knocked his block off the other day."

"At least we found out early," Mick says. "You have time."

I'm so rattled, I don't understand what he means. "Time for what?"

"To get lost before Inspector Reid comes after you."

Reid will be angry at me for not reporting Mrs. Fry's tip to the police and for the article that puts the entire justice system in a bad light. But he's not the person whose reaction I fear most. "I have to tell Barrett," I say.

"Don't go near the police station," Mick says. "Reid might be there."

"Barrett will have seen the paper already," Hugh says.

I should have told him yesterday, but I was distracted by our argument. Now he'll think I deliberately kept him in the dark. "I need to apologize."

"Do it later," Mick says. "Why don't you look for your father some more?"

"Good idea. Make yourself scarce until Reid and Barrett have cooled down," Hugh says.

I doubt that they're going to cool down any time soon. "But we have to investigate Mrs. Fry's story."

"Mick and I will do it," Hugh says. "Go!"

★　★　★

Before my father disappeared, my family lived in Clerkenwell, about two miles northwest of Whitechapel. I've been back only once since then, in 1888, to seek clues to my father's whereabouts. All I learned was that Ellen Casey's family still believes he murdered her, and so do the other local folks who remember the crime. There seemed nothing for me in Clerkenwell, but now I have new reason to go back. Now I'm on a hunt for Lucas Zehnpfennig. He and my father crossed paths in Clerkenwell, a logical starting point for my search.

I exit the underground train at Clerkenwell station. The day is so cold that my numb nose can barely smell the yeast and sugar from the breweries. Wagons and carriages skid on frozen puddles in the misnamed, long, paved expanse of the Green, and icicles hang from the eaves of shops and houses. A new sense of purpose arms me against nostalgia and fear, as do the modifications I've made to my appearance. This morning I raided the props cupboard in my studio, and instead of my usual plain bonnet, I'm wearing a hat made of indigo velvet, trimmed with blue silk roses, whose little black net veil obscures my face. A blue wool cape covers the top of my gray coat, and I carry a tapestry bag instead of my usual satchel. I feel as if I'm dressed for a masquerade, but there should be little chance of anyone recognizing me as Sarah Bain, daughter of the prime suspect in Ellen Casey's murder.

Walking along the Green, I avoid the Crown Tavern, where my father once drank with his friends. The last time I went inside was the day before my mother told me my father was dead. I'd gone there to look for him every day for the several weeks he was missing. Loath to revisit the scene of my lost hope, I head for the few shops I remember from my childhood—a clockmaker's, a confectioner's, and a jeweler's, wedged between new warehouses and factories. I peer in the window of the clockmaker's. The men at the workbenches are all strangers, Jews with beards and skull-caps; the shop has changed hands. At the confectioner's, the man behind the counter is too young to have known people from my father's time. But the jeweler polishing his glass case of baubles is

Mr. Sanders, still here though now ancient. As I enter his shop, the bell tinkles, and he looks up.

"Good morning," he says. "May I help you?"

I'm glad he doesn't seem to recognize me. "Yes. I'm looking for a man named Lucas Zehnpfennig."

"I'm sorry. I've never heard of anyone by that name."

My query produces the same results at other shops and from people on the streets. Now that I'm chasing the past instead of vice versa, it's eluding me like a will-o-the-wisp. An hour later, I'm standing outside the Crown Tavern, which occupies the ground floor of a three-story brick building on a corner of the Green. A new sign decorates it, and the frontage that surrounds the windows gleams darkly with fresh varnish, but when I open the door, I smell the familiar odors of tobacco smoke, ale, and the spiced pickles that the publican's wife used to serve. The Crown's interior is little changed, the walls paneled with wood that's stained the same deep brown shade as the bar and furniture. I'm suddenly ten years old again. My heart pounds, and a familiar flood of hope, fear, and desperation makes me feel faint. I look toward the back table where my father and his friends used to sit. It's vacant. Some dozen customers are having an early lunch of ale, bread, and cheese. On unsteady legs, I approach the only two women, both in their sixties, seated together.

"Good morning." I nearly blurt the words I spoke the last time I was here: *Have you seen my father? His name is Benjamin Bain. He's lost.* "May I have this seat?" I gesture toward the empty bench at their table and sit before they can refuse.

One of the women is lanky and gaunt, her nose curved downward and her chin jutting up. She's dressed in a black cloak and bonnet that add to her witch-like appearance. The other has a soft, plump face and body and a toothless, caved-in mouth. She wears a green knitted shawl.

"My name is Catherine Staunton." I say the false name with as much nonchalance as I can manage. "I'm a newspaper reporter." I pull the notebook and pencil out of my bag and hold them up.

"Are there lady reporters now?" The witch's genteel voice is oddly familiar.

"Some."

"What paper?" the plump woman asks.

"The *Daily World*. I'd like to interview you. May I buy you a drink?"

They accept, and I walk up to the bar. The publican is Mr. Aldrich, with the same curly mustache and red, cheerful face I remember, looking the same age as he was twenty-four years ago. I'm so astonished that when he asks me what I want, I stammer. Then I recall that Mr. Aldrich had a son; this must be him. I'm still shaken as I fish money from my pocketbook. The three glasses of ale slosh in my hands before I set them down on the table. Resuming my seat and struggling to compose myself, I open my notebook.

"What are your names?"

The women puff up, flattered that a reporter wants to interview them. The witch introduces herself as Agnes Hartwell and her friend as Millicent Johnson. I gulp. *I know them!* Miss Hartwell was my teacher at the local school; Miss Johnson is the parson's wife's sister. I desperately hope they won't recognize me.

"I'm looking for a man named Lucas Zehnpfennig. Do you know of him?"

Miss Hartwell and Mrs. Johnson furrow their brows as they sip from their glasses. I see the gleam of recognition in their eyes, and my heartbeat quickens. "That's a name I've not heard in a while," Miss Johnson says.

"Wasn't he that factory worker who always started trouble during the marches?" Miss Hartwell asks.

"You're right, Agnes. Always started it, always managed not to get caught. Remember the riot in 1865? He threw rocks at the police. That's why they broke up the march."

Miss Hartwell nods. "People were arrested, but not Lucas."

My father must have organized that march. Was that where he and Lucas became acquainted? Miss Johnson glances at my blank notebook and my pencil gripped in my motionless hand; she wonders why I'm not taking notes. I scribble some nonsense.

"He hasn't been seen here in more than twenty years," Miss Hartwell says, crushing my hopes. "Good riddance."

Miss Johnson fixes her shrewd gaze on me. "Why are you interested in Lucas Zehnpfennig?"

I suddenly remember that she was always quick to sniff out people's secrets—she caught servants at the vicarage stealing food—and now she suspects that I'm not who I said I am. Loath to let her and Miss Hartwell know my true motive, I lean toward them, cup my hand around my mouth, and lie, "This is about the Ripper murders." Their faces express the fearful thrill that any mention of the Ripper provokes. "I'm investigating an anonymous tip that my newspaper received. It said to look at Lucas Zehnpfennig."

"Could he be the Ripper?" Awe hushes Miss Hartwell's voice. Miss Johnson looks disconcerted because this man she knew might be the notorious killer, and she never suspected.

"At the moment, Mr. Zehnpfennig is just a person of interest," I say.

"The other papers haven't mentioned him," Miss Johnson says.

"Mine seems to be the only one that received the tip." It occurs to me that if Lucas learns he's been implicated in the Ripper murders, he'll make himself scarce. "I would appreciate your keeping our talk confidential. If Mr. Zehnpfennig is the Ripper and I'm the reporter who breaks the story, it will do great things for my career."

"Yes, of course." Miss Hartwell looks glad to be let in on the secret.

"I don't think it could be him," Miss Johnson says.

"Why not?" I ask. "You said he was a troublemaker."

"Not that kind of troublemaker. He never killed anybody."

"But Millicent, don't you remember, we thought he did?" Miss Hartwell says. "When that girl Ellen Casey was murdered, Lucas was the first person we thought of."

I gulp ale to hide my astonishment.

"The first person *you* thought of," Miss Johnson retorts. "*I* never thought he did it."

"But you gave me the idea."

"You're so forgetful, Agnes." Miss Johnson says to me, "The police didn't think Lucas killed that girl. He was never arrested." Her grimace says she *did* think Lucas was guilty and would rather forget her mistaken judgment. She frowns at my notebook.

I scribble, *Lucas killed Ellen Casey?* I press so hard with the pencil that the tip of the lead breaks. My heart gallops under my fancy cape. I came to Clerkenwell to discover what role Lucas played in my father's disappearances, and here is a connection between him and the crime for which my father was blamed.

Miss Hartwell cringes from her friend's rebuke. "But the police took him to the station for questioning."

This is the first I've heard that my father wasn't their only suspect.

"They let him go, didn't they?" Miss Johnson says with an air of triumph. "They decided it was that photographer—Benjamin Bain."

I flinch at the sound of my father's name. My elbow knocks my glass, and I grab it before it can spill. I take a deep drink of the sour ale, to calm my nerves.

"Oh, but it couldn't have been Mr. Bain," Miss Hartwell murmurs. "He was such a nice, gentle man."

I remember that a boy at school wrote "Witch" on the chalkboard in her classroom and I laughed; now I wish I could tell her I'm sorry. Her testament to Benjamin Bain's good character means so much to me.

"Agnes, he ran away, don't you remember?" Miss Johnson says, exasperated. "He wouldn't have unless he was guilty." Her glance at me is sharp, speculative.

I fear she's on the verge of recognizing me. "Have you any idea where I might find Mr. Zehnpfennig?"

Both women shake their heads. "He left Clerkenwell at around the same time Mr. Bain did," Miss Hartwell says. "I always thought it an odd coincidence."

Here is a hint that someone besides my father went on the run after Ellen Casey's murder. Then Miss Hartwell says, "I also thought it odd that Mr. Bain and Lucas were friends—a nice man like Mr. Bain and a troublemaker like Lucas."

If they were friends, why didn't my father want Lucas in our house? Comprehension strikes as I remember Lucas petting my hair while I sat on his lap. My father thought Lucas was going to molest me! He must have known or suspected that Lucas had an attraction to young girls. *Did he also know that Lucas murdered Ellen Casey?* I think he must have. But why didn't he tell the police? Why did he run away instead?

"Well, they came from the same village," Mrs. Johnson says with another sharp glance at me. "Maybe they both went back there."

Ambushed by this second surprise, I can't even pretend to take notes. I always thought my father was born and raised in London. "What village?" I say, breathless.

"I asked Mr. Bain once, and he just smiled and brushed me off," Miss Hartwell says.

"I always thought that was suspicious," Miss Johnson says darkly, scrutinizing me. "I managed to get it out of him that he was from Ely."

I can tell that she's about to ask me where I'm from and who my family is. I rise, thank the women for their time, and make a hasty exit.

★   ★   ★

I spent the rest of the day in Clerkenwell, questioning more people about Lucas Zehnpfennig. I considered traveling to Ely, but the railway map shows that it's some seventy miles from London—a good half day's journey each way. By eight o'clock in the evening, however, I was sorry I didn't go, for my inquiries in Clerkenwell were fruitless. Disappointed and weary, I gambled that it was safe to go back to Whitechapel.

There, a few cabs and a lone omnibus roll down the foggy high street. The shops are closed, their ground-floor windows dark except for those of the Angel and the White Hart public houses—and my studio. Apprehension puts me on guard, for my companions are usually upstairs at this hour. From inside the studio, a man's angry voice blares so loudly that I can hear it even though the door is closed. I see, through the moisture-clouded window, Inspector Reid gesticulating furiously at Hugh and Mick.

Staying away all day wasn't long enough to hide from the police.

Hugh sees me and covertly waves his hand, shooing me away. Reid notices, turns, and when he spots me, an ugly, wolfish grin spreads over his face. He flings open the door. "If it isn't the elusive Miss Bain."

My heart is beating hard, pumping so much energy through me that I'm sure I could outrun Reid, but I can't leave Hugh and Mick to take the brunt of his anger. When Reid bows with mock politeness and motions for me to enter the studio, I comply with as much dignity as I can summon. He shuts the door. The odor of his pine-scented shaving soap taints the air. My camera, flash lamp, and furniture seem to cower from his hostility. Two police constables lean against the fireplace. Reid knows better than to confront my friends and me alone.

"I've had half the police force looking for you," Reid says. "Where've you been all day?"

Holding his gaze, I don't answer. Hugh and Mick keep quiet. We mustn't let slip any information that might enable Reid to lay his clutches on my father.

"PC Barrett wasn't looking too happy today," Reid says. "What's the matter—had a lover's tiff? Or maybe he's just upset because you've been wreaking havoc behind his back."

My heart contracts. The shaky terms on which Barrett and I parted are getting shakier.

"But never mind," Reid says. "What I really want to know is, where did you get that tip about Amelia Carlisle?"

"From an anonymous source," I say.

"Right, that's what the story in the paper said. Who is it?"

"I'm not at liberty to say."

Reid grimaces in disgust. "I think there isn't any anonymous source. I think you made the whole thing up."

Hugh and Mick snort in indignation. I say, "I did not."

"Then tell me who the source is."

Either I give up Mrs. Fry or I'm a liar. Reid smirks at my uncomfortable silence and says, "That's what I thought—Amelia Carlisle didn't escape, and the story in the *Daily World* is just another of Sir Gerald's publicity stunts."

Mick leaps to my defense. "Miss Sarah didn't make it up."

"And you can't know for sure about Amelia," Hugh says. "You weren't at her hanging. Besides, I passed by Whitechapel Police Station today, and there were people lined up outside to report sightings of her."

The newspaper story must have inspired people to think they'd seen Amelia. Even if many are mistaken, perhaps some actually have seen her. I remember that thousands of sightings of Robin Mariner were reported after he was kidnapped. The power of the press is great indeed.

"You oughta be lookin' for Amelia instead of botherin' Miss Sarah," Mick says.

"Amelia could be walking around town, free as a bird." Hugh adds slyly, "Just like Jack the Ripper."

The three of us know Jack the Ripper is gone, but Hugh couldn't resist a jab at Reid's sorest spot. Reid clenches his fists, and his face is so livid with anger that I think he's going to strike Hugh. We back away from him, but the constables move in on us from behind, enraged by Hugh's allusion to the police's failure to solve their most notorious murder case.

Reid's expression turns ominously jovial. "We're about to settle the Amelia Carlisle business. She's going to be exhumed tomorrow. To prove that she's in her grave."

Surprise fills me. The power of the press is even greater than I thought.

"That's quite an extreme step," Hugh says. "And all because of an article about an anonymous tip."

"No, not all because of an article about an anonymous tip," Reid says, mimicking Hugh's upper-class accent. "The Home Office has been besieged with telegrams and visits from city officials, members of Parliament, the prime minister, and the rich and famous. Not to mention an envoy from Her Majesty the Queen. All of whom are outraged by the idea that there was a conspiracy to help the Baby Butcher escape justice."

The story has upheaved society at its highest levels.

"Well, digging Amelia up is the way to find out if she's really dead," Hugh says.

"Which brings me to the reason I'm here." Reid reaches in his coat pocket, removes a folded sheet of paper, and gives it to me by smacking it against my chest.

I gasp at the rude personal contact. Mick says, "Hey!" and lunges at Reid.

The constables grab him. Reid says, "Down, boy, unless you want to spend the night in Newgate."

Mick shakes the constables off, scowls, and jams his hands in his pockets.

Hugh takes the paper from me and reads, "'To Sarah Bain, Lord Hugh Staunton, and Mick O'Reilly: You are hereby summoned to attend the exhumation of Amelia Carlisle at Newgate Prison on Saturday the eleventh of January'—that's tomorrow—'at eleven o'clock AM.'"

"Crikey!" Mick sounds awed and tickled.

I quail at the thought of what could happen at the exhumation. "Why do we have to be there?"

"Because you deserve to face the consequences of your mischief." Reid grins.

"Wait, there's more," Hugh says, frowning at the summons. "'Should you fail to attend, a warrant will be issued for your arrest. Signed, James Monro, Chief Commissioner of Police.'"

"I dare you not to show up tomorrow," Reid says.

CHAPTER 17

"This is gonna to be so terrific!" Mick bounces with gleeful anticipation.

It's ten thirty in the morning, and he, Hugh, and I are crowded in a cab with my camera equipment, riding to Newgate. After Inspector Reid delivered the summons last night, Sir Gerald sent a message that instructed me to photograph the exhumation.

"I can't go through with it." Hugh's face is pale, moist, and sickly.

"Don't you wanna see if Amelia's there?" Mick says.

"I'm afraid that if she is, I'll disgrace myself."

I don't know which I'm more afraid of—that Mrs. Fry was telling the truth or lying. I suppose I should prefer to see a corpse and look a fool than learn that justice for Amelia Carlisle's victims was subverted.

At Newgate, police outside the main entrance are holding back a crowd of men, women, and children, reporters and photographers. Newsboys hawk copies of the *Daily World*, whose headline announces the exhumation. As we alight from the cab, laden with my equipment, a cry rises from the crowd. "It's Sarah Bain!"

I cringe from the mob that presses in around us. Reporters shout, "Miss Bain, who's the anonymous source? Do you think Amelia will be found in her grave?"

Cameras thrust at my face; exploding flash powder blinds me. I silently curse Malcolm Cross for making me a celebrity.

"Let us through!" Constables pushing the reporters and photographers aside usher my friends and me to the entrance. Two black horses draw a large black carriage up to the prison. The carriage bears a gold insignia—a ship in full sail. Sir Gerald steps from the carriage, his tall, stout person clad in a black overcoat and a silk top hat. The crowd keeps a respectful distance; his wealth and power form an invisible barrier around him that even the light from the flashes doesn't seem to penetrate. He surveys the scene as if he owns everything and everyone in it. The reporters address him with deference.

"Sir Gerald, are you glad that your newspaper has forced the government to exhume Amelia Carlisle?" "Sir Gerald, can you please give us a statement for our readers?"

On his heels follows Malcolm Cross, who behaves like a prince making a royal visit, waving to people he knows, his smile broad with self-importance. Sir Gerald pauses near the entrance and says, "All I care about is that Amelia Carlisle got her just deserts. If we find out today that she didn't, I'll move heaven and earth to make sure she does." His words have the gravity of a blood oath. Perhaps he thinks justice for Amelia will feed his hunger for vengeance.

Cheers from the crowd follow him and Malcolm Cross into the prison. Hugh, Mick, and I trail them. I try to appear calm while my insides quake. In the hall, we meet Governor Piercy, Sheriff Hargreaves, Dr. Davies, and the Reverend Starling. Their expressions are somber, composed; I can't tell if they're afraid of what the exhumation will reveal. Only the chaplain's jerking Adam's apple betrays any anxiety. They shake hands with Sir Gerald but disregard my friends and me. Dorothea Fry is absent. My uneasiness burgeons as I wonder why.

"Let's get started," Governor Piercy says.

He and Sheriff Hargreaves lead the way. We walk through the prison, as silent as a funeral procession, to a long, wide corridor lit by a ceiling made of glass windowpanes set in a metal grid. This must be Dead Man's Walk—the infamous passage between

Newgate and the Old Bailey, used by condemned criminals. Beneath the worn, grimy rectangular paving stones that cover the floor is the graveyard where hundreds of criminals executed at Newgate lie buried. But for the grace of fortune, my friends and I might have walked this path to our own deaths. Perhaps someday our earthly remains will rest here.

The gray masonry walls seem to close in on me. The cold, dank atmosphere sends a shiver rippling through the tension in my muscles. When I see Barrett and Inspector Reid waiting at the end of the passage beside two wardens armed with toolboxes, crowbars, and shovels, my anxiety turns to panic. Reid catches my eye and smiles faintly, as if he knows that I'd hoped he wouldn't be here. Barrett gives me a brief glance, his eyes dark with accusation and disappointment.

Our strife has gathered enough force to open a trapdoor, like the one in the execution shed, under my feet. He'll never forgive this. I can stop waiting for it to be over. Unable to bear looking at him, I study the crude letters carved into the walls—the names of the criminals on whose graves I'm standing.

Governor Piercy beckons to the wardens. They kneel on the floor and open their toolboxes. As Hugh and Mick help me set the camera on the tripod, I feel awkward, conspicuous. I put my head under the black drape that hangs from the back of the camera. When I peer in the viewfinder and crank the bellows, I see the two wardens wielding chisels and mallets against the mortar that cements a section of paving stones in place. The loud pounding, chipping noises echo in the corridor. Their rhythm quickens my heartbeat, heightens the suspense that hushes everyone. Hugh and Mick and the others stand motionless behind me. I hold up the flash lamp, take a photograph, and the powder explodes, lighting up the corridor. I change the negative plate in the camera and refill the lamp.

The wardens insert their crowbars in the cracks and pry up paving stones. They lean them against the wall and expose a pit that's some six feet long and three wide. An odor of decay infiltrates the darkness under my drape. Footsteps shuffle as everyone behind me backs away from the plain wooden coffin nested in the pit. I photograph the coffin. Then the wardens pry up the nails that seal it and raise the lid.

A vicious stench invades my nostrils like the tentacles of a monster. I taste rotten meat and blood, caustic lime. Nausea churns my stomach and dizzies me. The image in the viewfinder blurs. I hear exclamations of disgust.

"Oh, God," Hugh says in a hoarse, muffled voice.

Blinking to clear my vision, breathing shallowly through my mouth, I force myself to watch through the viewfinder. The wardens drop the coffin lid, turn, double over, and retch. The coffin contains a soupy brown muck and a figure that's barely recognizable as human. Scraps of black fabric clothe bones from which the flesh has dissolved. Strands of dark hair cling to the skull. All that's left of the face is patches of skin and gray sinews, the features eaten away by the lime, the pale teeth exposed in a ghastly grin. The muck roils as if from tiny vermin spawning.

"Gorblimey," Mick whispers.

Barrett and Reid cover their noses and mouths with their hands, their eyes wide with horrified revulsion. I hear gagging and moaning from the other men and the splatter of vomit. Sour, acrid bile rises in my own throat, and I swallow hard. My position behind the camera, viewing the corpse in a small rectangle of glass, distances me from the horrible reality. Concentrating on my job distracts my mind from my stomach. Moving like a wind-up automaton, I remove and load negative plates, change exposure times, and take photograph after photograph. Exploding flash powder lights up the corpse, and the sulfurous smell of the smoke joins the fetid reek.

"I hope you're satisfied," Governor Piercy says, gasping.

"How can we be sure that's really Amelia Carlisle?" Sir Gerald's voice sounds calm, normal; perhaps he's seen worse sights during his voyages to far continents. But I detect a rare note of confusion, as though he doesn't know which he prefers—that it is Amelia and justice has been served, or it isn't her and the *Daily World* story about her escaping execution is validated.

"Yeah, it could be anybody," Mick says.

Perhaps Governor Piercy, Sheriff Hargreaves, Dr. Davies, and the Reverend Starling buried someone else—a recently deceased prisoner?—in case Amelia's death were ever questioned.

"It's her," Dr. Davies says in a faint, thick voice.

"How do you know?" Sir Gerald says.

"Those are her false teeth."

Now I see that the teeth grinning inside the skull are too white and even to be real, rimmed with unnaturally pink gums. Made of porcelain and hardened rubber, they didn't dissolve in the lime. I move the camera closer, refocus, and photograph the false teeth that belonged to Amelia, who didn't escape the consequences of her past after all. Barrett picks up the coffin lid and slams it down over the corpse.

★   ★   ★

Sir Gerald, Malcolm Cross, Hugh, Mick, and I adjourn to a court-yard with all the others except Dr. Davies and the Reverend Starling, who have disappeared. The courtyard is cold, the fog condensing into sleet, but we breathe deeply, grateful for the fresh air. Hugh wipes his mouth with a handkerchief, looking weak and ill. He leans on Mick, the only one of us whose stomach seems unaffected. The other men's faces have a greenish cast, but Malcolm Cross, the governor, and the sheriff wear the same gloating, self-righteous expression.

"Gentlemen and lady," Sheriff Hargreaves says, with little bow in my direction, "can we agree that the issue of Amelia Carlisle has been resolved?"

"We can," Sir Gerald says, his manner rigid with displeasure. No matter if he likes that Amelia got her just deserts, he doesn't like being wrong.

Hugh and I nod. I can feel the egg on my face. Malcolm Cross hides a smile. Barrett, his mouth a thin line, won't look at me. This is probably the last time I'll ever see him. I won't be able to apologize or even say goodbye. Sorrow torments me.

"I ain't agreeing," Mick blurts.

"Are you suggesting that we killed another woman, pulled her teeth out, and put Amelia's false teeth in her mouth before we buried her?" Sheriff Hargreaves's gently mocking tone makes the idea sound ridiculous.

Cross snickers. Mick flushes. The sheriff's pitying gaze encompasses Mick, Hugh, and me. "That's Amelia Carlisle in the coffin. Whoever told you she's alive played a hoax on you." His expression turns reproachful as he addresses Sir Gerald. "I think you owe Governor Piercy and me an apology for your insinuations in the *Daily World*."

Anger reddens Sir Gerald's florid face. "Sorry." It's obvious that he hates apologizing even more than he hates being wrong.

"Maybe now you'll deign to tell us who gave you the tip?" Reid says to me.

I look to Sir Gerald; he nods. "It was Dorothea Fry." We feel no compunction to protect her after her allegations led us to this humiliating moment.

Governor Piercy regards us with scorn. "You're making that up to cover the fact that you invented the tip yourselves. Mrs. Fry is a trusted public servant; she wouldn't tell such a lie."

"I'd like a word with Mrs. Fry," Sir Gerald says in an ominous tone.

"Sorry, she's on leave," Governor Piercy says.

"How convenient," I say. I know why she's absent—so she needn't face the music after the hoax. "Did you put her up to feeding me the story about Amelia Carlisle?" I ask Governor Piercy and Sheriff Hargreaves.

"Not guilty." Hargreaves's smile at me contains a hint of mockery under its charm.

"Like hell you didn't!" Mick says. "You don't want us investigatin' Amelia's hangin', so you cooked up a plan to shut us down. Now you're hidin' Mrs. Fry so she can't rat on you."

"I'm sorry you think so." Sheriff Hargreaves manages to look regretful as well as amused.

I think Mick is right and there's still a conspiracy of silence even though it's not about Amelia being alive. And whatever is going on, the sheriff must be in the thick of it. I don't want him near Catherine. But I remain silent rather than make accusations I can't justify.

"You're not as smart as you thought. This'll teach you to believe everything you hear," Reid says to me.

Before I can protest that I'd had my doubts about Mrs. Fry, a stern look from Sir Gerald warns me to keep quiet and not make matters worse. Barrett looks as if he can't decide whether he's angrier with Reid, or me and glares at both of us.

"You're banned from Newgate," Governor Piercy tells Hugh, Mick, and me. "If you come back, you'll be arrested for trespassing."

"Much as I would enjoy continuing this discussion," Sheriff Hargreaves says, "it's time to make a statement to the public."

★   ★   ★

As we file out the main door of Newgate, cheers greet us. Sheriff Hargreaves stands on the top step while Governor Piercy, Inspector Reid, and Barrett position themselves below him to the right of the entrance, on the sidewalk against the wall of the building. To his left, I tremble as I stand with Hugh and Mick, Sir Gerald and Malcolm Cross, and my photography equipment. Constables push back the crowd that's expanded to fill the street as far as I can see. People shout, "Was Amelia there?" Flash lamps emit explosions like gunfire; their white light blazes through the fog. I flinch from sparks raining down on me. Sheriff Hargreaves raises his hands, and the crowd subsides into expectant murmurs.

"Amelia is in her grave, exactly where she's supposed to be," he announces.

Most of the people in the crowd cheer, but I also hear groans of disappointment.

"She's dead. She was executed." Hargreaves's voice rings out, full and rich. I can picture him performing a soliloquy on stage. "Justice has been served. We can all go home happy."

But the crowd pushes closer, and the reporters jostle their way to its forefront. "Sheriff Hargreaves! Does this mean there's no connection between the Warbrick murder and Amelia's hanging?"

"No connection at all," Hargreaves says with a pleased smile.

I still believe there is, but my credibility has been seriously damaged.

"I'm considering prosecuting the *Daily World* for libel," Hargreaves says.

Sir Gerald's expression, tight with controlled anger, increases my dread of repercussions.

"What bearing do today's events have on the contest between the *Daily World* and the police?" a reporter asks.

"I can answer that." Inspector Reid clambers onto the step beside Hargreaves and raises his voice above the noise of the crowd. "The contest is nothing but a publicity stunt gone wrong. The *Daily World* had no business investigating a murder. They knew they were going to lose the contest, but they didn't want to back down, so they fabricated evidence."

A stir sweeps through the audience. Reid is too excited to care whether he offends Sir Gerald, whose face darkens with rage. "The story about Amelia Carlisle was a hoax dreamed up by one of its reporters. A *female* reporter." Reid points at me. "That's her— Sarah Bain."

Dismayed, I shrink against the prison wall as the attention of the crowd turns on me like a many-eyed beast. Murmured speculation sounds like predatory growls.

"But it's no surprise that she would attempt such a hoax," Reid says. "Her father is Benjamin Bain. In 1866, Benjamin Bain violated and murdered a little girl named Ellen Casey. He's been a fugitive from the law ever since."

My own past has ambushed me. I'm sick with horror, dying of shame even though I think my father is innocent. My mother taught me to keep our connection with him secret. She said that if people found out that we were related to a troublemaker who organized protest marches, they would think we too were trouble-makers. Now it's as if she foresaw this moment when our secret would be revealed to the world, when I would become an object of disgust.

"What else could you expect from Benjamin Bain's daughter?" Reid jabs his finger at me like a weapon. "Sarah Bain inherited her father's bad blood!"

People crane their necks to get a better look at me. Hugh and Mick, indignant at Reid, move in front of me to shield me from the catcalls and disapproving stares, the cameras and exploding flashes. Stripped of my dignity, I'm furious at Reid, but it's the helpless fury of a child overpowered by the law that branded my father a criminal. I struggle not to cry.

"Sarah Bain deceived you," Reid tells the mob. "She did it to raise her status at the newspaper and line her own pocket. She didn't care about you or the truth, or about the people whose repu-tations she smeared. She's a selfish, ambitious, unprincipled, and immoral—"

Barrett clambers onto the step and yells, "Shut up!"

He's defending me? It must mean he still loves me! My heart rejoices even as I rue the cost to him—escalating his own feud with Reid.

"You're out of line, Constable," Reid says. "Back off."

"You leave Sarah alone!" Barrett seizes Reid by the arm and tries to pull him down from the step. Governor Piercy and Sheriff Hargreaves seem too surprised to intervene.

"Why are you sticking up for her?" Reid asks. "The little tart hoodwinked you." As he tussles with Barrett, he shouts to the crowd, "I'm launching a manhunt for Benjamin Bain. Anyone with information about him should report it at the nearest police station."

I'm horrified that he's making good on his threat.

"You sonofabitch!" Barrett punches Reid in the nose.

Their strife erupts in a tornado of fists and thrashing limbs. Now I'm terrified for Barrett. Although he's younger and stronger than Reid, and he can win this fight, he'll surely be fired for striking his superior and making a public scene; he could even go to prison. His parents will be devastated. I can't be glad that he's chosen me over his career and his family honor. I rush to stop him, but Sheriff Hargreaves and Governor Piercy are already trying pull him and Reid apart. The crowd swamps me in a flood of jostling, agitating people. Reporters and photographers battle for a good view of the action. I glimpse Sheriff Hargreaves gripping Barrett in a chokehold.

"Let go of him!" Mick jumps on the sheriff's back. "You killed Harry Warbrick! You put Mrs. Fry up to trickin' Miss Sarah. This is all your fault, you bastard!"

Goaded by jealousy over Catherine, yelling like a wild man, he seizes the sheriff's golden hair with one hand and punches his head with the other. Hargreaves releases Barrett and fends off Mick's blows. I'm horrified because assaulting him is a crime for which Mick could go to jail. The heightened emotions in the air infect the crowd. Women scream. People surge around me, press me against the wall of the building. Trapped, I shout with panic.

The crowd parts as four large, strong men, clad in dark coats and hats, plow a path through it toward Newgate. I recognize them by type: they're Sir Gerald's bodyguards. He must have had them waiting nearby in case he needed them. One of them hustles Sir Gerald away. Another grabs my arm. I barely manage to snatch my camera before he pulls me through the mob. We turn a corner, the mob thins, and I see Sir Gerald's carriage parked on the roadside. Sir

Gerald climbs in and hoists me onto the seat beside him. Two other guards arrive with Mick and Hugh, carrying my other equipment. Mick holds his hand over his bloody nose. Hugh has lost his hat. They jump into the carriage. The guards load up my photography equipment, slam the doors, and perch on the running boards. The driver cracks the whip. As the horses accelerate from a trot to a gallop and the carriage rackets down the street, reporters chase us and yell:

"Sir Gerald, are you sorry you published the story about Amelia Carlisle?" "How does it feel to look like a fool?"

CHAPTER 18

In the carriage, I sit beside Sir Gerald, who gazes straight ahead as if he's watching a bomb explode in the distance and knows the damage is bad. Hugh shivers in the cold, Mick wipes his bloody nose on his sleeve, and I smell a foul odor—our clothes have absorbed the reek of Amelia's corpse. I'm glad Sir Gerald's guards rescued us, but the dark frown on his face portends trouble.

"I'm terminating your employment," he says.

Hugh and Mick stare at him in surprise, but I've always known that as soon as I ran afoul of him or outlived my usefulness, he would jettison me. On top of losing Barrett, I'm losing my job—the job that I let come between us. Sir Gerald wants to put the blame for the fiasco on someone other than himself, and while I've no hope for myself, maybe I can save my friends.

"Hugh and Mick had nothing to do with Mrs. Fry's tip or what happened today," I say.

Unmoved, Sir Gerald says, "I no longer need their services."

"With all due respect, you're not being fair." Hugh's pale cheeks redden with anger. "Sarah reported Mrs. Fry's tip, but *you* decided to print the story. Without giving her time to corroborate it, I might add. She doesn't deserve to be punished, and neither do Mick and I."

I should have quit the day Sir Gerald started the contest, said no when he assigned me to photograph crime scenes, or never accepted employment with him in the first place. But it's too late to refuse the glass of milk that's now been spilled.

Sir Gerald regards Hugh with scornful pity. "Life's not fair. I need to clean house at the newspaper to save its reputation." And his own. "Miss Bain has to go. And so do her friends."

"So we're the scapegoats," Mick says. "After all we been through because of you!"

"You chose to work for me. You accepted the terms. You knew there were no guarantees."

This is but a reminder of everything I already knew: He's not a generous patron; he's a hard-hearted businessman. I knew we were living on borrowed time, but the rejection hurts nonetheless.

"The business about your father is another problem," Sir Gerald says to me. "It didn't matter when it was under wraps. I hired you in spite of it. Even if he's guilty, you had nothing to do with the girl's murder. But now that it's come out, having you at the paper is a liability."

Shock renders me speechless. How did Sir Gerald know the story about my father before Reid made it public? He must have investigated my background.

The carriage stops outside St. Paul's station. "You'll be paid through the end of the month," Sir Gerald says.

"No skin off your nose," Mick mutters.

My pride tells me to refuse the money, but we need it.

"What about the contest?" Hugh says.

"The contest is off."

"Don't you care about solving the murder?" Mick says.

"I'm leaving that to the police." Sir Gerald's voice contains a rare note of defeat. I sense that he's thinking of Robin rather than Harry Warbrick, realizing that the justice he craves is a shining, elusive quarry beyond his reach. "Remember, the confidentiality agreement still holds."

"Bugger the confidentiality agreement!" Mick says.

Menace darkens Sir Gerald's expression. Hugh says quickly, "Our lips are sealed."

We climb out of the carriage and unload my photography equipment. Now I'm too numb to feel anything but a desire to go home.

Mick gives Sir Gerald a bitter look. "I used to think that underneath everything you were a good man. I was wrong."

Sir Gerald regards Mick with a blend of pain and reproach, as though he's the injured party. He says to me, "Develop the photographs. I'll have them picked up tonight." He shuts the carriage door and rides away.

★ ★ ★

At home, in our rooms, Hugh, Mick, and I shed our stinking clothes. Fitzmorris bundles them off to the laundry before they can contaminate the house. We take ice-cold baths instead of waiting for water to heat. When I'm done, I'm shivering so hard that my teeth chatter. I dry my wet hair by the fire, then go to my darkroom to develop the photos of Amelia Carlisle's exhumation. Transferring negative plates from one tray of chemical solutions to the next in pitch darkness, my last job for the *Daily World*, I'm not glad there won't be any more summonses to crime scenes or grisly sights to photograph. We've lost our livelihood. Enlarging and printing the images by the light of the red gas lamp, I think of Barrett, and tears burn my cold cheeks. I hang the damp prints on pegs on the string stretched over the sink, wishing I didn't have to leave the darkroom and face the world.

Hugh and Mick are waiting for me in the dining room. It's four thirty, already dark outside. We've missed lunch, but not even Mick is hungry. Fitzmorris pours cups of scalding tea, which we sip gratefully. His somber face says that he's been told the bad news. Hugh asks the question that's on my mind.

"How long can we stay afloat?"

We all turn to Fitzmorris, who manages our finances. He sits down, looking glum. "About three months."

That's even less time than I thought. Mick puts on a cheerful face and says, "Don't worry—I can get a job in a factory."

I don't want to seem unappreciative, but I can't pretend that's a viable solution. "It won't pay enough to support us."

"We can revive our detective agency," Hugh says.

We need to face reality. "After the news about today spreads, who will hire us?"

"You still have your photography studio," Fitzmorris says.

Although he could find another position, I know he doesn't want to leave Hugh, who's as much a beloved younger brother to him as his master. "I haven't any clients," I say, vexed at myself for letting Sir Gerald monopolize my time. It was easier to coast on the salary he paid us than to get a fledgling business off the ground. "And after today, I'm not likely to get some."

As we sit drinking tea that soon grows cold, contemplating our uncertain future, the doorbell rings. "It must be Sir Gerald's messenger, come for the photographs." I go downstairs. When I open the front door, there stands Barrett.

Surprise is only one of the emotions that strike me speechless. I'm relieved to see Barrett, hopeful for a chance to make up with him. But he's in ordinary clothes, not his uniform, and his grim expression seems to confirm my fear that he's been fired and disgraced. Dread squeezes the air out of my lungs as I let him in the door. The studio seems too small to contain both of us and the tension that crackles in the air. My hands tremble as I light a lamp. Then I face Barrett and say the only thing I can say.

"I'm sorry." My voice hitches on a gasp. "I should have told you."

"You should have." Barrett's gaze is sober, unforgiving.

I'm afraid to ask, but I need to know. "Why aren't you in uniform?"

"It's at the laundry. I'll put on my spare one tomorrow."

His uniform must have reeked as badly as the clothes I wore to the exhumation. He hasn't lost his job. Cautious relief trickles into me as I think of his parents, so proud of their son who followed in his father's trade. If his police career were to end because of me, they would dislike me more than they already do. But the worst would be the fact that I had caused the downfall of the man I love.

"Then Inspector Reid didn't—?"

"Fire me? No." But Barrett's humorless smile is cold water dashed on the small flame of my hope that all will be well. He pauses as if reluctant to voice the rest of what he came to say. "Sarah, I need to warn you."

"Warn me about what?"

"Reid is serious about finding your father. He's put five men on the case and started a full-scale manhunt."

My father's past is gaining on him. It's no different from what I could have expected, so why should Barrett make a point of telling me?

He takes a deep breath, exhales, and says, "Reid gave me a choice—I take charge of the manhunt, or I hand in my resignation."

Incredulous shock thumps my heart, opens my eyes wide. "Reid put *you* in charge of the search for my father?"

Barrett nods, unhappy. "You can probably guess why."

Reid is using Barrett as a weapon against me, getting revenge on two birds with one stone. *"And you're going along with him?"* No matter how angry Barrett is at me, surely he won't spearhead Reid's effort to punish my father.

The look in Barrett's eyes is apologetic but resolute. "That's what I came to warn you about."

I moan with the pain of betrayal. "How could you do this to me? If it were the other way around, and *your* father was the fugitive, I would never—"

Barrett grasps my shoulders. "Sarah, listen."

"Don't touch me!" Writhing, I try to push him away.

He holds tight. "Let me explain." His eyes plead with me.

"What's to explain? I know you're doing it to save your job."

"My job be damned!" Barrett seems angry that I would think him so selfish.

"Then you should have resigned." I seethe with hatred toward Barrett because I think I know why he didn't quit. "Instead, you're getting back at me for keeping secrets from you. That's not fair! No matter what I've done, my father doesn't deserve to be punished for it."

"I'm not doing it to punish you or your father," Barrett says, adamant. "If I quit, Reid will just put somebody else in charge. It's better this way."

"How could it be better?" I demand.

"I have some control over what happens. If we find your father, I can prevent him from getting hurt when he's captured." Barrett adds, "Police don't go easy on men they suspect of murdering little girls."

The thought of what might happen to my father if he's captured is so awful that I've blocked it from my mind. That he would be hanged afterward was unbearable enough. To picture the police torturing him makes me so ill that the fight drains from me.

"So you understand." Relieved, Barrett drops his hands. "Now you have to help me find him."

"Help you?" I gape in fresh disbelief.

"Yes. If you've any clues to his whereabouts, you need to tell me."

Thoughts of Sally and Mrs. Albert come to mind. Again, I wonder if Mrs. Albert knows something she's not telling me. I force myself to hold Barrett's gaze so he won't suspect that I'm concealing anything. *"Why?"*

"We need to convince him to turn himself in. That way, there'll be no rough stuff when he's arrested."

Barrett seems to think there's a real possibility of finding my father. Hope lifts my heart at the same time that the thought of my father being arrested horrifies me. Should I tell Barrett about Lucas Zehnpfennig? If I can convince him that Lucas is a better suspect in Ellen Casey's murder than my father is, maybe he can make

Lucas the target of the manhunt. But I quickly discard the idea. Reid won't change course based on my say-so. He'll only suspect me of trying to trick him and be all the more determined to punish me through my father.

"You know something, don't you?" Barrett says, his eyes narrowed.

He knows me so well that I can't fool him into thinking I'm not hiding anything.

"Hiding from the law makes your father look guilty," Barrett points out. "Turning himself in will make him look more like an innocent man who wants to clear his name. Which might convince the jury to acquit him."

The argument sounds logical, but I balk as I realize that Barrett hasn't said whether he believes my father is innocent. Perhaps he thinks Benjamin Bain is guilty and therefore will try his best to deliver him to the gallows. My old habit of distrust braces me. Folding my arms across my chest, I say, "This is a trick to make me help you trap my father."

"My God, Sarah!" Barrett throws up his hands in indignation. "Don't you know I would never do that to you?"

Just because Barrett has never deliberately hurt me doesn't mean he wouldn't. Everything that's happened since Hugh, Mick, and I decided to catch Jack the Ripper has taught me that anything, no matter how improbable, can happen. Less than two years ago, I was a solitary woman with no worries except making ends meet. Now my situation is so different that I feel as if I've stumbled into foreign territory and found myself among people whose motives I can't understand. Maybe Barrett isn't the kind, decent, loyal man who loves me; maybe he's just a policeman who would stop at nothing to achieve his ambitions. I live a life of subterfuge and deception; maybe he's no different. I don't know what to believe. Nerve-wracked by today's events, I clasp my hands around my head, afraid I'm losing my grip on reality.

"Sarah?" Barrett is watching me with concern. "What's the matter?"

I know he has a job to do, and he's more objective about the situation than I am. But in this moment, all I'm absolutely sure of is that he's chosen his job over me, and I must choose between him and my father. My first loyalty is to my father, the first man I ever loved. That makes Barrett, who's determined to hunt him down, the enemy. My thinking may be irrational, but it's overpowered me.

I lower my hands, square my shoulders, and level an icy stare at Barrett. "Get out."

Barrett's mouth drops. "Sarah—?"

Furthermore, I believe Lucas is the magic ball of string that will lead the way through the maze to the Minotaur—my father. I mustn't give Barrett an opportunity to wrest the ball of string from me.

I point at the door. *"Get out!"*

CHAPTER 19

I spend a sleepless, tearful night reliving my argument with Barrett. Plagued by regrets, I wonder if he really is trying to help my father. But I can't shake my conviction that I mustn't betray my father to a policeman who's duty-bound to act according to the law rather than for love of me. I've made my choice. I've banished Barrett from my life; I've self-fulfilled my own prophecy that any man I love will leave me. Despite my sorrow, I can only try to convince myself that I'm glad it's over between us.

In the morning, I rise late and force myself to wash, dress, and go downstairs. Fitzmorris hands me a cup of tea. Mick, standing by the parlor window, gazing down at the street, says, "Miss Sarah, look."

I carry my cup over to him and see a crowd of people outside. It's too foggy to discern who they are; I can't hear what they're saying. More people join the crowd as I watch. "What is this about?"

"There's Hugh," Mick says. "Maybe he can tell us."

I see Hugh weaving his way through the crowd, toward the house. He went out last night to see Tristan Mariner. The bell jangles as he unlocks the door. I hear people shouting at him before he closes it. He vaults up the stairs and comes into the parlor, face grim, with a bundle of newspapers that he spreads on the table.

"The excrement has hit the wind," he says.

My own image jumps out at me from the front pages—photographs of me leaving Newgate Prison. This is worse than I expected.

"Dear God," Fitzmorris murmurs.

"Those people outside are reporters wanting to interview you and curiosity seekers wanting a good gawk," Hugh tells me.

Even worse than the pictures are the headlines—all variations on the one in the *Observer*, which proclaims, "Reporter's hoax exposed." Aghast, I say, "They're blaming me for the hoax!"

"Sonsofbitches!" Mick says.

The *Chronicle* contains fanciful illustrations of prison wardens opening a coffin and myself photographing Amelia's decomposed corpse. I skim the text that accompanies the pictures: *Sarah Bain is guilty of irresponsible reporting . . . tried to further her ambitions by deceiving the public . . . a grievous insult to the memory of the Baby Butcher's victims.*

Hugh puts his arm around me. "Don't pay any attention to that drivel. Anybody who knows you will know it isn't true."

"But everybody else will believe it."

Fitzmorris reads aloud from the *Star*: "'Sir Gerald Mariner made a splash when he took over the *Daily World*. His contest with the police has ended in a belly-flop. He should have stuck to banking.'"

"He ain't gonna like that," Mick says, "but compared with Miss Sarah, he got off easy."

Of course the press went easy on Sir Gerald. He's wealthy and powerful and can retaliate against anyone who crosses him, whereas I'm safe game. But now that I've had time to get over my initial anger at him for firing us, I can pity him. He's trying to keep his foothold on ground that crumbled after his nervous breakdown.

"Listen to this editorial from our friend Mr. Palmer," Hugh says. "'Sarah Bain, our reporter who claimed that Amelia Carlisle escaped execution, has been dismissed. We do not tolerate incompetence or unethical behavior from our staff. We are more committed to our pursuit of the truth than ever, and we shall continue to shine our light into the dark places where it hides.'" Hugh says with disgust, "The pompous ninny."

And now I see, in the *Telegraph*, a column about Benjamin Bain, the prime suspect in the rape and murder of Ellen Casey. The head-line reads, "Like Father, Like Daughter." The author is Charlie Sullivan, the drunken reporter that Hugh and I met at Harry Warbrick's wake. In the article, he speculates that the hoax is but a harbinger of many crimes I'll commit. He's taken his revenge on me for stealing his tip.

"My reputation is ruined." Little good it did me, keeping a low profile for most of my life; now the limelight has scorched me in the most shaming way possible.

Mick pats my hand. "Don't worry, Miss Sarah—we're gonna fix it."

"We certainly are," Hugh says, "and we'll knock some heads together while we're at it."

Although heartened by their support, I know their aim tends to exceed their reach. "How?"

Hugh responds with his usual bright-eyed, reckless, grandiose response to a challenge. "We'll start by solving Harry Warbrick's murder."

"And proving it had to do with Amelia's hangin'," Mick says.

I don't ask how we're going to accomplish that. Charting a course all the way to the end isn't our strong point.

"Sarah, you'd better stay home until the hubbub dies down," Fitzmorris says.

I'm loath to face the mob, but I say, "I can't. I have to look for my father."

"It can wait a few days," Hugh says. "Reid and all the king's men and horses couldn't catch Jack the Ripper. They won't catch your father. His trail is twenty-four years cold."

"Things have changed." Last night I didn't share Barrett's news with Hugh and Mick because I was too upset. Now I tell them that Barrett is in charge of the manhunt.

They frown in consternation. We all know Barrett is a clever, diligent detective, and his chances of finding my father, albeit probably low, must still be many times higher than Reid's.

"Well, well, another contest," Hugh says with glum humor. "I'm losing count."

The *Daily World* versus the police; my friends and I versus Malcolm Cross; and myself pitted against the man I still love. My father is the prize that I, not Barrett, must locate. "I'm going to Ely today."

"How're you gonna get past the mob?" Mick asks.

Fifteen minutes later, I'm dressed in the indigo velvet hat and blue wool cape I wore to Clerkenwell, the tapestry bag in hand, waiting while Hugh goes downstairs and opens the front door. I hear the crowd roar and Hugh say, "Sarah Bain is coming to speak to you, so if you'll just be patient for a few moments." I make my escape via the back door and down the alley.

★ ★ ★

An hour later, I'm at the townhouse in Chelsea, knocking at the back door. A manservant answers, and I ask for Sally. He nods and shuts the door, and I think he's gone to fetch her, but it's her mother who appears, bristling with rage.

"What is it this time?"

"I need Sally to come with me."

"Where?" Mrs. Albert demands. "What for?"

I can't tell her that I'm going to Ely to look for Lucas Zehnpfennig, or why. She wouldn't approve. When I hesitate to answer, she says, "It must be about your father again. Well, if you find him, tell him that the coppers were here looking for him yesterday."

Barrett must have seen the address written on the police report and followed the clue. He's already managed to track down my father's second family. I can't hide my shock or dismay. "What did you tell them?"

"I said that I don't know Benjamin Bain or where he is. But Inspector Reid already knew he'd been married to me and using the name 'George Albert.'"

Fresh shock assails me. "*Inspector Reid* was here?"

"Yes. He said he's going to flush your father out from whatever bush he's hiding in."

Reid obviously isn't satisfied to trust the search to Barrett. He's undertaken his own search, and the fact that he discovered Mrs. Albert means he's smarter than I thought. Does Barrett know about her? Maybe he does and deliberately neglected to tell me. That I've kept secrets from him doesn't make the idea any less hurtful. Reid's plan to use Barrett as a weapon against me has worked too well.

"He said your father's going to be arrested and hanged for the murder of that girl Ellen Casey." Mrs. Albert's manner blends dread and triumph.

I think that a part of her still loves Benjamin Bain and fears for him even while she hates him for leaving her. But she relishes the idea of him executed for the crime. "Did Reid question Sally?"

"I didn't tell him about her. He didn't seem to know that your father and I have a daughter. And I intend to keep it that way."

At least one secret is still safe from Reid.

"I don't want coppers bothering Sally. I've seen them hanging around outside the house. They must be watching it in case your father turns up." Fearful, Mrs. Albert glances up and down the alley. "I'm keeping Sally inside because if they see her and notice how much she looks like you, they'll know who she is. So don't come around and lure her out. Stay away."

I remember my suspicion of her. "Do you know something about my father?"

She slams the door in my face.

★　★　★

The train to Ely thunders through fens that spread as far as I can see from my seat by the window. Gray clouds hang low over snow-frosted black earth in fallow fields, brown reed beds, and stunted, leafless trees. A few cottages on stilts and windmills with skeletal arms dot the flat terrain. Human figures, dwarfed by the great expanse of land and sky, move here and there. A tiny hunter aims a rifle, and the inaudible gunshot sends a flock of geese flying upward. The scenery is desolate, beautiful, and unfamiliar. My father never brought me here on a photography expedition, even though it's no farther from London than the places we went. I'd thought he chose our destinations randomly, but now I believe he was avoiding the place of his origin.

I wonder if he ever returned to Ely.

In the distance, a great cathedral floats like a ship in full sail above the fens, at first as insubstantial as if sketched on gauze, then massively solid as the train rumbles nearer. Its stone towers loom over the station at which I alight. I walk through the cold, damp, smoky town that lies in the cathedral's shadow, along narrow streets past ancient houses. At the post office, I learn that there's no Benjamin Bain, George Albert, or Lucas Zehnpfennig on the mail delivery route, but there is a Mrs. Herman Zehnpfennig.

The Zehnpfennig house stands among several old mansions near the edge of town. The ivy that covers their stone walls gives them an air of forbidding privacy. The Zehnpfennig mansion has rose bushes, bristling with carmine thorns like barbed wire, in its front garden. I hope I've tracked my elusive quarry to his family abode, but I hesitate, with my hand on the iron latch of the gate. If I find Lucas here, what shall I do? I've no authority to question or detain him. I could pretend I'm soliciting donations for charity, strike up a conversation, and ascertain that he is the Lucas Zehnpfennig who lived in Clerkenwell in 1866, but what next?

As I vacillate, two women dressed in black come out of the mansion. One is elderly, with a dowager's hump. She leans on the arm of the thin younger woman as they walk down the steps and path.

"Good day," I call. "Are you Mrs. Zehnpfennig?"

The women lift their gazes to me. Similar double chins and downturned mouths mark them as mother and daughter. The daughter is some dozen years my senior. The mother, who must be over seventy, answers in a withered voice, "Yes?" She clutches her throat and stares.

"I'm looking for Lucas Zehnpfennig. Does he live here?"

She hobbles back into the house. The younger woman follows, glaring over her shoulder as if I've committed some atrocity, and the door slams behind them. Startled, I let myself in the gate and knock on the door, but they don't answer. I've traveled seventy miles to meet an impenetrable wall of silence.

A voice calls, "I've never seen Ada Zehnpfennig move so fast. What did you say to her?"

I turn to see a woman standing in the doorway of the mansion across the street. "I asked for Lucas Zehnpfennig."

"No wonder." The woman is perhaps sixty years old, top-heavy with a florid face and hair colored ginger with henna and done up in rolls. She smiles in sly amusement and puts a finger to her lips. "It's forbidden to speak that name in Ada's hearing."

I thought Ada Zehnpfennig seemed stunned even before I said Lucas's name, but maybe this trip isn't a waste of time after all. I cross the street. "Why is it forbidden?"

"Who are you?" the woman asks, curious.

I offer the same false identity I used in Clerkenwell. "I'm Catherine Staunton, a newspaper reporter for the *Daily World* in London." I bring the notebook and pencil out of my tapestry bag. "May I have your name?"

Her red nose quivers as she smells good gossip. Her eyes are like brown marbles, shiny with anticipation. "I'm Edith Maxwell." There's no ring on her finger, and her common manner suggests that she's a servant rather than the lady of the house. "What's a reporter from London want with Lucas Zehnpfennig?"

"He's wanted for a murder in London," I improvise.

"You don't say!"

"My paper received an anonymous tip that he's originally from Ely. I came to see if his family is harboring him here."

"Someone's set you on a wild goose chase," Miss Maxwell says in a pitying tone. "The Zehnpfennigs wouldn't take him in if he was starving and on his hands and knees begging. He's been gone more than thirty years. He knows better than to show his face in Ely."

Finding Lucas so fast would have been a miracle, but his past may provide clues to his present whereabouts. "Why wouldn't they take him in?"

"It's a long story." Miss Maxwell licks her lips, salivating with her eagerness to tell it. "Come in for a cup of tea."

"Thank you." As I enter the house, I glance across the street and see the curtains in Mrs. Zehnpfennig's window twitch.

The parlor to which Miss Maxwell ushers me is oddly arranged, with velvet settees, brass lamps, mahogany tables, cabinets of knick-knacks, and decorative screens pushed against the walls. Then I see an old, white-haired lady in a wheelchair by the front window. She wears a wool housecoat; a quilt covers her lap. The furniture is arranged for maneuvering her chair. Beside it is an armchair where Miss Maxwell presumably sits so they can look outside together.

"How do you do?" I say to the old lady. Instead of replying, she beholds me with a vacant stare.

"That's Mrs. Howard," Miss Maxwell says. "I'm her companion. It's all right to talk in front of her—she's senile, poor dear." She positions a chair for me next to hers, invites me to sit, and fetches a tea tray that she sets on a table between us.

Now there are three snoopy biddies spying out the window, but there's no sign of life at the house across the street. I prop my notebook on my knee and hold my pencil ready. "Is Ada Zehnpfennig Lucas's mother?"

"Not anymore," Miss Maxwell says, pouring tea. "And she wasn't to begin with." She smiles at my confusion. "His real mother was Ada's younger sister, Mary. Ada and Mary's father owned a hotel on the High Street. When Mary was fourteen, she got with child. She would never say who the father was, but everyone thinks it was a railroad inspector who stayed at the hotel. Ada was married to Herman Zehnpfennig—he was from Germany, and he built a sugar factory outside town. He's dead now. When Lucas was born, Ada and her husband adopted him. But Mary couldn't let him go. She was over there every day. When he was old enough to walk, he would follow her wherever she went, like a pet dog."

I'm scribbling notes to quell my impatience. I don't want to hear Lucas's entire life story, I only want to know where he is now, but if I interrupt her, she might think me rude and change her mind about talking to me.

"They were so close, it wasn't healthy. When Lucas misbehaved, Mary always made excuses for him. She never gave Ada a chance to be his mother. I once heard them arguing about it. But Ada had her own child a few years later, a girl, Josephine—that was her you saw; she still lives with her mother—she never married. So Ada let Mary take care of Lucas. And then one day, when Lucas was twelve"—Miss Maxwell pauses for dramatic effect— "Ada caught Lucas with Josephine—*if you know what I mean.*"

My interest perks up because I think I understand, but I want details. "No, I don't know what you mean."

Miss Maxell speaks in a loud whisper even though there's nobody except her senile mistress to overhear. "Josephine was lying on her bed with her skirts up, and Lucas was on top of her with his pants down."

Now I'm writing as fast as I can. This statement is evidence that Lucas has molested at least one young girl and indication that he's guilty of raping and killing Ellen Casey. "How do you know?"

"My sister worked for the Zehnpfennigs. She overheard the whole uproar."

"What happened to Lucas?"

"They sent him to a boarding school. I remember the day. Mary cried and screamed and clung to him. Ada and Mr. Zehnpfennig had to pull her off. She had a nervous breakdown, and they sent her to the madhouse. She was there for six months. But Lucas didn't learn his lesson. Two years later, one of his classmates invited him home for Christmas, and he was caught with the boy's little sister. He was expelled. Ada and her husband refused to have him in their house, even though Mary begged them to take him back. Mr. Zehnpfennig found work for him on a ship that was sailing to the West Indies. Mary had another breakdown and went to the madhouse again, for a whole year. When she came home, she was a different person—always cross and sad. She never got over losing her son. But life has to go on, doesn't it? She went to work at the hotel, and she eventually married a man she met there—a photographer. He came to Ely to take pictures, and he was staying at the hotel."

My heart gives a mighty thump; my hand stops writing. "A *photographer*?" Disbelief makes my voice shrill.

"Yes," Miss Maxwell says, puzzled by my reaction. "He took a liking to Mary. After the wedding—"

I clear my throat and interrupt, "Who was he?"

"A Mr. Bain. I don't remember his first name. He was far from rich, but Mary's family thought marriage would cure what ailed her, and she couldn't expect anyone better. And Mr. Bain was a nice, kind man."

My mind careens between so many thoughts that it can't fix on one long enough to examine it, let alone determine which is the most significant or shocking.

Mary was my mother!

Here's a secret from the past that I never imagined, that's completely taken me by surprise. I feel as if I've been digging for coal in a mine and excavated a hole down which I've fallen a thousand feet into the strange light of a different world. The story I've been impatiently listening to is about my mother's life before she met my father! 'Mary' is such a common name; I didn't realize that my mother and the girl Miss Maxwell is speaking of are one and the same.

And Lucas Zehnpfennig is my half-brother!

It was astonishing enough to learn about Sally, and now to find out that my father wasn't the only one of my parents to have a child whose existence I never suspected. I gaze out the window, dumbfounded because the old woman who lives across the street is my aunt. My resemblance to my mother must be the reason she was so stunned to see me. And the younger woman—Josephine, the relative that Lucas molested—is my cousin.

"After the wedding, Mr. Bain took Mary to London," Miss Maxwell says. "He was going to open a photography shop there. They never returned to Ely, and they didn't keep in contact with Mary's family. I've always wondered what became of them, and Lucas."

It was my half-brother who raped and murdered Ellen Casey! Now I'm wondering if my father was aware of my mother's past. "Did Mr. Bain know about Lucas?"

"Oh yes. There was no hiding it from him; everybody in town knew." Miss Maxwell says, "Moving to London was a fresh start for Mary. I like to think she was happy with Mr. Bain."

I piece together the sequel to her story. When Lucas returned to England, he must have looked up his mother. That's how he came to be in Clerkenwell.

"You said Lucas is wanted for a murder," Miss Maxwell says, eager for news in exchange for her old gossip. "Whose murder?"

I'm so upset that my voice falters as I say, "A young girl named Ellen Casey."

"How did she die?"

"She was . . ." Unable to voice the ugly, obscene word, I say, "She was interfered with and strangled."

"Dear me." Mrs. Maxwell's eyes shine with thrilled horror. "Well, I can't say I'm surprised. I hope they find him before he hurts anybody else."

"Do you know where he could be?"

"Haven't the slightest idea. I didn't know he came back to England. Neither does anybody else in town, or I'd have heard. But I can tell you this: the one person in the world who loved Lucas was his mother. I'll wager that if you find Mary, you'll find Lucas too."

CHAPTER 20

My mother had an illegitimate child.
Lucas Zehnpfennig is my half-brother.

The revelations pound in my mind like a deafening drumbeat as I ride the train back to London. My father is a mystery, but I never suspected that my mother had a secret. My discoveries cast a new, transforming light on my whole life, including the day I met Lucas. The quarrel between my mother and father must have arisen because she had let Lucas fondle me. And my perception of Ellen Casey's murder changes drastically. My parents must have suspected that Lucas killed Ellen, but my father's police file contained not a word about Lucas and no statement from my mother.

I think she was forced to choose between her son and her husband, and she chose her son. And my father and I aren't the only ones who've suffered because of her choice.

I dread telling Sally. I can't even soften the blow with new information regarding our father's whereabouts. All I've brought from Ely are more questions. Why did Lucas write to Benjamin Bain instead of his mother—*my* mother? After her death, I found no letters among her belongings, but she and Lucas could have been in touch while I was away at boarding school. I'll never know. Even if she knew where Lucas went, she can never tell; she took her secrets to her grave. And I can never tell her that I know what she did or how devastated I am by her betrayal.

When I arrive home, in dire need of comfort, I hear raised voices in the parlor. "You little sneak!" The shrill, angry voice belongs to Catherine Price. "How could you do this to me?"

I find Catherine and Mick standing in the middle of the room, she with her hands on her hips, her chin thrust at Mick. She wears her blonde hair in an elaborate confection of ringlets and has on a low-necked red satin gown whose full skirts are puffed out by petticoats. She must have come straight from the stage. Her face is bright with rouge, her sapphire eyes ablaze with anger.

"It was for your own good," Mick says.

Hugh and Fitzmorris are sitting on the sofa, an intimidated captive audience. Catherine whirls to face me. "Did he tell you?" She points at Mick, whose expression blends the same defiance and guilt that I used to see when he was a street urchin, when he confessed to stealing food in order to survive. "Today he went behind my back and talked to my friends, trying to prove that Lionel wasn't with me the night the hangman was murdered."

So Mick hasn't given up trying to pin the murder on Sheriff Hargreaves. "I did prove it," he says to me. "After the show, Catherine went to a tavern with some other folks. They say she went home by herself. Her landlady says she were alone in her room 'til the next morning."

I'm impressed by his detective work. He's poked big holes in the alibi that Catherine had provided for Hargreaves.

"My landlady is half-blind and deaf, and she sleeps like a log," Catherine says. "She doesn't know I went out late that night to meet Lionel, and I came back before she woke up." But Catherine's voice rings false.

I'm grieved to see her stand by her lover despite evidence that he could be guilty of murder. "Catherine, don't."

"You're lyin'." Affection gentles Mick's rebuke. "Lyin' for him. Lyin' to yourself too."

"Don't protect him, Catherine," Hugh urges. "He's not worth it."

Catherine ignores Hugh and jabs her finger at Mick. "*You're* jealous. That's why you're trying to get Lionel in trouble. Because—"

Mick suddenly looks cornered, frightened. We all know that Catherine knows how he feels about her, but she's never said so.

"That's enough," Hugh snaps.

She's too angry and reckless to desist. "You think that if you can get rid of Lionel, then you can have me." She tosses her blond ringlets. "Well, you're a fool. I'll never—"

Hugh, Fitzmorris, and I shout, *"Catherine!"*

She sputters into silence, too late. Mick cringes as if he wants to drop through a hole in the floor.

Now Catherine has the grace to be ashamed. "Mick, I'm sorry." She knows that she owes her life to him, that he risked his own to save her; she doesn't really want to repay him with cruelty. She reaches out her hand to him. "I didn't mean—"

His humiliation turns to anger. "You're more a fool than me. Hargreaves don't care about you."

"Yes, he does!" Catherine's indignation can't hide the doubt that flickers across her face. "We're in love. We're engaged."

"You think he's gonna dump his wife to marry you? Hah! He's just havin' fun with you and usin' you for an alibi."

"He promised." Catherine sounds like a little girl trying to convince herself that her dreams of becoming a princess will come true.

"You oughta run from that guy as fast and far as you can," Mick says, determined to protect her even though she's rejected and mocked him. "Before he hurts you."

"He's right," I say, reluctant yet obligated to make Catherine face reality.

Catherine turns to Hugh, whose masculine judgment she trusts. Hugh nods sadly.

"You're all wrong. I'm going to marry Lionel," Catherine declares. "Just wait and see!" Head high, she exits the room in a swish of red satin.

My mother chose Lucas Zehnpfennig over her husband; I chose my father over Barrett; and now Catherine has chosen Sheriff Hargreaves over Mick. Choices can have serious repercussions, but they have to be made, no matter if they set in motion a steamroller of consequences that will crush us into dust someday.

Mick gazes unhappily after Catherine, then flops onto the chaise longue. He blinks, trying not to cry. Hugh, Fitzmorris, and I tactfully avert our eyes. Fitzmorris says, "I think we could all use some hot cocoa," and goes to the kitchen.

In a gallant attempt to pretend that the scene with Catherine never happened, Hugh says, "Sarah, welcome home. What happened in Ely?"

I relate my discoveries. Hugh, flabbergasted, whistles. Mick, distracted from his woes, says, "Crikey!"

Something occurs to me that failed to earlier. "The conspiracy of silence between the witnesses to Amelia Carlisle's hanging isn't the only one. There was another, between my parents and Lucas Zehnpfennig."

"They covered up the truth about Ellen Casey's murder." Hugh shakes his head, regretful. "That was noble of your father, keeping quiet for the sake of his wife and stepson."

I smile despite my outrage at the situation. Hugh would find the most charitable way to view it. But I'm still furious at my mother because she chose Lucas over my father—and, in effect, over me, her second child. That I was less beloved than the first is apparent from the harsh way she treated me. These ideas are like a chest of serpents that I don't want to open.

Fitzmorris brings cups of steaming cocoa on a tray. I sip mine, and the sweet, milky chocolate soothes my spirits. I ask Hugh, "What did you do today?"

"I sat in pubs near Newgate, bought drinks for the regulars, and chatted them up. It appears that Governor Piercy wasn't telling the truth when he said he was in his residence the whole night of Harry Warbrick's murder. I spoke to the cab driver who picked him up outside Newgate at eleven thirty. He knows Piercy; he's driven him before."

I'm interested to learn that Sheriff Hargreaves isn't the only suspect whose alibi has evaporated. "Where did he take Governor Piercy?"

"He dropped him off at Spitalfields Market."

"That's not far from The Ropemaker's Daughter."

"It weren't Piercy." Mick lies on the chaise longue with his arms crossed over his face. "Hargreaves done it."

"Governor Piercy had the opportunity to kill Harry Warbrick," Hugh points out.

"So what? It don't mean he's guilty for sure," Mick says. Either he still hopes that if he incriminates the sheriff, he'll win Catherine's hand, or his mind is too one-tracked to change course.

"A witness has placed the governor near the scene of the murder," I say. "Have you found anybody to place Hargreaves there?"

"Nope. But give me time."

"There are still four other suspects," I say.

"Forget 'em and help me go after Hargreaves."

"Mick, we can't focus on him and ignore everybody else." Kindness softens Hugh's exasperation. "To restore Sarah's reputation and get our detective agency back up and running, we have to solve this case before the police do. We can't afford to be wrong."

"I know I'm right. I'm gonna get Hargreaves if it's the last thing I ever do." Mick runs upstairs, and his bedroom door slams.

The rest of us exchange troubled glances. Hugh says to me, "Any ideas?"

CHAPTER 21

Snowflakes gray with soot drift from the opaque sky as Mick, Hugh, and I walk past Newgate Prison the next morning. "Too bad we can't just barge in and grab her by the scruff," Mick says.

"What fun would that be?" Hugh laughs, always happy to start a new venture.

Yesterday we decided to confront Mrs. Fry about her false tip about Amelia Carlisle. But if she's inside the prison, she's safe from us; we're banned from Newgate, and the wardens won't let us in.

We go to the Copper Kettle, a pub near the prison, sit at a table in the back, and order hot whisky. Hugh reaches in his pocket and brings forth the letter we composed yesterday so that we can reread it one last time. *I saw you outside Harry Warbrick's pub the night he was murdered. Meet me at the Copper Kettle right now, or I'll tell the police.*

"Good?" Hugh asks.

Mick and I nod. Hugh seals the letter in its envelope and gives it to Mick with a shilling. Mick runs off. He seems deliberately cheerful today, as if he's trying to put his quarrel with Catherine behind him. As Hugh and I wait for him to return, I try not to think of Barrett.

"Don't worry about Barrett," Hugh says, perceptive as always. "He's a good detective, but if you couldn't find your father, I doubt he'll be successful. And you two will make up."

I smile. Although I don't believe him, I appreciate his effort to console me. "Thank you."

Mick returns. "I bribed a guard to deliver the letter to Mrs. Fry." He sits down, breathless from running. "Do you think she'll come?"

"Oh yes," Hugh says. "If she killed Harry Warbrick, she'd rather negotiate terms with a blackmailer than be arrested. If she's innocent, she'll want to tell the blackmailer to shove it."

We nurse our drinks, watching the clock. Twenty minutes later, Hugh points at the window. "Didn't I tell you?"

There, outside the pub, is Dorothea Fry in her blue-plaid wool coat and dark blue felt bonnet. We exchange triumphant smiles. Mrs. Fry reaches for the door, her expression stoic. I can't tell whether she's come to negotiate with or tell off her blackmailer. I feel a twinge of panic. Once we've lured her to us, how are we going to make her tell us why she played the hoax? Again, we've not planned far enough ahead.

Mrs. Fry pauses, then walks away. We gape at one another. Mick says, "She musta smelled a rat."

We run out to the street. The gray falling snow obscures the figure of Mrs. Fry, who's halfway down the block, walking fast. She turns, sees us, and breaks into a run.

"Mrs. Fry!" I call as we chase her. "Stop!"

She turns the corner onto Newgate Street. Following her, we come upon a crowd gathered outside the prison. We weave between people, searching for Mrs. Fry. She's gone. We stop, panting from breathlessness and frustration. I notice that the crowd is larger than the daily assembly of folks who loiter outside Newgate to watch the police bring in criminals. Reporters and photographers flock around a police wagon parked by the main entrance.

Mick speaks to a teenaged boy who stands near us. "What's going on?"

"They caught the bloke who hanged the hangman."

"No!" Mick exclaims. Hugh and I stare in dismayed surprise.

"Yeah." The boy points at the wagon. "He's in there."

"Who is he?" Mick asks.

"Dunno."

Two men climb down from the seat beside the wagon's driver. One is Inspector Reid, the other Malcolm Cross.

"Our friends have beaten us to the punch," Hugh says glumly.

I should be glad of justice for Harry Warbrick, but there goes our hope of solving his murder and restoring my reputation. Ashamed of my selfishness, I'm also avid to see who the culprit is. We jostle our way closer to the wagon and stand on tiptoe while Reid unlocks its door. Two constables drag out the prisoner—a stout man, hatless in a black overcoat with a fur collar. He looks to be in his fifties, his gray hair trimmed short around a bald crown. His hands are cuffed behind his back, and his pudgy face wears a dazed, terrified expression. I've never seen him before. He disappears from my view as the police march him into Newgate amid exploding flash powder. Reporters shout questions; the crowd roars and jeers. The heavy door yawns open, swallows the constables and prisoner, then slams shut.

Hugh shakes his head in amazement. "I was so sure it had to be one of the people at Amelia's hanging."

"Me too," Mick says, crestfallen.

I can tell he's thinking of Sheriff Hargreaves and Catherine. This new development has dashed his hopes as well as mine. "We were all wrong." I can't believe it. Every instinct still tells me that Amelia's hanging is germane to the murder, and the witnesses are still suspects.

Inspector Reid and Malcolm Cross stand on the steps in front of the main entrance, flanked by constables. Reid holds up his hand, and the crowd grows quiet. Our two foes, joined in an alliance we never expected, are about to make a speech. Flashes illuminate their self-congratulatory expressions as they pose for the cameras.

"I'm pleased to announce that I have arrested the man who murdered Harry Warbrick." Reid raises his voice above the murmurs of excitement. "His name is Jacob Aarons."

We exchange baffled glances: The name means nothing to us; the killer is someone we never came across during our investigation. But of course we focused on the suspects who were at Amelia Carlisle's hanging.

"Mr. Aarons is a dealer of curios and antiques," Malcolm Cross says. "I discovered that he had quarreled with Harry Warbrick. They were bitter enemies."

Mrs. Warbrick had said that her husband had been very well liked. It appears that by taking her word for it, instead of looking for his enemies, we were seriously negligent.

"Harry Warbrick had promised to sell Mr. Aarons the rope he'd used to hang Amelia Carlisle," Reid says.

Mick curses under his breath. Hugh mutters, "I'd forgotten all about the missing rope."

Malcolm Cross had profited by investigating the angle that we overlooked.

"Mr. Aarons had made a down payment, but Harry Warbrick decided he could make more money selling the rope in pieces." Cross savors the limelight, his voice shrill with excitement. "He reneged on his promise."

And here's a motive we failed to unearth—not a conspiracy of silence regarding a notorious criminal's execution, but a simple business deal gone wrong.

"Mr. Aarons was furious," Reid says. "He assaulted Harry Warbrick at The Ropemaker's Daughter. They fought. Some customers threw Mr. Aarons out of the pub. They heard Mr. Aarons threaten to come back and kill Warbrick."

I'm ashamed of myself for not questioning Warbrick's customers. Perhaps I deserve the ruin that the newspapers have made of my reputation.

"I paid a visit to Mr. Aarons at his shop in Bloomsbury," Cross says. "I found the rope hidden in a cupboard, and a pair of shoes with blood on the soles."

I close my eyes for a moment and see footprints in the blood on the floor of The Ropemaker's Daughter. Malcolm Cross had tracked them to their source while my friends and I had been chasing wild geese.

"Mr. Cross reported his discovery to me," Reid says. "I arrested Mr. Aarons."

The audience cheers. Reid and Cross beam. As the reporters shout questions, Cross calls, "Read the details in the *Daily World*!" The constables hold back the crowd to let him and Reid descend the steps and stroll down the street as if they're royalty.

But I realize that the story I've just heard is far from conclusive. I look at Hugh and Mick and see the same thought in their eyes, the same hope of getting ourselves out of disgrace. We hurry through the departing crowd, after Cross and Reid. Cross ignores us; he and Reid keep walking. Reid grins and says, "Case closed, no thanks to you."

"No, it ain't," Mick says.

"You proved that Mr. Aarons was at the scene of the murder," I say to Reid. "You haven't proved he's guilty of killing Harry Warbrick."

"That's for a jury to decide," Reid says, "but he's sure to be convicted. There's enough evidence."

"Evidence that he's a thief, not a murderer," Hugh says.

Scorn curls Reid's lip. "When he came to steal the rope, Warbrick must have caught him. They fought, and Mr. Aarons killed Warbrick. Then he tried to make it look like suicide."

"How do you know that's true?" I say.

"You're just trying to poke holes in the case against Mr. Aarons so you won't look so bad." Nettled, Reid walks faster. I think he's not as sure of himself as he would like to be.

Cross deigns to acknowledge me with a sneer. "You tripped yourself up once. Haven't you learned your lesson?"

I hurry to catch up with Reid. "You may be railroading an innocent man while the real killer goes free."

"You're entitled to your opinion. I stand by mine."

"If you're so confident that you're right, then why are you getting hot under the collar?" Hugh asks. "If you have any doubts, the time to admit them is now, not after Mr. Aarons is hanged."

Reid pauses and faces us. "Now that Sir Gerald's cut you from his payroll, you should be looking for another job. If you'll excuse me, PC Barrett and I have a fugitive named Benjamin Bain to catch." He aims an evil smile at me and stalks off.

I halt in my tracks, alarmed by the news that although he thinks the murder is solved, he and Barrett aren't going to drop the hunt for my father.

Hugh says to Cross, "You really shouldn't publish this story."

"That's up to Sir Gerald, and he's happy with it." Cross adds, "He's given me a raise."

"You're putting your career at risk," Hugh says. "If Mr. Aarons proves to be the wrong man, the same thing that happened to Sarah could happen to you."

Cross snorts. "Don't you wish?"

I feel oddly protective toward Sir Gerald. He's not only the cold-hearted businessman who used me and fired me; nor is he only the monster who's taken the law into his own hands and has blood on them. He's a father whose child disappeared, and I'm a child whose father disappeared; I can't help feeling a bond with him despite everything.

"You're endangering Sir Gerald too," I say. "He and the *Daily World* could suffer."

"No worry." Cross is more confident than Reid.

"We ain't gonna stop investigating," Mick says, "not 'til the real killer's behind bars."

"You three rotters listen up." Cross's perpetual smile and relaxed attitude vanish, unmasking the hard-bitten man behind them. "I've worked for newspapers since I was twelve. I quit school to sell them after my dad died, and I had to help my mum support my brothers and sisters. I've always wanted to be a reporter, and this is my chance to make it big." He points his finger at us. "Don't wreck things for me. Or else."

"Or else what?" Mick shoves his face close to Cross's.

Cross's smile returns, malevolent and cunning; he addresses Hugh. "How long have you and Tristan Mariner been lovers?"

I can't breathe. Mick's jaw drops. Hugh turns pale with shock.

"Yeah, I know about you two gal-boys," Cross says. "I followed you to the Bishop Hotel the other night."

Hugh sways as if he's going to faint. I grab his arm to support him. "You don't know anything," I say to Cross. "They're just friends."

"Friends who backscuttle each other." Cross's contemptuous gaze rakes Hugh. "If you didn't want anybody to see you going at it, you should've left the key in the keyhole."

I picture Cross kneeling outside the door of the hotel room, grinning as he spies on Hugh and Tristan. I behold him with hatred and revulsion.

"You bastard!" Mick raises his fists at Cross. "I'll—"

Cross says to all of us, "You'll back off the Warbrick murder case. Or I'll tell Sir Gerald."

★   ★   ★

Late that night I wait up for Hugh. The parlor feels empty despite Mick and Fitzmorris's company, cold despite the fire in the hearth. Hugh has gone to tell Tristan that the bomb has dropped, and their secret is in our enemy's hands.

The sound of the front door opening launches us to our feet. Hugh plods up the stairs, and we sit down before he joins us in the parlor; we don't want to seem too eager to barrage him with unwelcome questions. His face is weary, haggard. He tosses his hat and coat on the rack and carefully lowers himself to the chaise longue as if he's so fragile his bones might break. Fitzmorris hands him a cup of tea. Suspense thickens the silence.

Hugh wraps his hands around the cup, warming his hands, then looks up at us. His green eyes are bloodshot, their lids smudged with purplish shadows. "I told Tristan that if he wanted to call us quits, I would understand." The strain in his voice says how much those words cost him. "He said we should stop seeing each other."

Tristan, wracked with guilt about their relationship, terrified of exposure, has broken Hugh's heart rather than face the music. I'm too furious at him to be tactful. "The coward!"

"That's like closing the barn door after the horse is out," Mick says, indignant.

Right now I hate Tristan as much as I hate Malcolm Cross, but Hugh leaps to his defense. "Don't blame Tristan. Cross is more of a danger to him than me. The press has already let my dirty cat out of the bag. Tristan still has everything to lose. If the Church finds out about him, he'll be defrocked and excommunicated. Even worse, he'll have to reckon with Sir Gerald."

Sir Gerald, who's already disappointed with his son for choosing the priesthood instead of joining the Mariner family business. Sir Gerald, who isn't above wreaking violent punishment upon people who run afoul of him, even if they're his own blood kin.

"Tristan needs to put some distance between us. It's the only way he'll be able to deny Malcolm Cross's accusation and protect himself." Hugh's voice is leaden with sorrow. "He's going back to India."

"Like a weasel running off to hide in its hole," I say, disgusted.

"Sarah, please. I know you never liked Tristan, but you're not making things any better."

"I'm sorry." I want to tell him that he's better off without his faithless lover, but he won't believe it; he'll only resent me for saying so.

"You shouldn't be concerned only about Tristan," Fitzmorris says. "If Sir Gerald learns about his affair with you, it won't be only Tristan that he'll punish."

"We'll play along with Cross. We'll stop investigating the

murder," Mick says. I can see that he's reluctant to give up trying to pin it on Sheriff Hargreaves, but his loyalty to Hugh outweighs even his love for Catherine. "Then Cross won't rat you out to Sir Gerald."

I nod. Hugh is also more important to me than finding out who killed Harry Warbrick or salvaging my reputation.

"The hell he won't," Hugh says with a glum laugh. "Oh, maybe not right now, but someday, when he's feeling mean or bored, he'll play his card. Tristan told me that I should go away too."

A stab of panic contracts my stomach. "Go away where?"

"Maybe America. Or Australia. Someplace where nobody knows me and I can change my name and start a new life."

Fitzmorris, Mick, and I are too horror-stricken to speak. The thought of Hugh far away, never to be seen again, carves a painful chasm in my heart. He's my family, my dearest friend. I see from the expressions on their faces that Mick and Fitzmorris are feeling the same loss and grief that I am. We each wait for someone else to find the courage to speak the necessary words.

"You oughta go," Mick says, his voice gruff with reluctance.

"Yes," I say, swallowing a sob. "As much as we would hate to lose you, we want you to—to have a chance at happiness." Fitzmorris nods. I think of Barrett and my father. I suppose I can live without Barrett, and I've had twenty-four years to get used to my father's absence. But I don't think I'll ever get used to Hugh's.

"But there's no place in the world where everybody accepts men like me," Hugh says. "Wherever I go, I'll get in trouble and have to decamp again. Once I start running, there'll be no end to it, and that's no way to live. Besides, Sir Gerald has a long reach." Hugh smiles with wry humor. "You'll have to put up with me for the foreseeable future."

Relief fills the chasm in my heart. Mick whoops with joy, then claps his hand over his mouth, embarrassed. Fitzmorris coughs as he and I wipe away tears.

Hugh too is teary-eyed, touched by the love that he can see in us even though we're too inhibited to express it verbally. "If I have to suffer, it's better to do it among friends."

At least Hugh has us. He once told me that Tristan has few friends and none who truly know him. I experience a rare moment of sympathy for Tristan as I picture him alone in a dark, cold, empty church, praying. I hope God gives him comfort.

"Does this mean we're gonna go ahead with solvin' the hangman's murder?" Mick says cautiously.

"I think we'd better call that quits," Hugh says. "Not on account of Tristan or me, though. There's still Inspector Reid."

"But we have to revive our detective agency," I say. It's our only hope of supporting ourselves, of maintaining our household together.

"No, Sarah," Hugh says, gentle but firm. "We can't give Reid an excuse to keep gunning for your father."

"Yeah, you're right," Mick reluctantly agrees.

"We can't back down," I protest. "Not while we believe that Jacob Aarons didn't murder Harry Warbrick." My reputation is far less important than rescuing the man whose only crime was the theft of a rope.

"Sarah, I admire you for wanting to find the real killer," Hugh says, "but you have to protect your father."

I've been protecting my father all my life, first by keeping quiet about him like my mother told me to and later by trying to prove his innocence. But I suddenly feel as if for twenty-four years I've been walking in a deep, narrow, circular trench that gets deeper and narrower with every footstep. Hugh decided not to spend his life running. Maybe I shouldn't spend mine walking in the same circle. I love my father, but he may never come back to me no matter how much I protect him, no matter if he's guilty or innocent.

I look at my friends' concerned, sympathetic faces. A radical notion seizes me: it's time to start living fully in the present, for myself and for the people I love who are here now. I've lost Barrett; Hugh has lost Tristan; Mick has alienated Catherine. This investigation has cost us dearly, but my friends and I still have one another and our hope of bringing a killer to justice.

I take a deep breath and say, "Reid be damned. We won't give up."

If Hugh is courageous enough to fly in the face of danger, then so am I. Let the ills of the past catch up with me; I'll greet them with open arms—and an ax in my hand, if necessary.

We all I smile at one another, united by the same reckless bravado that spurred our hunt for Jack the Ripper. I feel as if I've levitated up from the trench, and the exhilarating freedom is also terrifying: I've been flung loose into the sky, with nothing to guide me or hold onto and no idea of where or how hard I'll land.

CHAPTER 22

At six o'clock the next morning, Hugh, Mick, and I walk through the streets of Stepney, a mile east from Whitechapel. Daybreak is an hour away, and the lingering night is foggy and chill. "Ernie Leach won't be happy to see us so bright and early." Hugh yawns. "I could've used two more hours of shut-eye."

"We need to corner him before he goes to work," I say.

"You really think he'll talk?" Mick asks.

"I hope so." His odd personality makes him an outsider among the witnesses to Amelia Carlisle's execution and perhaps less tightly bound by the conspiracy of silence.

"But you said he's a stickler for rules," Mick says. "Mum's the word about hangings."

"We'll see," Hugh says.

The fog grows thicker and bitter with smoke and the stench of gas, sulfur, and tar. We hold handkerchiefs over our noses and mouths. The sound of coughing from other people on the streets echoes. The sky glows a yellowish orange from the Stepney gasworks. I hear the roar of the furnaces that burn coal to make gas for lighting streets and buildings. Giant cylindrical gas storage containers loom high above the rooftops, amid clouds of steam. On White Horse Lane, we come upon a terrace of narrow, identical two-story houses, their front stoops flush with the sidewalk, their brick walls black with tar.

"This is like hell on earth," Hugh says, his voice muffled by his handkerchief.

I can taste the tar through mine. The haloes of light around the street lamps are dense with ash particles. We locate number 45, the address on the card that Ernie Leach gave me at Harry Warbrick's wake. It's across the street from the public gardens, whose trees look permanently leafless, suffocated by the tainted air. The windows are dark, but lights shine in others along the row. I knock on the door and call Ernie Leach's name. The house remains silent.

"Either nobody's home, they're all asleep, or they don't want to talk to us," Hugh says.

"I can get to 'em." Mick runs to the end of the row, around the corner.

"Mick, wait," I call as Hugh and I follow. He means to break into the house, and we could end up in jail.

The narrow alley behind the terrace is lit by the glow from the gasworks, lined with dustbins. Mick is standing at the bottom of the stairs that lead to the cellar of Ernie Leach's house, by the open back door. "The lock's broken," he says. "I didn't have to pick it."

Before I can warn him that a thief or other intruder who's up to no good may be inside, he and Hugh have slipped through the door. I follow. If they're in danger, there's no use my staying safe. Beyond a basement kitchen, Mick and Hugh are climbing the stairs. I join them in a narrow passage from which another flight of stairs leads to the second floor. The parlor and dining room, on the right, are dimly lit by the street lamp, and empty.

"I smell gas," Mick whispers.

I've been smelling gas for quite a while. "It's coming from outside."

"No," Mick says, "the gas is on in here. Don't you hear it?"

Now I do hear the hissing from gas jets, and the smell is poisonously strong. Hugh flings open the front door to let in air. We run about, groping along the walls, locating pipes, turning off the jets. We dare not light any lamps for fear of igniting the gas. We race up the stairs.

"Mr. Leach!" I call, nauseated and half-asphyxiated.

It no longer matters whether we get in trouble for entering his home without permission; his safety is paramount. The second-floor hall is completely dark. I fumble around, twist a doorknob, and pull. A flood of gas swamps me. I recoil backward, coughing. Light from a window in the room shines on two people in bed—a man and woman, gray-haired, elderly, their eyes closed.

"Wake up!" I cry. "You have to get out."

They don't move. The hiss of gas is the only noise. Hugh and Mick locate and turn off jets and open the window while I shake the couple. I can't rouse them.

"We have to see if there's anybody else in the house," Hugh says between coughs.

Mick opens a door across the hall. "Two more in here!"

It's a younger couple asleep in bed. The man isn't Ernie Leach. While Hugh tries to wake them and Mick turns off other gas jets and opens the window, I stumble up the stairs to the attic. "Mr. Leach! Are you there?" I totter into another room filled with gas.

In a bed beneath the slanted ceiling, Ernie Leach lies on his back, silent, motionless, his mouth agape. His chest isn't rising or falling; I don't hear breaths. I fall to my knees, overcome by the fumes. Hugh and Mick come and support me down the stairs. I resist.

"We have to save him!"

"We can't take all these people out by ourselves," Hugh says. "We need to get help."

At the bottom of the lower flight of stairs, wheezing and retching, we charge toward the open front door. Hugh pushes me ahead of him. I trip off the stoop and reel into the street.

An enormous bang erupts behind me, louder than the boiler explosion in the factory where my mother and I once worked. I scream as a blast of flaming-hot wind launches me off my feet. I fly through air filled with smoke and bricks. The world is on fire but silent; the bang has deafened me. Terrified for Hugh and Mick, I wail their names.

A crash like a black wall slamming into me obliterates all senses and thoughts.

★ ★ ★

The sound of voices echoing, brisk footsteps, and wheels rattling penetrates my groggy consciousness. Pain throbs in my forehead. My mouth tastes sour, and when I lick my lips with my parched tongue, they're chapped and scaly. The rough pillow against my cheek smells of bleach. My eyelids, gummed shut with sleep, crack open. Light sears my vision; my head throbs harder, the pain like knives jabbing my skull. A gray blanket covers my body, and metal rails surround the bed in which I lie. I touch my head and feel a bandage wrapped around it. Panic jolts me alert. I don't know where I am, and I'm lying wounded, at the mercy of strangers. I moan as I struggle to sit up.

"Sarah!"

Two dark figures loom over me, then they coalesce into one. It's Sally. She's crying, clasping my hands. "Thank God! I was afraid you weren't going to wake up."

I'm relieved to see her, but confused. "Where am I?" My voice is a raspy croak.

"In London Hospital."

My vision is still blurry, but now I see the long room where foggy daylight fills tall windows. My bed is one of many that are arranged in two rows against the walls. Nurses in gray uniforms tend women who occupy the other beds. Visitors sit beside the patients. In the aisle, tables display vases of flowers whose sweet scents mingle with the bitter odor of medicine.

"Thirsty," I mumble.

Sally raises my head and holds a cup to my lips. I feel dizzy, and as I gulp the water, it dribbles down my chin. I lie back on the pillow and wait for the world to stop spinning. "How long have I been here?"

"Since yesterday morning." Sally wipes my face with a cloth.

"What happened?"

"Don't you remember?"

I shake my head, wincing at the pain. The last thing I remember is walking up to Ernie Leach's house.

"There was a gas explosion. It knocked you unconscious. That's what Fitzmorris said the police told him. He told me you were here. You're lucky to be alive."

My panic resurges. "Where are Hugh and Mick?"

"They're in the men's ward," Sally says. "Don't worry—they weren't seriously hurt."

"I want to see them."

A nurse approaches. "Not today. You've had a concussion. You need to rest." She takes my pulse and my temperature, then departs.

My thoughts are fuzzy, as if swaddled in cotton. I squint at Sally to bring her face into sharper focus. "Your mother wanted you to stay home." I can't remember why. "She'll be angry."

"It's all right. I want to be here." Sally squeezes my hands. "I was so afraid I was going to lose you. The house you were in and the two adjacent ones were completely destroyed. The police think somebody left the gas on in that house, and somebody next door lit a fire that set off the explosion. Nine people were killed."

Memory comes seeping back. I picture Ernie Leach and the four other people in his house, unconscious in their beds. They must be among those who perished. I moan with horror.

"These accidents are so terrible," Sally says. "People ought to be more careful to make sure the gas is turned off before they go to sleep."

Barrett suddenly joins us. He's in uniform, carrying a bouquet of red roses. He looks worried and tired, but I'm overjoyed to see him; he's the most beautiful sight in the world. But he's never bought me flowers before, and I remember that we parted ways. Is he a figment of my wounded brain? When he sees that I'm awake, a smile lights up his face. Then he notices Sally. "Hello."

Oh, God. Now I know this isn't just a pleasant illusion. I knew I would have to introduce Barrett and Sally someday, and there couldn't be a worse time. "Sally, this is Police Constable Thomas Barrett."

She smiles shyly and curtseys. "I'm so glad to meet you at last."

As Barrett raises his eyebrows at me, I take a deep breath, then say, "This is Sally Albert. She's my sister."

Astonishment widens Barrett's eyes. "You never told me you had a sister."

He must be thinking that he knew I had secrets, but this is one he never imagined. In the awkward silence, I twist the blankets with my trembling hands, afraid that this is the last straw, that when he leaves again, it will be the last time.

"What beautiful roses," Sally says to Barrett. "If you'll give them to me, I'll find a vase for them."

Barrett wordlessly hands her the roses. She bustles off, leaving us alone. He drops into the chair by my bed as if someone just clubbed him behind the knees.

"I owe you an explanation." My mind scrambles to figure out what to tell him and what to leave out. Because of the blow to my head, gathering my thoughts is like trying to pick up lint that's been scattered into a river of treacle.

"Never mind." Barrett's eyes brim with concern. "I was at the police station with the other constables for the morning report when we heard the explosion. We rushed over and saw a big, burning pile of rubble. There were bricks and boards and broken furniture all over the street, and people lying wounded and crying. The fire brigade was spraying water on the fire. We rescued two men who were buried under debris, and I almost died of shock—it was Hugh and Mick. I knew you must be there too. I ran around like a madman, shouting your name." Vestiges of terror darken his gaze. "Then I saw you in an ambulance wagon. Your hair was full of blood. You were so pale and so still, I thought you were dead."

I try to say I'm sorry I scared him, but it takes extra time to translate thoughts into words.

Barrett leans close to me and cups my feverish face in his strong, cool hand. He looks into my eyes and says, "I was angry at you about the contest and the secrecy and everything, but it doesn't seem so important anymore. What's important is you're alive, and I love you." He kisses my lips.

It's the first time we've kissed in public, and I blush with embarrassment, but a rush of happiness lifts me above the pain in my head.

"I'm not going to ask you what you were doing at Ernie Leach's house." Barrett has apparently learned who lived there. "You also don't have to explain about your sister. I'm not letting anything come between us again. Life's too short."

I feel guilty because Barrett is more generous than I deserve. I haven't forgotten my decision to brave the consequences of my past. "No, I want to tell you." I begin with the address I found in my father's police report last year, which turned out to be the Chelsea mansion where Sally and her mother work. I relate my discovery that my father had been living under the name "George Albert," remarried, and had another daughter before he'd disappeared again in 1879.

Barrett scowls.

"I knew you'd be angry." I'd hoped that in his generous state of mind he would be willing to forgive me. If he isn't, this is a consequence I must accept.

"I'm not angry at you. I'm angry at myself. Because I must have acted like such a bastard that you couldn't trust me."

"That's not it," I say, eager to absolve him. "I kept quiet about Sally because of Inspector Reid. If he found out about her—" It's too awful to imagine, let alone speak of, Reid tormenting Sally to satisfy his grudge against me. "I didn't want to force you to choose between doing your duty by telling Reid and protecting Sally and me."

"Of course I'm not going to set Reid on Sally. I'm not a total bastard." Barrett's tone is fond, exasperated. "Besides, she hasn't seen your father in eleven years. She can't possibly have any clue to his whereabouts."

"But she has."

Barrett's eyebrows lift.

This is my chance to shut the barn door before all the horses are out, but I want to come clean. Barrett is right: life is short. I don't want to spend it distrusting and lying to the man I love. I tell him about Lucas Zehnpfennig, my trip to Ely, and my shocking discovery about my family. Barrett, stunned, exhales a gust of breath. It must have been shocking enough for him to learn that I have a half-sister whose existence I kept secret, and now he knows I also have a half-brother who's a pervert. I'm afraid he'll recoil from me in disgust.

Barrett lowers the rail on my bed, sits beside me, and takes me in his arms. "Oh, Sarah. I'm so sorry you had to bear it alone. I wish I'd been there with you."

His sympathy and understanding make me so happy that it's worth almost dying in the explosion. Despite nurses and other patients watching, I lean against Barrett, comforted by his embrace, relieved that my family history hasn't put him off.

"But this is good news, in a way!" Barrett says. "Lucas Zehnpfennig is a new suspect in Ellen Casey's murder. You should let me tell Inspector Reid."

I struggle to articulate my reasons for not telling Reid. "I think that if Reid were to arrest him for the murder, Lucas would accuse my father and turn him in to protect himself."

"But Lucas needs to be found and questioned. I'll help you look. I won't tell Reid."

I underestimated Barrett; my fear of trusting him was unfounded. "Thank you." Words can't convey the enormity of my gratitude. But I'm compromising his duty, putting his career at risk. I remember that Ernie Leach is dead; he took whatever he knew about Amelia Carlisle's hanging to the grave, and a man who's probably innocent is in jail. "When can I go home?"

"The doctor said you should stay here at least two more days."

"Two days! But I have to solve Harry Warbrick's murder." I remember what Sally and I were talking about when Barrett arrived. "And that's not the only murder. Sally said Mr. Leach's death was an accident, but it couldn't have been."

"How do you know?" Barrett says, skeptical. "Did you see something when you were in his house?"

"I don't remember." But my memory of events in the more distant past is crystal clear. "Mr. Leach worked for the gas company. He would have known better than to fall asleep with the gas on."

"Somebody else at the house could have forgotten to shut it off."

Another recollection surfaces in my mind like a thick bubble in a swamp. "All the gas jets were on, all over the house—not just one that somebody forgot. It had to be deliberate."

Barrett frowns, disturbed as well as interested. "Mick and Hugh didn't mention that when I talked to them yesterday. Are you sure?"

"Yes. We ran around shutting them off."

"One of the family could have done it to commit suicide and didn't care if the others were killed." Barrett sounds like he doesn't believe his own theory.

"Both hangmen from Amelia Carlisle's execution have died under dubious circumstances. It can't be a coincidence." I think the repercussions of whatever transpired at the hanging aren't finished, and the past won't stay safely in the past.

Convinced at last, Barrett nods. "It couldn't have been done by Jacob Aarons. He's been locked in Newgate since his arrest. Not to mention, he allegedly killed Harry Warbrick during a fight over the rope. That's not a motive for killing Ernie Leach or his parents or brother and sister-in-law."

"I still think the killer was one of the other witnesses to the execution," I say. "While Inspector Reid and Malcolm Cross were patting themselves on the back, he's killed again. I think he used gas because if the people in the houses smelled it, they would have thought it was coming from the gasworks."

Barrett looks as distressed as I am. "We got the wrong man."

The contest between the *Daily World* and the police seems a crime now that both sides have colluded to put the innocent Jacob Aarons behind bars and failed to prevent the murders of nine people.

"I have to solve the murders before anyone else is killed!" This is no longer just about saving my reputation or detective agency. With an enormous effort, I push myself upright in bed. My whole body hurts. Dizziness whirls the room. Nausea turns my stomach, and I break out in a sweat, but I kick the blankets off me. I'm dressed in a long white flannel gown, which I pull down to cover my legs as I swing them over the side of the bed.

"I don't think you should get up," Barrett says.

"If Sheriff Hargreaves is the killer, he's more ruthless than I thought. I have to warn Catherine." My bare feet touch the cold floor. When I stand, black spots swarm into my vision. My legs crumple.

"Sarah!" Barrett catches me.

Nurses come running. As they put me back to bed and raise the rail that Barrett had lowered, they scold me for trying to get up too soon. One says to Barrett, "She needs peace and quiet. You'd better go."

CHAPTER 23

I stayed three more days in the hospital. The nurses brought me soup and custard and medicine and gave me baths in bed while I listened to the other patients gossiping. Most of the time I slept. On the second day, the dizziness abated, I felt stronger, and the nurses walked me around the ward. On the third day, the doctor discharged me with strict orders to avoid excitement and strenuous physical activity.

Barrett comes to take me home. Dressed in fresh clothes that Fitzmorris sent for me, carrying my pocketbook—which was miraculously rescued from the debris—I lean on Barrett's arm as he escorts me to the men's ward. We find Mick and Hugh in adjacent beds, surrounded by nurses, other patients, and visitors who are laughing at their jokes. Hugh lies on his stomach because his back and scalp are bandaged. When he and Mick hear Barrett and me approach, they look up with expectant smiles that fade just a bit as they recognize us. Hugh must be hoping for a visit from Tristan, Mick from Catherine. I feel sad for them because I gather that Tristan and Catherine haven't shown up. But they greet me with a delight that warms my heart.

Mick, his face marred with bruises and scrapes, yanks open his hospital robe to reveal the cloth tape wound around his chest. "Look, Miss Sarah—I got two broken ribs."

"My goose was almost cooked," Hugh says, and his audience laughs.

Barrett had told me that the explosion set Hugh's clothes on fire. When I ask him and Mick how they're feeling, Mick says, "It only hurts when I laugh."

"I'm not bad, but I'm going to need a wig," Hugh says. "The hair was scorched off the back of my head."

They could have died! I'm angrier on their behalf than my own.

"When we get outta here, we're gonna catch the rotter who turned on the gas," Mick says.

"Unfortunately, the doctor said we have to stay for a few more days," Hugh says.

I don't think our investigation can wait that long. If I want to find out who killed Ernie Leach and the eight other victims, I'll have to carry on by myself. I've relied so much on Mick and Hugh for help with investigations that I feel bereft, forlorn.

After Barrett and I leave the hospital, he hires a cab, and as we ride along Whitechapel Road, he says, "My squad of constables is hot on your father's trail." I experience a jolt of alarm, which Barrett's sly smile quickly dispels. "I gave them a false lead. I said you'd told me your father had been sighted in Kensington three months ago."

"That was clever of you." I'm grateful to Barrett but afraid he'll get in trouble for misdirecting the police's search.

"That's kept them busy while I looked for Lucas Zehnpfennig. No luck yet, though." Barrett adds, "I'm also reinvestigating the Warbrick case. I found a streetwalker who saw a man go inside The Ropemaker's Daughter after closing the night of the murder. It could have been the killer. I've been looking for other witnesses who can describe him. But I'm sure it wasn't Jacob Aarons. He's short; the man was tall."

So are Governor Piercy, Sheriff Hargreaves, Dr. Davies, and the Reverend Starling. Barrett has reestablished them as suspects—a big help. But he's risking his career for my sake, again. "Inspector Reid won't like it." Neither would Barrett's parents.

"Tough," Barrett says. "It's the right thing to do."

I admire his principles, but I can't let him suffer.

At the studio, Barrett comes upstairs with me, helps me remove my coat, seats me on the chaise longue, and covers me with a lap robe. Fitzmorris brings the tea tray and asks Barrett, "Would you like a cup?"

"No, thanks, I have to go to work." Barrett pats my shoulder and says, "I'll come back tonight."

After he leaves, I wait five minutes. Then I set aside my unfinished cup of tea and throw off the lap robe. Fitzmorris says, "Sarah, what are you doing?"

"I'm going out."

"I don't think that's a good idea. You're not well yet."

But I can't sit idle. Even though my head still aches and I'm unsteady, I don my coat and hat, grab my pocketbook, and falter outside. I start down Whitechapel Road and peer through the fog for a cab . . . and bump smack into Barrett.

"Where do you think you're going?" he says.

Surprised, I say, "How did you know—?"

Exasperation tinges his triumphant smile. "I had a hunch that you wouldn't stay put. Now answer my question."

"I'm going to investigate the gas explosion. I thought I'd ask the neighbors if they saw the person who broke into Ernie Leach's house or anyone acting suspicious." I won't tell Barrett that I'm trying to find the real killer before he gets in trouble. If he thinks I'm trying to protect him, he'll stop me.

"Well, think again." Barrett grasps my arm and propels me back to the studio.

I drag my feet. "But the police won't investigate; they think it was an accident."

"I will," Barrett says. "Leave it to me."

"How will you have time while you're looking for Lucas and investigating Harry Warbrick's murder?"

"I'll make time."

"All right, I'll stay home." This time I'll wait longer to make sure he's gone.

He reads my thoughts. "Oh no, you don't." Flinging up his hands in exasperation, he says, "What will it take to knock some sense into you? The gas explosion didn't do it. What must I do to make you take care of yourself?"

Urgency makes me cunning. "Help me get to Mrs. Fry."

Barrett grimaces, vexed because I'm trying to manipulate him. He points at me. "You stay away from those people. If you're right and one of them murdered Harry Warbrick and Ernie Leach and the eight other victims of the gas explosion, he's dangerous."

"That's why I have to stop him. I still think he's Governor Piercy or Sheriff Hargreaves, although Dr. Davies and the chaplain are possibilities."

"By now he'll know that you and Hugh and Mick were at Ernie Leach's house, snooping around even though the Warbrick case is closed. He'll know you survived the explosion, and he'll come after you next."

I grip Barrett's arm. "So if you care about me, you won't wrap me in cotton wool—you'll help me do whatever I can to catch him."

Barrett frowns, removes his helmet, and rakes his hand through his hair. "Why do you want to see Mrs. Fry?"

I feel relieved because he's capitulating, guilty because I'm enticing him to the wrong side of the law again. "I need to find out who put her up to the hoax. I'm certain that person is the killer."

After a long, pensive moment, Barrett says, "I promise to find a way to Mrs. Fry if you promise to rest today."

★ ★ ★

By ten o'clock that night, I begin to suspect Barrett's promise was naught but a ploy to keep me at home. Then the doorbell jangles. Minutes later, Barrett and I are walking toward Whitechapel Station.

"Are you sure you're up for this?" he asks.

"I'm sure." My head pounds in rhythm with my footsteps, and I shiver in the wind that blows sleet against my face.

Riding together in the night train, I'm thankful that Barrett is with me, relieved that he's stepped in to fill the gap left by Hugh and Mick's absence. This venture is a new experience for us, the first time we've collaborated on an investigation. I don't know how either of us is supposed to act, and we'll have to play it by ear.

Newgate Prison is grim enough by day, a vision of hell at night. Lights from within the black granite walls make the fog glow yellow, as if the prison is a cauldron of fire and brimstone. Two police constables waiting by a side door greet Barrett and let us in.

"Thanks, mates," he says.

As they escort us through the prison, I try not to think about what could happen if we're challenged. We reach the women's quadrangle, where gas lamps turned down low illuminate the galleries. Moans and whimpers emanating from the cells sound unearthly, inhuman; the odor of urine seems more intense. Images of alien beasts in caves come to mind so vividly that goose bumps prickle my skin. I wonder if I'm experiencing after-effects from my head injury. It's so dark that I can barely see the iron staircase that we climb single-file. My inability to see what's below me is worse than seeing how high up I am. On the top gallery, one of the constables bangs on Mrs. Fry's door.

"Who is it?" Mrs. Fry's gruff, sleepy voice says.

"Police. We've got a new prisoner for you."

I hear rustling inside. Light shines under the door, the lock rattles, and Mrs. Fry appears in a quilted brown dressing gown and a white nightcap. When she sees me, the annoyance on her puffy face turns to dismay. *"You."*

She tries to close the door, but Barrett and his friends and I push our way into the room. A single flame burns in a sconce on the wall near the rumpled bed; the rest of the room is in shadow, the cold air fusty with the smell of sleep.

"Get out," Mrs. Fry says.

The constables lock the door and stand in front of it. Mrs. Fry grabs a small object from a table—it's a whistle. Before she can put it to her lips, I snatch it. She gasps, her usual stoic calm turned to fear. "What do you want?"

"You know what I want," I say. Barrett looks surprised; he must have assumed I would let him do the talking. "Why did you lie to me about Amelia?"

Defiance gleams through the fear in Mrs. Fry's eyes. "I was just pullin' your leg. And you fell for it hook, line, and sinker."

I ignore the taunt, refuse to let her distract me. "Who put you up to it?"

Her eyes shift, and I can see that I've hit the target, but she pretends not to hear the question. "Got fired from the newspaper, didn't you? That'll teach you to believe everything you're told."

Anger boils under my civil manner. Barrett doesn't intervene, but he's watching me nervously. "Was it Sheriff Hargreaves?"

Mrs. Fry laughs, disdainful. "You want to think it was a big, important man that hoodwinked you, not just little me."

It's true. I not only believe that Piercy or Hargreaves is behind every attempt to sabotage the investigation into Harry Warbrick's murder, but I want the person who made a shambles of my life to be someone of greater stature than Mrs. Fry. "Or was it Governor Piercy?"

"You can stuff your questions up your behind and go."

I glance at Barrett, who shrugs. Either he has no idea how to wring the information from Mrs. Fry, or he thinks that since I started the interrogation, I can finish it by myself.

"Don't look at your boyfriend. He's as stupid as you are," Mrs. Fry says.

Enraged by the insult to Barrett, scared that I won't be able to coerce Mrs. Fry, I look around the room for inspiration. My gaze lights on the framed photographs on the windowsill, and I snatch up the wedding picture of Mrs. Fry and her husband. I don't know what I intend to do with it, but Mrs. Fry reacts as if I've struck her in her most vulnerable spot.

"What the hell do you think you're doing?" She grabs the picture and tries to wrest it from my hands.

The wooden frame comes apart at the joints. Picture and glass fall to the floor. The glass breaks; fragments scatter. Mrs. Fry moans and drops to her knees. When she tries to rescue the picture, I clomp my foot down on it. I'm ashamed of myself for damaging someone's precious possession, but I believe she's shielding a murderer; I'm furious, and I pity her not at all.

"Sarah—" Astonishment rings in Barrett's voice; he's never seen me in full dudgeon.

"You bitch!" Mrs. Fry lunges up at me.

A spear of glass protrudes from the piece of frame in my gloved hand. I thrust it at Mrs. Fry, defending myself. The constables shout. Mrs. Fry recoils. She must have seen countless fights in Newgate and thwarted attacks from bigger, stronger women than I, but terror blanches her face. I've never seen myself in a mirror when I lose my temper, but I've gathered, from other people's reactions, that I'm more than a little menacing. Mrs. Fry reaches under the bed and picks up a truncheon. As she swings it at me, the constables grab her from behind. Barrett grabs me and twists my wrist.

"Sarah, that's enough!"

I drop my weapon, and when he turns me to face him, there's horror in his eyes—but also desire. The heat in my blood has heated his, and his desire enflames mine. We stare at each other, disturbed as well as thrilled by our mutual reaction. His grip on my arms tightens, then relaxes, then tightens again, as if he's reluctant to let me go, afraid of what I'll do next.

The constables seize the truncheon from the red-faced, huffing

Mrs. Fry. As Barrett pushes me toward the door, she yells at me, "If I ever see you again, I'll kill you!"

Now I'm appalled at my own loss of control. This is the last time Barrett will help me with an inquiry, and I've learned nothing. I retort, "You'll be lucky to live long enough to see me again, Mrs. Fry. Ernie Leach was murdered. You could be next."

Shock wipes the outrage off Mrs. Fry's face. "What? But they said it was an accident."

I resist Barrett's effort to get me out before I cause more trouble. "'They' weren't there. I was. Someone turned on all the gas jets in Ernie's house while he was asleep." I remember how he looked, acknowledge what I didn't want to believe at the time. "He was dead before the explosion."

"I don't believe you." But her eyes shine with new fear.

"He was killed by the same person who killed Harry Warbrick, and it wasn't the curio dealer. Whoever it was wanted to make sure neither hangman talked about Amelia's hanging."

Mrs. Fry manages a poor semblance of her usual calm self-possession. "Everybody knows I'm no snitch."

"Don't think you're safe," Barrett interjects. "All I have to do is spread a rumor that the police are reopening the case and you're cooperating with our inquiries, and you'll have a target painted on your back."

"You wouldn't."

"The killer will think you're talking whether you are or not," Barrett says.

Mrs. Fry crumbles. "Oh, God."

"The only way to protect yourself is to finger the killer," Barrett says. "Tell us who put you up to the hoax."

As she shakes her head, I say, "Which was it, Governor Piercy or Sheriff Hargreaves?"

"You got it all wrong." Mrs. Fry's face takes on the reckless, triumphant expression that I once saw on a pickpocket who jumped off a bridge to escape the police. "It wasn't the guv or the sheriff. It was Mr. Cross, the reporter."

I'm flabbergasted. *"Malcolm Cross?"* Barrett gapes, stunned too.

"Yeah," Mrs. Fry says, gratified by our reaction.

I sense she's telling the truth, but while Piercy or Hargreaves could have coerced her by threatening to fire her, I don't see what leverage Cross had. "How did he make you do it?"

She looks at Barrett and the other constables, then says to me, "I'll talk to you. Alone."

"Forget it," Barrett says. He doesn't want to leave me alone with her; he doesn't trust us to behave ourselves.

I need to hear what she has to say. "It's all right. Go."

Barrett exchanges glances with his friends, then says, "We'll be right outside."

When the door is closed behind them, Mrs. Fry and I sit in opposite chairs at the table, cautious and watchful, like rival queens negotiating a truce. She speaks in a low, hesitant voice. "Mr. Cross chatted up a warden who works for me. Took her out to a pub, got her drunk, and asked her questions about me."

So although Cross thought Harry Warbrick's murder had nothing to do with Amelia Carlisle's hanging, he'd investigated the witnesses anyway, hedging his bet.

"When she drinks, she can't keep her mouth shut. Otherwise, she never would've told. We're friends. That's why I'm not gonna tell you who she is. We go way back."

"Way back where?"

Mrs. Fry sighs and looks at the floor. "I started after my husband died and left me with nothing. It was that or the poorhouse. You know what them places are like—filthy with rats and lice and sickness, and they feed you garbage and work you to death. I was desperate. So I went to work at . . . another kind of house. That's where I know her from. Do I need to spell it out?"

Comprehension dawns. Mrs. Fry was once a prostitute in a brothel, and so was her friend the warden, who told Malcolm Cross about her past.

"I made up my mind I was gonna do better for myself," she says. "When I heard that Newgate was hiring female wardens, we both applied. They took us. Now . . ." She gestures around the room, proof of her success at the job.

Her lie about Amelia Carlisle cost my friends and me our jobs, but I can't help sympathizing with her. Whenever my own finances are precarious, I fear that I'll end up selling myself. Mrs. Fry sank to those depths and fought her way up from them. I'm not sure I would have the will or strength to do the same.

"Mr. Cross told me that if I fed you that tip about Amelia Carlisle, he wouldn't tell Governor Piercy about me." Mrs. Fry says, "When I applied to be a warden, I told the guv I was a respectable widow. If he found out the truth, he would fire me."

She gave in to blackmail because she didn't want to lose the security and respectability she'd regained. "I see why you didn't want the police to hear why you went along with Malcolm Cross."

"You can tell 'em if you want." Mrs. Fry's sly smile says she bets I won't.

"I won't if you tell me what happened at Amelia's hanging."

She folds her arms across her bosom and keeps mum.

Frustrated, I say, "I'm not leaving empty-handed. You have to give me something. Tell me what Amelia did and said and what happened to her here before she was hanged. That's not covered by the Official Secrets Act."

Mrs. Fry ponders, then seems to decide that granting my request can't hurt. "She asked me to bring her liquor. It's against the rules, and I wasn't gonna break 'em for her. She complained about the food and the bedbugs and the cold. They all do. She said she was being unfairly singled out for punishment, and she wanted me to help her get the mothers who gave her the babies she murdered arrested."

This is much the same information I heard from the Reverend Starling. I'm glad to know that Malcolm Cross is behind the hoax— and I intend to make good use of the information—but Mrs. Fry's account of Amelia's life at Newgate has cast no light on the crucial two minutes and fifty seconds in the execution shed.

"She only had one visitor, other than reporters and photographers and folks that paid three pence to see her like she was a freak at a carnival," Mrs. Fry says. "It was her daughter. Jane Carlisle. She came to say goodbye."

My interest quickens. The Reverend Starling had mentioned Jane, a mysterious figure in the Amelia Carlisle case, arrested with her mother at the house they shared but released soon afterward. The official statement from the police said she wasn't a party to her mother's crimes. No picture of her ever has appeared in the papers, and she disappeared before Amelia's death. Earlier I'd discarded the idea of looking for her, but now she seems my last chance of a clue.

"Do you know where Jane is now?" I say.

"She's in the Imbeciles Asylum at Leavesden," Mrs. Fry says.

★   ★   ★

On the way home from Newgate, Barrett doesn't say a word. At the studio, he silently follows me upstairs. Fitzmorris has already gone to bed, and the house feels empty and strange without Hugh and Mick. I pour whisky into two glasses. Barrett and I drink sitting on the sofa, a chaste distance between us.

"You scared the bejesus out of me," Barrett says.

"I'm sorry," I say, sheepish as well as contrite. Tonight's collaboration has helped him get to know me better, perhaps too well.

Barrett scrutinizes me warily. "Are you sure your head is all right?"

He thinks the blow made me crazy and violent. I don't want to confess that I had a temper before the explosion and probably always will. "It's fine. I just got carried away."

Barrett narrows his eyes, unconvinced. "So what did Mrs. Fry tell you?"

"Malcolm Cross has something personal on her. It has nothing to do with Amelia Carlisle's execution or Harry Warbrick's murder."

"And you're not going to tell me what it is?"

"I can't." I feel guilty about withholding the information from Barrett after he did me the favor of getting me inside Newgate.

Barrett frowns and purses his lips as if he can't believe he heard me correctly.

"Oh, God, I'm doing it again—keeping secrets from you after you've been generous enough to forgive me."

"Keeping secrets for a suspect in a murder case," Barrett points out. He seems resigned rather than angry. "But it's all right."

He must be remembering our conversation in the hospital, and he means to stand by his declaration that love is more important than complete honesty. I smile to express my gratitude and love.

"It's all right *this time*." His smile verges on sardonic. "My generosity's not a bottomless well."

I raise my eyebrows, surprised to discover that he's setting limits beyond which my secrecy won't be tolerated. He must have decided that his love for me won't make him a pushover, and his will is stronger than I thought. To my further surprise, I like it.

His gaze turns serious, intense. The arousal that flared between us in Newgate rekindles. I want him more than ever, and I'm thrilled to see that he wants me just as badly. If only we were alone in the house.

Barrett looks away from me and clears his throat. "Does this mean we went through all that at Newgate for nothing?"

"I did learn something." I tell him about Jane Carlisle, glad to have one piece of information I can share.

"The Imbeciles Asylum." Surprise lifts Barrett's eyebrows. "So that's where she is."

"I'm going to visit her tomorrow."

"Maybe that's not such a good idea."

"Why not? Maybe Amelia told her something that's a clue to what happened at the hanging."

"Maybe that blow to your head damaged your memory. Have you forgotten what happened tonight?"

"This is different," I say. "How could I possibly get in trouble at the asylum?"

Barrett chuckles glumly. "Oh, I think you could."

"Think whatever you like. I'm going."

"You just got out of the hospital," Barrett says. "You're supposed to rest."

I belatedly realize how exhausted I am. The headache is worse than this morning, and a touch of the vertigo has returned. "I'll be fine."

Barrett sighs with resignation. "Well, if I can't talk you out of it, I'm going with you."

I wouldn't mind his company, but I mustn't involve him further. "That's not necessary."

He groans and lowers his head into his hands for a moment. "If my mates and I hadn't broken up the fight you started with Mrs. Fry, one of you might have been killed."

I'm crestfallen because I needed his help and might need it again. "Don't you have to work tomorrow?"

Barrett pulls a wry grin. "Inspector Reid thinks I'm busy scouring London for your father. I can sneak a holiday and he'll never know." Then he looks hurt. "Are you making excuses because you don't want me?"

"That's not why," I hasten to say. "If there is trouble, you could be caught up in it."

Barrett waves away my protest. "If I am, I can handle it."

"Very well." I'm too tired to argue, glad to give in.

We walk downstairs to the dark, cold studio. Before I can open the door, he turns to me. Then we're kissing, his mouth hard against mine. I'm backed against the wall, our bodies pressed together. He breaks away from me, gasping.

I reach for him, but he opens the door and says in a hoarse voice, "I'll see you tomorrow."

CHAPTER 24

The cab we hired at the Abbots Langley station after we arrived this morning carries Barrett and me past cottages and fields, toward the village of Leavesden. Snow is falling; the scene is tranquil. Fifteen miles northwest of London, the air is cleaner, the snow white instead of gray, and we've escaped the fog. Traffic consists of a few farm wagons. Barrett and I smile at each other, sharing a sense of adventure. This is the first time we've been this far from the city together.

"Are you cold?" Barrett asks.

Bundled in my wool coat, hat, frock, flannel petticoats, and fur-lined gloves and boots, I'm warm enough, but I say, "A little."

He puts his arm around me. The driver can't see us, and there's nobody else nearby to look askance at us.

The Imbeciles Asylum comes into view—many buildings, a village unto itself, enclosed by an iron fence. I glimpse the cylindrical tanks of a gasworks, and suddenly I flash back to that early morning in Stepney. I see the fiery glow in the sky, smell the gas; I'm in Ernie Leach's house, finding him dead in his bed. The memory is as immediate and terrible as if I'm experiencing the actual event, as if the injury to my head has torn the veil between the past and the present. I force myself to sit still and calm until the vision fades minutes later.

The cab stops, and we unload my photography equipment.

Barrett asks the driver to wait for us. We enter the gate and walk through the falling snow, along a semicircular driveway. Pine trees exude a green, fresh, pungent scent. Ahead looms a massive three-story brick building like a castle, with a turret above the main entrance and ivy covering the walls. Rows of plainer brick buildings on both sides extend toward the back of the compound. The tinkle of laughter brightens the cold air as some dozen people run onto the snow-covered lawn beside the driveway. They chase one another, throwing snowballs. At first I think they're children, but they're men. One of them, stout with small, shifty eyes, approaches me, uttering gibberish.

I halt, unnerved. Another man, dressed in a dark blue overcoat with brass buttons and a matching cap, who looks to be an attendant, calls, "Don't worry, ma'am—he's harmless. All of 'em here are. The dangerous ones are in Bedlam."

Here, far from London, the inmates might be safe from harm or ridicule, but it seems to me that they're quarantined as if they have a contagious disease.

"Are you here to visit an inmate?" the attendant asks.

When Barrett and I say yes, he tells us to go inside the administration building and points to the castle. Entering, we find a hall where a porter directs us to a waiting room furnished like a parlor. The only people about are a female attendant in a gray frock and white apron and cap and a man sweeping the floor. The attendant asks us who we've come to see, beckons the man, and says, "Robert will take you to the ward."

Robert leaves his broom and dustpan and scuttles up to us. Perhaps forty years old, small and wiry as a boy, with bright blue eyes and close-cropped yellow hair, he wears a corduroy jacket and trousers and wool neckerchief. As he leads us down a long corridor, he talks in a rapid monotone without looking at us. "The Imbeciles Asylum opened in eighteen seventy. It cost eighty-five thousand pounds to build. There are one thousand five hundred sixty inmates—that's eight hundred sixty females, seven hundred males."

With his penchant for numbers and details, he reminds me of Ernie Leach. I suppose I'll be seeing shades of the assistant hangman from now on. He has joined Polly Nichols, Liz Stride, Annie Chapman, Kate Eddowes, and Mary Jane Kelly—Jack the Ripper's victims—in the ranks of the people I didn't know well when they were alive but whose deaths will haunt me forever.

As Robert rattles off statistics about how much food is consumed daily at the asylum, I notice similarly dressed men lugging coal scuttles and realize that they and Robert are inmates. I suppose they benefit from working for their keep rather than sitting idle. They may be harmless, but they remind me of odd folks I see on the streets, whose behavior is unpredictable and disturbing. In a passage that connects with the wards, Robert opens a door, and a female attendant greets Barrett and me. As she leads us into the ward, Robert calls after us, "Two thousand pieces of laundry are washed every day."

The large room has walls painted a cheerful light green, a high ceiling, and tall windows. It's cold despite the fire in the hearth, populated with women of all ages clad in drab woolen dresses, shawls, and white bonnets. Some of the women sit in chairs near the fire or at long tables decorated with vases of artificial flowers, some reading books or playing cards or checkers. Everyone seems well behaved, everything clean and neat. But for the inmates who yelp like animals, those who wander about with blank looks on their faces, and the middle-aged women playing with dolls, this could be a charitable community club. Attendants rove, keeping order. The attendant with us asks Barrett who we are. He gives her our names, explaining that he's a police constable from London and I'm his friend.

"If you were reporters, I would ask you to leave," she says. "We've tried to shield Jane from the publicity about her mother. The poor girl has enough troubles."

Today I'm glad I lost my job at the *Daily World*. "May I photograph her?"

"If she doesn't mind." The attendant leads us to a table where a small, slim young woman dressed in a dark blue frock, lighter blue shawl, and white bonnet sits alone. As we approach, I hear her whispering to herself.

"Jane, you have visitors," the attendant says.

Jane, in her early twenties, is a young, disconcerting version of her mother, Amelia. She has the same black hair parted in the middle, the same slanted dark brows. But her skin is smooth and pale, her lips delicate and rosy, and she's as lovely as a porcelain doll. She ignores us and keeps whispering.

"Good luck," the attendant says, and departs.

Barrett and I look at each other in dismay while we set my photography equipment on the floor. If Jane is unable to communicate, then our investigation has met a dead end. Barrett moves closer to Jane and bends so that his face is level with hers.

"Hello?"

She goes silent and looks up. Her eyes are aquamarine blue, fringed with black lashes. She surveys us with suspicion. "Who are you?" Her voice is high, little-girlish.

"I'm Thomas. This is Sarah," he says, as if he's decided that first names would be friendlier. "May we sit with you?"

She sizes him up with the bold frankness of a child. When she nods. Barrett pulls out the empty chair to her right for me, then sits in the one to her left.

"Don't sit on Friday Willie!" she shrieks.

Startled, Barrett bolts up from the chair. "Who's Friday Willie?"

"My friend," Jane says, as if it should be obvious.

An imaginary friend, I realize, to whom she'd been speaking when we arrived.

"I have lots of friends," Jane says happily.

"That's nice," Barrett says as he seats himself in the chair beside the invisible Friday Willie's. "Who are the others?"

"Well, there's Powell and Green Boy. But they aren't here." Jane turns away from Barrett and speaks to Friday Willie.

I can't understand the words, and they don't sound like any foreign language I've heard; I wonder if she made them up. I can understand why the police decided that Jane Carlisle wasn't involved in her mother's crimes. In an attempt to regain her attention, I open my satchel and pull out the box of chocolates I brought.

"Jane, would you and your friend like some candy?"

She appears not to hear. When Barrett sets the open box in front of her, she pops a chocolate into her mouth and says while she chews, "Friday Willie doesn't want any."

"Why not, Jane?" Barrett says.

She gives him a condescending look. "Because he's a cat. Cats don't like sweets."

After an interview of this sort, the police probably decided that her mother could have killed those babies right under her nose while she was living in her own world.

Jane's lips are smeared with chocolate, and she wipes it off with the back of her hand. "Don't call me Jane."

"I'm sorry," Barrett says, chagrined because we've treated her like the child she seems rather than the grown woman she is. "Miss Carlisle."

Just as he got to know me better last night, I'm getting to know him better now, seeing a new side of him. He's good at drawing people out—a talented policeman who deserves the promotion that he might have achieved if not for me.

"Green Boy and Powell are here now." Jane plucks two chocolates from the box and sets them on the table by two empty chairs. "Why do you think I'm Jane Carlisle? I'm not."

"Then who are you?" Barrett asks.

"I'm Maria Thirty-nine Kemp," she says.

Barrett wrinkles his forehead, as baffled as I am. Seeing a gray-haired attendant who has an air of authority, I beckon to her and say, "We came to see Jane Carlisle, but this doesn't seem to be her. Can you direct us to Jane?"

"That's her all right. If she says otherwise, don't listen. She's always playing games." The attendant hurries off to help an old lady who's fallen.

Jane chats with her invisible companions. Barrett rolls his eyes at me to signal that he thinks we're here on a fool's errand, but he doesn't give up. "Why is there the number thirty-nine in your name?" he asks Jane.

"I can't tell you," she says.

"Why not?" Barrett asks.

She puts her finger to her lips and smiles mischievously. "Shh, it's a secret."

Although frustrated, I feel sorry for her; she can never lead a normal life. For the first time, I pity Amelia Carlisle. There's no justification for her crimes, but having a child like Jane must have been a woeful ordeal. Our inquiries have reached a dead end, but at least I can document the experience.

"Maria, may I take your photograph?" I say.

"Oh yes," she says with delight. After I've set my camera on the tripod and filled the flash lamp with powder, she says, "My friends want to be in the picture." She curves her arms around their imaginary presences and smiles while I take the photograph.

Barrett turns the conversation to Amelia Carlisle. "Let's talk about your mother. Can you tell us about the last time you saw her?"

As I remove the exposed negative plate from my camera, I fear that the memory of visiting her mother in prison will upset Jane.

However, Jane seems unruffled. "I went to visit Mama at the black dungeon." That must be her fanciful perception of Newgate. "A witch put a spell on her, and she was locked in a cage."

Amelia must have played make-believe with Jane to shield her from harsh reality.

"What did you and your mama talk about?" Barrett says.

"She told me to be a good girl and do as I'm told so the people here will be nice to me."

Perhaps Amelia had loved her daughter even though she'd killed other children.

"That's good advice," Barrett says. "What else did she say?"

"She said that she's going to break the spell. Then she'll come get me. She said it might take a long time, but I should be patient and wait."

Barrett and I look at each other, disconcerted. Jane doesn't know her mother is dead! "Do you know why, uh, the witch put a spell on your mama?" Barrett asks cautiously.

Jane answers with blithe nonchalance. "She was jealous because Mama and I are more beautiful than she is."

Amelia must have borrowed a leaf from "Snow White." It seems cruel to deceive Jane, but perhaps a lie was kinder than the truth about what Amelia did and what really became of her.

"When Mama comes, we'll go away together," Jane says.

"Go away where?" Barrett's downcast expression says he's given up hoping for any useful information. "Back to London?"

Jane compresses her lips and shakes her head, as emphatic as a child who's been offered a spoonful of cod liver oil. "Not London. We don't like London. That's where the witches live. We're going to Leeds."

"Why Leeds?" Barrett glances at the clock on the wall. It's ten thirty, and if we leave soon, we can catch the return train at twelve.

"Because that's where our castle is. Mama was the queen, and I was the princess, and when we get there, we'll rule over our kingdom again." Jane flashes her mischievous smile again, puts her finger to her lips, and whispers, "Shh. It's a secret."

★ ★ ★

In London, Barrett and I part ways at the studio. He has to check on the men he sent chasing a false tip about my father, and I'm exhausted, my head pounding. I lie down for a nap, wake at five o'clock feeling better, and go to the hospital to visit Hugh and Mick.

In the ward, nurses are distributing dinner trays from wheeled carts. I find Mick devouring beef tea, custard, chicken stew, and rice pudding. Hugh lies propped on his side to eat. When he sees me, he smiles, but his eyes are sad, which I take to mean that Tristan hasn't deigned to visit. I sit in the chair between their beds and tell my friends what's happened since I last saw them, starting with my confrontation with Mrs. Fry.

"So it was Cross who put her up to the hoax," Mick says as he licks his pudding dish. "The bastard!"

"Well, that's one loose end tied up," Hugh says. "Are you going to tell Sir Gerald?"

"Not yet." I explain, "Mrs. Fry won't confirm it. She doesn't want her past to come out. It would be my word against Mr. Cross's, and my stock with Sir Gerald is so low that he probably wouldn't believe me."

"Yeah," Mick agrees reluctantly, "but I can't wait for Cross to get his comeuppance."

"First we'd better find out who killed Harry Warbrick and Ernie Leach and prove that Cross was wrong when he fingered the curio dealer," Hugh says. "Then Sir Gerald will be likelier to believe you, Sarah."

When I describe what happened at the Imbeciles Asylum, Mick says, "Jane Carlisle sounds like a real nut."

I can't disagree. "Even if she heard anything that relates to her mother's execution or Harry Warbrick's murder, it probably went over her head. But Barrett doesn't think our visit to her was a waste of time." I relate what Barrett said during our trip home. "There could be a clue in something she said."

Mick snorts. "You mean, the evil witch who put a spell on her ma killed Harry Warbrick?"

"Scoff if you like," Hugh says, "but our PC Barrett has a good head on his shoulders. If he says 'clue,' then I believe clue."

I want to believe it too. As Mick starts to protest, Hugh says, "Bear with me for a minute. Suppose there's a grain of truth in Jane's fancies."

It's just what Barrett suggested, but I'm having a hard time making sense out of nonsense. "Friday Willie the invisible cat? Or the Queen and the Princess of Leeds?"

"Well, maybe not him, and I doubt that Amelia and Jane are royalty," Hugh says, "but Leeds is a real place."

"Amelia musta been playin' games with Jane, and she needed the name of a city, so she pulled Leeds outta her behind," Mick says.

"Not necessarily," Hugh says. "What if they really did live in Leeds at one time?"

"The newspapers didn't mention it," I say.

Shh, it's a secret.

"I wonder if there's a reason Amelia didn't tell anyone she was from Leeds," Hugh says. "It might be worth a trip up there to find out why. I think there's more to the story of Amelia Carlisle than we know."

CHAPTER 25

The journey from London to Leeds, which was supposed to take five hours, actually takes seven because of a stalled train on the track. By the time Barrett and I near our destination, it's three o'clock in the afternoon. We watch from the window as our train leaves the sunny countryside and thunders into a dark fog that begins at the outskirts of Leeds and grows thicker as we pass factories whose chimneys belch smoke.

"Those must be the wool mills," Barrett says, his spirits high despite the tedious trip and the fact that the scenery isn't at all beautiful. "I've always wanted to see someplace besides London." He's never been this far from home. Enjoying our impromptu holiday, he smiles at me. "Aren't you excited?"

I am, but although he's half-convinced me that finding the origins of Jane Carlisle's stories could help us solve the murders, this could be a wild goose chase. Moreover, Leeds is some two hundred miles from London, far enough that we must stay for at least one night. The expense troubles me, and so does traveling with Barrett, which is improper because we're not married.

The train shudders to a halt inside the station. We and other passengers descend amid steam and smoke to a cold platform where we claim our trunks and my photography equipment. The people rushing to and fro speak with a Northern accent so thick that it sounds like a foreign language. When we venture outside the station, we discover that it is elevated high above ground level, the surrounding streets built atop stone arches that contain shops or businesses. The city is all but lost in dense gray fog. Street lamps wear auras of soot. The freezing wind reeks of sewers, coal smoke, and tar.

Barrett coughs. "It's no worse than London on a bad day." He looks as uncertain as I feel. Leeds is alien territory, and all we have to guide us are figments of Jane Carlisle's insane mind.

A line of cabs and horses waits in the street. A driver calls to us. It takes me a moment to translate his words: "Need a ride?"

"Yes," Barrett says.

The driver is a burly man in his forties with a swarthy complexion, dressed in a tweed overcoat and cap. A red wool muffler wraps his neck up to his dark-bearded chin. When he smiles, his eyes crease into slits. I've heard that Northerners are friendly, and he seems so. We climb in the cab, and he secures our baggage on top.

"Where to?" he says.

We look at each other.

"From London, are you? Need a hotel?"

"Shall we start with that?" Barrett asks me, and I nod, glad to address practical, simple concerns.

"I know a good one," the driver says. "Me cousin's a clerk there."

Even as we acquiesce, I wonder if the hotel will be too expensive or too squalid. The streets along which we're travelling don't calm my trepidation. Factories emit the roar of furnaces, steam from boilers, and the racket of machinery; the people I glimpse are faceless wraiths in the fog. The sewer smell grows so strong that I hold my handkerchief over my nose and mouth.

Barrett pulls his muffler over his. "God, what a stink! It's worse than the Thames."

We join the heavy traffic that clatters across an iron bridge. The river is black and glutinous, its banks lined with factories. Boats and barges float amid debris, foamy scum, and iridescent oil slicks. On its opposite bank, we pass terraced houses whose red bricks are grimy with soot. The cab stops outside a large, two-story, triangular brick building whose sign reads, "Swan Hotel."

The three-way junction of streets is too noisy with wagons, cabs, and omnibuses, but the hotel looks respectable, and lights shine invitingly from its arched windows. The driver escorts us inside and carries our baggage. The bright foyer smells of furniture polish. A doorway leads to a taproom; the Swan is a public house as well as a hotel.

The clerk at the desk greets our driver. "Hullo, Frank."

"Hullo, Jimmy. Brought you some customers."

The two men are so much alike that Barrett and I smile, but I'm nervous because I know what's coming next.

The clerk asks Barrett his name, then says, "Would you and the missus like a room with one bed or two?"

"Uh, we need two rooms," Barrett says.

"I understand." The clerk lowers his voice. "We're very discreet here."

Now he thinks we're illicit lovers. I blush and look at the floor while he tells Barrett the price, which is fortunately modest. Frank, our driver, hovers by the door, and Barrett asks him to wait because we'll be going out. The bellhop carries our baggage to the second floor and lets us into our adjacent rooms. Mine is clean and comfortably furnished, with striped wallpaper, a wool rug, an upholstered armchair, and a mahogany dressing table; the double bed has a thick mattress covered by a white counterpane. While I relieve myself in the bathroom, I hear Barrett doing the same next door. It's not that we've never attended to our bodily functions when we've been together at my home, but here is embarrassingly different. When we meet in the hall outside our rooms, we're oddly shy. Photography equipment in hand, we go downstairs and meet Frank.

"Where to now?" he asks.

I tell him that I want to look up some old friends—Jane Carlisle and Maria Kemp.

"Don't know anyone named Carlisle or Kemp."

I'm disappointed, but not surprised; Leeds is a big city. Barrett says, "Do any of these names sound familiar? Friday Willie, Powell, or Green Boy?"

"There's a Powell Street."

I'm glad of the slightest link between Leeds and Jane Carlisle's fancies. "Let's try there."

The ride takes only minutes. Less than a mile from our hotel, Powell Street is one among many occupied by rows of identical red-brick terraced houses built back to back. Women are standing on stools, hanging wet laundry on lines strung high across the road, while noisy children play ball around mud puddles. It's as poor as any slum in Whitechapel, but it gives the same impression of people making the best of hardships, and I feel at home. However, nothing I see has any apparent connection to Amelia and Jane Carlisle.

"Can we drive up and down the street?" I call to Frank.

He obliges. After a few moments, Barrett shouts, "Stop!" and points to a sign hanging from a pole mounted on a building. The sign reads "The Robin Hood." The building contains a public house on the ground floor. As our cab halts, I discern the painting on the sign—a boyish figure with a bow and arrow, dressed in green.

"Green Boy," Barrett says, proud because he's found a further grain of truth in Jane's stories. "He must be Jane's imaginary friend."

I set up my camera outside the pub and photograph the sign. When Barrett and I are back in the cab, I remember Jane's childish voice saying, "Maria Thirty-nine Kemp." I call to Frank, "Take us to Number 39 Powell Street."

We smile at each other, excited to be unraveling mysteries together, beginning a journey into the past that Amelia Carlisle left behind. I gain faith that the journey will lead us to the more recent past and the truth about the murders.

"There it is!" Barrett points to black iron numbers mounted on a house at the end of a terrace. We jump out of the cab. While I photograph the house, Barrett knocks on the door—repeatedly, in vain.

The door of the adjacent house opens; a woman appears and calls, "It's empty." She looks to be in her thirties, her sleeves rolled up, her apron soiled. Two children cling to her skirts.

"We're looking for Maria Kemp, who used to live there," I say. "Did you know her?"

"Must've been before I moved in. The name ain't familiar."

"Is there anyone who's been around longer?" I say.

"Try the doc. His surgery's at number twenty-seven Waterloo Road."

Frank drives us back to the busy main street on which our hotel is located. There, drab brick buildings house shops of all kinds. Pedestrians throng the sidewalks and dodge wagons loaded with goods and machinery in the street. The surgery occupies a storefront between a barber and a confectioner.

"Look at the sign!" I exclaim. "'William Friday, Physician.'"

"He's 'Friday Willie.' Jane named her imaginary cat after him." Barrett grins, as thrilled by the new clue as I am.

When we go up to the surgery, we find the door locked, and when we ring the bell, nobody answers. The sign says it's open from nine AM to six PM, Monday through Saturday. Today is Sunday. As I take pictures of the surgery, a wave of faintness sways me off balance.

Barrett steadies me. "What's wrong?"

"Nothing." But the painful throbbing in my head has begun again.

"You shouldn't have left the hospital so soon. We shouldn't have come here," Barrett says as he helps me pack up my photography equipment and get into the cab.

My stomach growls; we haven't eaten since our early lunch of sandwiches and tea on the train. "I'm just hungry."

"Let's go to the hotel," Barrett says. "We'll come back here tomorrow."

★ ★ ★

The dining room at the Swan Hotel is the nicest place that Barrett and I have ever eaten at together. It has gold-tasseled maroon curtains, a brass chandelier, oil paintings on the walls, and friendly waiters. Laughter issues from the taproom across the hall. Seated at a table set with candles and a white cloth, near the fire, we smile at each other. The thought of a whole night to ourselves makes my heart beat faster. Still, I'm uncomfortable among the other diners, who look to be businessmen. They glance at Barrett and me, and I blush to think they know we're lovers.

Barrett orders red wine to accompany our roast beef, potatoes, peas, and lemon tart. After the waiter fills our glasses and departs, Barrett raises his, smiles, and says, "A toast?"

"To the success of our investigation." As we drink, I blush hotter, for it feels as if we're celebrating something more personal.

"Three clues means we're on the right track," Barrett says.

"The right track to what? We've deciphered Jane's fantasies, but we're no closer to the truth about Harry Warbrick's and Ernie Leach's murders."

"Tomorrow will tell," Barrett says, confident.

When our food arrives, we don't talk except to comment on how good it tastes; we're both ravenous. I know we're both thinking the same thing: *We could spend the night together.* In London, we could have gone to a hotel, but how would I have explained my absence to my housemates? They would have guessed that Barrett and I had been having relations, and the constables at the police barracks would know he'd been with me. And I've always relied on the risk of being interrupted to keep us from going too far. We linger in the dining room until everyone else has left. Upstairs, we hesitate outside the doors to our rooms. Barrett raises his eyebrows at me with a hopeful smile. A tug-of-war wages inside me—desire versus fear.

Averting my gaze, I search in my pocketbook for my key.

"Well," Barrett says. The single word conveys his disappointment, his kind acceptance of what's best for me. "Good night, then."

"Good night."

Locked inside my room, I hear Barrett moving around inside

his. I feel relieved, safe, but also disappointed and lonely. The room is cold, and I light the fire before I disrobe, bathe, and put on my white flannel nightdress. Combing out my hair, I glare at my reflection in the mirror, angry at myself for wasting our chance for a night together. I turn off the lamp and climb into bed, listen to the clock tick and the muted noise from factory machinery. There's no sound from Barrett, who's probably asleep. I feel a desire so strong that I toss and turn as if I'm trying to dislodge a wild animal that's preying on me. Five days ago, I was almost killed. I could have gone to my grave without ever having known Barrett fully. I want him so much that I can't bear it any longer. I jump out of bed and tiptoe to the door, quietly open it and peer up and down the hall to see if anyone is about.

There is Barrett, doing the same thing I am.

We smile sheepishly. Then our smiles fall away. I let Barrett in my room, lock the door, and turn to him. He's wearing a dark blue wool robe over blue pajamas. I've never seen him in his pajamas. I'm naked under my nightdress, and he's never seen me entirely without clothes. This is different from other times we've been together, and it feels dangerous.

"Are you sure?" Barrett says, as if he's afraid I'll change my mind.

"Yes." I've never been so sure I'm asking for trouble.

Barrett offers me his hand. It's as cold and tense as mine. We walk to the bed and pause. Should we disrobe first? That would be so awkward. My heart is beating so hard that he must feel it in my fingers. I could still change my mind. Barrett peels back the covers. I clamber into the bed and lie stiff and flat on my back, trembling with fear and longing. Barrett climbs in and pulls the blankets over us.

Now the touch of his lips on mine, the clean taste of his mouth, are thrilling yet familiar. So is the catch of his breath as I press myself against him. Then we're tearing at each other's clothes and our own, hastening to undress. Barrett throws off the blankets, but

I pull them back up, not ready to see him entirely nude or for him to see me. The warmth of our bare skin against skin is a shock—an intimacy I've never experienced. I've never asked him whether he has done this before, and I'm too intent on exploring his body to care about women in his past. Beneath silky hairs and smooth skin, the muscles of his chest, arms, and thighs are hard and strong. He caresses my breasts, lowers his mouth to them, and his tongue describes circles around my nipples. I've always wished he would do this, but we've always been in a hurry to finish before we were interrupted. Gasping, I touch his hardness, but he pushes my hand away.

"I'm too excited," he says, his voice hoarse with arousal.

I want us to take our time, to enjoy the luxury of a whole night to experience all the possibilities of lovemaking, but our habit of haste is too strong to break. When his fingers slide between my legs, I already feel myself climbing toward the pleasure I crave. Our bodies act against our wills, our better judgment. He climbs on top of me; I spread myself. Instinct tells me what to do: I reach down to guide him into me. The mere feel of him thrusting at me sets off my crisis. As the ecstasy of release takes me, I clutch his back and yell. His thrusts plunge through my inner resistance, and tearing pain invades my pleasure. I yell again, in agony, fright, and triumph. Barrett groans and shudders with his own release. I hold him tight, as though we're fighting a battle for our lives and we'll both die if I let go.

Later, as we lie side by side, exhausted, Barrett turns to me and whispers, "I love you."

The fire in the hearth has burned out, and I can't see his expression, but his voice is so tender that it takes away the breath that I've just managed to catch. Moments pass before I can whisper, "I love you."

Barrett doesn't respond; he didn't hear me; he's asleep. I lie awake, listening to his quiet, steady breathing, and wonder, *What have I done?*

CHAPTER 26

At breakfast in the hotel dining room, I watch Barrett and the people at the other tables eat their eggs and bacon. I marvel that the world seems so unchanged although I'm no longer a virgin.

Barrett smiles at me with a new, proud possessiveness in his eyes. The carnal union supposedly joins a man and woman in a spiritual bond, making them one, but I hadn't expected to feel as if I'm not quite separate from him anymore. I dwell upon the potential consequences of last night. I don't think I could have gotten with child, but I'm not sure. Barrett loves me, but we've not discussed marriage recently, and how can he feel as if he's given as much of himself to me as I've given of myself to him? It was my blood, not his, that stained my nightdress. Our future seems more insecure than ever.

"That hit the spot." Barrett sets down his coffee cup and surveys our empty plates. I somehow managed to clean mine while I was musing. "Are you ready to go?"

★ ★ ★

We'd asked Frank, the driver, to pick us up at the hotel at nine o'clock, and he's waiting outside right on time. This Monday morning is cold, the air so dense with fog and acrid smoke that the street lamps are still lit. Carriages, wagons, and omnibuses rattle past us as we ride in his cab. People throng the shops. A display of fresh fish glistens outside a fishmonger's; sausages hang under the butcher's awning; and signs advertise boots, tea, oatmeal, and hair pomade. The cab draws up to Dr. William Friday's surgery. Barrett asks Frank to wait for us while we go inside.

The waiting room is full of women, some holding babies; children play with dolls and blocks at a little table. Beside a door that leads to the back of the building, a window cut in the wall gives a view of a stern elderly woman in a nurse's gray uniform and white cap.

"Good morning," I say. "We'd like to see Dr. Friday."

The nurse eyes us with suspicion; we're obviously not the doctor's usual patients. "He's booked up today. I can give you an appointment for tomorrow."

"I'm with the London police," Barrett says. "We need to speak with Dr. Friday about some people who may have been patients of his years ago. Maria Kemp and her mother."

The nurse's face shows recognition, surprise, and then grave concern. "Oh. Maria and Violet Kemp. I'll tell Dr. Friday," and goes into the back room.

"'Violet Kemp'" must be Amelia Carlisle," I say to Barrett. "She changed her name and Jane's when they moved to London."

Soon the nurse ushers us into the back office and seats us in chairs by the desk. The office is very full, the desk's cubbyholes crammed with papers, the walls hidden under anatomical charts and shelves of books. A glass-fronted cabinet contains medicine in bottles and tins. Galoshes and a medical bag stand beneath a coatrack draped with mackintoshes and hats. Dr. Friday comes in, his step brisk even though his bushy hair is pure white, his shoulders stooped, and he must be in his seventies. After we introduce ourselves, he sits at his desk and scrutinizes us through his spectacles.

"Must say, I'm surprised the London police are interested in Violet Kemp." His voice is dry, rough with age, but strong. "The Leeds police didn't take enough interest."

Barrett and I exchange glances, intrigued by this hint that Amelia Carlisle had been up to no good in Leeds. I say, "Just to make sure we're talking about the same people: Was Violet Kemp's daughter mentally abnormal?"

"Yes. I met Mrs. Kemp for the first time in 1873, when she brought Maria to see me." Dr. Friday apparently has excellent recall for dates. "Maria was five years old, and Mrs. Kemp was worried because she hadn't started talking yet." Pity softens his shrewd gaze. "Unfortunately, there's naught that a physician can do for children like that. I didn't charge Mrs. Kemp for the consultation because she was in a bad way. She was a widow; her husband had left her and Maria penniless when he died. The next time I saw her and Maria was a few months later. She'd set herself up as a baby farmer."

We frown, surprised that Amelia Carlisle's career as a baby farmer began longer ago than anyone in London thought, dismayed because we think we know what's coming next.

"She called me to her house because a baby she'd taken in had died. She needed a death certificate. I examined the baby and signed a certificate that said he'd died of natural causes. Nothing unusual about that—too many diseases with no cure; children die. I didn't get suspicious until after she'd asked me to certify three more deaths in less than two months. The last time, the baby's body was emaciated. There were three other babies in the house, all fast asleep and none too plump. I asked her if she was drugging them with laudanum to keep them quiet and not feeding them. She denied it, but I had my doubts. I told her I would have to write, 'Cause of death, possible foul play' on the certificate and report her to the police."

I'm horrified because my hunch was correct: Amelia Carlisle had murdered babies years before her arrest, before the hundreds of murders she'd committed in London.

"Oh, God." Barrett shakes his head. I can tell that he's distressed because his initiative led us to the discovery that the past that Amelia had tried to outrun was darker than we had imagined.

"Didn't the police investigate?" I say.

"Never heard from them," Dr. Friday says. "But Mrs. Kemp never asked me for another death certificate, so I figured that if she'd been killing babies, I'd scared her into quitting. A few weeks later, I went to her house in Powell Street to check on her, and she and Maria were gone." Apprehension clouds his face. "Is she in trouble with the law now?"

Barrett and I exchange another look, not wanting to break the news that he's afraid to hear, but better if we tell him now than he reads it in the papers later. Barrett says, "Have you heard of Amelia Carlisle?"

Dr. Friday's eyes widen with horrified realization. "But she and Violet Kemp can't be the same person. I've seen Amelia Carlisle's picture. She looked nothing like Violet Kemp."

"It's been seventeen years since you saw her." I open my satchel and remove the photo I took of Jane. She smiles from the black-and-white print, her arms curved around her imaginary friends. "This is Amelia's daughter Jane. She's an inmate at the Imbeciles Asylum in Leavesden. Does she look familiar?"

Dr. Friday stares at lovely Jane with her black hair and porcelain-doll face. As stunned as if he's seeing a ghost, he whispers, "Dear Lord. Maria Kemp. She's the image of her mother."

I remember his nurse's expression when I mentioned Maria Kemp. Dr. Friday must have told her of his suspicions about Violet. Now the lines in his face deepen. "Starving the babies to death must have taken too long, and a proper burial requires a death certificate. It was safer and cheaper for her to strangle them and throw their bodies in the river."

"She got what was coming to her," Barrett says, trying to ease the doctor's distress.

"But too late. How many babies has she murdered since?" Bitter with self-reproach, Dr. Friday says, "I should have kept after the police to arrest her before she skipped town."

"You couldn't have known what she would do." I think of Jack the Ripper's victims and Ernie Leach. I'll always believe that they died in part because I didn't do enough. There's nothing I can say that will relieve Dr. Friday's guilt. My camera is in the cab, but I haven't the heart to ask if I can take his picture; he won't want this occasion memorialized.

★ ★ ★

Outside the surgery, while Frank and his cab wait for us, Barrett and I exclaim over what's happened. "This is what we came here to find," Barrett says.

"Hugh was right—there's more to the story of Amelia Carlisle than anyone knew," I say. The murders that Amelia had been hanged for and suspected of in London were only the tip of the iceberg, and we're the first people to connect her with Violet Kemp.

"We should go back to London right now, so you can tell Sir Gerald," Barrett says. "It'll be a big story for the *Daily World*."

But he sounds as reluctant to go home as I am. I know we're both thinking about our rooms waiting for us at the Swan Hotel. I come up with a reason to stay. "I don't think our story is enough to get me back in Sir Gerald's good graces. It doesn't prove that Jacob Aarons didn't kill Harry Warbrick—or that Ernie Leach's death was murder."

Barrett seizes on my excuse. "And it doesn't solve either murder. We can't leave yet."

If we stay another night, I'll tempt fate again. Backpedaling, I say, "What more can we hope to discover? Where else can we look?"

"I can think of one more place," Barrett says.

As we ride in the cab along the main street, he explains, "I want to know whether the Leeds police investigated Dr. Friday's complaint about Violet Kemp."

The idea of visiting a police station plunges me into my old fear of the law.

"I also think we should tell them that Violet Kemp was Amelia Carlisle," Barrett says. "I don't want them to be blindsided when the news comes out."

It's the last thing I would have thought of—warning the Leeds police, giving them a chance to prepare for bad publicity. It's an unwelcome reminder that despite last night, Barrett is still a police officer, and I'm the daughter of a fugitive.

The Leeds police station, constructed of dirty red brick, occupies a plot of land shaped like an arrowhead, where several busy streets lined with factories and houses converge. At the point is a clock turret with a conical roof. As Barrett and I walk toward the entrance, a group of constables comes out. One holds the door open for me. Even with Barrett to protect me, my heart thuds as we enter the lobby. Its smell of mildew and stale tobacco smoke and sweat makes me feel sick. I remind myself that the Leeds police don't know me or what I've done.

Confident despite the fact that he's a stranger in town with no official standing, Barrett strides up to the constable who's posted behind a desk. "I'm Thomas Barrett from the London Metropolitan Police."

The constable is raw-boned, with bad posture and a sandy mustache. "Really?" He seems glad of a novelty to enliven a dull day, impressed by his big-city counterpart. "What can I do for you?"

"I'm investigating a case that has a connection with Leeds," Barrett says. "May I speak with the officer in charge?"

"He'll want to know what case," the constable says, fishing for information.

"Amelia Carlisle," Barrett says.

"The Baby Butcher? But wasn't she already hanged?"

"Yes, but we're tying up loose ends," Barrett says.

"What kinda loose ends?"

Barrett stifles a sigh of impatience. "We had a tip that she once lived in Leeds."

"Criminy!"

Three constables walk in through the door, and the man at the desk calls to them, "Hey! This copper from London says the Baby Butcher was from Leeds."

They exclaim, flock to Barrett, and fire questions at him. "Did she kill babies here?" "How many?"

Caught unprepared for the attention, Barrett says, "We don't know for sure that she—"

"When was this?"

"I really should discuss it with—"

"How'd you find out?"

"—the officer in charge. Could you please tell him I'm—"

A door at the back of the room opens. The man who emerges is some fifty years old; his paunch strains the brass buttons on the coat of his blue uniform. Medals decorate its front. His head is small for his size, his face pudgy, with a neat gray beard and mustache. "What's all this commotion?" His voice is like a large dog's bark.

The constables stand at attention. The one behind the desk points at Barrett. "He's from the London Police, Inspector Driscoll. He says Amelia Carlisle was from Leeds, and this is where she started killing babies."

Inspector Driscoll scrutinizes Barrett and me with sharp, narrow eyes. He beckons to us, saying, "We'll discuss this in my office," and points his thick finger at the constables. "Not a word about this to anyone."

"Yes, guv," they chorus.

He marches us down a passage. We're not under arrest, but when he shows us into his office and shuts the door, my anxiety spikes. I calm myself by focusing on my surroundings. The desk holds a brass nameplate, pipes in a rack, an ashtray, and stacks of neatly aligned papers. A shelf on the wall displays trophies—gilded miniature statues of men shooting rifles.

Inspector Driscoll points to two plain wooden chairs. "Please be seated." It sounds like an order rather than a courtesy.

We obey. The chairs are unusually low, as if two inches have been sawed off their legs. When Inspector Driscoll sits in the tall, leather-upholstered chair behind his desk, he towers over us. "Now." He addresses Barrett. "Who are you?"

"Police Constable Thomas Barrett, London Metropolitan police, H Division, sir."

Inspector Driscoll looks askance at him. "May I see your credentials?"

Barrett reaches in his pocket, pulls out the badge from his helmet, and slides it across the desk. Inspector Driscoll studies it for a long moment, as if to determine whether it's genuine, before passing it back. He ignores me.

"Who's your superior?" he asks.

"Inspector Edmund Reid," Barrett says. I admire his poise, enjoy the novel experience of watching him in action in a place where I'm ill-equipped to cope.

"Are you here on his orders?"

"Yes," Barrett answers without missing a beat or shifting his gaze.

"Suppose I telegraph Inspector Reid and ask him to confirm that he sent you."

Panic jolts me, but Barrett, unfazed, says, "Go ahead."

I pray that Reid is away from the station and beyond reach of telegraph messages.

"I'm surprised that London would send a man up here. It doesn't happen very often," Inspector Driscoll says.

I breathe easier; Barrett's passed muster.

"So." Inspector Driscoll pulls a notepad toward him and takes up a pen. "How did you trace Amelia Carlisle to Leeds?"

I don't like his making a written record that may wind up in Reid's hands, but Barrett remains calm as he says, "I questioned Amelia's daughter. She indicated that she and her mother had once lived here."

Inspector Driscoll jots on his pad. "What's the daughter's name and address?"

"Jane Carlisle." Barrett hesitates. "The Imbeciles Asylum in Leavesden."

I resist the urge to wince; Barrett has just diminished his

credibility. Driscoll looks up, surprised and amused. "So you followed a tip from an imbecile." His manner suggests that Barrett is an imbecile himself. "What else did she tell you?"

"She said her real name is Maria Kemp." Defensiveness tinges Barrett's polite tone.

Inspector Driscoll makes a show of writing down the information. "And you believed her. Is that what passes for detective work in London?"

Barrett flushes, shifting in his low chair, angry because the inspector has insulted the Metropolitan Police. "I found a witness in Leeds who confirmed that it's true."

Driscoll frowns, displeased because Barrett has scored a point. "Who might your so-called witness be?"

"Dr. William Friday. Maria Kemp was his patient. Her mother was Violet Kemp."

"I know Dr. Friday. When did he last see Violet and Maria Kemp?"

"1873."

Inspector Driscoll smirks while he writes. "That was a long time ago. Dr. Friday is almost eighty. Supposing his memory's not flown the coop, how did he identify Violet and Maria Kemp as Amelia and Jane Carlisle?"

I muster my nerve, pull Jane's photograph out of my satchel, and slide it across the desk. "I showed him this. It's Jane Carlisle, Amelia's daughter. Dr. Friday said Violet Kemp looked just like her."

Inspector Driscoll merely glances at the picture before sliding it back to me. His eyes are cold, hostile; Barrett's story is holding more water than he likes. "So you've some flimsy evidence that Amelia Carlisle is from Leeds. You can go back to London and tell your superior that he wasted the ratepayers' money sending you up here."

I don't like him, I'm afraid of him, but I can't help feeling sorry for him. I know what he's afraid of, and now Barrett says it: "That's not all. Dr. Friday said Violet Kemp was a baby farmer. She asked him to sign death certificates for babies. He thinks she murdered them."

"'He thinks.'" Driscoll speaks with scorn, but perspiration glistens on his forehead. "There weren't any babies murdered in 1873. I was here; I know." Of course he doesn't want to believe that the Leeds police let Amelia Carlisle slip through their fingers. He must be imagining the official censure, the public outcry, and the hell to pay if they did.

"Dr. Friday reported his suspicions to the police," Barrett says. "As far as he's aware, nothing came of it, and Violet Kemp, better known as Amelia Carlisle, skipped town."

"She didn't murder any babies here," Driscoll says, adamant.

"How do you know?" Barrett says. "Was Dr. Friday's report ever investigated?"

"I'm sure it was. We run a tight ship."

"I'd like to see the investigating officer's report."

"Oh, you would, would you?" Goaded into fury, Driscoll rises from his chair, leans across the desk. "I know what else you'd like— to pin the blame for the dead babies on us, so your outfit won't look so bad for taking years to get wise to Amelia Carlisle."

Barrett and I stand too, rather than be forced to look up at him. Barrett says, "I just want the whole story."

Driscoll shakes his finger at Barrett. "I'm going to report you to Inspector Reid. He'll be interested to know that you came up here and violated professional courtesy."

Although Barrett keeps his head high and his gaze steady, I know he's afraid that a report from Driscoll is just what Reid needs to get him fired. I also know he's angry at having his motives misinterpreted. Before he can say something he'll regret, I say to Driscoll, "The public will be interested to know that you had a chance to stop Amelia Carlisle and you blew it."

Driscoll turns his rage on me. "And who are you?"

Barrett looks dismayed that I've jumped into the line of fire.

"Sarah Bain. I'm a crime photographer and reporter for the

Daily World," I lie. Barrett makes a shushing motion that I ignore. "This story will make the front page."

The inspector laughs, but the expression in his eyes is deadly serious. "You won't make it back to London to print it. I'll arrest you for soliciting. A word from me to the judge, and he'll sentence you to two years' hard labor."

Now I'm horrified that my attempt to help Barrett has backfired.

"Sir, we don't mean to cause trouble for you," Barrett says in an attempt to placate Driscoll. "The other reason I came was to alert you so you can get ready for the publicity when the story about Amelia Carlisle comes out."

"It won't. Because I'm going to arrest you for conducting an investigation outside your patch. That should put an end to your police career. Unless, however, you swear to keep your mouth shut."

Appalled by the trouble we've gotten ourselves into, I want to escape while we still can, but Barrett stands his ground. "It'll come out no matter what happens to us. Do you really think your boys are going to keep quiet? Cooperate with us and make the best of a bad situation."

Driscoll glares as he considers his choices and their possible ramifications. Then he braces himself on the arms of his chair, hobbled by defeat. "Make the best of it how?"

"Look up your file on Violet Kemp," Barrett says. "If it shows that Dr. Friday's complaint was documented and investigated and no evidence of murder was found, then your department will be in the clear—you couldn't have known she would turn up seventeen years later as the Baby Butcher."

"Very well. I'll have the file brought up from the cellar." Driscoll regains a semblance of his authority. "Wait outside."

In the lobby, Barrett and I sit on a bench and look out the window at some constables gathered on the sidewalk. They're talking excitedly, and Barrett smiles at me as if to say he was right—they're spreading the story; it'll be all over Leeds soon. Forty minutes tick by on the clock before we're summoned back to Inspector Driscoll's office.

The inspector stands behind his desk with two papers in his hand and a smug look on his face. He reads aloud from the first: "'The third of August, 1873. William Friday, Physician, of 27 Waterloo Road, lodged a complaint regarding Mrs. Violet Kemp, baby farmer, of 39 Powell Street. Dr. Friday stated that Mrs. Kemp had asked him to certify the deaths of three babies who were in her care. He suspects foul play.'" Inspector Driscoll shuffles the papers, reads from the second: "'The fifth of August. Investigation of the complaint against Mrs. Violet Kemp. I went to Mrs. Kemp's house and questioned her. She stated that the babies had died of fever. There are two babies currently in her care. They appear healthy. I searched her house and found no sign of foul play.'"

Inspector Driscoll slaps both reports down on the desk, turned so that Barrett and I can read them. They're yellow with age, the ink faded, and therefore apparently not forged for our benefit.

"So there." He gloats with triumph. "Dr. Friday's complaint was duly recorded and investigated. Even if Violet Kemp really was Amelia Carlisle, there's no evidence that she killed any babies in Leeds." He says to Barrett, "So don't try to blame us for letting her get away with murder." To me he says, "And don't print it in the newspaper that we're the ones who slipped up."

I'm staring at the second report, at the line provided for the name of the officer who wrote it. The name, signed in bold, black letters, is "PC Leonard Hargrove."

CHAPTER 27

"Leonard Hargrove is Lionel Hargreaves," I say. After the long trip back to London, I'm seated in the conference room at the *Daily World* with Sir Gerald. It's six thirty in the evening, and I've just told him about the revelation that shocked Barrett and me in Leeds.

Contrary to practical expectation, we found the information we'd journeyed there to find, although we never could have foreseen what it would be.

"Their names are similar," Sir Gerald says. He looks unhealthy, his rough complexion pale, his eyes bloodshot. Raising the *Daily World* from the depths of disgrace has taken its toll. "But how do you know they're the same person?"

I knew that it seems improbable and after Mrs. Fry's hoax, he wouldn't jump to believe anything I said. Maybe somebody in his past once gave him a second chance and he's only repaying the favor. I pull my notebook out of my satchel. "This is what Inspector Driscoll said when PC Barrett and I asked him about Leonard Hargrove." I read from my notes:

"'Len was a handsome devil—a cut above the other constables. He could have risen in the ranks, but Leeds was too small a pond for him. He went to London to make his fortune. We never heard from him again. He's probably living the high life, counting his piles of money.'"

"It could be a coincidence that the description seems to fit Hargreaves." Sir Gerald sounds irritated; he rubs his forehead. "Besides, I happen to know he's from Birmingham, not Leeds."

This is news to me, an unpleasant surprise that I ignore while reading the rest of my notes: "'He was good at imitations. All he had to do was hear a person once, and he could imitate their voice and ways. He could talk posh like a duke even though his father was a mill worker and he'd been born and raised in Leeds. When he entertained us over a pint at the pub, he had us laughing our heads off. Everybody told him he should go on stage.'"

Barrett and I started out chasing Amelia Carlisle's past and stumbled onto Sheriff Hargreaves's.

Sir Gerald glances at his watch. "Suppose Hargreaves was once Leonard Hargrove, and he changed his name when he went on stage. Suppose he did investigate Amelia Carlisle back then. It doesn't mean he killed Harry Warbrick. I'm not going out on a limb to accuse him, and I'm not going to make the police reopen the case, if that's what you're asking."

It's what I'd hoped for. Uncomfortably aware that Sir Gerald's patience is running out, I say, "What if Amelia recognized Sheriff Hargreaves when she saw him at her execution? What if she told the others that he'd investigated her in Leeds, he missed seeing evidence that she'd murdered babies, and let her go free to kill hundreds more? I think that's a secret he would have killed for, to protect his reputation."

"That's two big 'ifs.'"

"Either he was negligent or Amelia outsmarted him." I point out, "If the story became public, he would never be Lord Mayor."

Sir Gerald frowns at my third big *if*. "It was seventeen years ago. He was young, inexperienced, he made a mistake. People can forgive that."

"He might not have been willing to take the chance that they would."

"Why would he have gone to Amelia's execution, knowing she

was a skeleton from his closet? He could have had someone stand in for him. That's legal."

"I don't think he knew. When he met Amelia in Leeds, her name was Violet Kemp. He wouldn't have recognized her from the picture in the newspapers. She'd changed considerably. Much more than he has, I daresay. He seems quite well preserved."

Sir Gerald strokes his beard. I sit on the edge of my chair. The clatter of the printing presses is loud in the silence before he says, "Miss Bain, thanks for taking it upon yourself to go all the way to Leeds and follow clues from Amelia's daughter. At your own expense too. I like that—it shows initiative and dedication."

His approval warms me despite how he's treated me, despite the terrible things he's done. My heart beats faster with hope that he's ready to believe me.

"Here's the big problem—Jacob Aarons has confessed to the murder of Harry Warbrick."

Hope dissolves into shock. "That can't be possible."

"I had it straight from Inspector Reid this afternoon."

"But he's innocent! Reid must have forced him to confess." I can imagine the brutal methods Reid employed.

Sir Gerald shrugs as if to say this is a battle he's not going to pick. "The trial is set for next week."

Horrified, I protest, "Even if he confessed, he didn't kill Ernie Leach."

"The gas explosion has been ruled an accident," Sir Gerald says.

I'm too stubborn and desperate to give up. "Sheriff Hargreaves must have been afraid that Ernie Leach would tell people what Amelia said about him at her execution. He or someone he sent must have turned on the gas while Ernie and his family were asleep."

Sir Gerald leans across the desk and regards me with something like sympathy. "Listen, Miss Bain. I like you; you have good instincts."

Startled because this is the most personal manner in which he's ever addressed me, I feel a blush suffuse my cheeks. In spite of everything, I'm not immune to his rare praise.

"When I hired you to find Robin, you went above and beyond the call of duty," he says. "You risked your own life. Because of that, I trust you as much as I trust anyone."

I'm too flabbergasted to reply. This is the first time he's mentioned Robin, and he's expressed a personal regard for me that I didn't know he had.

"Just between you and me—I smell a rat too," Sir Gerald says. "I'm not quite convinced that Aarons is the real killer and the explosion was an accident. But after the fiasco at Newgate, I need to be cautious. Circulation of the *Daily World* is down. So is investment in the Mariner Bank. I can't let my businesses suffer."

He looks wounded, vulnerable—a man whose shield of wealth and status is cracked. "The power of the press is stronger than I thought." He sounds surprised and chagrined, as if he can't believe that he's no match for words on paper.

"The truth is stronger." I believe that despite evidence to the contrary.

Sir Gerald smiles, rueful. "The truth is whatever the people with the most influence are willing to believe. But I knew that already. I've been one of them for a long time. And you can understand why I can't rehire you and Lord Hugh and Mick O'Reilly."

We're poison that would make him more vulnerable to public opinion. The trip to Leeds was for naught. Exhaustion catches up with me, and the noise from the presses worsens my headache.

"If you can prove your theory about Sir Lionel," Sir Gerald says, "I might change my mind."

That's a generous offer from a man who rarely changes his mind, but I can't imagine what proof or where to look for it. I rise, thank him for his time, and open the door.

There stands Malcolm Cross. Malcolm Cross, who helped Inspector Reid close the Warbrick murder case with circumstantial evidence against Jacob Aarons, who did everything he could to undermine Hugh, Mick, and me. If he was eavesdropping, he's unembarrassed, as cocky as ever.

"What are you doing here?" he asks me. "Trying to worm your way back into a job?"

My hatred for him revives my spirits, and I grab my chance to wring some value out of this occasion. I say to Sir Gerald, "By the way, I found out who's responsible for the hoax about Amelia Carlisle. It's him." I point at Cross. "Mrs. Fry told me so."

Cross is too caught off guard to hide his guilt. His smile vanishes for once; his eyes bulge with horror and fright.

"If you want proof, just look at his face." Relishing my vengeful triumph, I walk out of the room.

★ ★ ★

Peele's Coffee House, where I left Barrett with our baggage, is full of reporters talking and arguing about the latest news stories. He's sitting alone at a table, a steaming cup by his hand. When he sees my expression, the hope in his eyes turns to disappointment.

"So Sir Gerald didn't buy our story." He signals the waiter to bring me coffee.

I collapse in the seat opposite him. "It's worse than that." I tell him about Jacob Aarons's confession.

Propping his elbows on the table, Barrett presses his hands against his temples and groans.

"We can't let an innocent man be hanged," I say.

Barrett sits up straight and rubs his tired eyes; he inhales a deep breath as if to brace himself for trouble. "Inspector Reid won't reopen the Warbrick murder case on our say-so. I'll have to go over his head to the commissioner."

That would be a drastic move, revealing his clandestine investigation. "But what about your job . . . your parents . . ."

"What about them?" Barrett seems resigned to risking his livelihood and family honor.

I love him for his willingness to go out on a limb for me and for a wrongly accused man, but I can't bear the cost to him. "It'll be your word against Sheriff Hargreaves's. Who are they going to believe? And our tip came from a patient at the Imbeciles Asylum."

Barrett hardens his jaw. "It's the right thing to do."

"Wait one more day," I urge. "Let's look for more evidence against Hargreaves before you tell."

"One more day. That's enough time to find the fountain of youth too." Barrett's forced humor quickly fades. "And to warn Catherine."

"I don't think she'll believe anything bad I say about Sheriff Hargreaves." The waiter brings my coffee, and I draw sustenance from the hot, fragrant drink.

"At least you got Malcolm Cross," Barrett says.

It's small comfort. We think we've solved the murders, but we can't protect Catherine or deliver Lionel Hargreaves to justice. "No matter how angry Sir Gerald is at Mr. Cross, he's not going to take Hugh, Mick, or me back."

Barrett puts his hand over mine. "We're not giving up. We'll get Hargreaves."

I appreciate Barrett's attempt to cheer me up, but I gently withdraw my hand, uncomfortable with displaying our affection in public. "We haven't much time. The curio dealer's trial starts next week, and because he's confessed, he'll likely be hanged soon afterward."

Barrett eyes me with concern. "You're tired. So am I. Things will look better tomorrow after a good night's sleep. I'll take you home."

"I should stop at the hospital first and see Hugh and Mick. Maybe they'll have ideas about what to do next."

★　★　★

The ward is quiet, the lights turned down low, and many of the patients asleep. When Barrett and I arrive, our baggage in hand, we discover an old man with his leg in a cast lying in Hugh's bed and a young fellow with bandages on his face in Mick's.

Alarmed, I ask a nurse, "Where are Lord Hugh Staunton and Mick O'Reilly?"

"They just discharged themselves." She frowns. "Against the doctor's orders."

"Why?" I say, concerned despite my relief that they're alive.

"They didn't say. But they were in a big hurry to go."

★ ★ ★

Outside the hospital, attendants are unloading a patient on a litter from an ambulance wagon. A cab materializes from the dark fog. "Hugh and Mick probably left because they got bored," Barrett says, hailing the cab.

As the driver stows our baggage, I say, "I hope they're not out investigating the murders. They're not well yet." My vision blazes with a sudden, breathtaking memory of the gas explosion. "I'm afraid they'll get in more trouble."

Barrett helps me into the cab. "We'll probably find them safe at home."

I doze off during the short ride and awake when the cab draws up to the studio. Lights in the upstairs windows are a good sign that indicates Hugh and Mick are home; it's almost nine o'clock, and Fitzmorris goes to bed early. Relief calms my fears. Barrett pays the driver and takes our baggage while I unlock my door.

"Shall I come up?" he asks.

I'm not ready for us to separate, but I'm still exhausted and not ready to have my friends see me with Barrett after what happened between us last night. "No, thank you, I'm going straight to bed."

"Oh. Well. I should stop by the station and find out what's happened since I've been gone." He puts my baggage inside the door and kisses me. I cling to him, and desire rekindles. He gently disengages from me and caresses my cheek. "I'll see you tomorrow."

When I'm inside, I lock the door, leave my photography

equipment in the studio, and trudge upstairs with my suitcase, satchel, and pocketbook, calling, "Mick? Hugh?"

In the parlor, Fitzmorris lies asleep on the chaise longue. Wakening at the sound of my footsteps, he says, "Sarah. Thank goodness you're back."

"What's happened?" Dreadful premonition seizes my heart, and I drop my belongings. "Where are they?"

"They came home from the hospital about an hour ago. After they received this letter. It was left there for them." Fitzmorris picks up a white envelope from the table and hands it to me.

The address, printed neatly, reads, "Lord Hugh Staunton and Mick O'Reilly, care of the London Hospital." I remove and unfold the single sheet of plain white paper. I read the message written in script as careful as a penmanship exercise but spattered with ink-blots when the author's hand shook.

Dear Lord Hugh and Mr. O'Reilly,

My conscience will no longer allow me to remain silent. I must make a clean breast, with you and God as my witnesses. I beg you to come to me at Newgate Prison tonight and help me walk the difficult path to atonement for my sins.

Sincerely yours,
The Reverend Timothy Starling

I crumple into a chair, breathless with astonishment and confusion. This letter could mean that the chaplain merely wishes to divulge information about Amelia Carlisle's hanging, but it appears to be his confession that he murdered Harry Warbrick and Ernie Leach. If the latter, then Barrett and I are wrong about Sheriff Hargreaves, and the time we spent piecing together Amelia Carlisle's past was wasted. But I can't believe that everything we learned in Leeds led us to a false conclusion!

"They wanted you to go with them," Fitzmorris says, "but it got late, and we thought you'd decided to stay in Leeds another night. They were afraid the Reverend Starling would change his mind if they waited until tomorrow." He looks at the clock on the mantel. "They left about twenty minutes ago."

This development has taken me so much by surprise that a moment passes before I begin to wonder if it's too good to be true. I reread the letter, examine the handwriting, but can't tell if it's genuine or whether the letter is indeed a confession.

"They said that if you came back in time, I should tell you what happened, and you should meet them at Newgate," Fitzmorris says.

Sir Gerald said I have good instincts, and now I think I smell a rat. "This could be a trap." I grab my pocketbook, head for the stairs.

Fitzmorris hurries after me, snatches his coat from the rack. "I'm going with you. We have to stop them."

"No. It's too dangerous." I can't let him risk harm. A thought occurs to me. I run to the desk and open the drawer. The gun isn't there. "They have the gun. They're not defenseless. You stay here, and if we're not back by midnight, go to Mariner House and tell Sir Gerald we're in trouble at Newgate. Ask him for help." I'm making this up as I run down the stairs.

Fitzmorris, close on my heels, says, "By then it could be too late."

And I don't even know if Sir Gerald would exert himself to save us. "I'll go to the police barracks first and get Barrett to come with me."

Fitzmorris hovers in the studio while I open the front door. "Well, all right."

But I'm not going to get Barrett; it would take too long. My best hope of protecting Hugh and Mick is catching them before they get to Newgate. The chance of a confession from the Reverend Starling isn't worth risking their lives.

Chapter 28

The fog cloaks me in icy swirls as I run toward Whitechapel Station, my head throbbing with my every footstep. Inside the station, laborers wait for the underground train to take them to night shifts at the factories. I ask the ticket seller, "Have you seen a tall blond man and a red-haired boy?"

"Lady, I see all kinds. How do you expect me to remember any of 'em?"

"When is the next train?"

"When it comes."

I pace the platform, waiting fifteen long minutes. Once in the train, I sit on the edge of my seat, willing it to go faster. From St. Paul's station, I run to Newgate. I stop, gasp for breath, and will the pain in my head to diminish. The fog, stirred by the wind, creates the illusion that the black granite structure of the prison is moving, escaping the bounds of gravity and rigid stone, and growing like a cancer to infinite, monstrous proportions. There's no sign of Hugh and Mick. I trudge toward the prison's main entrance, where a shadowy, three-headed figure stands.

My heart thumps. I freeze in my tracks. It's Cerberus at the gates of hell.

The figure separates into three men, prison wardens. My fancies must be the product of exhaustion and the blow to my head, but the instincts that Sir Gerald praised are telling me to run away as fast as I can. Disregarding them, I walk up to the entrance.

"Who goes there?" calls a warden.

This is the time to escape, but I say, "My name is Sarah Bain. I'm looking for Lord Hugh Staunton and Mick O'Reilly. Did they go inside to see the Reverend Starling?"

"A few minutes ago."

My heart sinks.

"They said that if you came, to bring you in." The warden opens the door.

Exuding sulfurous light into the fog, it's like the entrance to the labyrinth where the Minotaur waits for live meat. I walk in. There's no point in my being safe if Hugh and Mick aren't. The door slams behind me like the lid of a coffin. The warden escorts me along a passage and up a flight of stairs I remember from my first visit. The familiarity seems an illusion meant to fool me while the prison rearranges itself into uncharted tunnels from which I can never escape. If this isn't a trap, why else would it be so easy for my friends and me to get in after Governor Piercy banned us from Newgate? Maybe it's Piercy who set the trap. If only I hadn't let Barrett leave me. Still, I'm not sorry I came. I feel a familiar sensation—the rush of energy I've experienced during other crises, the reckless determination to do whatever is necessary despite fear.

The warden leaves me at the chapel, which is dark except for the orange glow from the iron stove in the middle of the floor and the faint light from street lamps outside the barred windows. Crossing the threshold, I hear low voices echoing in the cold, cavernous space. Hugh, Mick, and the chaplain are seated in chairs by the stove. The husky Reverend Starling, clad in a black coat with a cape over the shoulders, gestures with his hands. Above his white clerical collar, his face is woeful; Hugh and Mick lean toward him, their expressions vivid with fascination. They look like figures in a medieval religious painting—disciples witnessing the martyrdom of a young saint. Neither they nor the chaplain seem to notice me. Relieved to see Hugh and Mick unharmed, I want to run to them, but intuition warns me to conceal my presence. I keep to the shadows near the bars behind which the male prisoners sit during sermons. The chaplain's image wavers, and I think it's an effect of the firelight, but as I draw closer, I see that he's trembling.

"I'm sorry," he murmurs between gasps.

"It's all right," Hugh says in a gentle voice.

"Why don't we talk someplace else?" Mick says. I'm not the only one who thinks it's not safe here.

Hugh pats the air to silence Mick. "Take your time," he tells Starling. "Breathe."

Starling's breaths snag on sobs. "I've done such a terrible thing. I've compromised my principles and sinned against God."

It sounds like a bona fide confession. Maybe this isn't a trap after all, but I'm still too wary to come out of hiding.

"This is your chance to make things right." Hugh's face is pale, drawn. He sits stiffly, as if in pain from his injuries. I see the bandage on the back of his head. "Tell us what happened."

Starling gathers his cape around him as if to pull himself together. "We were in the execution shed. Governor Piercy, Dr. Davies, Sheriff Hargreaves, and the two hangmen and me. Mrs. Fry brought Amelia Carlisle in." His wet, shining eyes are unfocused, watching the scene unfold in his memory. "Ernie Leach put the straps around her. Harry Warbrick put the noose over her head. Amelia stood there as if it were happening to someone else."

My mind works a strange magic on time, space, and geography. The chapel dissolves and rematerializes into a small room with brick walls, a plank floor, and a gallows—the execution shed. I'm standing among the somber, silent witnesses, invisible to them, the illusion so real that I can smell Governor Piercy's foul breath. Amelia, stoic in her gray prison frock, doesn't resist while Leach fastens the buckles on the straps that immobilize her and Warbrick tightens the rope around her neck. My heart races with excitement because I'm finally going to learn what happened during those two minutes and fifty seconds.

"Then she turned to us. I'll never forget the look in her eyes." Starling's voice quavers. "I think she wanted to kill us all."

Amelia pivots on the trap door. Her eyes are blue, icy pools of hatred.

"Then she smiled," Starling says.

I watch her lips curve with ugly contempt.

"She said to me, 'Hey, I know you.'" Starling's voice becomes hers, coarse but feminine, then shifts back to his own. "I was puzzled. Of course she knew me—I'd visited her while she was in prison. But she said it as though she'd suddenly recognized me from somewhere else."

Surprise jolts me. After Barrett and I discovered the connection between Hargreaves and Amelia, I'd been sure that whatever happened at the execution must have involved the two of them. Now it seems that Amelia also had a history with the Reverend Starling.

"Then Sheriff Hargreaves said, 'You're mistaken.' He was standing behind me. Amelia was talking to *him*."

My interpretation of the scene in the execution shed reverses. Amelia *had* recognized Sheriff Hargreaves, just as I'd speculated. Her connection had been with him alone.

"Like hell I'm mistaken." Amelia speaks through the chaplain as though he's a medium who's summoned her spirit from hell. "You're that copper from Leeds. You came to my house after the doctor told the police I was killing babies." Starling, Governor Piercy, Dr. Davies, Mrs. Fry, and the two hangmen stare at her, bewildered; they think she's talking nonsense. But I, the invisible trespasser, understand. The scenario that Barrett and I imagined really occurred.

"We all turned and looked at Sheriff Hargreaves," Starling says, his disembodied voice narrating the scene from across time and space. "He looked as if he'd seen a ghost."

In the execution shed, the man who was once Leonard Hargrove beholds the woman who was once Violet Kemp. His eyes widen with horror because his past has caught up with him.

"He recognized Amelia. What she'd said was true. We all saw it," Starling says.

The other witnesses gape in astonishment at Sheriff Hargreaves as Amelia says, "You knew I killed those babies. You found the bodies in the cellar where I hid them. But you let me get away with it. We made a deal."

There's apparently more to the story of their encounter in Leeds than Barrett and I guessed. The events at the execution take on such a vivid reality that for me it's as if they're happening now.

"She's lying." Sheriff Hargreaves says. The panic in his eyes contradicts his words. He says to Harry Warbrick, "It's time."

Warbrick stands unmoving, the white hood in his hands. "What deal?" he asks Amelia.

"Go ahead," Hargreaves orders.

I will her to answer the question before she dies. Amelia says, "His mistress was with child. He didn't want it, and he didn't want her. Because he wanted to marry some other girl who was somebody important, and she wouldn't have him if she knew about them. He said that if I took them in, he wouldn't tell on me." She faces Hargreaves, her blue eyes bright with gleeful accusation. "You wanted me to make them go away, and that's what I did. When the baby was born, I smothered it. Then I let the woman bleed to death."

I'm choking on incredulous horror. This is so much worse than if Hargreaves had been merely a negligent or incompetent policeman. I also feel a sense of inevitability, as if I've been watching a ball circle and circle the rim of a hole and finally drop in. I've thought all along that the motive for the murder of witnesses to Amelia's execution must be something extreme. I only wish Barrett were here to listen.

Sheriff Hargreaves shouts at Warbrick, "Hang her now, or I swear to God, I'll do it myself!"

Warbrick puts the white hood over Amelia's head. She struggles and screams at Hargreaves, 'It's not fair! Why should I be the only one to die?" She'd wanted to punish the mothers who gave their babies to her, and Faith Ingham, who'd reported her to the police.

Now she wants Hargreaves to share her death sentence. "If I'm going down, so should you!"

Warbrick pulls the lever. The trap doors bang open, Amelia drops through them, and her neck breaks with a loud snap. The witnesses silently gaze at the pit where her limp, hooded body dangles from the taut rope. My heart feels like a battering-ram inside my chest. Harry Warbrick looks at his watch. Dr. Davies opens the small trapdoor beside the pit and climbs down the ladder. He checks Amelia's pulse, climbs back up, and nods to confirm that she's dead. Governor Piercy, the Reverend Starling, and Sheriff Hargreaves sign the document that states that the condemned prisoner has been executed. Hargreaves gives each hangman a sealed envelope that contains his pay. This all seems a callous response to the ending of a human life, a mundane prelude to the hangmen's murders, which I'm now sure resulted from the scene at Amelia's execution.

Sheriff Hargreaves turns to the other witnesses. "Not a word about this." Now that Amelia is dead, they're the sole repositories of the ugly secret from his past.

Governor Piercy blurts, "It's true, isn't it?'"

"We won't discuss it." The sheriff's statement is a command.

"If she killed babies in Leeds, shouldn't the police there be informed?" Dr. Davies says.

Sheriff Hargreaves's expression deems the question absurd. "Why would they care? She's dead."

"That was some deal you made with her." Harry Warbrick's tone blends disgust with admiration for Hargreaves's ingenuity. "What would your wife think if she knew?"

His wife, the daughter of the owner of the theater troupe in which former police constable Leonard Hargrove had risen to fame as Sir Lionel Hargreaves. Lady Anne, the honorary chairwoman of the National Society for the Prevention of Cruelty to Children. She wouldn't stand by him if she learned he'd had his own child and its mother murdered by the Baby Butcher so that he could marry her and make his fortune. And if the public knew, his fall would be as steep as his rise.

The sheriff puts his finger to his lips. "I'll remind everyone that the Official Secrets Act prohibits us from divulging what happened here."

"Then we went our separate ways," the Reverend Starling says.

His words are the magic spell that dissolves my illusion. I find myself with him and Hugh and Mick in the chapel again.

"See? I was right," Mick says triumphantly to Hugh. "It had to be the sheriff."

And I was right when I told Sir Gerald that Leonard Hargrove was Lionel Hargreaves.

"A pat on the back for you, my boy." Hugh suits action to words, then asks Starling, "Did you ever discuss it with the others?"

"No." Starling bows his head in shame. "I was afraid that if I brought it up, I would have to do something about it."

"So why are you talkin' now?" Mick asks.

"Because too many people have been killed. First Harry Warbrick. Then Ernie Leach. I don't believe the explosion was an accident. I'm afraid I'll be next." The Reverend Starling explains, "Governor Piercy, Dr. Davies, and Mrs. Fry are beholden to Sheriff Hargreaves for their jobs. Harry and Ernie weren't. And I serve the Church."

It's just as I thought: Hargreaves is eliminating the witnesses he couldn't trust. Starling is the next weak link.

"When I read your letter, I thought you were going to confess to the murders," Hugh says. "It reeked of guilt."

"I am guilty—of protecting a murderer and letting innocent people die."

"So why're you tellin' us?" Mick asks.

"I was hoping you could take me to Sir Gerald," Starling says.

I once saw a sheep fall off a boat into the Thames. It bleated wildly, treading water, until the sailors rescued it. Starling's face has the same expression as the sheep's.

"The police won't believe Sheriff Hargreaves conspired with Amelia or murdered Harry Warbrick and Ernie Leach," Starling says. "Maybe Sir Gerald will. Maybe he can protect me from Hargreaves and see that I'm not punished for violating the Official Secrets Act."

It's as though Sir Gerald is a higher authority than the court itself. I've seen him use his money and power to bend the government to his will before.

"Good idea," Hugh says. "Let's go to Sir Gerald." He and Mick stand, eager to leave Newgate.

This isn't the time to tell them I've spoken with Sir Gerald and that he wants evidence before he'll publish a newspaper story, let alone grind Sheriff Hargreaves under the wheels of justice. The chaplain's testimony without corroboration may not be good enough.

Starling remains seated. His eyes shine with sudden apprehension. Hunching his broad shoulders, he pulls the sleeves of his coat over his hands as if he wants to disappear inside it.

Mick tugs his arm. "Come on, what're you waitin' for?"

I start to step out of the shadows to let Hugh and Mick know I'm here and help them hurry the Reverend Starling, who seems to have undergone a change of mind. Then I hear the sound he's heard: footsteps mounting the stairs, hastening toward us.

CHAPTER 29

Sheriff Hargreaves strides into the chapel. Governor Piercy trails him. I freeze. They stop so close to me that I can smell the damp wool of their overcoats and Piercy's bad breath. The shadows in which I stand are so dark that they can't see me. Hugh's and Mick's faces blanch with dismay.

"What have you told them?" Hargreaves asks the Reverend Starling.

"Nothing." But Starling's face is the picture of guilty fright, and I see Hargreaves and Piercy realize he's spilled all the beans. "What took you so long?"

Hargreaves aims an irate glance at the governor. "Piercy had second thoughts. I had to talk him into coming."

"We were right when we thought this could be a trap," Mick says to Hugh. "The Rev's in on it with those two."

Piercy glances over his shoulder as if he wants to turn tail and run. "This is a bad idea."

"This is the only way to stop their investigating," Hargreaves says.

Hugh speaks with regret and pity to Starling. "You ought to be ashamed of yourself."

"Rat!" Mick says.

The chaplain hangs his head. "I'm sorry."

Mick turns his disgust on Sheriff Hargreaves. "You made a deal with the Baby Butcher. You killed Harry Warbrick and Ernie Leach to cover it up." He points his finger at Hargreaves. "You think you're so high and mighty, but you're just a lousy, lowdown, murdering scumbag." Triumph rings in his voice. He's finally got the goods on his rival.

"They know everything." Piercy's voice tightens with panic. "And they're not bound by the Official Secrets Act."

"Sheriff Hargreaves promised that if I lured you here, he wouldn't hurt me," Starling tells my friends. "I was afraid to say no." His eyes are brilliant with shame. "I told you everything because I decided that I really did want to make things right. But I changed my mind too late."

"It doesn't matter. Nor does your elegantly worded opinion of me," Hargreaves says with a mocking smile at Mick. "They won't live to tell." He reaches in his coat pocket and pulls out a gun.

"The hell we won't!" Mick says.

Hargreaves has eliminated two people he thought likely to make his secret past public, and now it's my friends' turn. Terror stabs my heart.

Piercy cowers with dread. Starling falls to his knees, raises clasped hands to Hargreaves. "Please, don't! There's been enough bloodshed."

Hugh reaches down, yanks his gun out of his boot, and aims at Hargreaves. "Drop your weapon." Sweat gleams on his pale, sickly face, but his hand holding the gun is steady.

"So there." Mick grins at Hargreaves.

The sheriff blinks in surprise, then points his gun at Hugh. "Drop yours."

Neither man moves. Suspense paralyzes the rest of us.

"Where's Sarah Bain?" Hargreaves asks.

A skewer of fear runs through me. He plans to kill me too.

"Safe in a place where you can't get her," Hugh says. He and Mick glance around the chapel, looking everyplace except where I'm hiding. I realize that they've been aware of my presence all along. "She knows we came to see the chaplain."

Disconcerted and suspicious, Hargreaves keeps the gun trained on Hugh.

"She's waiting for us with Sir Gerald Mariner," Hugh says. "We were supposed to join them half an hour ago. By now they'll have figured out that something's wrong. His private cavalry is on its way."

Hugh is making up a story, telling me to run, save myself, and bring help. But it's too late, and I won't abandon him and Mick.

Hargreaves responds with a scornful laugh; he knows Hugh is bluffing even though he doesn't know I'm here. "Dream on."

"If you kill us, Sir Gerald will smear you in the newspaper," Mick says, defiant in spite of his fear. "You can kiss your chances of bein' Lord Mayor goodbye."

"I'll take the risk," Hargreaves says.

Someone's going to die. Hugh and Mick are counting on me, their ace in the hole.

"Drop it," Hargreaves says to Hugh, "or the boy's dead." He points his gun at Mick.

Things happen in a rapid blur of motion, all at once—I don't know which first. Hargreaves pulls the trigger. Mick dives behind the harmonium. I see flashes of light and hear gunshots—I can't tell how many or who fired. I fling myself on Hargreaves, knock him off balance. He shoves me. Reeling, I trip on my skirts; I fall with a crash that jolts my aching head. I look up to see Hugh lying facedown on the floor, Piercy straddling him. Hugh curses at the pain from the pressure on his burned back. His gun lies a few feet from them. Mick dashes toward it, but when he bends to pick it up, Hargreaves aims his gun at Mick and says, "Back away."

Mick obeys, scowling. As Hargreaves picks up Hugh's gun, Starling moans and runs toward the door. Hargreaves fires Hugh's gun at Starling, who screams, falls on his face, and lies still. Blood from the bullet wound in his back spreads in a dark puddle on the floor.

The others and I stare in horrified shock. Piercy climbs off Hugh and asks, "Why did you do that?"

"Loose lips." Hargreaves is as nonchalant as if he'd swatted a fly.

I run to Starling, kneel beside him. I touch his soft, downy cheek and cry his name. His lips, pressed to the floor, don't move in response. His one eye that I can see is open but lacking any spark of animation. My chest heaves with grief for this idealistic but weak young chaplain who had the misfortune of crossing paths with a condemned murderess and a corrupt man desperate to hide his guilty connection with her. If only Starling had revealed what had happened at Amelia's hanging and exposed Sheriff Hargreaves sooner! His conscience won out over his fear of violating the Official Secrets Act too late to save his life.

Piercy looks aghast; he didn't realize the extent of Sheriff Hargreaves's ruthlessness. Hugh, gasping and prone on the floor, yells, "Sarah, run!"

I lurch to my feet. Hargreaves aims Hugh's gun at me. "Don't even try." Despair sickens me because I've let my friends down, and we're all doomed.

Footsteps pound up the stairs. Two wardens who must have heard the shot rush into the chapel. They gape at Starling's dead body. "What happened?"

"He shot the chaplain." Hargreaves points at Hugh.

"It wasn't me," Hugh says, indignant. "You did."

Unfazed, Hargreaves says, "He tried to force the chaplain into confessing to Harry Warbrick's murder. I took the gun away from him. Governor Piercy and I will handle this. You can go."

The wardens hesitate, then leave.

"Bastard!" Mick says to Hargreaves.

Getting Piercy on our side seems the only way to save our lives. "If you help him, you'll be an accomplice to murder," I say.

"That's as good as if you pulled the trigger yourself," Mick says.

"Do you think you can kill all three of us and get away with it?" Hugh says. "Come on, man, use your head!"

Piercy stares, appalled by his dilemma. Hargreaves says to him, "Either we put a lid on things right now, or you'll go down for killing Harry Warbrick and Ernie Leach."

Piercy, astonished, says, "But I didn't kill them."

"We went to the pub that night because you said we should warn Harry to keep quiet about Amelia's execution," Hargreaves says.

"It was your idea to go. Not mine!"

Hargreaves speaks as if he hadn't been interrupted. "Harry was drunk and belligerent. You got in a fight with him, and you strangled him."

"I didn't strangle him—*you* did!"

I believe Piercy. I see what Hargreaves is doing—he's spinning a version of the murder that casts Piercy as the killer and exonerates himself.

"It seemed like an accident at the time," Hargreaves says, "but later I realized you deliberately instigated the fight, and you meant to kill Warbrick."

Piercy gapes, bewildered. "Why would I?"

"To make me a party to a crime and put me in your power." Hargreaves sounds so sincere, I would believe it if I didn't know he's a former star actor. "When I'm Lord Mayor, I'll have lots of favors to grant, and you wanted some."

Enlightenment dawns on Piercy like the sunrise revealing a wrecked ship. "I suppose you're going to say it was my idea to make Harry's death look like suicide."

Hargreaves nods. "It was a good idea, but too bad Harry's head came off. That was quite a mess."

"And you're going to claim you protected me by helping me hang him instead of calling the police." Anger kindles in Piercy's expression.

Hargreaves smiles. "We're friends. That's why I haven't told anyone that you sneaked into Ernie Leach's house and turned on the gas." His accusation against Piercy is tantamount to a confession that he himself murdered Leach.

Piercy doesn't bother to refute it; we can all see that Hargreaves isn't going to change his tune. "And this is how you repay me for helping you cover up Harry's murder—by turning things around to make me look guilty." Bitterness permeates Piercy's voice.

"Yeah," Mick says. "So wise up. Don't go along with him anymore."

"Call the wardens and tell them to fetch the police," Hugh says. "Turn Hargreaves in."

Even as Piercy glances toward the door, Hargreaves says, "It will be your word against mine. Do you really think that anyone who matters will believe you?"

Piercy bites his lips; his gaze skitters.

"There's the three of us to back you up," I say.

Hargreaves eyes us with disdain. "The sodomite, the street urchin, and the woman behind the Amelia Carlisle hoax." He strides over to Hugh and kicks his leg. "Get up. We're going for a walk."

Despair crushes my heart. There seems nothing we can say to make Piercy our ally or change Hargreaves's intentions. Hugh grits his teeth, clambers to his feet. Hargreaves says to Piercy, "I'll take him. You take the other two." He offers Hugh's gun to Piercy.

Piercy reluctantly reaches for the gun. My last hope vanishes. In the moment while the gun changes hands, Mick picks up a chair and flings it at Hargreaves. The sheriff dodges, bumps into Piercy. Piercy stumbles.

"Run, Sarah!" Mick says.

"Bring the cavalry!" Hugh says.

The force of their commands propels me toward the door against my will. Hargreaves says to Piercy, "Catch her!"

Piercy chases me as I bolt down the stairs. Hargreaves calls, "Bring her to the coal room under Old Bailey."

It sounds as though Hargreaves doesn't intend to kill anyone right away, but is there enough time to fetch help? From the bottom of the stairs, I race to the main door. Piercy shouts to the wardens loitering in the hall, "Don't let her out."

They block the door. I turn and run through the prison, down dim passages. Voices and footsteps pursue me. I hear a distant gunshot and can't tell where it came from. Is Piercy shooting at me? Has Hargreaves killed Hugh or Mick? I round a corner, and a warden grabs my arm. As I struggle to free myself, he opens his mouth to yell that he's caught me. Then he flinches as if someone jabbed him from behind. His grip on me loosens. I pull away, see him spin around, and hear the meaty thump of a blow. He grunts, doubles over, and falls at my feet, curled up and wheezing. Above him stands Barrett.

I exclaim in shock. He steps over the warden, then his arm is around me and he's hurrying me along the passage.

"What are you doing here?" I say, relieved to have him yet hardly able to believe that his presence isn't just another illusion.

"Ask questions first, thank me later," Barrett says with a wry smile. "I followed you."

"How—?"

"After you went in your house, I stood outside for a while." Sheepish, Barrett admits, "I was hoping you would come back and ask me in. A few minutes later, you rushed out the door in such a hurry that you didn't see me. I thought you'd decided to go off on some secret mission, and you didn't want me around."

He still doesn't trust me. Whatever else has changed between us, that has not.

"I was curious about what you were doing. I hid in the fog and got in the train car behind you."

Of course I can't blame him. Only three days ago, I'd tried to do exactly what he suspected me of tonight. Now I have to be thankful for his distrust.

"When we got to Newgate, along came Inspector Reid. He was working late, just brought a criminal to jail. He asked me where the hell I've been. By the time I got rid of him, you were inside. I've been looking all over for you. Now let's get out of here. You can explain later."

"We can't go. Something bad has happened." I spill a rapid, confused account.

"Sheriff Hargreaves can't just shoot Hugh and Mick in here," Barrett says, trying to reassure both of us. "That plus the chaplain would be a lot of deaths to explain."

"He's taking them to the coal room under Old Bailey."

"Oh, God." Barrett breaks into a run.

Panting to keep up with him, I say, "What is it?"

"There's no time to talk."

"I'm sorry." Sorry that he'll be caught up in whatever calamity he's foreseen.

"No time for sorry either."

He hurries me through a passage so narrow we have to walk single file. White brick walls with grimy mortar close us in. We pass through a series of low archways, each narrower than the previous one.

"Where are we?" I say.

"This is the old route that prisoners used to take to the gallows when hangings were public. It connects Newgate with Old Bailey. Hurry!"

In a labyrinth of eerie tunnels that reek of cesspools, gas lamps at long intervals illuminate exposed pipes like black snakes on the low ceilings. Barrett leads the way down a stone staircase that angles ten, then twenty, then forty feet into the bowels of Old Bailey. At the bottom is a room like a vast underground cavern. I taste bitter coal dust and sulfur. Light shines in the distance beyond large bins of coal. Barrett puts a finger to his lips. We advance on tiptoe.

"You really don't need to kill us." Hugh's jaunty tone doesn't hide the terror beneath it.

"We'll have to agree to disagree on that," Sheriff Hargreaves says.

"So you're in a jam—you're an intelligent chap; you can find another way out of it."

"Save your breath."

Barrett and I hide behind a coal bin and peer at Hugh, Mick, and Hargreaves. They stand near the brick wall in a small space lit by a flaming gas jet that casts their shadows on the dirty floor. Hargreaves, his back to us, points his gun at Hugh and Mick. Barrett makes a move to step out from behind the coal bin and rush Hargreaves.

Hargreaves turns slightly toward us. The sputtering orange light gives his features a feral aspect, as if it's burned off the urbane, charming, human mask. Barrett freezes. My terror mounts, for I know he's not going to spare Hugh and Mick.

"Governor Piercy ain't coming," Mick says, and I hear hope and desperation in his voice. "Sarah musta got away."

"If Piercy has half a brain, he'll get away too," Hugh says.

"They know what you done," Mick says. "They'll tell."

"I'll be tupping Catherine tomorrow night." Hargreaves bares his teeth in a wolfish smile.

"You sonofabitch!" Mick lunges at Hargreaves, but Hugh restrains him.

Without turning away from us or taking the gun off Hugh and Mick, the sheriff moves toward the wall. There, shovels, crowbars, and other tools hang on hooks. He takes down two thin objects, each about the length of his forearm, and slides them across the floor to Hugh and Mick. They make a metallic rasping sound. They're iron shafts with a ring on one end and notches at the other.

"What are these, the keys to the kingdom?" Hugh says.

"Pick them up. Slowly," Hargreaves says.

With no other choice but immediate death, Hugh and Mick obey. Hargreaves moves so that he's facing Barrett and me. Hugh and Mick are between us and Hargreaves; we're all in his line of fire. Barrett and I exchange despairing glances. Hargreaves points with his free hand at the floor, at a metal trapdoor about three feet square with two holes on opposite edges.

"Put the keys in the holes." When Hugh and Mick hesitate, Hargreaves says, "Do it!" They insert the keys. "Turn them and pull." They obey. The trap door lifts. "Set it aside."

Hugh and Mick drop the metal panel on the floor, the keys stuck upright in it. From the space below issues a fetid reek and the sound of water rushing.

"Pee-yoo!" Mick gazes into the square hole. "What's that?"

"The River Fleet," Hargreaves says.

I recall that the Fleet once flowed through London, but it became so polluted that the stench was terrible and it was covered over; it now runs beneath the city. Horror fills me as I realize what Barrett deduced earlier about Hargreaves's intentions.

"You're going for a swim," Hargreaves says.

"If you think you can make us disappear, think again." Hugh's voice is reedy with panic. "Our bodies will float up in the Thames. That'll raise some serious questions."

"I'll worry about it later." Hargreaves steps closer to Mick, lashes out with the gun, and hits him on the temple.

Hugh shouts. Mick goes limp, unconscious. Hargreaves shoves him, and he falls into the hole. Hugh and I cry, "Mick!"

I hear the distant splash of his body hitting water. Barrett and I launch ourselves toward Hargreaves. Hugh is in the hole, descending a ladder mounted on one side of the shaft below. Hargreaves aims the gun at us. The bang deafens me. Sparks from the muzzle sear my vision. The bullet whizzes between Barrett and me and shatters against something in the darkness.

"Get back!" Barrett yells at me.

As the gunshot reverberates, we duck behind a coal bin. Peeking out, I see Hargreaves reach for the trap door to seal the shaft down which my friends have vanished. Barrett charges at Hargreaves, knocks him sideways. They fall to the floor and wrestle for control of the gun. I run to look down the shaft. It's more than ten feet deep. At the bottom is black, glimmering water. I call Hugh and Mick. There's no answer. I kneel on the floor and then lower myself into the shaft. Awkward in my long skirts, I grasp the rough, rusty ladder and climb down. The smell of sewage and dead things is a thick, gaseous miasma that makes me gag. I'm in a brick-walled tunnel that must be thirty feet across, with curved walls and an arched ceiling. The tunnel is half full of water, the foot of the ladder submerged. I can't tell how deep the water is, but it's flowing fast—too fast.

"Hugh! Mick!" I don't see them. A loud bang above terrifies me. Has Barrett been shot?

Barrett yells, "Sarah! Watch out!"

I look up and see Hargreaves crouched at the top of the shaft, aiming the gun at me. I scream as Barrett grabs Hargreaves. Then they're tumbling down the shaft toward me. I duck, but their weight hits my back with a jarring thud, breaks my grip on the ladder, and I plunge into the water. It closes over my head, so cold that I'm instantly chilled to the bone, so deep that my feet don't touch bottom. Its fetid sliminess invades my nose and mouth. My skirts billow up around me, tangling my arms as I frantically swim upward. I break the surface, gasping air, spitting water that tastes like chemicals, excrement, and rotten meat and burns my eyes. Near me, Barrett and Hargreaves fight amid wild splashes and gurgles. It's so dark that I can't see anything except a faint glow receding into the distance as the current carries us away from the shaft. I want to swim back to the shaft like a drowning animal desperate to survive, but I have to help Barrett; I have to find Hugh and Mick. Shivers wrack my body as I tread water. My feet kick lumpy objects—garbage or corpses? Something with a long tail slithers past me—a rat or snake?

The tunnel brightens. High overhead a crisscrossed circle of light appears. It must be a street lamp shining through a storm sewer grate. I see that the water level has risen; the tunnel is two thirds full. Some ten feet from me, the black surface of the water shatters and a hulking, dripping figure rises. It's a monster with seaweed for skin, crusted with barnacles. I scream in alarm. The light gleams on its wet, coppery hair, and I recognize Sheriff Hargreaves. Barrett surfaces by him, panting. Hargreaves raises his hands, claps them down on Barrett's head and pushes. The water roils as Hargreaves holds Barrett under it. I swim across the current toward Hargreaves. Breathless and exhausted, I grab him. My hands slide on his wet, slimy face. He kicks backward and pain bursts in my knee. I gouge his eyes with my fingernails. He bellows and thrashes, then plunges deep into the water.

I gulp air before I'm pulled down. In a maelstrom of kicking and hitting, Hargreaves seizes hold of my coat. He's trying to keep me submerged until I drown. My chest is bursting with the urge to inhale, my heartbeat thudding in my ears. I can't see him through the dark, cloudy water. I strike out blindly, and my fist connects with flesh as we slam against a wall. His grip on me releases. I fight my way upward. My head clears the surface; blessed air inflates my lungs. I don't see Hargreaves; he's still underwater, stunned or dead.

I don't see Barrett either.

Panic-stricken, I shout his name as I swim in frantic zigzags, searching for him. The light grows faint as the current carries me away from the storm grate. I bump against a large, heavy shape that floats just beneath the surface. I clutch it and feel a rough wool coat, then the features of a face that I don't need to see to recognize. I pull Barrett up, hold his head above the water. I wail with terror because I think he's drowned.

He coughs and sputters. Moaning in relief, I hold him tight, sure that if I let go, he'll die. Barrett, gasping, says, "Where are Mick and Hugh?"

"I don't know. We have to find them!"

We swim side by side with the current. The water is still rising, the tunnel three-quarters full, the ceiling a few feet above us. The pain in my head throbs. My heavy, sodden skirts weigh me down. I'm beyond exhaustion; I can't go on for much longer. Barrett's breathing is ragged, and I fear he was injured while fighting Hargreaves. The tunnel goes completely black. We're going to drown without ever seeing the light again.

"Mick!" I call. "Hugh!"

A faint cry answers. Barrett and I swim faster. In the distance, the water ripples with light from another sewer grate. I see Hugh by the wall, one arm hooked around a ladder that extends up to the grate, standing on a submerged rung. His other arm is around Mick, holding Mick's head above the water.

I cry with relief. Barrett says, "Thank God."

Hugh sobs. "I can't revive Mick. I don't think he's breathing."

Mick's eyes are closed, his mouth slack. Terror thumps my heart. "Oh no. No!"

"We've got to get out of here," Barrett says.

We swim to the ladder and catch onto it. Barrett gasps as he climbs a few rungs. Hugh and I lift Mick. His drenched body is inert, heavy. The effort strains my muscles and tears a groan from Hugh. Barrett hangs onto the ladder with one hand, circles his arm under Mick's, and pulls. Step by laborious step we scale the ladder. Barrett presses his face against the storm grate and calls, "Help! Is anybody there? Help!"

The rising water floats Hugh, Mick, and me upward. Only inches remain between our heads and the ceiling. The current, all the more powerful, threatens to tear my hand off the ladder. We haven't time or strength to swim back to the shaft in Old Bailey. Hugh and I add our pleas to Barrett's.

"Who's that?" a man's gruff voice calls.

"We're trapped down here," Barrett yells. "Get us out!"

A clamor of shouts, running footsteps, and metal clanking on metal begins above us. Something big and heavy thuds against me. It's Sheriff Hargreaves, his blue eyes fierce with determination to survive. He seizes my coat. The sewer grate lifts. Hands pull Barrett to safety, then Hugh and Mick, then Hargreaves and me. We collapse on cold, wet cobblestones. People flock around us. Hugh and I spread Mick on the ground and push on his chest. Mick lies still, silent. My heart clenches; tears of grief flood my eyes. Then his chest swells with a big, wheezing breath, and he coughs so hard that his whole body jerks. His eyes pop open, and water spews from his mouth.

"Thank God," Hugh moans.

As I sob with relief, I see Sheriff Hargreaves crawling away. Barrett lurches toward him, grabs his legs, and says, "You're under arrest!"

CHAPTER 30

The women's ward of London Hospital is noisy with nurses distributing lunch trays and patients chattering while they eat. There's no tray for me; the curtains around my bed are closed. I've just finished dressing, and after three weeks here, I'm ready to go home, eager to see Barrett, Mick, and Hugh. After our rescue, an ambulance wagon brought us to the hospital, where we fell ill with terrible nausea, vomiting, diarrhea, and fever contracted from the polluted River Fleet. For many days, I badly wanted to die. Thank heaven and Sir Gerald that we survived.

The din in the ward quiets; voices lower to murmurs. When I pull back the curtains, there stands Sir Gerald himself, portly and dignified in his fur-collared overcoat. Nurses and patients stare with the awe that his presence commands. "Miss Bain. How are you?" he says.

"Much better." I'm surprised to see him; this is the first time he's visited me. I'm glad of the opportunity to say, "Thank you for all you've done for us." He's the reason that my friends and I are alive: he paid for the best doctors in London to treat us.

"It was the least I could do. You people risked your lives to set things right. I respect that. And you gave me a big story. Circulation's up thirty percent." Sir Gerald smiles. "I should thank *you*."

After we were rescued, he caught wind of it and sent a reporter to the hospital for an interview. I've been following the sequel to our story in the newspapers. Sheriff Hargreaves has been charged with the murders of the Reverend Starling, Harry Warbrick, Ernie Leach, and the other eight people who died in the gas explosion, and the attempted murders of Hugh, Mick, and me. Governor Piercy was caught at the London docks, trying to flee the country. Hargreaves swore he was innocent, but Piercy gave evidence against him in exchange for a prison sentence instead of the death penalty for his own role as an accomplice in the crimes. Hargreaves is in Newgate, awaiting trial and probable hanging. The whole story of the intersection between his past and Amelia Carlisle's ran with the photos that I took in Leeds, which the staff of the *Daily World* developed while I was in the hospital. All the newspapers in town have sung the praises of Sarah Bain, Lord Hugh Staunton, Mick O'Reilly, and Police Constable Thomas Barrett, the heroes who risked death to solve the case. My reputation has gone from mud to gold.

"I don't often apologize," Sir Gerald says, "but I'm sorry for the shabby way I treated you and Mick and Lord Hugh. Will you forgive me?"

I'd have thought he would think paying our doctor bills was compensation enough. And this is the second time he's saved my life. "Yes, of course."

"I want to rehire the three of you at a twenty percent increase in wages," he says.

"That's very generous of you." But my thoughts fly to Barrett, whose dismay I can picture. I remember that Sir Gerald has done terrible things, and his favor is unreliable. Should I commit myself and my friends to another stint at photographing crime scenes and the prospect of new, dangerous investigations? The thought excites as well as daunts me.

Sir Gerald sees my hesitation. "Here's a little sweetening for the deal—you won't have to work with Malcolm Cross. I fired him, and I've hired a new reporter. It's Charlie Sullivan, the fellow who gave you the tip about Amelia's hanging."

I smile, glad that Cross got his comeuppance and Sullivan his belated reward. "I should consult Hugh and Mick."

"You can do it now. They're waiting for us. I'm driving all of you home."

We find them with Barrett in the foyer of the hospital. Mick and Hugh embrace me and kiss my cheeks. I'm delighted to see them, though dismayed at how thin and pale they are. I turn to Barrett. He too has lost weight; the bones of his face are sharper under his dark whisker stubble; but his gray eyes are as clear and keen as ever as he smiles at me.

"It's good to see you," he says.

Suddenly shy, I murmur, "You too."

"Tell them about my offer," Sir Gerald says.

After I obey, Mick says, "Criminy!"

"My sentiments exactly," Hugh says.

"So, are you ready to start work tomorrow?" Sir Gerald says.

"Yes, sir," Hugh and Mick say.

If they're back in the game, then so am I. I nod, afraid to look at Barrett.

A gust of cold air from the street ushers in a woman who stalks toward us. It's Catherine, resplendent in a fur coat and bonnet, her beautiful face contorted with turbulent emotion. Mick's eyes light up. "Catherine!" I can see that he thinks his wish has come true; now that Sheriff Hargreaves is out of the picture, she's turning to him, the hero who saved her from the villain.

Catherine slaps him hard across the face. Hugh, Barrett, and I gape in astonishment; Sir Gerald frowns; the people at the reception desk stare.

"Ow!" Mick touches his reddened cheek. "What was that for?"

"Lionel is in jail for murder, and it's your fault!" Catherine's voice shakes with anger.

"He's guilty. He deserves to be punished," Mick says.

"Well, he's not the only one being punished. I've been fired from the theater!"

"Why?" Mick says, alarmed and puzzled.

"They're afraid of bad publicity. Everyone knows I was Lionel's mistress. Just imagine: 'Now playing.'" Catherine points up at an imaginary theater marquee. "'The whore who slept with the man who hanged the hangman!'"

"You can get another job, can't you?" Mick says.

"I've tried. Nobody at the other theaters will put me on stage. At least not the decent theaters. I'm poison!"

I say, "Oh, Catherine. I'm sorry."

"I'm sorry too, but we tried to warn you against being involved with a murder suspect. You didn't listen." Hugh's rebuke is gentle but firm. "Don't take it out on Mick."

Catherine turns on us. "All right, so I've been stupid." Her blue eyes spark with anger at herself as well as us. "But if all of you had minded your own business, this wouldn't have happened!"

Now Mick's own temper ignites. "And a murderer would be walking around, free as a bird. Is that what you want?"

Catherine sniffles, her eyes tear-shiny. "I want things to be the way they were before."

I put my arm around her and say, "I know." I myself long for the simpler time before I learned that my father was wanted for murder.

"You'll get through this, Catherine," Hugh says. "People have a short memory. Pretty soon there'll be another scandal, and they'll forget this one. Your stage career will recover. So will your pride."

Incredulous, Catherine pushes me away. "Is that all you think this is about—my career and my pride?" Her face crumples. "I'm in love with Lionel. I've never been in love with anyone before. And he's going to die!"

Sobs burst from her. Her naked devastation gives a hint of how she'll look when she's old, her beauty gone. I'd thought her a shallow, selfish, fickle girl who liked Sheriff Hargreaves mainly for his wealth, his status, and the prestige that her association with him lent her. Never had I imagined that her feelings for him were so deep. Mick looks devastated because his plan to win her has gone terribly awry, and reality has dashed his naive hopes.

Catherine glares through her streaming tears at Mick. "I'll never forgive you. I never want to see you again!" She stalks out of the hospital.

Mick blinks away his own tears as he watches her disappear.

★　★　★

"Home at last," Hugh says with a sigh of contentment as Sir Gerald's carriage stops outside the studio.

The fog, crowds, and traffic in Whitechapel High Street have never looked so good. I turn to Sir Gerald, seated beside me, and thank him for the ride. He's gazing out the window at a man who stands near the studio, a dark-clad figure hazy in the fog. As Hugh, Mick, Barrett, and I climb out of the carriage, the man approaches us.

"Tristan?" Hugh and Sir Gerald say in unison. Jubilation raises Hugh's voice; puzzlement inflects Sir Gerald's. I'm surprised and not altogether happy that Tristan has finally put in an appearance.

"What are you doing here?" Sir Gerald asks.

Tristan's handsome face is somber, tense. "I came to see Hugh." He hesitates a moment. "We need to talk to you."

My heart lurches because I realize Tristan means to tell Sir Gerald about their relationship. Hugh's expression turns grave.

"All right." Sir Gerald beckons Hugh and Tristan, and they join him in the carriage. As it rattles away, I say a silent prayer.

In the studio, Mick runs upstairs to his bedroom and slams the door, still upset about Catherine. Fitzmorris welcomes me home, then tactfully leaves Barrett and me alone in the parlor. We sit on the sofa, gazing into the fire. There's so much to say; we don't know where to start. I take a deep breath and tackle the most immediate knotty issue.

"I don't suppose you're glad that I'm going to work for Sir Gerald again."

"I can't say I am." Barrett's tone suits his words. "But I can't kick up a fuss either. While I was in the hospital, the police commissioner came to see me. He reprimanded me for going absent without leave and conducting an outside investigation. Then he gave me a promotion—for going above and beyond the call of duty to bring Sheriff Hargreaves to justice." Barrett's teeth flash in a jubilant grin. "You're looking at the newest detective sergeant."

I gasp with delight. "That's wonderful! I'm so proud of you." He's achieved his goal, and his parents will be thrilled.

"It wouldn't have happened if not for Sir Gerald and his contest." Barrett's grin turns rueful. "So if you go back to work for him, I'm not in a position to complain."

Relief eases my mind. His higher rank will make him more duty-bound to his superiors, and if I cause trouble, he'll have more to lose, but that's a bridge to jump off when we come to it. The matter closer at hand is our future. I summon my courage, clear my throat.

"About that night in Leeds . . . It can't happen again. Not that I don't want it to, but . . ." I blush with embarrassment. "I'm afraid that . . ." While I was in the hospital, I was relieved to find myself not pregnant. "There's nothing to worry about now, but . . ."

Barrett nods; he understands everything I haven't said. "It won't happen again." He sounds disappointed but resolute.

"You know it will." I feel the heat of desire, see it in Barrett's eyes. The line has been crossed; we can't uncross it. If we were alone in the house, we would be in my bedroom making love right now.

"Then there's only one thing to do." Barrett gets down on his knee, takes my hand, and gazes into my eyes. "Sarah Bain, will you marry me?"

I thought my happiness had reached its full capacity, but now joy overcomes my fear of committing myself, of risking all for love. My brushes with death have made me want to live life to the fullest, with Barrett. But I have to say, "Your parents won't approve."

"They want me to be happy. They'll come around," Barrett says with confidence.

I remember the current of the River Fleet, sweeping us through the tunnel. I feel a similar sensation inside me—our love and all our past experiences that have led up to this moment, carrying us toward the future that I'm ready to brave after we faced death together and survived. The last resistance in me crumbles.

"Then, yes! I'll marry you."

We sit holding hands, basking in bliss. Before we can discuss announcing our engagement or work out the practical details of our marriage, Hugh comes home and wanders into the parlor. We jump to our feet.

"I should go to the police station and get ready to start my new duties," Barrett says.

We kiss goodbye, self-conscious because it's the first time we've done so in front of Hugh. But Hugh doesn't notice. He collapses on the chaise longue and lies staring at the ceiling as Barrett leaves. I perch on the sofa, eager to know what happened but afraid to ask.

"Tristan told his father about us," Hugh says. "It didn't come as a surprise to Sir Gerald. He already knew."

"Because Malcolm Cross told him?"

"No. Cross did tell him, but Sir Gerald knew long before that. He didn't say how he found us out, but he must have had spies watching Tristan."

"Oh." I'm not surprised to hear that Sir Gerald keeps tabs on his son; I'm surprised that he let Tristan's affair with Hugh go on without objecting.

"He's not exactly thrilled, but he's a practical man. Tristan also told him that he's quitting the priesthood, which is what Sir Gerald has always wanted. He'll take it even though it's been served to him on a dirty platter." Hugh grins.

"So he's willing to tolerate your relationship?"

"As long as we're discreet. He wants to be on good terms with Tristan and hopes to convince him to join the Mariner business.

Tristan isn't against it. He'll need an occupation when he leaves the church. And oh, by the way—Sir Gerald told Malcolm Cross that if he exposes us, he'll wind up in jail for the Amelia Carlisle hoax as well as obstructing justice, and when he gets out, Sir Gerald will make sure he never works for another newspaper."

I think it's a safe bet that Cross will keep his mouth shut. "How about a drink to celebrate?" I rummage in the liquor cabinet and find a bottle of champagne that I forgot to bring out after I accepted Barrett's proposal.

Hugh rises. "I'm going to see if I can get Mick to join us. A little bubbly should raise his spirits." He bounds up the stairs, whistling happily.

When they come, I'll tell them that Barrett and I are engaged. I sit watching the fire crackle and glow, thinking over recent events and tallying what went wrong and what turned out right. I'm glad that one investigation was successful, but unfinished business disturbs my tranquility. Lucas Zehnpfennig and my father are mysteries that I can see no way of solving.

The past is biding its time, coiled around its secrets like a hibernating serpent, waiting to strike when I'm least prepared.

EPILOGUE

On the fourteenth of March, Barrett, Sally, and I ride in a cab through a fog that smells of verdant earth and chimes with birdsong. Our mood is somber; no one feels like making conversation. Yesterday Barrett told Sally and me that he'd found Lucas Zehnpfennig, but this isn't how we had hoped the search would end.

Out of the fog materializes a tall stone portal—a large arch flanked by two smaller ones, surmounted by a cross. Their black iron gates stand open, and we ride in through the middle entrance, along a quiet, empty road, beneath trees whose branches are hazy green with new foliage. Crocuses and daffodils bloom in the grass around rows of tombstones. Ghostly stone angels spread their wings, clasp their hands in prayer, or weep over graves. This is the City of London Cemetery. When we reach an area of small, modest gravestones, Barrett tells the driver to stop. Fresh, dewy spring air veils us as we climb out of the cab. Our footsteps squish the damp ground as Barrett leads Sally and me to a gravestone that's far from the road.

"Here he is," Barrett says.

The gravestone is a plain, rectangular slab, crusted with lichen and green with moss, its base covered by dead weeds. I can barely see the inscription: "Lucas Zehnpfennig, 1840–1880." By a cruel trick of fate, his ultimate destiny caught up with him before I could.

"When I couldn't find any trace of him in town, I checked the death records," Barrett says. "He was easy to find because he has an unusual name at the end of the alphabet."

Sally crouches by the grave and lays down the small bouquet of lilies she brought. She has a kind heart, and Lucas is my blood kin, no matter what he's done.

"How did he die?" I say.

"He was run over by a train," Barrett says.

I briefly close my eyes against the vision of an oncoming train, the whistle blaring, a shadowy figure of a man standing on the tracks, and the violent impact. No matter that I believe Lucas murdered Ellen Casey and my father took the blame, it's a terrible way to die. And I'm sorry he's dead, for he was my last link to my father.

"How did it happen?" Sally asks.

"I wish I could tell you," Barrett says. "The police record says it was a foggy night. The man driving the train didn't see anything before it hit Lucas. And no witnesses came forward."

We've reached a literal dead end in the search for Lucas, but my father is still at large, and my investigation of the hangman's murder taught me that there are many paths to the truth. This moment, this grave, has just opened up another path of inquiry.

"We'll get to the bottom of it all." My voice has the weight of a promise, an oath. I stand shoulder to shoulder with Sally. We'll walk the path together, and when we finally catch up to our father, he can stop running from the past, and Sally and I will find resolution if not peace of mind.